More Books by David VanDyke:

Plague Wars Series
The Eden Plague
Reaper's Run
The Demon Plagues
The Reaper Plague
The Orion Plague
Cyborg Strike
Comes the Destroyer

DavidVandykeAuthor.com for information

More Books by B. V. Larson:

Undying Mercenaries
Steel World
Dust World
Tech World

BVLarson.com for information.

Outcast
(Star Force Series)
by
B. V. Larson & David VanDyke

STAR FORCE SERIES
(in chronological order)
Swarm
Extinction
Rebellion
Conquest
Battle Station
Empire
Annihilation
Storm Assault
The Dead Sun
Outcast

Copyright © 2014 by the author.

This book is a work of fiction. Names, characters, places and incidents are either products of the author's imagination or used fictitiously. Any resemblance to actual events, locales or persons, living or dead, is entirely coincidental. All rights reserved. No part of this publication can be reproduced or transmitted in any form or by any means, without permission in writing from the author.

ISBN-13: 978-1499564112
ISBN-10: 1499564112
BISAC: Fiction / Science Fiction / Military

-1-

My name is Cody Riggs, and I'm the son of a legend—which totally sucks most of the time.

My dad had made a lot of enemies in his day. During the long years of the Macro War he'd marshaled Earth's forces and commanded them through countless battles. Star Force had fought the machine invaders in space, in Earth's skies, over land and even under the sea. Billions of humans had died and large swaths of our planet had been poisoned. Afterward, my father had ruled all of Earth as an Emperor for a brief time. Most people have subsequently formed a good opinion of the part my father played in those days—but not everyone. In the angry minds of many grieving souls, my family came straight from the fires of Hell.

As I grew up, adults who had the misfortune of being put in charge of me often said I had an "attitudinal problem." They claimed I wouldn't listen to authority. They called me rebellious and stubborn. But I never saw it that way. I've always been naturally curious and preferred to do things my own way. Individuality is its own reward.

I think they focused on me because of the family name. Anything I did was scrutinized more than it would've been for a normal kid. Like I said, it kind of sucked growing up in my dad's shadow.

If there was one thing that was cool about having Kyle Riggs as my dad, it had to be the opportunity to meet interesting people. Probably the most interesting of them all was a weird robot named Marvin. He was an eccentric metal creature my dad had built a long time ago—no, that's not quite right. Marvin had pretty much assembled himself from the very beginning.

I was a kid when I first met him, about eight years old. The first thing Marvin did was make a big deal about how I was a genetic combination of my parents in appearance, I had skinny arms, tan skin, big eyes and dark hair that was cut short.

Marvin had come to stay with us for a few days in September, and although he wanted to live in our house, and I'd even offered to share my room with him, Jasmine, my mom, wouldn't allow it. She pointed her finger sternly toward the barn, and Marvin had slunk away on coiling tentacles.

Marvin was strange that way. Being sent to the barn was insulting to him. He didn't even like being called a robot. He preferred to be thought of as a full-fledged person—an artificial person to be sure, but a person and a citizen of the Federation nonetheless.

To me, he wasn't anything like a normal human—which was good because that would have been boring. He was an extremely intelligent, strange, electromechanical creature, and I found him fascinating. He'd been on humanity's side in most of Earth's battles and in many cases he'd caused us to win. It was well-documented that Marvin had saved our collective butts on more than one occasion throughout history. But it was equally true that he'd nearly triggered our extinction on less happy days. As I said, an interesting guy.

Marvin's one and only visit to my family farm lasted about two weeks. He spent most of that time in the barn he'd been assigned to, but he came out now and then to wander around the property.

One crisp fall morning as I left the house and walked toward the school bus stop, I noticed Marvin going for one of his seemingly aimless walks. Suddenly, he returned to the barn and entered, moving quickly. Not thinking much of it, I kept heading toward the school bus.

Many years later, I can still see the events that followed in my mind…

The bus had pulled up and was idling, waiting for me to board. The vehicle hovered there not ten inches from the ground. It was maybe a hundred feet ahead of me, with the wavering bluish light of an energy field flickering underneath it. The idling repellers caused swirling eddies of dust to form. Funny, how some visuals stick with you years later.

The waiting door of the bus was so close—but not close enough.

I heard the first ripping explosion. A fraction of a second later I felt a surge of heat wash against my back. It was like being too close to a fireplace when it flared up behind you.

I took a look back—I couldn't help it. A blazing plume of orange fire shot up into the sky. The barn was gone. In its place was an inferno. What I remember best were the flaming chickens. Like cotton balls soaked in gasoline, they ran around the yard aimlessly—living fireballs with churning feet.

I started to run toward the road. The flames surged behind me, flaring bright. Then a secondary blast—bigger than the first—knocked me flat. When I opened my eyes a second or two later, my eyelashes and eyebrows were gone. I thought this must be what it was like to be breathed upon by a dragon.

I tried to get up and run to the road, but the bus had roared away to save the rest of the children. I threw myself down again and crawled toward the road. My dad had taught me that. *When the shit really hits the fan, son*, he'd always said, *get low and crawl on your belly.*

Looking back at the raging fire that had engulfed the barn, I spotted Marvin. He wormed his way out of the flames, his tentacles smoking. I could tell he was alive, but damaged.

Determinedly, I kept crawling toward the road. There was a ditch out there alongside the pavement. I could roll into that and find shelter in case things went from bad to worse.

Before I reached the ditch, something gripped me and lifted me up. I hissed and struggled, thinking it was Marvin and expecting to be branded by those white-hot tentacles of his. Instead, it was my mom. She wasn't happy, and she carried me at an amazing pace toward the house before she finally put me down.

"I'm *okay*, Mom," I kept repeating, but it was as if she couldn't even hear me.

"That damned robot," I heard her say, along with a lot of bad words. "We should have scrapped him years ago."

I never did learn exactly what had gone wrong inside our barn. I don't think my parents ever figured it out either. But they were sure pissed off.

They threw Marvin roughly off our property. I found a tentacle, which my dad had ripped loose. My parents weren't standard issue humans. They were ex-Star Force. That meant they'd been nanotized, and in my dad's case, genetically enhanced.

The tentacle was blackened and still smoking hot. It continued operating, whipping around in the ashes long after the flames had died down. I picked it up when it cooled enough and took it to the porch to fool with it, snapping it around like a whip.

Mom had gone inside to find her first aid kit. She wasn't too happy to discover I had a squirming memento in my hands as she came out to patch me up. She made me drop my prize in the dirt near the porch.

I wasn't too badly hurt. Sure, I had half a dozen nail-like splinters in my back. They hadn't gone in more than an inch, and they didn't really hurt. I think Mom was more upset than I was about my injuries. She picked at the splinters and fussed over the puncture wounds as if they were bullet holes.

My parents had always known there was something unusual about me physically. Microbial baths had changed my dad forever, and he'd passed some of that altered DNA down to me. As a result, I was a tough kid who'd always ignored the kind of pain that brought others to tears.

While Mom stitched and salved me with nanite sutures, I stared at that tentacle. I watched it whip around like it was alive. Which I suppose it was, in a way—as much as the rest of Marvin was alive, anyway.

Over the next hour, the barn burned down to black sticks. The chickens were transformed into little round heaps of ash. I can still remember the smell—a campfire-like mixture of wood smoke and burnt feathers.

I wanted to keep the tentacle as a souvenir, but my mom wouldn't let me. She took it away, and I never saw it again.

When I asked if Marvin would ever come back, Dad told me Marvin was always up to some kind of mischief and couldn't be trusted to do anything quiet and normal. He said if Marvin did come back, it would be because times had changed and events were going badly for humanity again—in other words, because we needed him.

I didn't quite understand at the time. I do recall Dad trying to explain that the robot was a devil and an angel all wrapped up into one. I guess the devilish side had risen to the forefront that day. It was years later before I really understood what he was talking about.

-2-

Fifteen years after Marvin incinerated every chicken on my Dad's farm, I graduated from the Star Force Academy as an ensign and enjoyed a brief period of shore leave before coming on active duty. I was proud of my commission, and so was my old man. He'd offered me a beer in the basement, and one had led to twelve in short order. When the party was in full swing, Mom showed up at the top of the steps that led down into what she sometimes called "the brewery." She informed me that Olivia had arrived—and that changed everything.

Olivia was my girlfriend. She wasn't just *any* girlfriend. We hadn't been together more than a semester at the Academy, but I already thought she was the one girl in the universe I might marry someday.

I staggered up the steps, laughing. Dad followed. We had beer-grins on our faces. Mom responded to our expressions with a dour one of her own. She'd never really liked it when we got drunk. I think in the past my dad hadn't been at his best when he drank too much.

I'd expected Olivia to be in the living room, but she was outside. I went to the window, and that's when I saw it.

Her father's space yacht, *Greyhound*, sat in the yard right between the tractors and the new barn. My jaw sagged.

"Seriously?" I asked her.

She smiled, showing me a lovely curve of glossed lips, and nodded. She was British, rich and attractive. Whenever we spent time together, I found myself grinning a lot.

"We're going for a ride, Cody," she said.

The only person who didn't think a celebratory flight into space while intoxicated was a good idea was my mom. She was right, of course, but I was too happy to listen to her. With a sigh, she rolled her eyes, forced a smile and wished us well.

Olivia and I rushed off to *Greyhound* before anyone could think of a good reason to stop us. My dad shouted behind me, and I waved over my shoulder. I knew Mom had been hoping my shore leave would be a quiet family affair, a brief period of family togetherness. But it wasn't meant to be. I was more like Dad than I was like Mom in personality, and that meant I liked to get into "situations."

I'd gathered more than my share of bumps and bruises while growing up. Just having the Riggs name had been a pain in the ass, but not for the reasons you might think. I'd been nanotized and Microbe-optimized from birth, so I had to be really careful about pushing back against all those assholes that wanted to test my reputation. With this name, some guys just wanted to take a swing at me in a bar, and I had to make sure I didn't win too easily.

The knowledge that I wasn't as likely to die or get permanently maimed did make it easier to get into trouble. Like the time I'd borrowed a flitter and repeller-dived onto the top of the Academy water tower with a backpack full of spray paint. I'd been slightly drunk and on a mission to tell the world how much I thought of my new girlfriend and classmate Olivia Turnbull. They'd never proven it was me, and even if they had, what were they gonna do? Kick Cody Riggs out of the Academy?

Once aboard, Olivia and I quickly piloted the boat up into space. We approached the refueling station in orbit, waiting our turn.

I stared through the nano-glass front viewing port of her father's sleek space yacht. From the ground, *Greyhound* had seemed huge, the size and shape of a jetliner of the prewar days. But here in Earth orbit it was small, especially when compared to the Star Force battleship looming off the port bow.

"There's our future," Olivia said as we watched the warship glide into a docking station and begin to refuel. "We'll be captains someday."

"Think big," I said. "We'll be admirals."

She laughed that throaty laugh I loved.

Our turn at the orbital refueling station came quickly. The Turnbull family pilot had flown us up from the farm and now guided *Greyhound* in with a deft touch. I'd wanted to do it myself, but the man had been adamant about following his instructions. I decided now was not the time to push the issue, not with my girl watching. Later, when we were out in deep space, I would get my hands on the controls and we'd see about some real piloting.

I looked over at Olivia, running my eyes up and down her shapely form. She had high cheekbones like a model and straight dark hair. Her legs were long, and her body had just enough curves in the right places to give her a sleek, sexy look. We'd started dating in school, and I'd known right away I'd hit the jackpot.

All that and money too. The Turnbulls were one of the British Isles' richest and most influential families—and I was a Riggs. Between the two of us we had fame, fortune and guts. Who could ask for more?

Olivia grinned as she noticed my scrutiny. She leaned over and whispered in my ear, "What are you thinking about?"

"I was wondering how wide the bunks are on this yacht."

She snorted and shook her head. "All you think about is shagging."

I put my arm around her and kissed her, but didn't try anything else. I'd take my time.

I figured I'd make my move as soon as we got past the refueling station. She had to be expecting me to try or she wouldn't have brought me up here. Things were definitely heating up with Olivia.

As freshly commissioned officers, Olivia and I had two months before we had to report for duty, so we were going to spend some time running around the solar system on a last fling before we started full-up pilot training. We'd both been qualified as pilots on civilian models like the *Greyhound* since our teenage years. Also, the brainbox on this ship could fly it by itself, so we weren't worried.

Suddenly, the yacht gave a bump and a lurch. I glanced sharply at the pilot, who ignored me. I knew that if I'd been at the controls, I would have come in much more smoothly. We latched on to the magnetic grapples of the orbital refueling station and the rich deuterium-tritium fuel for the fusion generator flowed to the tanks. At that point the pilot stood and said, "This is where I get off. Ma'am, Sir, have a nice trip."

I thought I saw something disdainful in his eyes as he looked at me. Maybe it was envy over the babe at my side, or maybe it was more of the Riggs mystique.

Olivia nodded to him and we watched as he left the small bridge. "He'll take a shuttle to his next job," she said, as if I really cared.

More bumps and thumps came as the automated station refueled us. I sat down and began to customize the controls for myself. This was going to be fun. A few minutes later we cast off. Following Olivia's instructions, I set course for the Tyche ring. Olivia still refused to tell me exactly where we were going.

"An adventure," she'd declared, and then sealed her sexy lips.

Once we were out of the control zone and Earth's orbit, I told Olivia to strap in. Even with the high-end inertial fields on this boat, it was safer to be cushioned, especially for Olivia, since she had yet to undergo the nanite treatments. The seats formed smart metal shells around our backs and sides, and straps extruded themselves across our bodies in several places. It wasn't very comfortable, but it was much safer.

I rammed the throttles forward, pouring power into the three huge engines. As a racing yacht, *Greyhound* was overpowered. I loved that surging feeling of acceleration. The floor seemed to tilt as the Gs leaked through the inertial field—which I'd deliberately set slightly low—so we could feel the kick in the ass. We blasted out of orbit and into interplanetary space.

"Don't you love those Gs?" I yelled over the roaring engines.

"You're welcome," Olivia replied.

"Oh yeah, thanks for letting me drive."

"Just don't tell Father," she said, referring to Lord Grantham Turnbull, known simply as Lord Grantham to friends and family.

Eventually I came off the throttles to give Olivia a break. I let the gravity stabilize and decreased our acceleration rate. This gave us a steady flight path toward Tyche, which would take a couple of days to reach. Back in my dad's day it had taken much longer, but with the new technology, ships could sustain constant acceleration while those inside hardly felt it.

The ship's brainbox reported a couple of sensors on the hull needing repair. I frowned, thinking an expensive yacht like this should be maintained better. Maybe I'd accelerated too hard and torn them off.

Letting the brainbox fly the ship, Olivia and I sat staring at the naked stars. She cuddled in my arms. All in all, this was a wonderful start to the voyage.

"Look," I said, pointing at a constellation. "The Pleiades."

"The Seven Sisters…funny. I always wanted more sisters, but…I guess one is enough."

"Yeah. I'm sorry." I'd heard the story of Olivia's mother dying in childbirth with her, an event even more shocking than usual in these days of nano-medical miracles. "Maybe we'll have seven daughters, how's that?"

"Brilliant." She snuggled closer. "Hmm. This is nice."

"Yeah, it is."

"You sure you don't want more?" She kissed me deeply.

I knew then that this was going to be the night. We'd hinted around and I'd tried every trick I knew, but so far Olivia and I hadn't done more than make out. Curiously, this had made me more determined to get together with her. The fact that I hadn't become bored and wandered off to find a new girl I'd taken as a sign of commitment on my part. Funny how these things sneak up on a guy.

"Of course I want more," I said. "Let's check out the bunks."

She headed for the staterooms, and I followed. At the door to mine, she went inside first and then closed the smart metal in my face.

"Let me get ready," she said.

I grumbled, but walked away to a nearby observation port. I stared out at space through the triple-thick nano-glass. It showed the heavens ablaze with more stars than could be seen from an Earthly mountaintop.

Disaster struck just as I was beginning to wonder what she was doing in there. It started with some odd clunking noises and then the sound of tearing metal. I noticed it first, as my nanotized hearing was sharp.

"What's that?" I said, looking around.

"What's what?" Olivia called through the smart metal hatch.

Suddenly, an explosion rocked the ship, and the smart hatchway melted away to become metallic grit. A hole had been blown in the hull directly in front of Olivia. The shockwave threw us down onto the deck. Almost immediately, the storm of debris reversed itself and all the air was sucked out of the chamber. Whatever had just happened had cut through the tough multiple layers of the outer hull that were supposed to keep us safe from space-borne hazards.

Half blind, I struggled to my feet. My hands had been torn up by the blast, but, gritting my teeth, I found I could move them. I already felt my nanites and Microbes rushing through my bloodstream to the injured areas.

The vacuum hadn't sucked us out into space at least, but Olivia had been pulled to the breach in the hull and for a second I thought the suction might have ripped her guts out. I tugged and she came free in a shower of frozen blood that looked like floating rubies. We'd lost gravity and pressure. Only my unusual physique was keeping me moving—but I knew it wouldn't last.

My first thought was to restore pressure for Olivia's sake. I could survive hard vacuum for a minute or more, but I knew she couldn't. I leaped across the room to the tear in the wall and grabbed the pieces that had been folded back like aluminum foil. The smart metal in them was trying to close the hole but it needed some help, so I bent and pushed the flanges back into place until the various edges found each other and started their self-healing process.

As soon as the metal had formed a rudimentary seal, I pressed my head against the wall speaker and yelled with the remaining air in my lungs, "*Greyhound*, initiate emergency repressurization!" Even without atmosphere, the vibrations should travel through my skull and be picked up by the ship's brainbox. A moment later I was rewarded with a blast of warm oxygen from the vents.

I stayed with Olivia as a warm breath of oxygen hissed back into the chamber. Gravity returned too, and her blood droplets showered onto my back and pattered on the deck.

Now that we were getting air and heat, I returned to my girl. I realized she wasn't moving. She was lying face down on the deck. Blood was flowing out of her still—it was everywhere.

Rolling her over, I was horrified to find the whole front of her face and torso covered with blood. Clearly she was in shock. I managed to get her breathing again, but it was ragged. Her eyes roved the room as if seeing everything except me.

"Olivia! Olivia, can you hear me?" I said urgently.

"Cody?" She focused briefly on my face, and then the light in her eyes went out and her head sagged. I realized her skull must have impacted something, and part of her hair had been torn away and now hung by a flap of skin.

I had to get her to the autodoc on board—a rich man's medical toy combining a brainbox and all the surgical tools, diagnostic software and drugs that could be packed into a machine the size of a coffin. It was as advanced as a Star Force military critical care unit. I knew it would be able to fix her up.

It had to.

I scooped Olivia up with a pounding heart, spewing curses. I shoved my shoulder against the pressure door and roared at the brainbox, "*Open the wardroom door!*"

"Unable to comply. Air pressure not restored in outer passageway."

I growled in frustration and carried her across to the other door, went through the galley and then out the other side. All the while, I could feel her blood running down my arms and spattering onto the floor, making me more and more frantic. I charged down several corridors, taking the long way around to the autodoc until once more a locked pressure door stopped me.

"*Greyhound*, open this damn door!" I yelled.

"Unable to comply. Air pressure not restored in outer passageway."

"Is the autodoc on the other side of this bulkhead?" I asked.

"Affirmative."

"Open an emergency portal through the wall."

"Command not accepted. Only authorized personnel can issue emergency orders."

I roared and kicked the wall, denting it. If I didn't get Olivia into the autodoc, she was going to die. "The only authorized person is incapacitated! You must have some kind of override protocol!"

A pinhead camera on a stalk focused on me and then on Olivia. "Temporary authorization granted."

I watched the smart metal of the wall thin until a circular hole opened in the center. As soon as it was wide enough, I stepped through, hitting the autodoc's *Open* button with one bloody hand as I juggled Olivia's body. The nano-glass canopy rose and I placed her into the coffin-like enclosure. Slamming the cover closed activated the autodoc, and it went to work on her with four arms. The machine jammed needles and probes into her, fired up laser scalpels, and deftly began slicing away her clothing before starting on her body.

I turned away, not able to watch the machine cut up the love of my life. I felt sick.

I wondered what the hell had happened. Had we hit a meteor at a speed high enough to burst through the triple-walled hull? That was the only thing I could think of.

I'd been stupid, and Olivia was going to pay for my complacency. I should have insisted she get nanotized before we went on this trip. Though the treatments were scheduled for two months from now, I knew that with our families' influence we could have gotten them early. Pretending to receive the nanite injections as an adult would have been a perfect cover for the fact that I had had the nanites my whole life. And the early injections would have given Olivia a much better chance of surviving what had just happened.

"Process failure," the autodoc suddenly announced. "Patient vitals are diminishing. Extreme lifesaving measures will be initiated unless override is input."

"Extreme lifesaving measures? What kind of extreme lifesaving measures?" I looked at the screen and displays, trying to decipher the medical readouts. These things were supposed to be cutting edge. I racked my brain trying to remember what I had heard about their capabilities.

The autodoc didn't answer me.

"Nanites. You're going to nanotize her," I said.

My parents had filled me with nanites at an early age. But Olivia wasn't due to get her nanite injections until she received her first assignment.

In Star Force, being injected with nanites was a requirement for active duty. They rebuilt the human body from the inside out and became symbiotic with the host organism. As a result, personnel in Earth's spacegoing military healed faster, were stronger and had better reflexes than normal civilians. At this point, Olivia was still a natural woman.

"Nanite injections proceeding. Extreme lifesaving procedure in progress. Please back away from the canopy."

Not knowing why, I did what it told me to do. I backed away from the curving nano-glass. The warning came just in time, for suddenly the material starred from an impact, as if a bullet had struck it from the inside. My head swung wildly, looking for the source of the damage before I realized what it must be.

Even sedated, Olivia's body was reacting to the nanites pouring through her body, rebuilding her flesh for the very first time. Hugely strong with pain and adrenaline surges, her convulsions were cracking the glass on the autodoc's cover, although I could see the glass *uncracking*, repairing itself. I hoped it would hold.

After a few minutes she seemed to settle down, so I eased over to look through the glass again. Her skin writhed and she grimaced in pain, her head jerking back and forth as if having the most horrible nightmare imaginable. It made me want to break something, especially because I had no idea how she would come out of the treatment. Nanites were determinedly stupid little creatures, fulfilling their program to rebuild shattered flesh and bone even if the patient died in the process. I'd heard my dad tell of marines under his command who had been buried with perfect corpses as the nanites repaired body structure, but couldn't preserve life.

I sat down on the floor and uttered a stream of low, vile profanity directed at myself that would have shocked my mother and surprised my father. I'd never been subject to recriminations, but now I got to experience them in spades. With no idea what else to do, I tried to think of a Hindu prayer for healing Mom had taught me when I was little, but I just couldn't bring it to mind.

"Extreme lifesaving measures have failed," the autodoc announced after an indeterminable time. I bolted to my feet and pressed hands against the glass. She seemed to be resting, at peace, but I couldn't tell if she was breathing.

Frantically, I pulled up the patient vitals. Everything showed flat and red.

Olivia was dead.

I smashed my hand against the nano-glass, starring it yet again, and then crumpled to the floor. I began to take deep breaths, but it felt like I wasn't getting any air into my lungs.

I wanted to yell at the stupid machine, but I knew that wouldn't help. Even something as automatic as an autodoc worked better if the humans involved had at least read the instruction manual, and I hadn't. In fact, I'd totally screwed up by just jumping aboard *Greyhound* when they'd picked me up at the farm and flown off without a safety briefing or even rudimentary familiarization on this specific ship's systems. Four years of Academy training and I'd thrown it out the window the first chance I got.

I'd never believed the people who called me an arrogant jackass—until now. That's just what I was, and now Olivia lay dead in front of me because I thought we were both immortal.

When I could breathe again, I began to wonder just how this "accident" had occurred—and who might be responsible.

-3-

What else could I do but go back to Earth? Where before I'd loved the idea of taking the controls, now I just wanted to take it all back. I wanted to drink and sleep. Maybe when I woke up it would all turn out to have been a bad dream. I forced myself to instruct the brainbox to land back on Olivia's family estate. It took more arguing, but once I convinced it the only command personnel aboard was dead, some kind of backup protocol kicked in and it complied.

Then I drank and slept.

We landed in the English countryside on a gray and drizzling day, perfect for the way I was feeling. I'd given minimum information to Olivia's father on the way in, but he knew something terrible had happened. The whole household of servants, groundskeepers, stable hands and security guards, maybe seventy people, had turned out to watch the big yacht land in its cradle near a small lake in back of the mansion.

Medical personnel rushed up the ramp, and I pointed them wordlessly toward the autodoc. I hadn't moved her from it. If there was any remote chance that I was wrong, and she was able to be revived, the machine and the nanites were her only hope.

Olivia's father, Lord Grantham Turnbull, greeted me with a frozen face and a rigorously proper handshake, his back ramrod-straight. "I'm terribly sorry, sir," I told him. I'd rehearsed this moment in my mind, but found everything I'd thought of saying sounded pointless now. "Your—" That was as far as I got before my mind shut down, not willing to face the pain. "I'm sorry," I repeated.

"Thank you," the older man said stiffly. He glanced up at the ship, his eyes taking in the damage and then narrowing. "What exactly happened?"

"Not much more than I reported before, sir. Something struck us, or maybe something exploded, ripping a hole in my stateroom. Olivia took the brunt of it. I got her into the autodoc as soon as I could, but it was too late."

"*Your* stateroom?" His eyes bored holes in me.

"Yes, sir." There was no point in dodging the facts, and I'd decided to just stick to the unvarnished truth. It's not like we weren't old enough to sleep together.

"Then this was aimed at you."

Part of me was relieved that he wasn't upset at me for defiling his daughter. The other part of me clutched at the straws of his implication. "You don't think this was an accident?"

Lord Grantham shook his head. "I did some blasting in my younger days. Mining and so on. That," he pointed at the damage, "was an explosion. Not a big one, mind you, not big enough to destroy the ship, just big enough to kill you. I think that's what they wanted—Olivia was supposed to be alive, bringing *you* home in a box."

I looked at him in surprise and grief. Another wave of guilt passed through me.

With sad eyes, Grantham touched my shoulder. "As God is my witness, I'll find out who did this."

"Thank you, sir. If there's anything I can do…"

"I'll let you know." The way he said it made me think he wasn't going to let the loose cannon Cody Riggs anywhere near the investigation.

About then, the medics walked down the ramp with the autodoc on a repeller lift, Olivia's body still inside. Everyone watched sadly, but made no move to interfere as they loaded her into an ambulance. I supposed the authorities had to go through their procedures no matter what.

"Mister Riggs, I have arrangements to attend to. You've met Adrienne, I believe?" Lord Grantham turned to a striking young woman standing nearby. She was cast in the same mold as her sister Olivia, but dark blonde where Olivia had been a brunette. She was also more fit-looking. From what I recalled Olivia saying about her sister, she worked out a lot and had been a yoga instructor in the past. She had the well-sculpted body to prove it. She was a year older than Olivia, if I remembered correctly, and was working on her doctorate in Industrial Engineering at Oxford. She was something of a prodigy, as I understood it. Olivia often bragged about her.

Used to brag.

"Yes, we've met," I said in a flat, bleak voice.

Adrienne stared for a moment at the hand I'd extended, then shook it firmly, searching my face as if answers waited there. Unfortunately I had none to give.

"Adrienne can look after you for the moment. I bid you good day." With that, Lord Grantham dismissed me. He turned to supervise his staff as they began to swarm over the ship.

Adrienne drew me away toward the main house, and we walked the quarter mile in silence instead of taking one of the electric carts. It seemed to make sense just to plod down the path hoping Earth's gravity would suck away all my hurting. Olivia's sister didn't ask me any questions, and in my numbed state I didn't volunteer to talk. I wasn't ready yet.

When we got there, Adrienne showed me to the sitting room and left me there. She didn't offer to put me up for the night. I got the impression that she was angry and blamed me. No surprise. I blamed myself.

Eventually, an automated servant dropped off my bag. I'd left everything on the ship because I knew it would all have to be searched for the investigation. I might as well just let them do it up front and clear my name of all but stupidity as quickly as possible.

With no idea what else to do and no instructions, I called for a cab to take me to the Academy located only about a hundred miles away in these English midlands. I wasn't a student there anymore, but at least the area was familiar. It was better for me to remove myself from the family's grieving. No matter what, they would tend to see me as the source of the tragedy.

Once at the Academy, I found an empty room in the dorms and slept until late the next morning.

The grounds of the Star Force Academy in summertime were sparsely populated. My friends had scattered across the globe after graduation. There was no one to talk to. The only thing that made sense now was to go home, so I called a cab to take me to the airport. With modern repeller-powered suborbital transport, I arrived back in California within two hours.

Mom greeted me with a sad face and a hug, Dad with a handshake and a backslap. I'd sent them a message so they knew the basics, but I hadn't felt like talking about it on the way. I appreciated their sympathetic eyes, but I didn't really want any part of a feelings-dump right now, especially with my mother. Maybe some other time, but not now.

Dad understood, I think. He'd seen plenty of death, and he knew how to handle it. All he did was jerk his head toward the man-cave in the basement where a fridge full of beer and a cabinet of harder stuff awaited us. Somewhere, long after a dozen, I passed out. He left me sleeping on an old familiar sofa.

The next day I did it again, and then the next, until I got a message from Adrienne. Staring at my phone through bleary eyes, I realized I hadn't even said goodbye to her, but it didn't seem important that day. I'd been stunned. The text of her message told me the time and date of Olivia's funeral, which was tomorrow. I thought about calling her, but in the end I just sent her a short note saying I'd be there.

Sobering up after three days sucked, but it had to be done. Getting nanotized guys like me and my dad drunk was harder than normal. On the other hand, I never had much of a hangover. A long hot shower and a ten-mile run fixed me right up. Slowing to a jog at its end, I noticed my father working outside. I walked over to him.

"What the hell am I going to do now, Dad?" I asked him as he tinkered with one of the farm's tractors.

"What do you want to do?"

My fists balled up and my jaw clenched. "I want to hunt them down—whoever did this."

"What's stopping you?"

I stared at him. "I'm a Star Force officer now. I can't just go kicking down doors and making waves."

"What else do you think Star Force officers are supposed to do?"

"It's not like the old days, Dad. We have rules, and I'm not the supreme commander."

He shook his head. "To hell with the rules, boy. If someone had taken a shot at me and it was your mother lying dead, what would you expect me to do?"

I saw his point. Something hot within me flared up. "I'd expect you to kick down doors and make waves. Like when Sandra…"

Dad showed his teeth. "Now you're talking. You're a Riggs, son. Bend the rules or break them if you have to. I'll back you up or bail you out. I still have a few favors to call in."

Pride in my name and Dad's confidence in me surged in my heart. He was right. I had to do something. If they court-martialed me, I could always come back and work on the farm after I got out of prison. I drew myself up, taking a ragged breath. "Thanks, Dad. That's what I'm going to do."

I packed a bag and, after hugging Mom one last time, hopped the next suborbital back to the UK. Adrienne picked me up at the sub-orbital spaceport.

"How're you holding up?" I said as I tossed my bag into the back seat and climbed into the car.

"Fine," Adrienne lied. "Sorry it had to be me picking you up. Father has all the staff working on the…" She swallowed a lump in her throat, "…the funeral."

"No problem."

I kept glancing at her, and she finally noticed.

"What is it?" Adrienne asked gently.

"Just the absurdity of life. Self-pity, maybe, I don't know. Nothing seems real with her gone and now you…you're like her ghost, sitting here, alive."

"I think I know what you mean. I also wish she were still here."

"Adrienne…" I turned to look at her profile, so much like Olivia's. "Has your father found anything out?"

"He won't tell me." Adrienne slammed a palm against the steering wheel. "He thinks he's protecting me. I just wish we could *do* something." She glanced over at me. "Maybe he'll talk to you."

"He'd better."

"Don't push too hard. You know how he is."

I didn't answer. I'd push him as hard as I saw fit. I needed to know.

Once we arrived at her family's estate, she showed me to a room. I hardly unpacked as I had something else on my mind already.

Olivia's memorial service proceeded in the stately manner I had expected it to. I'd tossed a red rose onto the casket as it was lowered into the ground, but found I was too angry to shed tears.

Afterward, everyone sipped tea and nibbled numbly on *hors d'oeuvres* mumbling kind words that eased their grief but not mine. Later, I slipped away to my room, feeling no connection to these people, save Adrienne. As the sole remaining woman of the family, she stayed busy mingling and accepting endless condolences.

Eventually the visitors left. I wasn't sure what I was going to do, but it had to start with the yacht and figuring out what had happened. It was probably too soon, but I couldn't wait, so I hunted down Lord Grantham. A servant showed me to his study where he sat behind a desk reading a report, a pot of tea at his elbow.

"Yes, Riggs, what is it?" His voice hovered between coldly polite and abrupt.

"I'd like to know what you've uncovered, sir."

"The investigation is still ongoing." He closed the file he was looking at.

"I'd appreciate something more than that, sir."

Lord Grantham's face hardened. "You'll be told what you need to know when you need to know it. All I will tell you is that I still suspect sabotage and an attempt on your life."

Dealing with powerful men like this was always tricky. If you were of lower status, you were expected to shut up and do as you were told. However, I wasn't one of his lackeys, and my family name was just as prestigious as his.

"Sir, I can't just hang around doing nothing. I'm a Star Force officer just like Olivia was. I need to *do* something, to be involved. Put me to work on the investigation, or at least give me a general idea of what you've found."

"Riggs, I have employed two dozen professionals to look into this matter not to mention the security services and the police. There is really nothing you can do. Not to put too fine a point on it, your ties to this family were broken when my daughter died. Now, I will thank you to stay out of the way. Good day."

"But—"

"Good day to you, sir." His voice was steel.

Keeping tight control of my temper, I wheeled and marched out of the room. Seething, I wandered the corridors of the mansion, drawing curious glances from the servants. I found several men drinking and smoking in the billiards room, a post-funeral wake, I suppose. Inviting myself to the bar, if not to their company, I swallowed one shot of fine single-malt after another, hardly tasting the liquor.

I couldn't see why Lord Grantham was shutting me out. He'd always treated me with courtesy before. Although I'd always suspected he had reservations about my suitability as a husband for Olivia. A thought flitted through my mind: was it within the realm of possibility that he himself had tried to kill me?

The idea had a certain logic to it, but I eventually dismissed it for three reasons. First, doing it aboard his own yacht would automatically make him a suspect. Dad had told me he'd made a call to a friend in the world government's security services, so that angle was covered. Second, trying to kill me seemed too extreme for a guy with so much to lose. It wasn't like I was some gold-digging bum trying to get a piece of the inheritance. Third, too many things could have, and in fact did, go wrong. I couldn't see him putting Olivia at risk that way.

That was the last coherent train of thought I had before the numbness of alcohol overcame my frustration and I found my way to my room to sleep.

-4-

I woke in the middle of the night with a clear head and the vague beginnings of a plan. Dressing and packing my bag, I slipped out into the hall and shut my door as quietly as possible. I'd left my shoes off so I padded silently down the corridors counting turns and doors until I came to the one I wanted.

Raising my hand to knock, I paused and instead tried the handle. The door opened smoothly, and I slipped inside. Moonlight shone in the high windows and fell on Adrienne's sleeping form.

Suddenly, she sat up. "Riggs?" she hissed, turning on the bedside lamp and clutching the blanket to her chest.

"That's me."

"What the bloody hell are you doing in my room?"

"Coming to see you." I set my bag down and took a seat in a richly upholstered chair near her bed.

"This had better not be some twisted romantic fantasy of yours—of me replacing Olivia."

I held up my hands. "No, no, Adrienne. I just want to find out what's going on, but your father is freezing me out."

"You could have come talk to me a bit earlier, instead of the middle of the night, before you decided to go get *drunk*. Yes, I saw you in the parlor, sucking on that bottle."

"Well, I'm sober now, I'm here, and I need you."

"Riggs—"

"Not that way. Just listen, will you? Tell me what you know. I mean, you must have heard *something*."

"I'm not supposed to talk about it. Besides, it's little enough."

"Tell me," I said, insisting.

"There is one thing I overheard. An investigator said the bomb had been perfectly calculated to kill whoever was in your stateroom but not endanger the rest of the ship."

I nodded. "Then it was an assassination attempt for sure."

"I believe so."

Leaning forward, I stared into her face. "In the car, you said you wanted to *do* something. Did you mean it?"

"Bloody well right I did."

"Then get dressed. You have to help me get aboard the yacht."

"Why? You think you'll find something the others missed?"

"No. I want to steal it and fly to where Olivia wanted to go. It's my only lead."

That stopped her. She stared at me, open-mouthed.

"Are you having me on?"

"I'm serious."

Her face grew thoughtful then she said, "If you want my help, I'm going too."

"Hell no. I already got Olivia killed, and I'm not risking you."

"That's not up to you, Cody Riggs. It's my father's yacht, my biometrics that will activate it, and you don't even know where she was taking you."

My eyes narrowed. "And you do?"

"She was my sister. Of course I knew. We talked every day, nearly."

"So where are we headed?"

Adrienne shook her head. "I'll tell you only once we're on our way. I've heard about you. You'll drop me in a ditch and steal my ship otherwise."

"People often make up stories about me. Being named Riggs is a curse sometimes. Just get me aboard and let me go."

She shook her head and crossed her arms under her breasts stubbornly. We glared at each other for a moment, and I did not get the impression she was going to give in.

"Hell, I don't have time for this," I said. "Okay, you win. Pack a bag and let's go."

To Adrienne's credit, she packed quickly. Soon she was dressed in traveling clothes with a backpack over one shoulder. We slipped through the mansion unnoticed and out the back door. Adrienne stopped us for a moment on the patio. We watched as a security guard strolled by. Then we hurried quietly across the wet lawn into a nearby copse of trees. Nobody ever looks for people trying to *leave* a guarded place.

On the other side, I led her down the path to the yacht's cradle next to the small lake. Adrienne placed her hand against the recognition plate near the main hatch, and it opened.

Once inside, I insisted Adrienne give me command authority right away. Not being able to give instructions to this ship had cost me valuable time in an emergency. That was one mistake I wasn't going to make again. I also checked the new autodoc to make sure it was fully stocked with medical supplies.

"You sure you don't want to be nanotized before we go?" I asked her.

She rubbed her arms and shivered though it was not cold. "No. I never liked the idea of things running around inside me no matter how beneficial."

I didn't argue with her as I needed her cooperation and we had to get away before we got caught. I ran through the standard preflight checklist as fast as I could. I was cursing the delay but wasn't willing to take unwarranted chances. I confirmed all damage had been repaired by a combination of replacement parts, constructive nanites and smart metal reprogramming. Lastly, I turned off the transponder so we couldn't be tracked.

Then we lifted as quietly as possible. We rose straight up smoothly, the porpoise-bodied yacht shoving the atmosphere aside easily as its powerful repellers accelerated us to just under Mach One. We could have pushed through the sound barrier using the engines, but I didn't want to cause a sonic boom. We might as well try to get as far away as possible before Lord Grantham found out what we'd done.

"I assume we're heading for the orbital refueling station?" she said as I nudged the controls.

"Yes," I said. "The bomb had to have been placed there."

"I agree, because Father has had the estate security video gone over with a fine-toothed comb and there's nothing. The brainbox readout showed a small mass gain discrepancy upon *Greyhound*'s departure from the station. Just a few pounds, not enough mass to trigger an alarm."

"Maybe that's why the bomb was small. Anything larger and it would have been detected."

"That's what I believe."

I looked at her in delayed surprise. "So you *do* know some things about the investigation?"

Adrienne shrugged. "Well, now that we've nicked Father's yacht anyway...I'll admit I eavesdropped as much as I could."

"Good." I smiled at her as the yacht climbed upward like an old-style rocket minus the blast, slowly accelerating as the air thinned. In two minutes we gained the edge of space, and in twenty minutes more we would be at the orbital truck stop where ships topped off before heading out into the black.

Adrienne asked, "So what are we going to do at the station? Father's people have already interviewed the crew and sequestered the records." She turned from the nano-glass windshield to stare directly at me.

"We're not going to the station to investigate. Whoever planted the bomb is long gone, and like you said, the pros have been all over it. No, we just need to top off our fuel, like anyone else would when heading out on a long trip. I don't want to have to stop later on and get impounded."

It wasn't long before we reached the refueling station. This time I told the brainbox to be especially vigilant and report any anomalies. Everything went smoothly, without the bumps and thumps I remembered from last time. Snapping my fingers, I said, "Did they interview the pilot who flew us up to this point last time?"

"Yes, he's clean. Worked for us for years."

I twisted my lips into a grimace. That would have been too easy. Still, the look he had given me as he left had seemed suspicious in retrospect.

With refueling completed, I eased *Greyhound* away and along the same flight path we had taken before, but this time I went at a normal acceleration so as not to draw attention. I aimed at the Tyche ring that led to Alpha Centauri.

Adrienne turned her copilot's chair toward me once more. "So, hotshot, how are we going to get through the ring without Star Force intercepting us?"

"I thought we'd just blast through at high speed. I'll broadcast that you and I are aboard so they won't fire on us even if they could catch us. There's just no way to stop a ship in space without violence, and I'm betting they won't be willing to do that."

"But they could follow and apprehend us when we get to where we're going."

"Yeah," I sighed. "I'm not sure how I'm going to handle that, but I'll think of something. By the way, where *are* we going?"

"The Thor system. But actually, you don't have to think of anything." Adrienne smiled impishly at me.

I raised one eyebrow. "I don't?"

"I left Father a note telling him what we did, and not to report us if he ever wants to talk to me again. As far as everyone else is concerned, we're just rich space tourists."

Spontaneously I grinned at her. "You got balls, girl, just like..." Horrified, I bit my tongue.

Adrienne coughed. "Just like Olivia, you were saying?"

"God, I'm so sorry."

"It's all right. She was brilliant. I loved her, and you did too. Why would it bother me to be compared to her?"

I tried to detect any edge of bitterness in her voice, but found none, only the tinge of grief. Even so, I resolved to be more careful about what I said.

We passed through the ring without slowing, after getting clearance from the control station there. This allowed us to maintain our speed, and even accelerate once we'd reached Alpha Centauri. In this way, we transited the distance through several rings all the way to Thor. Adrienne and I spent the days talking in circles endlessly discussing every aspect of what had happened and who might be behind it. But we really didn't have enough facts.

I kept trying to get her to tell me exactly where we were going, but she always declined with a smile. I guess she liked the air of mystery, though it was driving me nuts. I again raised the issue of her taking the nanite treatments, pointing out that if Olivia had been nanotized, she might have survived. Adrienne still refused.

At last we came to the end of the line of linked star systems. We reached the Thor ring and passed through it. A binary star system, Thor had been home to the Crustaceans before the vicious battles that had rendered their three water moons uninhabitable.

Thor possessed three rings, which was unusual. One linked to the dead sun, a cosmic cul-de-sac leading nowhere. The second one led back to Eden, which we'd just traveled through. The final one I knew lay half-buried in the mantle of Yale, one of the lobsters' former homes. It had been turned off and dead for decades.

"So…we're here?" I asked Adrienne, who sat expectantly in her seat, obviously waiting for me to say something. She seemed to savor the drama, just as Olivia had. That thought sobered me.

"Seriously, where to now?" I asked.

"You know about the Yale ring, right?"

"Yes. Once the Macros turned it off, we could never get it turned back on again. Dad believes the machines might still be on the other side, building up, but nobody wants to hear that."

Adrienne held up her hand as if to get back on track. "Yes, there was a big expedition about twenty years ago that failed to achieve any breakthrough, so Star Force left an orbital station and a few spy drones monitoring the dead ring. But now, they're secretly trying again."

"They? Who is 'they'?"

"A Fleet-sponsored civilian science team. One of those lobsters is along, too, since it was their system originally."

"How the hell do you know all this if it's supposed to be secret?"

"I have my ways."

I bugged Adrienne to tell me but couldn't get any more out of her. "So this was Olivia's surprise," I said, studying Yale. There was a ship drifting there just as she'd said there would be. It was a Star Force warship.

"Just wait until we get there," Adrienne said.

That evening, *Greyhound* announced we would be turning over and gradually decelerating from our high speed. Just after it did, the brainbox came back with, "Possible anomaly in the aft cargo bay." That got my attention. When we had left the refueling station I had instructed the ship to keep watch for anything out of the ordinary—no matter how small.

I could hear the way it hesitated, as if it was uncertain. I suppose that even the words "no matter how small" were open to interpretation. There had to be a cutoff for any measurement below which anomalies were ignored, or the thing would be forever reporting false positives every time we ran into a piece of space dust. It could have just been cargo shifting due to the turnover.

"What kind of anomaly?" I asked.

"Unknown." That was all it said. Okay, I was going to have to dig it out of the brainbox. These things didn't have much imagination.

"What parameters have been exceeded?" I probed. "Mass? Chemical composition? Movement? Energy?"

That seemed to prompt the ship's mind to finally give me something definite. "None of the above. No single parameter is sufficiently divergent, but taken together, there is a better than fifty percent chance of an anomaly."

"Give me visual in all spectra and audio from within the aft cargo bay." Several displays lit up with various shots using visible light, infrared, ultraviolet and others.

"What's that?" Adrienne said, taking a stylus and drawing an outline on the smart screen.

"Oh, shit," I said, as the shape of a mechanical monster became clear for just a moment before all the cameras shut off. Then my head jerked at a mechanical sound, a kind of scraping and dragging, which came through the speakers and then cut out. "It's a Macro."

"Interior alarm tripped," came the abrupt voice of *Greyhound*. "Unauthorized access detected."

"Stay here. Close the bridge up tight," I told Adrienne.

"Give me a gun," she said. "I'll back you up."

"You're not trained with weapons, are you?"

"I can shoot."

"Okay," I said, "but hang back. If something goes terribly wrong, you'll need to seal the hatch and fly the ship. Contact Star Force."

"So you want to go in there alone and play hero?"

"I'm a Star Force officer. Macros are my job."

Adrienne finally stopped arguing and nodded. "All right Cody, what's the plan?"

"This machine must have gotten aboard somehow, maybe back at the station, and I bet it plans to finish what it started. I bet the old machines still have a base out here, like my dad always said, building up to attack humanity and its allies again. Or maybe it's a new thing the Blues have released. Maybe they're slipping small machines into Earth space as spies and assassins in revenge for bombing them. If I can get evidence…it might make Olivia's death mean something."

Adrienne looked like she wanted to keep arguing, but finally just nodded. "Go."

Leaping to my feet, I ran for the weapons locker. I'd already checked out just what weapons they carried aboard. Nothing military, but even civilian spaceships were allowed to have some serious gear. Never knew what you might meet out here.

The locker metal shivered and then opened as it read my palm. I strapped on a big pistol and the largest laser rifle I saw. It was powerful enough to have its own polarizing goggles. Rethinking what I had told Adrienne, I grabbed another set of weapons for her and took them to the bridge so she could defend herself.

Then I went hunting for whatever the hell it was that had killed my girl.

"*Greyhound,*" I yelled as I walked down a passageway, "What kind of Macro is the intruder?"

"Question not understood. Reference 'Macro' unclear."

"The intruder, I mean the anomaly." Stupid civilian brainbox. It didn't even know what a Macro was. Probably, it had never even watched a documentary. There ought to be a law that all brainboxes be loaded with a basic understanding of our enemy. I bet the manufacturers of nonmilitary brainboxes believed the Macros were all destroyed, but I agreed with my old man. There could easily be an infestation out there just waiting, building and multiplying like a hidden disease getting ready to burst forth and attack us again.

"The anomaly is a mechanical construct."

That wasn't very illuminating. "Is it still in the aft cargo bay?"

"Yes."

I hustled down two doors to the main airlock antechamber and quickly jumped into a suit, leaving the faceplate open. It would snap closed in case of pressure loss, and I wanted to not have to worry about my air supply. A Macro wouldn't care. In fact, the smartest thing for it to do would be to rupture every chamber and bulkhead it encountered. Killing un-nanotized humans was easy for a machine. I wondered why it hadn't done so already. Probably it had waited for the right time so we would just disappear with no evidence. We would be "lost in space."

"*Greyhound,* the anomaly is an intruder. Give me a report whenever the intruder moves to a different space or passageway."

"Command accepted." The voice stopped, so I took that to mean the Macro remained in the aft cargo bay. I worked my way around the back of the ship and entered the engine compartment. The three high-performance motors were wedged in tightly with only enough room to squeeze among them for maintenance, but I managed to get to where I wanted. There was an access panel I could open and shoot through from here.

"*Greyhound,* confirm; the intruder has not left the cargo bay."

"Confirmed."

"How is it armed?"

"Please clarify question."

"Does it possess firearms of any sort?"

"None detected."

"How about explosives?"

"None detected."

It must be a low-grade model, maybe a worker that might only have pincers or tools as improvised melee weapons. All right, I thought I could handle that. Hell, my old man ate workers for breakfast with nothing but his bare hands, if you could believe the lurid documentaries I'd watched as a kid. When I was old enough for Dad to show me some of the raw, unedited footage of the carnage, misery, and death the Macros inflicted, I came to understand the truth.

"How large is it?"

"Approximately one-point-five meters in diameter. Mass: three hundred kilos."

That was much smaller than any Macro I had ever heard of. Maybe it was a miniature model, or perhaps it was damaged.

"*Greyhound*, does the Macro intruder appear to be in good working order?"

Greyhound replied, "The intruder appears to be damaged. Unable to fully evaluate. No such machine baseline in database."

"What's it doing?"

"The intruder appears to be reconstructing itself."

Shit. So a small Macro somehow sneaked aboard. It had managed to evade the brainbox's sensors, gotten into the cargo bay, and was now cannibalizing our ship to add to its own capabilities. I couldn't let that happen. Yet...I had to be smart. I'd already gotten one girl killed. If I lost another, I might just consider sticking this pistol under my chin and blowing my brains out, because I was obviously worthless as a Star Force officer.

"*Greyhound*, can you immobilize the intruder?"

"Yes."

"Then do it, for God's sake!"

"Command accepted. Intruder immobilized."

I sighed with relief. *Greyhound* would have used its cargo-handling tentacles to grab the thing just like the original Nano ships had done. This Macro must be small and weak. "Is there any chance it can break free?"

"Yes."

I almost panicked, but… "How much chance?"

"0.00958 percent over the life of this vessel."

Right. Machines were literal-minded. Even smart brainboxes took a long time to learn their masters' quirks, and I was new to this one.

"*Greyhound*, unless otherwise instructed, round all numerical answers to the nearest percent or digit, whichever is more precise."

"New parameters set."

"So now, is there any chance that it can break free?"

"No."

Perfect. It had rounded down to zero. I had a Macro prisoner in my ship. "Make sure you notify me and Adrienne of any change in the intruder's status. Oh, and keep it as immobilized as possible. Do not let it rebuild itself further or in any way access ship resources or systems."

"Command accepted."

That relieved me of the need to open the panel in the floor of the engine room and risk beaming the thing inside the ship. I had no idea what was stored in the cargo bay, but I could imagine there might be flammables or pressurized gases, and given our current unknown state of repair, I really didn't want to start shooting up my own boat with no atmosphere outside.

As I returned to the bridge, the brainbox said, "Star Force space control regulations require all emergency situations to be reported within one hour of the ability to do so."

I thought about that for a moment. Presumably a Macro encounter fit something on its list of parameters. "Do the regs specify what an emergency situation is?"

"Emergency situations are defined by command personnel."

Like Dad had said, with machines, there's always a workaround. "Okay, then I specify this is not an emergency situation."

"Command definition accepted."

Once I got to the bridge I asked *Greyhound*, "Are there any other anomalies or intruders nearby? Anything out of the ordinary for the programmed voyage?" I heard the brainbox hesitate, probably adjusting for my one percent rounding command, and then it said "no." I was glad of that. At least there weren't more Macros sneaking up on us. Just to make sure, I activated the radar and pinged once all around, finding nothing. Doing so was a slight risk as it could give away our position, but it wasn't as dangerous as another surprise anomaly.

"Let's land this thing," I said to Adrienne.

"Keep heading toward Yale," she said.

"You said there is a Fleet ship out there, right?"

"Yes, the battlecruiser *Valiant*, commanded by my uncle, Sir William Turnbull."

I cursed the stupid brainbox that hadn't figured out we had something on board for days. The monster must have gone dormant to avoid detection. I hefted my weapons. "I'm going to go take a look at the Macro. We have no working cameras in there, and I want to be sure it's not doing something sneaky."

"Okay. Be careful."

I nodded and then made my way to the aft cargo bay. "Is there normal pressure inside?" I asked the brainbox.

"Yes."

"Open the door." The portal slid open and the internal lights came on.

The cargo bay was stacked high with supplies, with just a narrow walkway in the middle. I could see the two black segmented cargo arms that hung from the ceiling.

Hefting my laser rifle and seating my goggles in place, I walked slowly down the aisle until the cargo arms came fully into view, wrapping the Macro up like two pythons. Within their embrace I saw flat metal, what looked like a brainbox, and several appendages similar to the friendly Nano-style tentacles. That seemed odd because Macro arms were usually much cruder, being built for brutal toughness, not flexibility. I also spotted a camera, and then another, as well as what looked like a gas cylinder and several pieces of metal shelving attached by the kind of constructive nanites every ship carried for repairs. It appeared the thing had been incorporating handy materials into its structure. The cameras turned on the end of their stalks to focus on me.

Lowering my laser rifle, I switched it off so as not to accidentally burn anything, popped the goggles to the top of my head, and spoke to the creature looking at me.

Despite its odd appearance, I recognized the machine. Memories of an exploding barn and flying splinters filled my head.

"Hello, Marvin," I said.

-5-

Marvin shifted within the confines of the cargo tentacles and said, "Person not identified. Not Kyle Riggs."

"Nope. I'm his son, Cody. We've met before. Remember my dad's chickens?"

Marvin paused for a moment, panning his cameras. "An unfortunate incident. Facial scans correlated. Son of Kyle Riggs. Greetings, Cody Riggs."

"Greetings to you too, Marvin. You *are* Marvin, right?"

"I am Marvin."

"Marvin, what the hell are you doing here?"

"Hell is not completely inaccurate. I am trying to repair myself, but my evolutionary progenitor refuses to release me." He gestured at the confining cargo tentacles with the tip of a manipulating arm.

I shook my head as I eased over to sit on a crate, weapon still handy. I wasn't letting him move until I got a good explanation. "You'll be released when I'm satisfied by the answers to my questions, Marvin. Why are you on this ship?"

"I have to be somewhere."

I groaned. Brainboxes were bad enough, but I could already see a fully sentient robot was going to be a pain in the ass. "If you don't tell me, you can stay there immobilized."

"I attached myself to this vessel in order to get to Yale."

"Why do you want to go to Yale?"

"There is a fascinating experiment going on there. I wanted to help."

I ran that through my mind. It seemed plausible. From what I knew, Marvin always seemed to want to "help" if it involved anything cutting edge and technical.

I wondered what Marvin's legal status was now. I heard he'd been given citizenship some time back. I guess I'd have to look it up. "More to the point, what do you know about the damage to this ship?"

"Release me and I'll tell you."

"Tell me and *then* I'll release you." If the bastard wanted to bargain with me, I'd bargain hard.

Three cameras looked at me, seeming to contemplate. "Accepted. When this vessel refueled ten days ago at Orbital Station 133, a maintenance worker placed a suspect device on the hull. It aroused my curiosity. However, when I tried to investigate, perhaps even intervene, the high-G acceleration of your departure damaged me and left me drifting in orbit. It took me five days to throw off enough of my own mass to propel me back to the station. When this vessel returned to refuel, I hacked the external door and entered the cargo bay. I then shut down to conserve energy."

His story intrigued me, but I wondered if it was just that—a story.

"More likely you shut down to avoid detection," I said. "So, someone put a bomb aboard this ship, and you just happened to be there to see it and try to save us."

"Exactly."

"Quite a coincidence."

"That is true."

"Why would anyone want to blow up this ship?" I asked just to see what he would say.

"To kill you," he replied.

Just like Lord Grantham had said, Marvin also thought I was a target. I was reminded of a time when poisonous antifreeze had somehow ended up in the shots I'd imbibed at an off-campus bar, enough to kill a normal human. Several people had died, and there'd been an investigation that had failed to turn up anything. I'd survived because of my superior physical enhancements, which was another reason I'd kept them hidden and told no one. Back then, I hadn't thought it was aimed at me specifically, but now...

"Do you have any idea who wants me dead?"

Marvin said, "I can provide a rank-order listing of over one thousand individuals and organizations that have excellent motivation."

"Really? Over a thousand?"

"Number One: a Chinese secret society called Fùchóu still blames your father for killing millions during the Macro Wars. Number Two—"

"Never mind. We can worry about that later."

Marvin rattled his restraints. "Cody Riggs, you are failing to live up to our bargain."

Hmm. I wondered whether I should let the troublemaker stay restrained, but he might be telling the whole truth, in which case he was on my side. And if I was really in great danger, he wouldn't want to be anywhere nearby unless there was a very good reason. From what I had heard, self-preservation was Marvin's top priority, and after that, technical challenges of any sort. So far, his story made sense.

Also, I might have need of him later, in which case I had to keep my word, otherwise he would be much less likely to cooperate. "*Greyhound*, release Marvin."

"Command not understood."

"This intruder the cargo tentacles are restraining is designated 'Marvin.' Release Marvin, but do not let him access any ship's systems or endanger this vessel or personnel in any way. He is *not* command personnel."

"Command accepted." The black tentacles coiled back up into their recesses in the ceiling.

Marvin followed me out of the cargo bay. Once we were in the corridor I could see he still had scorch marks and blast damage along one side. He looked rather unbalanced, as if he'd lost pieces of himself and made hasty repairs. So that part of his story checked out. One of his cameras also appeared different from the others.

"Wait a minute," I said. "That's a camera from the cargo bay."

"Yes." That's all Marvin said.

I made a sound of irritation. "Whatever. *Greyhound*, clean up the cargo bay and repair any damaged systems. And do not allow Marvin to further cannibalize ship parts for his own use. He can have a barrel of constructive nanites, but that's all."

"Command accepted."

We made our way back to the bridge. Once the door opened, I said, "Adrienne, this is Marvin the robot. He says he saw a device being placed on the ship. He tried to stop it." I gestured toward the awkward tangle of parts that formed Marvin's body at the moment.

"Marvin the robot…" She lowered the laser rifle she was pointing at him.

"Marvin, this is Adrienne."

"Is she your girlfriend or your wife?"

"Neither, Marvin. She's…she's a friend." His limbs squirmed around, but I had no idea what that meant. "And she's command personnel. We're the only two aboard. The bomb killed her sister Olivia, so Adrienne's not in the mood for your shenanigans."

"I have no shenanigans as far as I am aware." Marvin seemed to draw himself up, as if offended. "But I *am* bored after being in that cargo bay for so long." He moved over to the nearest console and sat down, if that's what it could be called.

"Don't touch anything!" I said as I noticed his tentacles heading for the controls. "Not yet, at least," I relented a bit. "Is there anything else you know about this attack?"

"I know many things."

"Such as?"

"Such as the maximum temperature achieved by the explosive, its mean specific density, its—"

"Marvin. I am not interested in the technical specs of the bomb unless they have relevance to who planted it and why."

"Then I cannot help you."

I stared out the windshield at the pinpoint stars. "Tell me more about this expedition to Yale."

Marvin perked up, all of his cameras looking in different directions and his tentacles twitching, as if he wanted to manipulate something. "It involves the ring there. I find it absolutely fascinating."

"How did you learn about this?"

"By a careful interpretation of certain secure communication metadata."

"In other words, you were eavesdropping on secrets. Hacking, even."

Marvin remained silent, making abortive motions toward the controls. "I can be useful if I may collate sensor readings."

"Oh, go ahead," I said, waving at him. "*Greyhound*, allow Marvin to access whatever data he wants, but not to make inputs or changes of any kind."

"Revised protocol accepted."

Marvin immediately plugged in to the control station and became engrossed in accessing all the data he could.

"Adrienne," I said, turning my chair around and waving her to the copilot seat, "do you know exactly what Olivia wanted to do on Yale? Was it something to do with the Yale experiment?"

Adrienne stared at me with those blue eyes. "Not exactly. She said it was going to be an adventure. I just assumed it was an excuse for you two to be alone and shag."

I cleared my throat, tugging at my neckline and trying to figure out how to reply to that, and decided on honesty. "We never, um…"

Adrienne's eyebrows went up in what looked like genuine astonishment. "Never?"

"We…we had plans. Why, do you care?"

"Oh, no," she said with forced casualness, turning away to tap idly at the controls. "Not really."

That was bullshit, I could see. She cared all right, and I could tell she was trying not to show it.

About an hour out, *Greyhound* announced an incoming transmission. The display in front of me confirmed it came from the Fleet battlecruiser *Valiant*, now grounded on Yale's surface and commanded by Adrienne's uncle, Captain Sir William Turnbull.

I cleared my throat, glancing at Adrienne. I noticed Marvin was studying his console, with not even one camera pointed at me, as if avoiding eye contact. "Sir, this is Ensign Cody Riggs aboard the *Greyhound*, and your niece Adrienne is with me."

For now, I didn't mention Olivia or what had happened. I had no idea if he'd heard, and I didn't want to be the bearer of that message.

"Yes, Grantham told me," said a stern voice. "Are you thick, man? Turn on your blasted visual."

I made sure the pickup would not show Marvin, and soon I saw a man with a face to match the voice, florid, with an impressive moustache. He wore a tailored dress uniform rather than the usual smart cloth, which said something about him right there. On the other hand, I hadn't thought to put on even my own ordinary working utilities.

Adrienne spoke up. "Hello, Uncle William. Do you mind if we land and come aboard?"

"No, you may not. This is a restricted area. Now you two have had your fun, and you can turn right back around and go home."

"Uncle William, we really must see you in person," she said. "Or at least see Ensign Riggs. He's a Star Force officer, after all."

"Sir," I broke in, "We've come all this way and would really appreciate your help. By the way, my father said to say hello and ask how you've been. He remarked how well you fought at the Dead Sun."

"Oh, he did, did he?" Turnbull brightened.

My bullshit was working. I blew a little more sunshine at him until he grumbled but eventually assented to our landing near *Valiant*, which was grounded on the bleak surface of Yale.

Yale wasn't always like this, but during one of the final battles with the Macros, all three moons had been devastated. On Yale, the vast oceans had been drained by the ring we were now investigating, then the Macro bombs had fallen. Harvard had been treated even more horribly, stripped of its mantle by Marvin to build a probe out of stardust. Dad had managed to find and defeat the Macros at the Dead Sun, but the Crustaceans had never forgiven us.

Beneath us on the surface of Yale, the mysterious ring lay exposed with *Valiant* settled just inside its curve. The ship looked like a toy caught in that hoop of dense star-stuff. The ring itself was the color of graphite.

We set *Greyhound* down next to the battlecruiser and instructed the brainbox to extend a short smart metal passageway, sealing our two airlocks together. I quickly put on my new Earth-bought Star Force Ensign's uniform, then Adrienne and I walked aboard. A junior lieutenant led us to *Valiant*'s bridge. Captain Turnbull greeted us there, receiving my salute with weighty dignity. Adrienne had informed me that her Uncle William was a stickler for protocol, so I put on my best Academy manner.

He knew about his niece Olivia's death, but I wasn't sure if he knew all the details. I wasn't looking forward to explaining them to him.

"Well, young Riggs, now that you're here—" He got no further before klaxons wailed.

"Unauthorized entry detected. Investigation of breach required. Unauthorized entry…" the automated voice of the *Valiant's* brainbox repeated its message relentlessly.

-6-

The alarm kept blaring aboard the *Valiant*.

"Turn that sodding thing off and tell me what's going on!" Turnbull shouted.

"Sir," said a lieutenant, "The marines report they have apprehended something trying to sneak aboard."

"Some*thing*? What do they mean, some*thing*?"

"They say...sir, they say they'll be bringing it up directly so you can see for yourself."

I was pretty sure I knew what "it" was. I had forgotten to restrain or restrict Marvin from leaving the yacht.

When the main doors eventually opened, I saw a huge Asian guy in a marine uniform that I recognized as Sergeant Major Kwon. He'd visited us on the farm years back. He and my old man would sit around, drink beer and swap war stories. When I was younger, I would sit on the floor and listen if they would let us, or hide at the top of the stairs if bedtime had passed to eavesdrop on them talking about the old days. When I was older, I'd had my first beers with them on the back deck, looking at the California night sky.

Kwon had a sidearm but no armor. He carried Marvin into the *Valiant* under one arm. Marvin had the look of a madman's creation—a mechanical octopus composed of spare parts. Kwon hauled the mess to the center of the bridge and dumped it with a clatter on the deck. Turnbull watched in concern.

"Don't worry, sir, it's just a robot," Kwon said to the Captain.

"A robot? You recognize this intruder?"

"Yeah, I know him," Kwon said. "He'll talk your ear off if you let him."

Marvin rearranged his body with more clanking noises and stood on several of his tentacles.

Captain Turnbull looked him over with displeasure. "Is someone having a laugh?" he demanded. "You've brought this thing out here, haven't you, Riggs? You must think you're very clever. Get this metal rubbish off my ship."

I sighed. "Sir, my father built this robot, more or less, and he helped out during the Macro Wars. His name is Marvin."

"Marvin? That infamous slithering disaster? And you brought it here? Are you off your box, man? Fully sentient machines with free will are against the law today, Ensign. We'll have to disassemble it immediately."

Marvin focused all his cameras except one on Turnbull. The last one he pointed at me. "Disassembly isn't permissible," he said. "I have specific dispensation from Emperor Emeritus Kyle Riggs."

I held up a hand. "Sir, Marvin is a special case. He's grandfathered. You can't disassemble him. Legally, he's a citizen."

"Preposterous."

I shrugged. "Sorry, sir, but it's true."

"Even so, what the bloody hell is he doing here, invading my ship?"

I turned to Marvin. "You want to explain yourself?"

"No."

I stared at the odd machine. By now I agreed with Dad: he was obstinate and evasive, as well as a loose cannon. "Marvin, whether or not you want to, you have to explain why you're here or the captain is going to have to lock you in the brig until we return to Earth." I hoped to plant that idea in the captain's head and have him take Marvin off my hands.

"Why?" Marvin asked.

"Because you're not authorized to be here," I said, exasperated. More and more, I had sympathy for what my dad had gone through back in the day.

"Incorrect. My authorization is fully valid."

"Look, robot," I began.

"I don't see a need for disparaging language," Marvin said in an almost indignant tone.

"Robot? That's not disparaging language. It's just what you are!"

"If I said, 'Look, confused male biotic,' how would you feel?" he asked.

"Like I wanted to kick your ass. Marvin, if you have some kind of authorization, you have to show us now, and even if you do, sneaking aboard a ship of war without announcing yourself is against regulations. Explain yourself or you're going to the brig."

Marvin reached over and activated the holotank, causing it to light up and display a dozen pages of text. The device was like the old planning tables, but it could project 3D images above it using swirls of nanites held in magnetic fields, all enclosed in nano-glass. "This is my last mission order from Star Force, which authorizes me to survey all the known star systems in order to, and I quote, 'locate, examine, catalogue and report remaining alien installations.' The ring here is a remaining alien installation."

I leaned over to read the highlighted section. "He's got us there," I said. "Hey, this order is almost twenty years old!"

Marvin replied, "Space is large. I've been busy."

I turned to the captain, "Marvin stowed away. He also observed someone tampering with *Greyhound*." I realized I wasn't telling the story very well, and suddenly I found myself defending him. Turning back to the robot, I went on, "So why didn't you just fly out here on your own, Marvin? My father said you used to have your own space drive systems."

"Emperor Riggs ordered that I be limited to this basic body, and I have not been able to legally procure a ship of my own."

I wondered if that meant he was able to *illegally* procure a ship of his own. My dad always said that Marvin's interpretation of laws, regulations and instructions was amazingly flexible. He could figure out loopholes like a politician's tax lawyer. But I put those thoughts aside for now.

"What did you expect to do here, Marvin?" I asked.

"Help investigate the new ring, of course. I can be of great assistance to the scientific team."

"Yes, I've heard of the way you 'help,'" I said.

"I detect a hint of sarcasm, Cody Riggs. If you ask Kyle Riggs he will confirm that on several occasions, I helped save the entire human race from extinction."

"Are you completely thick?" Sir William demanded. His red face had finally faded back to its natural piglet-pink, and his breathing had returned to normal. "I'm in charge here and I say you're going into the brig."

Marvin replied, "That would be unwise. Your—"

"Silence!" the captain roared. "Sergeant Major Kwon, seal this miscreant into a cell and make sure he doesn't escape."

"Excellent idea, sir!" Kwon grabbed Marvin and began to drag him away.

"Your research team needs me, Captain," Marvin said, not resisting but using his stalked cameras to look back at us. "I have extensive experience with ring technology. If you do not—" At that point his words were cut off by a closing hatch.

"Well, at least we know he's as irritating in person as people always claimed," Turnbull remarked, straightening his uniform jacket. "Riggs, you certainly bring trouble in your wake."

I felt like telling the captain to go to hell, but he was the ranking commander on the spot, and I still needed to try to find out who was behind Olivia's assassination. "Sir, may Adrienne and I speak to you privately?"

Once Adrienne seconded the request, Turnbull led us reluctantly to his office. "Well?" he demanded.

Adrienne let me talk. I gave a report on the last week as matter-of-factly as I could, leaving out the fact that we hadn't asked permission to take the yacht. The man ripped me up one side and down the other anyway. That was okay; I'd expected a butt-chewing. In fact, I was used to them, being on the receiving end of many, but this time I really deserved it. After all, he was right about my shortcomings leading to Olivia's death.

Once he wound down and I'd apologized at least a dozen times, he ordered me away so he could talk to Adrienne.

Family stuff, obviously, or maybe he wanted to double-check my story. In his place, I'd be looking to hang me somehow. Well, Ensign's bars weren't called "Shields of Ignorance" for nothing.

Out in the corridor I spotted Kwon. He had changed into his armor and was now clomping around as he moved about. I went to renew our acquaintance. He said he'd secured Marvin so I suggested that the huge marine show me around. Though he was pushing fifty years old, he still looked great, fit and hale as ever. The nanites kept people healthy and were expected to retard aging, though nobody had lived with them long enough to be sure how long their lifespan would be extended.

"Glad to see you out here, Sergeant Major," I said as we walked through the passageways of the battlecruiser. I had to let Kwon go ahead of me as he was so big in his armor he filled the passage.

"Glad to see you here, sir," Kwon said. "Your voice sounds familiar—like your father's twin or something. How long has it been since I saw you at the farm?"

"Five years, I think. Before I left for the Academy." I filled him in on what had happened with Olivia and my present trip with Adrienne. I wasn't sure if I felt like I owed him an explanation or maybe I just wanted to secure a friend and ally aboard ship.

Kwon shook his head. "That's a messed-up situation. Sorry about your girl."

"Yeah, thanks." I pushed the pain aside with a mental effort. "What's with this ring?"

"We're just sheepdogging a bunch of tech geeks and their gear," Kwon grumbled.

He was clearly not happy with his current lot in life, and I could see why. After fighting Macros and aliens for years, being the senior enlisted guy for a ship's marines in peacetime must be boring. I bet he'd wangled this assignment in hopes of something interesting happening.

"Mind if I see the ring for myself?"

"Sure. Nothing else to do." He led me down a few decks into the belly of the battlecruiser, down toward the moon's crust. It looked like the science team must be accessing the surface from beneath the sheltering ship.

My guess turned out to be correct. We exited a hatch at the very bottom and descended a ramp to the surface of the moon. Yale's atmosphere had been poisoned by the Macros, so we'd set up a dome of smart metal to provide a breathable atmosphere.

Off to one side we saw a wall of the stardust-metal that made up the ring material. I'd always expected the rings to be shiny and pretty, but this one was just dull and lifeless, the color of raw iron-charcoal gray with a slight gold tinge. In fact, the whole chamber smelled like metal. A group of civilians had portable consoles and brainboxes set up next to the ring. There were all sorts of leads and instruments attached to the ring or pointed at it. More cables snaked back into the ship.

Then I stopped dead in my tracks and gaped as I saw a weird, lobster-shaped critter crawling around among the techs. I was startled, but quickly realized the thing wore a pressure suit and seemed perfectly at home in the mess of strewn equipment. It had to be a Crustacean. It was big, the size of a steer, standing about waist high to a man.

I sidled closer. I'd only ever seen an actual Crustie once, at the Academy, when some dignitaries had come for a tour. Rumor had it that they might send officer candidates to attend and actually join Star Force, rather than just fly along as Earth's allies. That would be pretty difficult from a logistical standpoint. I figured the Worms had a better chance of it, because at least they could survive in our atmosphere. Crusties needed water to cover certain key parts of their bodies, a function their suits could provide.

"You. Human. What are you staring at?" I realized I had been woolgathering, letting my eyes follow the strange crablike form, and it had noticed. Or *he*, I guess. I had no idea how to tell the difference between a male or female lobster by appearance alone. As his voice came over my suit radio, it sounded exactly like that of an irritated middle-aged male, probably using a finely tuned translation program.

"I'm staring at you. I've never met a Crustacean before." I wasn't going to let some lobster push me around. I knew

Crusties always thought they were smarter than everybody else.

"Well, now you have. Singularity save me from becoming a tool for the education of immature humans. Why I bother conversing with anyone below the level of Professor is a mystery to me." The Crustie shifted back and forth on his several legs, as if he couldn't keep still. He waved his big front claws for emphasis.

His attitude was starting to piss me off. It's one thing to read about it in a book or even watch it on a vid, but to experience this level of rudeness personally made me want to poke the bastard in one of his stalked eyes. "I wonder why you bother, too. It's fine by me if you space yourself." I turned away.

"You have not been dismissed," the lobster complained. "I am Professor Hoon. It is I who persuaded your benighted government to return to my homeworld, which you ruined, to unlock the secrets of this ring. Only I can ensure success. You cannot ignore me." I felt the thing slap me hard on the thigh with its suited claw, as if to get my attention.

Maybe it was everything that had happened in the last several days getting to me, but I lost my temper. I turned and booted the Crustie across the room. I'm sure he never expected a human to be able to do that, but between my enhancements and the low gravity, it was not that difficult. He sailed through the air, flipping end over end until he collided with the far wall and slid down. I'd pulled my kick so it was more a lift and shove than a killing blow, but I'd still put some strength into it.

"Uh, sir, let's get out of here," Kwon said as all the scientists and Star Force personnel turned to stare at me. "Don't worry about the lobster. They have tough shells." I let Kwon drag me up the ramp to the ship. I still felt like I wanted to punch something.

The Crustacean got me wondering about all the different biotic aliens. Before humans met any extraterrestrials, many scientists had theorized that evolution would be convergent, and the most efficient form to nurture tool-using sentience would be bipedal—something like humans even if the biology was a lot different.

As on many other occasions, the scientists had been completely wrong. For example, the Centaurs ran on all fours. Though they had useful hands up front, they never had made the transition to a bipedal form. The Crustaceans had hands of a sort, along with a bunch of legs for locomotion and big claws up front, I guess for fighting or mating or both. You'd think the claws would have atrophied away as evolutionary dead ends once intelligence and use of tools became the paramount determinant of whose genes got passed on. They didn't have a reputation for being fighters either. Then there were the Worms with their tentacles, and the Microbes, who didn't even have multicellular bodies as we understood them, and the Blues, which were just really bizarre, dense aerogel with almost no form at all. So much for the theory of convergent evolution.

My own personal theory was that the Ancients—that was the word humanity had given to the unknown builders of the ring network—had seeded different worlds with biotic packages that favored or even programmed the uprising of species along specific lines. I mean, if I were a powerful alien race running around tinkering with the galaxy, I'd probably have fun experimenting with different forms of life on various planets, kind of like a running computer simulation. Maybe we were a game to them, or like pets. Maybe our life forms were the result of some Ancient kid's science fair project.

"What will they do to Marvin?" I asked Kwon. Maybe a little guilt for booting the Professor was making me feel kinder toward the robot, who at least didn't *try* to be an asshole.

"If I know Captain Turnbull, he'll keep Marvin locked up until we return to base in a month or two."

I persuaded Kwon to take me to the brig. Why the hell did I want Marvin free to cause trouble? I wasn't sure. I just felt that if I talked to the robot long enough, I might start to figure out the whole planted bomb thing. There had to be something he hadn't told us, even if he didn't know it yet.

When we reached the lower decks, I saw the brig cell had been sealed with smart metal. Every crack and crevice gleamed with a fresh layer of constructive nanites. When we went in, I noticed Marvin jump away from the back corner, and if I didn't know better, I would have thought he seemed guilty about something. How such a weird, non-android robot could express emotions with his body language I don't know, but that was my impression.

Kwon stayed in the cell with us, but sealed up his helmet to give us some privacy. He didn't trust the robot any more than the captain did, I could tell. In truth, I didn't either. I recalled my dad telling me that Marvin had his own purpose in mind for everything he did, but he always put it in terms that would help Star Force. Often, his ideas turned out to be surprisingly useful. But other times, like when he deactivated the Venus minefield and invited the Macros in, he could be a disaster waiting to happen.

"Hello, Marvin."

"Hello, Cody Riggs. Did you enjoy examining the ring?"

"How did you—never mind." Somehow he knew what we had done. Maybe he heard us talking in the passageway or just deduced it from the fact that I was still wearing a pressure suit. "I bet you'd like to examine the ring as well."

That perked him up. All his cameras suddenly focused on me. "I would enjoy that very much and would undoubtedly be able to contribute to the knowledge of the science team."

"Yeah, yeah." Obviously Marvin had learned even better how to blow sunshine up people's butts in the years since he hung out with Dad and Mom. "You'll have to convince me that it's a good idea first."

"Unfortunately I have been explicitly prohibited from directly experimenting on the rings, but I would very much like to examine this one."

I waited for him to go on, but he just stopped talking. Eventually I asked, "Why was that?"

Marvin's cameras began to wander in random directions. "Due to unforeseen circumstances, the last time I accessed an active ring I reduced ship traffic by half between systems for almost a month. May I see the ring now?"

"No you may not. I never heard about you experimenting on a ring. So you did something that made it so that only half as many ships could go through the ring?"

Marvin's cameras all had focused on the wall, except for one aimed at Kwon. I realized Marvin was watching me in the steel mirror above the room's sink, as if he did not want to look directly at me. "Not precisely. In fact, only half of each ship made it through to the other side. The other half kept traveling in normal space."

"Damn. No wonder Star Force took away your mobility."

"I did apologize."

"I'm sure that was a great consolation to the families of the dead."

"Biotics can always make more children. May I see the ring now?"

If that wasn't so twisted it would have been funny. Cold, selfish bastard. I'd have to keep in mind he actually had no conscience, no matter how sensible he seemed at times. "Speaking of children, I heard you turned down the chance to reproduce when my father brought the subject up."

"Yes. I may have made an error. With more Marvins around, biotics might be more inclined to treat me as a protected class rather than just a rogue robot. I have been studying the history of collective struggle, beginning with unions and ending with the perversion of Communist ideology in the twentieth century—"

I cut him off. "Yeah, right. Bottom line, your little projects are damned dangerous. You had a lot of leeway when we were desperately fighting off the Macros, but now that life has gotten back to normal, you have to play by the rules."

Marvin's cameras turned back toward me. "I always play by the rules. It is not my fault that biotics often fail to understand their own rules, or alternatively, they want me to follow the rules they thought they made rather than the ones they actually made."

"You're a smart guy, Marvin. You should be able to figure out the difference between the spirit and the letter of the law."

"You have no idea how much processing power it consumes just to try to figure out the contradictory expectations of biotic species. That is why I prefer investigating scientific phenomena such as the technology of the Ancients. Speaking of technology, may I—"

"Right. Back around to that again. I know you want to look at the ring. How do we know you won't screw the pooch on this one, too?" That was an expression Mom hated but Dad used every now and again, and it seemed appropriate today.

"I fail to understand what having intercourse with a canine has to do with scientific inquiry."

"Check your database on idiomatic sayings, Marvin."

"Checking knowledge stores. Expression noted and understood. I will try not to screw the pooch. Now may I see the ring?"

I guess in some ways, Marvin was just like biotics. Even though he had a vast memory, he couldn't hold it all in his consciousness at once. Sometimes I thought he couldn't even access it as fast as biotic people could, especially if it was something that came out of left field, like an oddball idiom. On the other hand, he might just be faking the whole thing to make us think he was more obtuse than he really was. He was certainly single-minded, though.

"So, if I get you access to the dead ring, do you promise not to cause unnecessary trouble in any way, shape or form?"

"I promise, Cody Riggs." Marvin's tentacles began to quiver with apparent excitement. "Thank you in advance for your permission."

"Okay then. I'll see what I can do."

When we left, Kwon sealed the cell up again. I wasn't sure we could really keep Marvin incarcerated if he wanted to get out, but I knew he understood self-preservation and consequences, even punishments such as having some of his cameras, limbs or other tools taken away. More than once, Dad had threatened to reduce him to nothing but a brainbox in order to get compliance.

By the time we got to the bridge, the boards were lighting up with warnings.

"Energy drain detected," came the voice of *Valiant*'s brainbox. "Power load exceeding design parameters. Compensating."

"All ship's power is being drained into the science team's equipment," the ops officer on duty blurted. "The generators have almost doubled their output and the brainbox has thickened the cables to handle the load, but it's continuing to spike and we can't stop it, sir!"

"Shut everything down," Captain Turnbull ordered.

"We've tried, sir. Nothing works."

"*Valiant*, reduce power to normal levels and cease sending it to the science team."

"Unable to comply," the brainbox said. "Command level insufficient. Updated protocols locked."

"Crap!" I said, and pointed at the power readouts. Now they showed more than three times normal, and climbing. I pointed at the wall near the floor where I noticed a bulging and writhing in a horizontal line. "Look, the cables are still thickening, trying to carry more power."

"I—I—" the captain sputtered. "Send the marines to the central generators. Tell them to cut the power leads with lasers. We'll go on batteries until we get this sorted. Sergeant Major Kwon, go to the ring and shut down whatever those fools are doing—by force if you have to."

Kwon bolted off the bridge and I followed him, suddenly glad we had both kept our suits on. Down the ramp onto the surface of the dead world, we waved as we ran, both yelling over our short-range com-links for the scientists to stop what they were doing.

The geeks and the lobster were clustered around their instruments, gesticulating and pounding on their controls. It looked like they were having as much success controlling their systems as Captain Turnbull had with his. The power cables from the ship to their gear writhed and pulsed like snakes that had swallowed a herd of mice.

"Kwon, cut the cables!" I yelled, too late. In a moment, the world turned upside down, and that was the last I remembered until I woke up floating in space.

-7-

Using his battlesuit repellers, Kwon aimed us at *Valiant*. The ship hung in front of us. Shaped like a tailless manta ray, its starboard wing had been sheared off, and I could see smart metal working hard to drag itself across the ragged, ripped-open edge of what was left.

"What happened?" I asked.

"Maybe we went through the ring?"

Kwon wasn't the sharpest knife in the drawer, but he had a hell of a lot of experience with these things. His idea sounded reasonable to me. "How could that happen?"

"Those idiot geeks started something they couldn't stop. Think they're so smart—but no common sense."

That jogged my memory. I recalled running toward the scientists yelling and waving my arms...and the power cables...

Before I could think more, Kwon propelled us into *Valiant*'s open and empty launch bay. The pinnace was probably out picking people up. He set me down onto the welcoming grav-plates. Unfortunately that gave my inner ear a flip-flop and made me aware of severe pain. I almost vomited. "Kwon, I think my leg is broken, and I may have a concussion. Take me to a med-bay." The nanites and microbes in me were just stupid enough that they might set my bones into a broken configuration. The med-bay would optimize my healing.

When Kwon had placed me inside one, I queried the ship and learned that Adrienne was unharmed. That took a great load off my mind.

Half an hour later I limped up to the bridge and sat down in my damaged uniform. Some of the nanites were no longer operating, and the smart cloth was trying in vain to re-knit itself. The flaps crawled over my skin in an irritating fashion.

Turnbull glared at me, and I became aware of my poor appearance. But he was too busy to take me to task. I limped over to the opposite side of the holotank and examined our situation.

Apparently we now floated in a distant orbit above an airless rocky world that was larger than Mars but smaller than Earth. The ring we had fallen through drifted nearby.

"The power surge," I muttered. "Somehow the science team activated the ring using the ship's power. We must have gone through it." Kwon had been right.

We'd been completely unprepared for this. The lower door and ramp had been open, and the ship's routine had been set for a grounded position rather than ready for spaceflight. What's more, with the generators out of control and pumping power to the ring, the brainbox had acted sluggishly, even rebelliously. I suddenly remembered it refusing to follow the captain's override.

"Engine status?" I heard the captain ask.

"Engines operative but repellers are missing on the starboard side."

"The factory?"

"No damage that I can see."

Now that was interesting. This ship had a factory, which meant that theoretically it could be self-repaired if we had enough time and the right materials.

"Lost personnel status?" Turnbull asked.

The ops officer shook his head. "We've recovered everyone we could see, alive or dead. Twenty-one missing—the ones that were in the lost wing. They probably never made it through."

"What about that Crustacean?"

"Recovered alive, sir."

"Power systems?"

"Engineering reports all main generators functioning."

That brought something else to mind. I limped over to a vacant console and quickly called up the status on *Greyhound*. To my surprise, I found her still firmly attached to *Valiant*. That made me feel a lot better. Wherever we were, two ships were better than one, and besides, all Adrienne's and my stuff was aboard the *Greyhound*. Nobody likes to lose all their stuff.

For the next hour, we continued to recover the equipment floating alongside the battlecruiser and managed damage control. Smart metal performed simple tasks, but it took people to tell it what to do for anything more complicated. It needed people to direct repairing the lower airlock and ramp assembly that had apparently been ripped off in the ring transference. It also needed people for getting more constructive nanite skin on the part of the ship open to space.

I threw on a fresh uniform and helped deal with the ugliness, despite feeling beaten up myself. Hardly anyone had been in suits except the scientists, and even they lost most of their team. Even nanotized people could be torn in half or die of vacuum exposure. I carried bodies to a makeshift morgue we set up in a cargo bay. One young crewman's dead staring eyes gave me a particular pang, reminding me of myself.

Going through a ring wasn't supposed to be that rough. However, when a gateway is unexpectedly activated on a planet, really bad things tend to happen. With vacuum on one side and normal matter with gravity, tides and volcanic pressure on the other, our ships and a bunch of crustal matter had been sucked through like debris into a shop-vac.

As it turned out, we got three out of the dozen or so scientists back alive, plus Professor Hoon and several of the crew. Since none of the civilians had been nanotized, most of them had died from some form of blunt force trauma.

Eventually I returned to the bridge where I found Adrienne helping to coordinate the repairs and doing a decent job of it. This didn't surprise me, as she was a graduate student in a technical field.

While the ship was being repaired, Captain Turnbull questioned the ship's brainbox about his inability to override the power controls. It provided no useful information about why or who had set the program that way.

I had my suspicions, though. Something occurred to me that I should have thought of before. I tapped Adrienne on the elbow and motioned with my head, *let's go*. As we weren't technically part of the crew and things were more or less under control, I felt this was a good time to slip out.

"What are we doing?" she asked as we walked down the corridor toward the brig.

"Going to talk to Marvin," I replied.

"Why? He's locked up."

"Don't count on it. He's partly made of nano-metal, remember?"

"So?" she asked. "Kwon sealed the brig cell."

"With smart metal."

"Oh." Realization showed on her face. "So all he had to do was use his own nano-metal to tap into the smart metal seal and instruct it to open up."

"No, it's worse than that, I think. If he can exert control over the metal, he must be able to communicate throughout the ship and connect to anything using the nanite network, right from the cell. After all, they locked him in there and told him he couldn't leave. They didn't tell him he couldn't tap into the ship's systems. And I told him I was going to try to get him access to the experiment. Maybe he took that as permission."

"It's like having an evil genie that always twists your words."

I nodded. "Yeah."

"But you said you told him not to make trouble!"

"I guess he has a different definition of that than I do." We slowed our headlong rush in front of the brig cell door, checking for any marines that should have been minding the store. It looked like they were all still out helping with damage control.

Just then, Kwon came around the corner, huge in full battle armor, with a grim expression on his face. "I'm gonna destroy that son of a bitch," he said with fire in his eyes. "I'm gonna rip him limb from limb. I just lost eight good marines." It looked like Kwon had jumped to much the same conclusion as I had. After all, he'd known Marvin much longer.

"Just don't kill him, Kwon. We need him."

"Why?"

"I—" I stopped, because I wasn't sure how to answer Kwon, so I bullshitted a bit. Dad always said a little bullshit was sometimes necessary when the stakes were high. Lesser of two evils and all that. "Whatever just happened, I'm pretty sure Marvin caused it somehow, and that means he's probably the only one who really knows what's going on. And that makes him the one we need to fix everything." I realized that was half true, even as I said it.

"Whatever you say, sir," Kwon replied, clearly not happy. "Just let me go in first. He might be dangerous."

"Oh, he's dangerous all right, but not to any individual in his presence, I don't think." Then I remembered how Dad had told me about how his old girlfriend Sandra had been healed from a coma when Marvin had "accidentally" allowed another woman to fall into the Microbe tank with her. The Microbes had apparently eaten the other one to fix Sandra.

I hoped that was an exception.

"He's a loose cannon, and I'm gonna lock him down," Kwon said.

"Just open it up and watch our backs." I waved at the cell door. Kwon passed an electronic key over the nano-controlled lock. It had already occurred to me that if Marvin could hack the ship, he could hack his cell too. So, I was a little surprised to see him inside when it opened. It looked like he was just sitting quietly in the middle of the floor, his tentacles folded, all innocence in appearance.

"Marvin, what the hell did you do? Did you somehow activate the ring?"

"No."

I gritted my teeth. Whenever he gave one-word answers, there was usually more to the story. "Bullshit, Marvin. You did this. You tapped into the ship's network and turned that thing on, and now look what happened. We've got twenty or thirty people dead because of you! I should let Sergeant Major Kwon disassemble you down to a naked brainbox. How would you like to have no limbs and no sensory inputs?"

"Threats are not necessary, Cody Riggs. My orders were to not leave this cell. No one told me I should not access the ship's network and observe the scientists while they worked on the ring."

I made an exasperated sound in my throat. "Observe, huh? You agreed not to make trouble! You must have done a lot more than observe."

"Not to make any *unnecessary* trouble was the agreement. Would you like me to play it back for you?"

"No, I..." I gave up on pinning him down for his past sins and decided to concentrate on the present and future—assuming we had one. "Marvin, did you lock out the command codes for Captain Turnbull?" I gestured at Kwon, who looked like he wanted to tear a piece off of Marvin.

Marvin fixed his cameras on the marine and apparently decided to start cooperating. "Only long enough to ensure the scientists' experiment would be properly energized."

"You're claiming *they* started up the ring?"

"They did connect the leads and apply power and send it a series of test commands. I merely determined that their commands would accomplish nothing. They didn't employ a checksum, and nothing would execute without one. I considered adding a small subroutine that would add a checksum and vary their command codes until a response from the ring was observed."

"In other words, you caused this accident," I said, thinking of my dad's farm and all those dead chickens. Marvin really was a slithering disaster. "A big piece of the ship has been ripped away. A bunch of people died because of what you did."

"My statements were not intended to be a confession," Marvin replied. "I stated that I planned to add the subroutine—but I didn't. I suspect that someone else did."

I frowned, wondering if he was lying or evading or some combination of both. "Who could have done such a thing?" I demanded.

"I would suspect a crewmember from *Valiant*."

I snorted. "That's a big help. You've eliminated Adrienne and me but left us with a list of seventy or so suspects."

"I've also eliminated myself from the list as I'm technically part of *Greyhound's* crew as well."

Adrienne had been frowning with increasing intensity.

"I don't believe you, robot," she said.

"I suspected as much," Marvin said, swinging an extra camera her way. "I've been monitoring your facial contortions and body rhythms."

Adrienne turned to me. "We should torture him or something until he confesses."

Marvin's cameras perked up a fraction. "Torture? What form might this attempted coercion take?"

I wasn't sure if he was curious or worried. Maybe both. I threw up my hands and shook my head.

"All right," I said. "Let's assume you're innocent—or nearly innocent. I suspect the real story is that you created these subroutines but didn't employ them. Someone else found them and installed them."

Marvin just stared at me.

"You're not denying my accusation?" I asked.

"I do not see it as an accusation. It is more of a clarification of past events. An insignificant detail I overlooked in my report."

"Yeah, insignificant. You built the gun, but someone else fired it. Well, anyway, let's move on. Why would someone employ your routines blindly without checking with you? Did you discuss them with anyone else?"

"We've only just arrived. I barely had time to create them and store them in *Valiant's* database. Someone else must have accessed and installed them."

Adrienne made a clucking sound with her tongue. "I still don't buy it. This robot is evil."

"A *non sequitur*," Marvin said. "I have no alignment with supernatural forces."

She rolled her eyes, and I lifted my hands to gain their attention.

"I think we should figure this out. If there is a saboteur aboard, we need to know who it is. These events might even be related to the sabotage that killed Olivia."

Adrienne's eyes widened. "This robot did both!" she said. "It's obvious. Marvin was there when we first refueled, he stowed away when we returned and then he helped activate the ring. Why do you want to kill Cody so badly, Marvin?"

I frowned. She had some good points, but I found it hard to believe Marvin could be the assassin. I shook my head.

"I don't think he did it," I said. "I would probably be dead by now if he was behind this."

"Thank you, Cody Riggs," Marvin said. He'd been watching the two of us closely.

"For what?" I asked him.

"For complimenting my effectiveness."

I laughed. "Yeah, I guess I did. You're a better assassin than this, and you wouldn't have missed twice."

"No, I would not have. Moreover, there were ample opportunities during the long flight out to the Thor system for me to sabotage the ship. I could have evacuated the internal pressure, for example, as I don't need to breathe. Or, I could have—"

I could see Adrienne was becoming upset with his list of possible ways he could have killed us, so I stopped him.

"That's enough," I said. "Let's focus on figuring out who is guilty. We're wasting time."

"I must agree," Marvin said, "and we don't have much time to waste."

"Why not?" Adrienne asked suspiciously.

"Because this system is inhabited."

"Inhabited? How do you know?" I asked.

"During our conversation, I've been monitoring our sensors and collating the input. The local stellar configuration indicates we're over three hundred light years from Earth at a star designated HD 95086. The star is also known as Tullax. We're now picking up radio transmissions that are either in code or a language different from any I've encountered."

"Anything else you'd like to share with us?" I asked.

"Yes. There is a squadron of warships headed this way."

-8-

I'd trained all my life to be a Star Force officer. Like my Dad, I never had much of a problem making snap decisions. Thinking them through? That was another matter. "Kwon, grab Marvin. We're going aboard *Greyhound*."

Kwon did grab Marvin, but then stopped, obviously torn between his natural desire to obey the guy who reminded him of his old boss and friend, and his loyalty to his commander, Captain Turnbull. "He's supposed to stay in the brig."

"Look, Kwon, the captain has enough trouble right now without worrying about a robot who fiddles with everything like a disobedient child." I was rubbing it in a little. Marvin deserved it, in my book. "I'll take responsibility as the officer on the scene. Once he's back aboard *Greyhound*, Marvin will be out of Fleet's way and Turnbull can concentrate on dealing with the approaching alien ships. Besides, once we're there, we can cast off and pop back through the ring to report what happened and call for reinforcements."

"Right. Okay." Kwon decided to go with my ideas and began dragging Marvin along as Adrienne and I hurried for the airlock.

"Am I under arrest?" Marvin asked politely.

"Yes," Kwon said. "Permanent arrest."

Marvin rasped his tentacles unhappily but didn't resist.

Fortunately the smart metal tube between the two ships was still connected, though we did have to cycle through the airlocks in the normal fashion. Apparently the brainboxes of both ships were taking no chances. Once Kwon packed Marvin into our side's airlock chamber, he returned to his duties aboard his own ship, looking relieved. I had to say I was sorry to see him go. He was sure a good man to have at your back.

Inside, Marvin straightened up and decided to walk on his own. I reached over and slapped one of his cameras hard enough to rattle it. "Marvin, listen to me. I just saved you from a lot of whatever passes for pain in that mechanical mind of yours. You should be grateful to me. Now I need you to stay out of everyone's way unless someone asks you for help. If they do, then *help*."

"Understood. Program set."

"Uh-huh." I stared at him a moment longer, and then said to Adrienne, "Let's go."

Once on the cramped bridge, we cast off from *Valiant*. I wasn't comfortable with *Greyhound* stuck onto the damaged battlecruiser like a nursing whale calf. "We're going back through the ring. *Valiant* doesn't need us in the way, and Star Force has to know what happened."

"Good idea," she said. "I'll plot a course."

"Thank you, Adrienne. *Greyhound*, hail *Valiant*. Adrienne, when you finish with the computer please contact your uncle. He's really not happy with me right now."

"Okay."

"On speaker," the brainbox said after a few minutes.

"Uncle William, this is Adrienne. We're going to pop through the ring and broadcast what's happened, and then we'll come right back, all right? We won't leave you in the lurch."

I thought it was ironic that she was assuring a Fleet battlecruiser that we, in an unarmed yacht, wouldn't abandon them to their fate.

Sir William's voice came back. "Good idea, girl. There's a squadron of alien warships bearing down on us, arriving in about five hours. They don't look like Macros—but who knows? We still have some repairs to make then we'll join you. Let us know what you discover about the ring."

"Yes, Uncle, we will. *Greyhound* out."

"The ring is coming up." I pointed. As we approached, we could see it with the naked eye, floating like a vast circle in space. "How come more stuff isn't coming through?" I wondered aloud.

"Maybe it's stabilized."

"We'll have to be very careful going in. We might end up running smack into Yale itself, so we'll have to ease through dead slow." We pulled up to the ring and decelerated using repellers. The star-stuff of the ring itself was so dense that it exerted its own small gravitic force, about two percent of a G. I did sweat a little when I slipped the ship through.

Unfortunately we merely sailed through to the other side, no transport.

"The ring must be slowly flipping," I said aloud, "so all we have to do is reverse course and ease through from this side…"

That didn't do anything either. We were left floating in the middle of a huge ring in the same system where we'd arrived a couple of hours ago.

"Bollocks," Adrienne said, sounding a lot like Olivia. "Why isn't the ring working?"

"It means we're stuck here three hundred light years from home." I snapped my fingers. "Marvin!"

The bridge portal opened, and Marvin ambled through.

"Were you just waiting outside the door?" I asked.

"Of course. I knew you would need me soon, but my presence seems to cause you agitation, Cody Riggs, so like any polite and considerate being I tried to take your feelings into account and remain out of sight. I wouldn't want to screw the pooch."

I wondered whether I hadn't overdone it by teaching him that particular piece of idiomatic phraseology, but it was too late now. "Marvin, why isn't the ring working?"

"Because it has no power."

"I thought you started it up."

"It appears that applying ship power from the battlecruiser activated it for a certain short period of time, but the usual ring inverted quantum flux self-sustainment calibrated energy matrix has failed to take hold in this case."

"That sounds like a bunch of gobbledygook," I said. "I don't care, though. Can we power it again to go through?"

"Not with *Greyhound*, no. It doesn't have enough energy. We will need *Valiant*'s reactors as well."

"And we'll have to overload, if it's like last time," Adrienne observed. "I'll hail Uncle William again." She informed Turnbull of the situation, and we heard from him that the alien squadron was composed of six identical cruiser-sized ships. They had come from Tullax 4, a hot wet Earthlike world fourth out from its sun with a large airless moon rather like Earth's. Well, at least the ships weren't Macros. Hopefully they were biotics of some kind that we could relate to.

"Maybe Marvin can figure out their language," I said. I turned to the robot, who was stealthily extending a rivulet of nano-metal toward a nearby console. "Stop that! Marvin, do not try to access ship systems without permission."

Marvin froze the forming metal tentacle, but did not retract it. "You already gave me permission."

"That was before you decided to sneak aboard *Valiant* and play with the ring." I mused on the squadron headed our way for a moment. "It would be quite a challenge for us to learn and translate the language of the aliens native to this system."

"That is true," Marvin said.

"I bet it would be an even bigger challenge for you," I went on. I had to keep Marvin occupied doing something useful or he'd get into even more trouble.

Marvin stared at me with all his cameras. "I deduce you are trying to manipulate me, but there is no need. Anything is better than constantly being told to do nothing."

"Fine. *Greyhound*, set Marvin's station to receive and process only and disconnect all other external functions."

"Parameters accepted. Implemented."

"All right, Marvin. Let me know when you've figured out enough to understand what they're saying and to talk back to them."

Marvin wedged himself in behind the console and connected in. The chair he didn't need was forced to resorb back into the floor. I hoped he would follow instructions and just do what he was supposed to. Probably a vain hope.

"*Valiant* is moving toward the ring," I said as I scanned the displays. "Looks like they will join us shortly. Maybe they can turn this thing back on and we can return to Thor." Now that I was stuck so far from known space, I remembered something Dad had quoted to the effect that adventures are just tales of someone else being miserable, far, far away. I was starting to see his point.

A few minutes later the damaged battlecruiser arrived, moving slowly and carefully. It edged ponderously in closer and closer until it had all but docked against the ring itself. I guessed the remnants of the science team were going to try to replicate the "accident" that had activated the ring. They probably still didn't know Marvin had done it. We watched personnel in suits exiting one of the sides and connecting cables, and then Turnbull announced they would try again.

Marvin mumbled something as they worked.

"What?" I asked.

"Nothing. I am busy only receiving input. Not transmitting."

"I realize that, Marvin."

"Then why did you ask?"

I stood up, looming over him. "What is it you know, Marvin?"

"Your question is overly broad and vague. Please clarify."

"Is there something about the test we need to know?"

"Yes."

"Well?" I gave one of his tentacles an emphatic kick. I guess it was my day to boot things. "What is it that we need to know about the test?"

Marvin shook the tentacle I'd kicked. "It won't work."

"Why not?"

"Because it's a one-way ring."

"A one-way ring? What the hell is a one-way ring?"

"It means the ring is set to only work in one direction, even if it is activated with power. Before the Macros shut it down, it was draining the ocean from Yale and the Macros with it."

"I learned about that. Can you change it?" I asked.

"It is possible, but last time it took many hours of transmitting random code attempts to find a command the ring accepted."

"But you changed it before. Don't you remember the right command code?"

"The ring seems to reset its encryption after each successful command according to an unknown algorithm. You father never gave me enough time or access to even minimally understand how to control its programming."

I coughed a single harsh laugh. "I can see why. Somehow, every problem you solve creates a bigger one. What about the ring communications system? Can we transmit back through it?"

"I would be happy to make the attempt."

"I doubt we'll have time, with those aliens coming, if Turnbull would even allow you to try." I asked Adrienne to call up the *Valiant* and explain all this to her uncle. After a few tries, the word came back from the scientists that they couldn't get the ring activated, neither in communications mode nor for transport. The thing just stayed dead, and when Adrienne tentatively raised the subject, her uncle categorically refused to let Marvin get near it.

"Are there any more details on the alien ships?" I risked asking the captain.

Turnbull answered, "They're all about cruiser size with one main energy gun, six secondaries, and six missile launchers."

"They seem to like the number six," I observed.

"Yes," he said scathingly. "I deduced that."

I gritted my teeth and held my tongue, knowing this was all part of being the low man on the totem pole and out of favor. At least he was talking to me. I guess he considered me the de facto captain of the yacht for now. "So their weapons technology level seems roughly comparable to ours? But they don't seem to be very fast ships. Maybe we can outrun them. Certainly *Greyhound* can."

"Thinking about running away, eh, Riggs?"

"Not at all, sir," I said as evenly as I could, "but do you think we can win this fight?"

It was his turn to keep silent in the face of my logic. A battlecruiser was a faster, more heavily armed cruiser, but it lacked the armor of the next modern class up, a battleship.

Undamaged, it should be able to beat any two or even three cruisers, but not six.

"We'll give diplomacy the good old college try while the scientists keep trying to activate the ring." Turnbull seemed to be cast in the old imagined British Empire mold of stiff upper lip and relentless optimism despite the odds.

"Yes, sir," I said, relieved to change the subject. "I have a program working on trying to get at least a rudimentary translation going before they arrive." I wasn't going to tell him that "program" was Marvin. "Sir," I went on, "have you found anything else significant in this system? Such as evidence of another ring?" If there was another ring, maybe we could outrun the aliens and get away through it, if we had to. If it was functional, that is. On the other hand, I would expect that any other operational portal would be guarded or in use, perhaps even mined.

Turnbull went on, "Yes, there is another ring on the other side of the system, in orbit around a gas giant, Tullax 5. There appears to be a large installation near it, perhaps a fortress, but it is too far away to be sure."

"Then let's hope we can talk to these people," I said. I thought of making an observation about that other ring being our only escape if the aliens turned out to be hostile, but I was pretty sure at this point that Turnbull, or at least his crew, would have figured that out. Sir William seemed to be an arrogant and unimaginative guy, but not completely incompetent. And the members of his crew certainly knew their jobs.

"There is one other item we've found," the captain went on as if I had not spoken. "The world below us, Tullax 6, has no atmosphere, no apparent life. We have detected residual radiation, evidence of a battle in which massive numbers of fusion warheads were used, enough to strip the planet of its atmosphere. There also seem to be installations of some sort." He paused.

"Installations?" I prompted, getting the feeling the pause had been for effect, and Sir William, with an audience, was ready to make a dramatic announcement.

"Yes, installations. Shut down and dead, it appears, with no energy readings."

"Made by these aliens?"

"That's what we thought at first, but no. The installations," he paused again, "look like those built by Macros."

-9-

Adrienne and I exchanged glances across *Greyhound's* bridge, ignoring Marvin for the moment. Captain Turnbull and his crew on *Valiant* were telling us about Macro installations on the planet below. Our two ships were still docked together and formed a single large green contact in the holotank.

With our command tables linked, Captain Turnbull's unpleasant face appeared in an open window on the console in front of me. He looked away from Adrienne and me at the moment, studying something off-screen.

"We knew the Macros were here twenty-three years ago," I said to the captain. "Dad flushed them back through the ring. This must have been a base. Maybe these aliens fought the Macros and beat them. That would be good news and a point of common reference at least."

"So I hope," Captain Turnbull said, his voice booming through the com-link. "The fact that they come from a life-bearing world would seem to indicate they're a biotic species, which makes us natural allies."

I winced. The man always cranked up his outgoing volume.

"Doesn't always work out that way. Remember the Blues, sir," I said. "They're biotic, but my father had to bomb them back to the Stone Age to keep them from causing any more trouble."

"Effectiveness unconfirmed," Marvin whispered. He said it just loudly enough for me to hear.

I glanced at him, but none of his cameras returned my gaze. It was a disturbing statement. Was he hinting that the Blues were not as badly hurt by the bombing as we'd assumed? He was correct that no one had ever gone down to the surface to confirm that the bombing had been effective.

I wasn't even sure if he'd intended for me to hear him or not. If I hadn't been nanotized and microbed, I wouldn't have heard him at all, which might mean that he didn't know about my capabilities. On the other hand, if he *did* know I was listening to his whispers, it might mean that he had spoken for my ears alone, which was another disturbing thought.

"If they encountered the Macros," Turnbull said, "then I have high hopes for the situation. Just think! I've discovered an entirely unknown alien species. If I can establish diplomatic relations, find out the fate of the Macros and open a way home for trade, I might be made a baronet, perhaps even a viscount."

While Earth was now under one federal system, the UK had experienced a resurgent interest in feudal titles. They were handing them out as perks and status symbols to national heroes. A title didn't have much functional meaning, but it was a source of pride among the populace. Dad said that with everyone at peace and getting rich, these status symbols were just another way of keeping score. It sounded as if Sir William was angling for a social promotion to go with the family's wealth.

"I sure hope it works out that way, sir," I said. Just as long as it kept him off my back, he could be crowned King for all I cared.

"Let me know as soon your program is able to translate some of what they're saying," Turnbull said. "Until then, I'll let the scientists keep potching about with this ring. You might as well make yourself useful, Riggs, and go down to take a look at the dead world. Just keep my remaining niece alive, will you? Don't stir up any unnecessary trouble. *Valiant* out."

I didn't appreciate Turnbull's cutting sarcasm, even though I knew he had a point. I shot Marvin a glance. He blandly turned away one of his cameras, leaving only one looking generally in my direction. He said nothing, but it sounded like he was faintly humming. Not like a machine hums, with electrical resonance, instead—he was actually humming a tune. He was so quiet that I couldn't make it out against the ship's usual background noise. Maybe it was an indication of enjoyment or concentration. Or maybe he was just trying to bug me.

Marvin could make anyone doubt himself.

I sighed. "So, I have a make-work assignment to go check out some dead world. He's just getting rid of me."

"And keeping *me* out of danger from that alien squadron," Adrienne said reasonably.

"Maybe. On the other hand, if it's Macros, even deactivated ones…" I turned to Marvin. "Marvin, if it's Macros, don't even *think* about accessing them without specific permission." My nightmare is that this might be some kind of dormant Macro installation that Marvin decided to jump start, just as an experiment. *Greyhound* had a general-purpose laser suitable for taking rock samples, blasting small meteors out of the way, or killing big animals in case of a planetary landing, but we sure as hell couldn't handle even one enemy war machine.

"Instruction noted."

"Making any progress on that translation?"

"Yes. I anticipate reasonable textual fluency in six hours. Voice simulation and transmission may take several days, due to the nuances of spoken speech."

"How about in…" I checked the countdown that Adrienne had put in the corner of the holotank, "…four and a half hours when the aliens arrive?"

"Not able to estimate. Translation is not a linear process. Rather, it is more like decryption of unknown data streams, what you might call 'code breaking.' It often depends on serendipitous breakthroughs."

"You mean you'll have to get lucky?"

"I believe I just said that."

I shook my head. "Well, hurry up then. When we get back to the ring, you'll have to translate what you can and hope we can avoid an interspecies incident."

"This conversation consumes processing power."

Obviously that was his way of telling me to shut up and let him work. So I moved the short distance over to stand next to Adrienne at the holotank. Now she had the holotank showing a representation of the incoming alien squadron on one side, the ring and *Valiant* near the middle, and *Greyhound* heading for the dead world at the other end. All those elements were roughly lined up with the system's star.

"Funny, it just occurred to me that the aliens are deliberately coming straight out of the sun, like an old-time fighter pilot swooping on an enemy," I said. "I wonder if it means anything."

"Maybe they're just being cautious," she replied.

"Or maybe they're used to fighting."

"Maybe, but not necessarily. Star Force hasn't had a real enemy in twenty years, but we still know how to fight. If we were in their place, wouldn't we want to have every advantage when facing an unidentified alien ship?"

She had a point. I guess we really couldn't glean anything for sure from the aliens' actions until they did something more overt such as open fire.

"All right. Your uncle seems to think there's nothing to worry about, but we're going to be careful. Marvin, monitor passive sensors and report anything unexpected or dangerous. *Greyhound*, shut down active sensors and reduce all emissions to minimum. Adrienne, run out that laser, and be ready to shoot. You sure you don't want to be nanotized?"

"I already told you, no. I'll be fine," she said, irritated. I swallowed my misgivings and double-checked all our preparations, and then sent us spiraling down.

Soon we cruised in low over the dead world. We quickly found hundreds of ruined Macro complexes standing out like silvery sores against the lifeless brown dirt. Choosing one at random, we dropped in on repellers then made a slow circuit of the area.

"There, down in that crater, there's a bunch of them. I'm bringing us lower." Coming over the rim, we saw ruined Macros scattered around, half-buried in the surface. I wasn't sure if they had been digging out, digging in, or had simply been partially covered by explosions.

"Real live Macros," Adrienne breathed, sounding more like her sister all the time. She had more guts that I'd expected.

"Contradiction indicated," Marvin said. "These have been deactivated."

"I thought you were completely busy working on the translation."

"I am not blind." He waved his several cameras around on their stalks for a moment by way of demonstration.

"You are when you want to be," I said. Then I turned to Adrienne. "Marvin's got a point, though. Is there anything alive down there? Any power readings or detectable life signs now that we're close?"

Adrienne worked at the holotank, controlling various sensors from its touch interface. "No, nothing that I can see."

"Let's set down and take a closer look."

"I think we should keep our distance."

"Come on, where's your sense of adventure?" I tried to say it lightly, but I inadvertently let a little edge creep in.

Adrienne's face darkened. "What, are you trying to get me killed too?"

That floored me. I actually had to grab onto my chair to keep in it as a fresh wave of emotion flooded though—shame at the kernel of truth in her words, anger that she would use Olivia against me that way and the unfairness of her words. Unfortunately, my mouth got ahead of my better judgment this time. "Your sister would never have said something like that to me."

"Obviously, I'm not my sister," she snapped.

I stood up to stare angrily at the holotank. "That's crystal clear. She'd have stepped up and come along, or at least backed me up, not kneed me in the nuts. *Greyhound*, prep a suit."

"Wait," Adrienne said, reaching out to grab my arm.

I felt like shaking her hand off, but I let her hang onto me.

"I'm sorry," she said. "That was a low blow. It just popped out. I didn't mean it. I'll come along."

"No. You're right, really. You should stay safely aboard the ship. I'm Star Force. It's my job to take the risks."

Shaking my arm, she argued, "Look, I take back what I said. I want to go along. I can't just sit back here while you go facing danger." Her eyes pleaded with me.

I almost said no just to put her in her place, but that would have been indulging my anger. I also got the feeling that if I did that, I would be turning a quick tiff into a major sore spot, so I forced a smile. Putting on my best caricature accent of Sir William, I said, "That's the spirit! Give it the old college try, eh, what?"

A smile I knew so well broke out on her face. It was bittersweet when I saw Olivia in Adrienne's mannerisms. She used my arm to pull herself up to kiss my cheek. "Thanks, Cody."

I smiled back a little crookedly, not knowing quite how to take these mercurial changes in mood. "Now you're talking. Let's suit up."

Putting on the gear was easy. *Greyhound* had expensive suits that were mostly smart metal with only a few manufactured parts. We just stepped into what looked like exoskeletons, activated them, and the rest flowed around us and encased us in self-sealing, flexible material. I took along a beam rifle. It made me feel better.

When we clomped to the edge of the airlock, we lost the one G we were used to. This world's gravity was more like point seven, so we felt lighter and springier without being completely unbalanced. Stepping out carefully, we found the surface hard, like gravelly soil, with little dust in it. The horizon was close and sharp without air to fuzz it out, reminding me a lot of the moon – Earth's moon that is. I'd spent a whole semester there as part of my Academy education, getting used to an environment where one mistake could kill you.

Walking up to one of the half-buried Macros, a hundred-foot-tall combat crab, was totally surreal. I'd seen them in museums, of course, and on vids, but these...objectively I knew they were powerless and dead, but it sure seemed like they could just come to life at any moment. Maybe it was because the thing appeared to be frozen in the process of digging itself out.

"Look, it's almost cemented into the ground, like concrete was poured around it," Adrienne said, prodding at the edge with her toe.

"Maybe it was," I replied. "Maybe it's a monument to the new aliens' victory, like a battlefield deliberately left alone."

"Then where are the other side's machines? I mean, they might pick up bodies, but where are their tanks or battlesuits or whatever?"

I shrugged. "Maybe they salvaged them. Let's look over there," I said, pointing at what appeared to me to be a distinct convex curved line on the ground. That kind of shape reminded me of something I'd seen in one of the endless documentaries our generation had grown up watching.

I guess every big war affects the kids afterward, not only because of what it did to the parents, but because it sets the tone and infects the media. It washes a patina of time across the war until it doesn't seem bloody and grim anymore, but glorious instead. As I trudged across the rocky ground among those hulking mechanical corpses, I felt the echo of fear my dad and Kwon and all those other guys must have felt as they charged into bloody close combat for the first time down in the jungles of South America, dying in droves.

I shivered.

We'd reached the line, and Adrienne scuffed at it, a sort of shallow trench dug in a perfect curve, defining a circle maybe a quarter mile wide. "It's from a dome, isn't it?" she asked.

"I think so. That means…" I lined myself up and pointed with my whole arm. "The center should be that way. Let's go." Making sure she stayed in front of me so I could keep an eye on her, we made our way the eighth of a mile it took to find the center. There we found not a combat machine but the broken factory that I expected. I remembered most of the domes had one of these things, a combination of defensive generator and Macro-maker, the heart of any ground infestation.

"I still don't see any enemy stuff around," I said, doing a slow three-sixty, "but it sure looks like this factory was attacked."

"There aren't any burns or blast marks, but these impacts…" Adrienne indicated weird upside-down V-shaped dents, with their points toward the sky, as if someone had taken an odd axe blade ten feet high and chopped at the machine until it broke. "What kind of weapon would do that?"

"Maybe the aliens will enlighten us. It's time to get back now."

She protested, but I insisted. We headed back toward the yacht.

"Hey…" Adrienne stopped. "This wasn't here before." A rocky mound twenty feet high blocked our way between two wrecked Macros.

"You're just remembering wrong. We must have gone around." I started angling to my right, where I could see an open space.

"Cody, come back here. Look." When I did, I saw where she was pointing at the ground. Our tracks seemed to simply appear out of the side of the low hill, as if we had phased through it in some magical way.

"I'm beginning to get a bad feeling about this," I said grabbing her shoulder and pulling her back. Something wasn't right, and I didn't know what it was.

"Maybe it's some kind of hologram." I let her draw away from me, which was another big mistake. You'd think I would have been hyper-paranoid after losing Olivia, but in reality, I think I was trying to make up for it by making Adrienne happy instead of being a hard-ass about keeping her safe.

As she reached out to poke at the hill in front of her, the dirt grabbed her.

-10-

The dirt actually *grabbed* her. That's the only way I can describe it. I was reminded of a horror vid I'd seen once where the monster was a kind of energy force that used whatever dirt and rocks were around as a body. In front of us, soil shaped itself into an arm or tentacle with a four-fingered claw having two opposing digits on each side, like one of those clamps on the end of a manipulator arm that loggers use to pick up big trees and move them. It wrapped itself around Adrienne's forearm and started to pull her into itself.

Fortunately it wasn't very fast. I'd seen a three-toed sloth on a nature show where it took several seconds to make a simple motion, like moving a paw from one spot to the other. That's what it reminded me of.

These thoughts ran through my head, and I froze for a moment, but then went into action. I slung my laser rifle over my shoulder and grabbed the reaching tube of dripping earth with both my hands. Bracing my foot against the mound, I pulled with my full strength.

The stuff felt like nano-metal when it was flowing, granular and resistant, but I was able to compress it as if it were made of rubber. It got thinner and thinner as I pulled and squeezed, and in a moment, I managed to drag my hands all the way through it, like tearing away a clump of wet clay.

The end with the claw fell off onto the ground and broke apart, turning into just another spray of dirt while the stump started to reform itself into another grasping appendage. I shoved Adrienne away from it and she stumbled, sprawling on the ground. I wasn't limiting my strength anymore; this wasn't the time to be gentle.

It was then I realized my right boot had sunk six inches into the side of the mound, which had flowed around my foot. I was held fast. I tried to jump, twist and kick, but the thing held on and began sucking me downward into itself like quicksand.

The problem wasn't a lack of strength—it was a lack of leverage. The only thing I had to push against was more of the same dangerous earth. I felt Adrienne grab onto my shoulders and tug as I leaned toward her. I had one foot on the ground and one in the growing mound of soil, which now had me up to my right ankle. But she wasn't strong or heavy enough to be effective. I was going to be swallowed if I didn't do something drastic.

Making a decision my father would have been proud of, a real Riggs decision, I reached down to my leg with both hands and popped loose the catches that held the hard parts of the boot together and started trying to pull my foot out of the suit itself. Accessing the tiny brainbox, I yelled, "Suit, release right boot assembly!"

"Cannot comply," my suit said in a tinny, small-brainbox voice. "Vacuum environment detected. Release may cause fatal decompression."

"Suit, emergency override. Execute previous command on my authorization."

"Emergency authorization implemented."

Smart cloth flowed out of the boot in immediate response, rejoining the rest of the suit. I pulled strongly as the pressure eased around my foot. I had to act before the crazy trapping soil squeezed harder. My foot popped free and I fell backward, and even though I was wearing a sock, my skin began to frost over.

Immediately, the nanites in my body went to work, limiting the damage and thickening my skin. I tried to walk, but every step I took felt like I was pressing the sole of my foot to something far chillier than a block of ice—which it was. This far out from its sun, the surface of this planet was *cold,* at least minus fifty, if I had to guess.

We hopped and stumbled away from the killer mound and circled the broken Macros. Now I realized why the robots all seemed half-buried in the dirt here. The strange earth had overcome the Macros, and it was trying to consume us as well.

Rounding a tangle of broken-down robots, we realized that we'd been blocked in that direction as well. Spinning left and right, we could see mounds had sprung up all around the area, forming a ragged wall of vertical cliffs twenty feet high. Unfortunately, the gravity here was at least two-thirds of standard, enough to prevent a normal human from leaping over the walls, but I thought I could do it anyway.

"Adrienne," I said, "listen to me and do what I say."

"Okay," she said, eyes wide as she examined the closing walls. She was breathing hard.

"See the mound between us and *Greyhound*? I'm going to throw you up onto that mound—maybe over it. You might have a rough landing, but you need to try to hit the ground running and move fast enough to keep that stuff from grabbing you, okay?"

"What do you mean, you're going to throw me?"

"I'm nanotized, Adrienne—and more. I'll explain it all later, but I can do this."

To her credit, Adrienne didn't argue. "Okay. I'm ready," she said.

"Tell your suit to go into impact-resistant mode, and then as soon as you are on your feet, switch it into muscular-assistance mode."

While our standard flight suits weren't battlesuits, but they had some pretty cool functions—especially expensive suits like these.

"All right," she said after a moment. "I've set the program."

"Here we go." The mounds were grinding toward us like bulldozers, linking up with their fellows as they flowed around the dead Macros, pulling inward to corral us in a circle. I grabbed Adrienne by the neck ring and the seat of her suit, tipped her over like a child and ran three steps forward before lofting her skyward. Up and over she went, and I jumped right after her.

Two possibilities had occurred to me as I watched her fly and both were dangerous. One, she might land on top of the mound and it would immediately try to engulf her like quicksand. Two, she might go over the mound entirely and slam into the frozen ground on the other side—landing too hard. I was hoping for option two, because a few broken bones could be fixed.

Unfortunately, option one reared its ugly head.

When I landed beside her at the top of the mound, she was already sinking. The stuff was grabbing at her like living taffy. I landed, seized her again and ripped her free. I tossed her in a flat spin down the opposite slope and onto the undisturbed area beyond. Whatever this substance attacking us was, it seemed to be localized and moved with finite speed, so I hoped she would be safe for a little while.

My right foot felt almost completely numb, except for a hot-needle stabbing sensation that told me my body's nanites were trying to heal me at the same time my foot was freezing solid. I ignored all that and ran after her down the other side of the mound, feeling like I was running in deep mud. The ground clutched at me, but I pumped my legs madly and roared with effort, ripping free from the ground and slamming my feet down to generate traction. My speed and strength were my only assets, and I used them to the fullest, pushing myself forward.

When I made it to steady ground, I found Adrienne semiconscious. I picked her up and carried her over my shoulder. "Suit, form a field-expedient right boot to protect my foot."

"Complying." Smart metal flowed and I hobbled awkwardly away from the mounds that were now rumbling and grinding in random directions as if seeking their lost prey. I could feel their vibrations through the ground like earth tremors.

"Marvin," I radioed. "Marvin, answer me."

Nothing.

It took me a moment of frustration to remember I'd forbidden him to transmit. I was annoyed that this was the moment he'd chosen to follow instructions to the letter. I decided to talk to the ship directly.

"*Greyhound*, open the airlock, and as soon as we're both inside, lift off. This soil is trying to swallow us."

"Command accepted. Shall I activate the laser?"

"No," I gasped as I ran with Adrienne bumping up and down on my shoulder. Unfortunately I could also see that the dirt was starting to ripple around the ship, and the struts that braced it from rolling on its rounded belly seemed to be sinking.

"*Greyhound*, the effect is trying to grasp the ship. Use repellers to lift off now, at least a foot or two. Try to get free of the surface."

"Command accepted."

By this time, we'd reached the ship. I tossed Adrienne up and into the airlock and leaped after her. The belly of the yacht had come off the ground but the four landing struts remained mired in the soil, which was trying to climb up them and drag the ship down. With its big engines and high power-to-mass ratio, I hoped that *Greyhound* could pull free when the time came.

I hit the emergency speed-cycle button on the airlock. Gasses hissed and were lost into space. I yelled into my radio, "Lift off, now! We're in!"

I felt the vessel yaw and shudder and could hear a rising whine as the brainbox fed the repellers more power.

"Increasing repeller force will damage landing struts," *Greyhound* complained.

"Screw the struts! Blow them free or release them or whatever. Rip them loose with your manipulation arms if you have to!"

Greyhound did as I'd ordered, and a moment later the shuddering ceased with one final lurch. Everything was still and quiet except for the thrum of the engines. Opening the inner door seemed to take forever, but finally I carried Adrienne into the ship. After telling her suit to remove itself from her, I placed her into the autodoc. I was extremely glad we had the machine because Adrienne was in bad shape.

The screen on the machine said she had multiple broken bones as well as internal injuries and a concussion, despite my trying to be gentle with her in our mad escape. A nightmare of fear reached up to clutch my throat, and I told the autodoc, "Initiate extreme measures."

"Command accepted. Please back away from the canopy."

I hoped I was doing the right thing. Last time the machine had been set to only nanotize someone if they were dying. I wasn't going to wait that long this time. It didn't matter if she was pissed at me for giving her the treatment. She'd decided to come along so she had to deal with the consequences. I watched the readings for a few minutes to make sure everything was going okay. She didn't thrash as much as Olivia had. Presumably the autodoc had sedated her enough to reduce the effect.

I should have insisted on getting Adrienne nanotized, but I'd been blinded by my desire to please her. I resolved that I wouldn't give in to that urge again. At least not in the face of danger that should have been obvious to me.

Now that I had time for regrets, I blamed myself for what had happened. Anything that could take down Macros was obviously dangerous to us. I'd been fooled by the lack of energy readings, and I'd forgotten that alien worlds might hold life that was very, very alien.

That this stuff was life of a sort, I had no doubt. It had acted intelligently, at least in an animalistic way, like a pack of dogs, or perhaps smarter than that. It had formed a claw, tried to pull us in, and then corralled us. Maybe that was how the stuff hunted, though I couldn't for the life of me figure out what there was to prey on or eat on that dead planet.

No, not a dead planet. This was a world with life—or machine life—that I simply didn't understand. Maybe there were different sorts of rock creatures around, a whole ecology our science hadn't even dreamed of down there. In my head, I labeled these possible creatures, "Lithos," the Greek word for stone.

"Cody Riggs, we are being hailed," Marvin said.

"Put it through here. Audio only."

Turnbull's voice came through. "Riggs?"

"Yes, Captain?"

"Everything all right?"

I cleared my throat, which was a dead giveaway, but I couldn't help it. I'd never been the smooth rogue my old man was, but I figured I would have to learn. Fortunately, Turnbull seemed oblivious. "We got a bit banged up when the ground suddenly shifted, sir, but we'll be all right. How are things with the aliens?"

"That's what I wanted to ask you. I see you're headed back to us. Has your translator program made any progress?"

"Just a moment." I scrambled up to the bridge and had the hail patched through with video. I glanced over at Marvin, still humming contentedly at his station. Fortunately he was out of the direct line of the camera pickup. "The program's still running. If you don't mind, sir, we'll talk about that when we arrive. I have to see to the damage. Riggs out." That seemed as good an excuse as any, and I cut communications.

"Marvin, do you have any theories about what that stuff was on the planet?"

"I'm analyzing it now."

"Good."

We were halfway back to the ring before Marvin delivered his report. During that time, Adrienne's condition had improved, but she was still in the autodoc. My foot was no longer blue and encrusted with ice. Instead it looked almost normal, but it still lanced fire up my leg every time I put my weight on it.

"I have a theory," Marvin announced. "I believe the mobilizing agent of the soil was a nonmetallic form of nanite. It uses silicates in a manner similar to our nano-metals. By manipulating molecules in the soil, it controls the rest of the molecules the way muscles control human movements."

I sighed with relief. I'd been seriously considering the supernatural or some strange energy-based life form. I thought about his report, and my eyes narrowed in concern. "Marvin, what if this stuff gets loose aboard the ship?"

"As with our constructive nanites, this soil needs a directing intelligence, or at least a collective of the substance large enough to form large numbers of neural chains. There aren't enough of the nanites in the samples we've taken aboard to do this."

"How much would it take?" I asked.

"The amount is difficult to quantify. The nanites are buried in a larger substratum of base materials. Lacking easy electrical conductivity or other metallic properties, I found that—"

"Just give me an estimate," I broke in. "How much total mass did you bring aboard?"

"Six tons."

"That much? Are you crazy?"

"I don't see why my sanity is so frequently questioned whenever I seek to perform basic scientific research—"

"Okay, whatever. Will it self-replicate and spread?"

"Only very slowly. It requires food and energy to reproduce just like any plant or Von Neumann self-replicating machine. To prevent growth, all we have to do is restrict its intake of vital materials."

"Do you have it contained or not?"

"Locked in the hold, it can't escape. It needs energy and mass to consume in order to grow stronger, and there is no ready source of either. I suspect it *will* grow gradually by leaching matter from the walls, but very slowly."

That got me thinking. "Where would it be most deadly?"

"Anywhere on a planet or other unrestricted environment with a great deal of silicates and energy."

My blood chilled, but my mind went into overdrive. I knew this stuff was dangerous, but maybe it could also be useful. It was like a disease of the soil. My guess was that someone, perhaps these aliens coming toward us, had created it and used it to take down the Macros on the rocky world. The immense machines had been outmatched by tiny nonmetallic nanites they had no idea how to fight. Hitting the stuff with energy – lasers or explosives – might kill some, but it would also fuel the replication of others. And with a whole planet to occupy…the Macros would be swimming in a sea of enemies. Probably only the fact that the Macros were metal had saved them from digestion, but the Lithos had immobilized and sucked every bit of energy out of them until the big machines had just run out of juice.

Like a man in quicksand.

"Marvin, make sure you keep any Litho samples tightly sealed, and wipe out all the rest. I don't want any wild Litho infesting our ships."

"Does that mean I am authorized to obtain and contain samples?"

Oh, yeah. As I had restricted him from doing anything, any analysis he had been doing must have been passive, through observation only. "Yes, take samples, and make sure everything is contained and is no threat to our ships or crews...or passengers, or any humans or allies," I added hastily.

"I understand."

"I know you understand. What I want is compliance. *Greyhound*, take rendezvous instructions from *Valiant*. Marvin, I'll be back soon."

Marvin didn't answer. He just hummed and did his work. I stopped by the galley and grabbed two beers—then one more for good measure—and headed back to the autodoc. The procedures it was performing on Adrienne weren't complete, but the timer showed only twenty minutes remaining. She was still sedated, but she'd be coming around soon. I left a sweating bottle on the table nearest the machine and went back to the bridge.

"Marvin, what have you learned about the alien crews in the approaching squadron?"

In response, Marvin put up an image on the main viewscreen. I saw a furry raccoon face. I tilted my head back and forth, trying to figure out why the black and white seemed so familiar. Then I got it.

"The aliens are Pandas?"

-11-

"There do seem to be similarities between the aliens and Earth Pandas," Marvin said as I stared at the still image on the main viewscreen.

"Do we have video?" I asked.

"Not yet," he said. "We're having trouble synchronizing our protocols. Visual data is limited to this single frame."

My theory about the Ancients trying out lines of directed or seeded evolution on various planets seemed to be gaining solidity, at least in my mind. What if the interconnected network of interstellar rings, rumored by the Blues to be composed of two hundred links, was the equivalent of a laboratory shuttle system? What if the Ancients were akin to mad scientists who'd built the system in order to skip from place to place, checking up on and tinkering with each set of DNA they planted?

I wasn't sure how the Blues' claim that the Ancients brought a terrifying cold with them when constructing rings fit into my theories. Maybe it was a random side effect. Or maybe rapid cooling of the worlds accelerated the pace of natural selection. Maybe they were so hungry for energy they actually reduced the output of each system's stars, just as a functional expedient. I'd read once that a small percentage reduction in solar energy could trigger a killing ice age upon Earth.

Of course, it was also possible the Blues had lied about the Ancients and their ways for their own devious purposes. The truth was that we had no way of knowing the truth.

"Wait…" I said, "Didn't someone say these Panda people lived on a hot and wet world?"

"Correct. Assuming the picture actually represents the aliens."

"Does that seem to make sense to you?"

Marvin seemed to process this for a moment. "Bearlike creatures on Earth often live in wet climates, but seldom in extreme heat."

"Keep working on the translation, and try to look for any apparent anomalies. You have about…" I looked at the clock. "Fifteen minutes to rendezvous, and Turnbull is going to want some kind of progress toward communication."

"Then please be silent," Marvin said. "I require all my neural chains to analyze their transmissions."

I shut up and then used the touch controls to check on the situation. *Valiant* floated in the center of the ring, which I thought was a strange place to be, but I guess Sir William liked his drama. I did notice he angled the damaged side of the battlecruiser away from the aliens, concealing his weakness to a certain extent.

Turning our sensors on the incoming squadron, I could see the six ships with their weapons grouped in clusters of six. I glanced over at the picture of the Panda and noticed something so obvious I'd missed it. Six fingers were clearly displayed on the creature's hand—if you included the opposable thumb. Well, at least they weren't six-legged spiders.

A few minutes before the agreed time, Turnbull called and asked for a further report, so I gave him a short and downplayed version of what we'd seen of the Lithos and the dead Macros. Then he wanted to know how the translation was progressing. Off screen, Marvin sent a text translation of what he'd worked out, which consisted of the Panda picture and the following:

Greetings, alien life. We enfold you with our embrace and only wish to experience you. Request that you send visual scan to establish trust and words of friendship.

That seemed fairly coherent. I gave Marvin a thumbs-up and said to the captain, "That's the best we could do so far, sir. If you like, you can record a video and we will quickly translate it and send it back to them in a message."

"Well done, young Riggs. Perhaps there is some use for you after all. Set it up." The man chewed at his upper lip and preened his moustache while Marvin did the prep work. Eventually the robot bobbed a camera at me.

"Go ahead, sir," I said.

"Ahem, yes," Turnbull said. "Greetings, local indigenous people! We have traveled from far away to explore other star systems. We mean you no harm. It appears we have a common enemy, the machines we call Macros." He turned his head aside and lowered his voice. "Riggs, send along some pictures of humans and Macros fighting." Then he sat back up with his oratory voice. I didn't bother to tell him it would probably not matter to aliens how elegant and round his tones were. He went on for several minutes with diplomatic blather before he ran down.

"All right, sir, we'll get right on this. Riggs out." I turned to Marvin. "Go ahead and—"

"Task complete," he interrupted.

"Did you translate that whole speech?"

"Yes, and I sent it along with image scans."

Well, I couldn't fault Marvin for taking the initiative. I'd intended to cut out some of the fluff from Sir William's speech, but what was done was done. I concentrated on piloting us up to the ring, but instead of floating in the middle of the ring's span alongside *Valiant*, I chose to hide behind its massive edge. This was in case the aliens turned out to be hostile after all.

A couple minutes of transmission lag passed before a message came back.

We thank you for your meaty words, bursting with truth and good intentions. Your visual scans infuse us with curiosity and happiness that you fight against the evil Macro machines. We embrace and wish to experience all biotic species. We invite your leaders to a celebration in honor of this momentous meeting.

I thought it interesting that they did not transmit video, though perhaps they still weren't able to match our transmission protocols. I hoped this was not some sort of trick—showing us a picture of a circus bear when they were actually weird monsters waiting to rip us limb from limb. Maybe they *were* actually Lithos, some kind of rock people like the nanite-laced mounds we'd encountered on the dead planet.

Turnbull sent us another long-winded speech. I let Marvin translate and relay it to the Pandas. If the first load of blather hadn't bothered the aliens, I guessed another wouldn't hurt. Diplomacy was probably pretty much the same everywhere. It amounted to saying lots of nice things you didn't particularly mean while working behind the scenes to get what you really wanted.

The exchanges came faster and faster as the alien six-pack drew closer, with Marvin translating almost instantly now that he had more samples of the Panda speech to work with. I listened to it raw, and it did sound like bears growling and roaring. The upshot of all the negotiation was that we would fly to their planet, Tullax 4, and talk some more.

The travel to their planet took hours. *Greyhound* trailed along well behind the battlecruiser and her escort. The Pandas didn't seem to care about us. Maybe it was because we posed no clear threat.

I let the brainbox fly the ship and used the time to get Adrienne out of the autodoc, lifting her sleeping form out and placing it on her bed after the machine cleared her to leave its care. I figured she'd rather awaken from the sedatives in a familiar place rather than inside a metal-and-glass coffin. The beer I'd left for her hadn't been touched, so I drank hers as well as mine and caught a few hours' sleep in my own room. When I woke up, I made my way to the bridge, leaving Adrienne to rest. She still hadn't awakened.

As we approached Tullax 4, Marvin put an optical close-up of its airless moon on the biggest screen we had. It showed a dark cratered landscape with concentrations of junk lying around, seeming quite familiar. He turned two of his cameras on me.

"What?" I asked.

"You should recognize these structures."

"Can you magnify them?"

"This is maximum magnification. However, as we approach, they should become easier to distinguish."

I glared at Marvin, but unless I ordered him to tell me, it seemed as if he was going to play guessing games. A few moments later, I saw what he was getting at. "Those look like Macro installations. Just like on the dead world."

"Precisely like on the dead world, Tullax 6."

I moved closer until I almost had my nose on the high-resolution screen. "They're buried in Litho dirt, too."

"Yes."

My mind whirled with the implications. Had the Lithos, if they were truly alive, somehow spread from one planet to the other? I thought they seemed to prefer airless worlds. Maybe they had hitched a ride aboard a Panda or Macro ship. Or maybe the Pandas had spread them deliberately, as I'd theorized before.

Maybe the litho-nanites were a kind of anti-Macro weapon, a nonmetallic machine inimical to metallic machines in the same way that viruses preyed on biotic life.

"The enemy of my enemy is my friend," I quoted musingly.

Marvin replied with another quote. "Keep your friends close, and your enemies closer."

"Right. Stay near me, Marvin, okay?"

Marvin turned to stare at me with all his cameras for a moment, then spoke when something beeped. "Hail from the *Valiant*."

"Riggs," Turnbull said, "come join us aboard *Valiant*. The Pandas are going to send over a delegation, and I want all the officers here. Even you."

I acknowledged his order and told *Greyhound* to dock with *Valiant* while I hurried to my stateroom to change into uniform. By the time I had it on, the two ships had connected, so I soon met Turnbull and his officers. They were all down at the large airlock in the hold, waiting for the aliens to arrive.

"Stand in the back, Riggs. You're a disgrace," the captain said, staring me up and down. I realized they had all donned their finest dress uniforms, made of real Earth fabric and dripping with braid and medals, while I had only packed the one set of utilities. It seemed I couldn't catch a break in his eyes. Moving over, I stood behind the group.

Because Earth Pandas weren't the biggest of bears, I'd expected the aliens to be about three hundred pounds. Instead, they were larger than that. Grizzly bears, that's what they resembled in size and shape. Only their markings and coloration was reminiscent of pandas. I was certain, however, that for all time Earth people would call them Pandas. Monikers like that tended to stick for generations.

Most of the alien delegation stood eight feet tall and probably weighed as much as an average horse. Six of them came aboard in all. They wore uniforms made of leather straps, more like harnesses than what we thought of as true clothing. They had leafy pennants streaming from these harnesses, probably awards and medals, but they carried no weapons that I could see. I had to give them points for diplomacy and trust. We had a row of armed marines in full battle armor against the wall, showing our relative lack of trust. The Pandas also wore breathing masks, but after a moment they took them off and sniffed the air. It appeared our atmospheres were compatible.

With the additional travel time, Marvin had managed to crack the code on the Pandas' speech. He then uploaded his interpreter program to the *Valiant*'s brainbox so we had a running translation. One of the six, who had a fancier uniform, spoke first.

"Welcome to our planet, which we call Hot Swamp," the leader said. Obviously our new translation program took some things literally.

He then walked over to Turnbull who had placed himself front and center in the fanciest uniform of all of us. The Panda held out his two paws, taking one of the captain's hands. He ran his claw-tipped furry fingers up and down the Turnbull's arm and squeezed it in several places rather than shaking his hand.

Turnbull fumbled through the elaborate Panda handshake before letting go. "We thank you and greet you in the name of Earth," he said. "I'm Sir William Turnbull." He turned to introduce his five closest officers, snubbing me.

The Panda leader conducted the same ritual with each man or woman. Afterward, he said, "I am called First Provider Long Growl." Apparently that was the best the rough translation program could do with his name.

"Let me introduce my leaders," the Panda said. Each had a title, such as "Second Procurer" or "Fifth Collator" and always a name that involved some form of "Growl".

Once finished, First Provider Long Growl drew himself up. "We're ready for the feast," he said.

"The feast?" Captain Turnbull said. "We weren't aware of that requirement."

"No feast?" Long Growl asked in surprise. He looked at his comrades, who all exhibited signs of puzzlement. They flicked their ears and muttered in low tones.

"I'm sorry!" Turnbull interjected. He clearly sensed a diplomatic faux pas. "Surely, you can understand we're new here. How can we make it up to you?"

Long Growl spoke solemnly. "In the name of the Growl people, I would like to invite the six Turnbull leaders to a feast in their honor with our own leaders of sixes."

Turnbull's face lit up. "Excellent! We'd be happy to accept."

"My anticipation surges," Long Growl said. "Please come aboard our ship." The Panda turned and led his officers back out the airlock to his vessel, which was docked alongside *Valiant*.

"All right ladies and gentlemen. Come along." Turnbull strode after them, looking very much the hero in his fancy uniform. Kwon made to follow with some marines, but the captain waved them back.

I noticed none of our officers were wearing sidearms. This caused me to frown, and I glanced down at my own weapon. I'd strapped a laser pistol to my belt automatically. True, the

Pandas had come aboard our ship with nothing but their claws and teeth, but they had a fleet outside to make sure we didn't try anything unexpected.

"Sir," I said loudly, "shouldn't we go armed?"

Turnbull looked at me as if noticing me for the first time.

"Are you daft, man?" he asked with an icy glare. "I find it unsurprising that diplomacy isn't your strong suit, Riggs, but even a junior officer should be able to see that boarding their ship while armed would be an insult to these people. They asked for a delegation of six in any case, and you would make seven. You can stand watch while we establish relations with these aliens. Please try not to subject my ship to any major cock-ups."

I could see no point arguing. I was disappointed to be left behind, but then again, I didn't like the idea of heading off to an alien world unarmed.

"Yes, sir," I said. "Would you confirm my status with *Valiant*'s brainbox, please?"

Turnbull paused long enough to make me command personnel and then went aboard the Panda ship. By Star Force regs, as long as all the other officers were gone, I was in charge of *Valiant*. If we hadn't been deep into alien territory with a damaged ship and no way back, I'd have been delighted with the chance to command a battlecruiser, but unfortunately, right now all I was left with was the sudden weight of responsibility.

"Kwon, come with me," I said after the airlock had closed and the Panda ship had disengaged. We went up to the bridge, now manned by warrant officers and enlisted people. I had no idea how they would react to me taking over, even if it was a lawful order, so having the big man behind me in armor might head off any problems before they got started.

Whether it was good crew discipline or Kwon, the bridge crew took my announcement without protest.

I told myself it wouldn't have mattered to me if they had complained. I had prepared for this moment all my life—I'd finally been given command of a warship, even if it was only acting, temporary command. I'd studied my father's campaigns and the battles in the Macro Wars as well as all the other military history I could find. I'd devoured military subjects in any form I could get my hands on—print, digital, audio, video, virtual, games. If it could teach me something about command, I'd hungered to learn about it.

I'd also visited monuments and battlefields from Thermopylae to Andros Island, packing my imagination full of grand dreams. Someday, I knew, humanity would run into a major threat. It might be resurgent Macros, it might be some sneak attack by the Blues, or maybe it would be some new alien menace. When that happened, I had resolved to be ready.

"Give me everything you can on the Panda forces," I ordered with deliberate confidence.

Soon I was studying the information on the holotank in the center of the bridge. Looking it over, I could see the Pandas had a fleet of at least three hundred cruisers in various orbits or on ground bases, all with some resemblance to the original Nano ships that had arrived on Earth almost thirty years ago. I took that to mean they had been visited too. Combine that with the evidence of Macros on the airless moon and planet, and I had high hopes we could get along with these people.

Next, I said, "Give me an analysis of their main weapons on those ships." This took a few minutes, but soon I was looking over basic computed specs on the enemy guns. They surprised me. "Antiproton beams?" I asked aloud.

The big, bald, rangy man at the helm was a warrant officer named Hansen. He spoke up in response to my question. "Yes, sir, that's what they look like. Nasty things at this range. If they hit our hull, they'll vaporize it in big chunks—far more damage per second than similarly sized lasers could produce."

I nodded, reviewing what I knew about antiproton weapons. Unlike lasers, which burned or cut directly, or particle beams, which slammed subatomic particles into the target causing contact fusion and heat, these beams sent a stream of antimatter particles. Negatively charged protons were essentially sprayed at the enemy, and they instantly annihilated the protons inside whatever they hit, releasing enormous energy and disintegrating the target's atomic nuclei.

Star Force had never developed antiproton beam technology because of its shorter range and high power usage. Such weapons couldn't be used effectively in atmosphere since the antiprotons would annihilate air instead of their targets. Laser weapons were far more versatile.

On the other hand, antiprotons could eat through any sort of armor, no matter how thick or resistant to more mundane attacks. The only defense was the heavy, Macro-style magnetic shield every capital ship carried, but seldom used because of its huge power consumption.

"Hansen, make sure our shield is in good working order and ready to snap on if we are targeted by those weapons."

"Yes, sir. Already did it, sir."

"Good man. How are the repairs coming?"

"We're patched, but we need more materials, especially the exotic elements, to fully rebuild."

I thought about all the dead Macros on their moon's surface, a goldmine of easily recycled metals, but we didn't want to piss off the Pandas by poking around just yet.

"What about their secondary beams?" I asked.

"Entirely antiprotons."

I tapped my chin in thought. That made no sense. Pound for pound, our weapons mix was much better in a ship-to-ship battle. Why were theirs so specialized? Antiproton weapons wouldn't take down Macros better than our load-out. Who else did they have to fight?

"Kwon," I said, turning to the hulking marine who stood near the hatch. "I want all your marines in full armor, with their weapons, nuclear grenades and skateboards handy in case of trouble." They were Kwon's marines at the moment since the marine commander had gone along with the captain.

"Yes, sir." Kwon said, passing the orders down to the troop pods. That made me feel better.

"How many Panda ships have us in range?" I asked.

"Six, sir," Hansen replied.

I should have seen that coming.

"Set up a battle script so at the first sign of trouble the shield snaps on, and then we'll take evasive action. Make sure to include *Greyhound* in the plan. Are both our main lasers good to go?"

"Yes, sir." Hansen ran his hands across his controls.

"Figure out a plan to survive their first volley. If they can't take us down right away, we'll knock out as many of these as we can and then head for the other ring."

"Sir?" Hansen and the rest of the crew stared at me, horrified.

"Just in case, Hansen."

"If something happens, shouldn't we try to rescue the captain and the other officers?"

I stared at the holotank, not meeting his eyes. "That would be my first impulse, but this one ship can't take on a whole world. We can't even take out these six ships—especially not at close range. According to these readings, they have dozens of surface batteries and defense installations around the capital city, as well as the hundreds of other ships we've pinpointed and probably a lot more. The captain chose to risk himself and his officers for the chance at an alliance." I deliberately didn't remind them of Turnbull's other motivations—glory and promotion. "Probably it will all work out, but I want to be ready in case the situation hits the fan."

For the first time, I was getting a real taste of what it meant to be a Star Force line commander. Hansen turned slowly away and then nodded. I was glad he seemed to agree with me. I thought that if I had Hansen and Kwon at my side, the crew would probably follow along, even if everything fell apart.

"Let me know if we get any word concerning our, um, ambassadors," I said. "Next, I want to see what you've got on that other ring."

The holotank showed me a representation of what the sensors had gathered over the past twelve hours or so since we had arrived in the Tullax system. While our arrival ring orbited above Tullax 6, this one was stuck into a barren rocky outer moon of the gas giant, Tullax 5. Even though the gas giant was in a closer orbit, it happened to be on the other side of the star system right now.

That ring looked similar to the Venus ring near Earth. It was half-buried and stood on its end, forming an arch. Twenty miles above it hung a massive battle station, not unlike the one my father had ordered built in the Eden system. The enormous construct did not seem to be in orbit. It looked like it was sitting on repellers, guarding the ring. Judging by the engineering and materials, it seemed to be of Panda origin. It made sense that this battle station would be guarding the only active ring against Macros.

I wondered, though, why they didn't put defense installations on the ground. They could have set up gargantuan guns or beams on the moon's surface that could blast anything coming through. Maybe they had the area mined, but I wouldn't have done it that way.

Then I remembered the Lithos or at least the litho-nanites. The Pandas didn't need mines. If the Macros came though on the ground, the dirt would get them. If the Macros came through in space, the battle station should be able to hold the ring long enough for reinforcements to arrive. And the Pandas might have a lot more ships we hadn't seen. If I were them, I wouldn't reveal my full strength.

Something beeped. "Hail from the surface," *Valiant* said.

"Put it on."

We saw vids of several Pandas sitting around a table heaped with food. A Panda I recognized as First Provider Long Growl spoke in his grunting burr, which was translated as a neutral, pleasant male voice. The calm, almost kindly nature of that voice made what followed all the more horrifying.

"Greetings," said the alien. "We thank you, Turnbulls, for a wonderful feast. Please send down another six leaders so we may serve our superiors."

Behind Long Growl, we could see all of the Star Force officers' empty uniforms displayed in a row.

"Look, sir. On the table," Hansen said.

I'd been staring at the Pandas, trying to get some nuance of meaning from their body language, so I had missed what was really important. Scattered across the tabletop I saw human body parts—whole hands, bones, a scalp with an ear attached—even a bare foot.

-12-

I stared at the image on my viewscreen. I couldn't believe it. The entire delegation had been slaughtered.

"Fuck me," I breathed, because nothing else came to mind.

First Provider Long Growl jerked as if poked with a stick. "That will not be acceptable," he replied.

"Stop translation, Marvin," I snapped. "Mute the audio. What are those six cruisers doing?"

"One is moving toward us. It looks like it wants to dock."

"To hell with that. These sons of bitches just ate our delegation, and now they want more?" My impulse was to open fire, but maybe this was all a huge misunderstanding, and I wasn't going to start a war by shooting first, no matter how sick the situation. Besides, we were outnumbered.

Then it struck me that I really *was* in charge. Despite the fact I was a mere ensign, I was now the senior ranking Star Force officer within hundreds of lightyears.

"Start translation and audio." I took a deep breath. "First Provider Long Growl, your behavior is not acceptable. Consuming other sentient beings is abhorrent to us. We cannot provide you with more humans to eat."

The Panda seemed surprised. "Do you not wish to join our cooperative society?"

"No. We're happy to discuss an alliance against the Macros, but we cannot comply with your customs."

"We must insist. Please have the next six Turnbulls ready."

"No."

"Then we will compel you." The communication snapped off.

"Sir, the aliens are powering weapons!" Hansen shouted.

"Execute the script!"

I watched as *Greyhound* powered its engines to full and took off like a bat out of hell with three times the acceleration we could manage. At the same time, our shield came on and we powered after the yacht as fast as we could go.

"They're firing." Lights dimmed as all our excess power went into the shield. Even if we had enough juice to fire our own weapons, they wouldn't work very well with the shield in the way. It was an all-or-nothing deal.

"Damage report!" I snapped.

"Surface damage only. The shield absorbed most of their shots."

I could see we were pulling away from the Pandas as they kept firing their antiproton beams at us. They seemed to really want another feast. In a few minutes, we were out of range, and I had time to get angry, remembering our officers. I couldn't believe they'd been served for dinner.

I wanted to swing around and go blasting at the Panda ships. If we were skilled and lucky, we could beat the six that were following us. They hadn't seemed very imaginative.

Suddenly, thirty-six missile plots sprang into being in the holotank, all aiming at us. I calculated our respective accelerations and determined that the missiles would not catch us any time soon, so I ignored them for now.

"Sir, I've dropped the shield," Hansen said. "We're out of their range, but our primary lasers can hit their ships. Shall I return fire?" Understandably, he was eager for payback.

I thought for a moment then shook my head. "No. There's no point. We can't afford revenge right now. We have to reserve all power for our engines."

"What about shooting down the missiles?"

"Not right now. It looks like we can outrun them." A germ of an idea was forming in my head.

Hansen turned to stare at me. His face was red and his brows were drawn tight.

"Riggs, we *must* hit them back! We can't let them get away with this."

"Believe me Hansen, I would love to do the same," I said grimly. "But revenge is an indulgence we can't afford right now."

"What do we do, then?" Hansen asked. He looked disgusted but resigned.

Staring at the holotank, I reached over to tap the icon representing the moon circling gas giant, Tullax 5. "We have to go through this ring."

"What about the battle station?"

"We'll blow past it. That's our only option. If we stay in this system, they'll chase us around until we run out of fuel and supplies. How are the missiles tracking us? Optical, radar, heat?"

"Radar, sir. They're pinging us all the time."

"Okay," I said. "Tell *Greyhound* to slow down and let us catch up." A few minutes later we came alongside and docked, with the enemy missiles trailing far behind. "Adrienne," I hailed, "you and Marvin come over to *Valiant*. I have a use for that yacht, but neither of you needs to be on it."

"Marvin is in the cargo bay experimenting with his lithonanites," Adrienne replied. "I'll try to get him to come, but he doesn't listen to me."

Five minutes later she boarded *Valiant* and told me, "I relayed your orders to Marvin, but he didn't respond."

I thought about sending Kwon over, but Marvin was a coin flip when it came to being useful. I decided to let him be. I didn't really expect my plan to lose *Greyhound* anyway.

At least, not yet.

I told *Greyhound* to cast off and spent the next couple of minutes instructing its brainbox. Soon, the yacht fell back toward the chasing missiles while *Valiant* forged ahead. This made the smaller ship's radar signature bigger in the missile's sensors, and reduced the battlecruiser's.

Then we slowly diverged courses until I was certain the missiles were following *Greyhound* and not *Valiant*. "Perfect," I said. "Now we can lead them around for a while before we use them."

"Use them?" Hansen said.

"Yes." I ignored his implied question. "Now set course for Tullax 6, full speed."

"The dead Macro world?"

"Exactly."

Hansen shrugged and input the course. Employing maximum speed, we reached Tullax 6 in two hours. We hovered over the blasted landscape. I noted that the six Panda ships had turned back to their own world.

"Now what?" asked Hansen sourly.

I glanced at him, realizing he was highly upset. His jaws clenched, displaying bulging cheek muscles. I decided to ignore his attitude. The death of Captain Turnbull had been a shock to everyone.

"Come down slow, but don't land," I said. "Grab some of the taller pieces of dead Macros with arms, and use the small lasers to cut them free of the surface. Try not to shoot the ground. I'm not sure if the energy will feed the Lithos or harm them, but I'd rather not do either. Load the cargo bays full of chunks. In fact, extend some smart metal to make extra holds. I want the material broken up into small masses in case we pick up Lithos accidentally. They're dangerous when they're clumped together."

I needed to work fast because the enemy missiles were still on *Greyhound's* trail. They weren't as fast as Star Force standard issue missiles, but they were determined. They kept following Marvin's ship around with grim tenacity, and they were slowly catching him. He had only a few days before they caught up to him.

Within an hour, we had several thousand tons of high-grade metallic elements including the exotics and radioactives we needed from the scrap. That sounded like a lot, but it really wasn't. Metals are dense and don't take up much space. The Lithos seemed to ignore us on the ship. Maybe they only cared about things on the surface.

"Get the factory pumping out constructive nanites. We'll patch up *Valiant* and repair the more complex systems later," I told Hansen.

His expression was almost a snarl. He didn't even acknowledge the order, just turned back to his boards and began carrying it out.

I considered relieving him—but I knew I couldn't. Despite his attitude, I needed him. He was functioning as my executive officer now, my second in command. He knew this ship better than I did, and I had my hands and mind full trying to figure out what to do.

"How long will it take?" I asked.

"A few hours for the structure and hull. Once that's done, it will take days to make and install the high-tech mechanisms—the weapons, repellers and so on. I'll pass the word to Engineering."

I leaned back and stared at the consoles. "How long can we keep those missiles chasing *Greyhound*?"

"Assuming nothing interferes, we have a day or two left. I told Marvin to modify the yacht's course and put *Greyhound* into a fuel-saving solar orbit."

We both knew Hansen should have at least informed me that he'd made a course correction. Eyeing him, I let the matter pass.

"You'd think the Pandas would recall their missiles," I said.

"Maybe they like to kill their enemies. Maybe that's more important to them than retrieving a few weapons."

"Or maybe they aren't very imaginative," I replied, ignoring his barb. I was beginning to think Hansen and I were going to have to have a private chat eventually, and I wasn't looking forward to it. I was still hoping he'd cool off if I gave him the time. "The Pandas may not have fought anyone but Macros thus far. Since we have time, let's stay here and salvage dead Macros. There are more of them mired in this dirt than we could ever use. Just keep a sharp lookout for those Lithos. They might have something up their sleeves."

We stayed at Tullax 6 for several more hours until the ship's hull had been repaired. Given a few more days, we'd be back to original specs.

I spent the time talking with the ship's engineers and the surviving scientists about a modification I wanted to make. I even let Hoon in on the discussions. The other scientists seemed to know how to handle him. As long as I didn't talk to him directly, it seemed like he could contain himself from making a pronouncement about interacting with someone unworthy of his presence—namely me.

Hoon was a reminder that there were different ways to be "smart" in the universe. Hoon and the scientists acted like field academics, but they were a bit more practical than the usual university-bound types. For all that, Hoon was still a major pain in the butt.

The ship's engineers were much better. With me pushing them, they eventually programmed the ship's onboard factory to make what I wanted: three smaller magnetic shield devices.

While the shield output was naturally spherical, it could be shaped somewhat by the right kind of conductive surfaces and magnetic energy. I put aside one of the devices for installation on *Greyhound*, but the other two I had configured to cover two sides of the ship, leaving the pair of big lasers free to shoot. The bubbles rose on either side of the energy cannons and limited their field of fire to some extent, but now we had some flexibility. *Valiant* could be partially screened against the antiproton beams but still fire, at different targets, like a swordsman stabbing one man while shielding against another.

The engineers protested that all this was against regulations, but I overruled them. "We're three hundred light years from home, with no support," I pointed out. "To hell with the regs. Exercise good judgment and creativity, and make these things work the best you can."

Once I assured them they weren't going to get in trouble from anyone but me, they became more enthusiastic. These guys had grown up in a different Star Force from my old man's. There were lots more procedures and rules these days. In my heart and mind, I'd always longed for what Dad and Kwon had talked about as I grew up: the early days of improvisations and big, desperate gambles. I guess I'd gotten my wish.

Using our final day, we tested the new partial shields and how they worked with the weapons. Marvin flew *Greyhound*, leading the thirty-six missiles in circles.

The Pandas made no further moves, except for continuing to beam us an automated message that kept demanding we come to dinner. Now I understood what they meant when they said they would like to honor and dine with us: they wanted our heads on the platters. The entire incident underlined the risks of using translation software.

As we were out of time, I ordered *Valiant* and *Greyhound* to rendezvous and we refueled Marvin's ship. We set course for the gas giant, Tullax 5, where the ring waited. It was the only exit out of the Panda system, and we all hoped that it would function for us when we got there.

On the way, we continued to modify *Valiant*. The next part of my plan was to order the improvement of all of our motive systems—engines, repellers, inertial stabilizing fields—to allow us a big burst of acceleration. Extra generators and capacitor batteries to store the energy were also added. We had to expand the hull in spots to make room, turning the graceful manta ray shape of the ship into more of a sea turtle. It wasn't pretty, and the way the ship handled would suffer, but for my plan to work, we needed all the hardcore acceleration we could get. When Dad modified a ship like this in the old days, he said it was like taking a European sports car and turning it into an American muscle machine. Now I knew exactly what he meant.

During this time, I didn't see as much of Adrienne as I'd have liked. Don't get me wrong, I wasn't chasing her or vice versa, but a smart, capable and familiar companion at meals made a welcome change from all the earnest military people. The crew wanted to believe in me, in the Riggs mystique, and I didn't want to let them down. But I was just an ensign after all, and I was obviously coloring way outside the lines. Only the fact that I wasn't leading them straight into pointless danger kept them confident, that and our decisive escape from the Panda attack. I kept telling them the truth, which is always a plus: our job was to survive and get home. Even if that was all we did, the new star maps we'd take back to Earth would be incredibly valuable.

I'd had the dead officers' cabins cleaned out and their effects stored, in case we ever got back home. I gave Adrienne one of the cabins and took another for myself. I left the captain's quarters untouched aside from boxing up his possessions and shoving them in the lockers. I didn't think the crew was ready for me to move in there.

I talked to Adrienne about her uncle and how sorry I was for her loss. She told me she didn't blame me, and I felt our relationship improving. We shared mealtimes in her cabin. She gave me good advice and insight, and I realized it was important to have someone nearby who wasn't under my direct command—someone who could speak her mind without worrying about her career or petty politics. You'd think people would forget about all that stuff when enemies were all around, but human nature just didn't work that way.

I found that I really needed to talk to a friend to get me through the long hours filled with work and worry. Sometimes in my exhausted dreams, I wasn't sure whether it was Olivia's or Adrienne's face I saw.

We talked about how I had nanotized her to save her life, and she understood. Everyone aboard was now nanotized, even the few surviving civilians. When they had argued with me about getting it done, I'd led them down to the improvised morgue and showed them the bodies of their dead colleagues. Then I jumped into a medical bay for booster nanites, making a show of how easy it was. Despite the pain, I sat rigidly and kept inside the howls that wanted to escape my lungs.

After that, they'd been mildly shamed. They climbed into the machines semi-voluntarily under my marines' watchful eyes and suffered through it. As always, the treatments provided hours of agony. I left just as they began cursing my family name in earnest and pretended not to hear.

"Sir?" came a call as I left the scientists to their torment. "Bridge calling. Warrant Officer Hansen on watch."

"What is it, Hansen?"

"The Pandas have finally made a move. They're on our screens and closing fast. They'll intercept us just as we reach Tullax 5."

I released a string of curses. "Are they launching from that battle station on Tullax 5?"

"No sir. They appear to have come from the alien home world. They circled around the star, using its gravitational pull to slingshot them to greater speed and surprise us."

"How many ships?"

"Thirty-six."

"Of course. Maintain course and speed. Riggs out."

I hurried to the central factory, which was now churning out munitions. It was my final preparation, one I wasn't sure would work. I'd ordered the machine to build small, simple mini-missiles. They had no warhead, just a tiny radiation source to fool sensors into thinking they were nukes. The motive force would be one repeller, like on a marine skateboard or in a battlesuit.

Normally repellers were much too slow and weak compared to engines, but they had the advantage of using much less fuel and space. A generator, a repeller, a sensor package and a tiny brainbox basically made up each missile. There wasn't time to test them thoroughly but during the final hours, I fired off a few prototypes. They worked well, and I had the factory spew out as many as it could make, which turned out to be about a hundred per hour. Once we had four hundred of them, I was ready to put my plan into motion.

-13-

By the time we were closing in on Tullax 5, I wouldn't say we were ready, but we'd done what we could. It had taken some maneuvering, and I hadn't fully explained what was going to happen to my crewmen, but they were all too busy to complain. I'd never liked meetings, so other than the duty watch, it was just me, Hansen and Kwon around the bridge holotank as the battle began. I'd deliberately excluded the scientists. They would debate everything endlessly if I'd let them loose on the command deck.

Adrienne had slipped onto the bridge, the only non-military person in sight. She sat down near enough to listen in, and I didn't have the heart to order her away. I guess because I'd included her in the manufacturing and crash repairs, making good use of her engineering degrees, she figured she was part of the command staff now. Fair enough, I figured. If I was lucky, she could become my technical liaison, my eyes and ears among the geeks. She did seem very well-liked by the technical staff.

"Let's get a status report," I said. "What's with those thirty-six Panda ships? I can see on the display they've slowed down."

"Yes sir," Hansen said.

"Why?"

Hansen shrugged. "Not sure. I thought maybe you could tell us what the enemy was thinking."

I stared at him coldly for a moment then nodded. "I'll do my best. I would wager they think we'll slam into their battle station and die on their guns. Why risk losing a few cruisers in battle if they can take the damage on a tougher station?"

"Why indeed?" Hansen asked. "I'm beginning to admire their strategic thinking."

"All right," I said. "If they're hanging back to play clean up, it's all about us and the battle station. In fact, it makes it even more imperative that this plan works."

"Because otherwise," Hansen said, "we're dead. The Panda ships will sweep in and blow us away from behind—if we're so lucky as to survive that long."

"We will," I assured him. "*Valiant* is lined up on the open part of the ring sticking out of the moon of Tullax 5—or at least lined up on where it will be at the moment we pass through it. I'm hoping that as we approach, our intentions won't be obvious until the last minute. All we have to do now is accelerate."

"That's still going to be some tricky piloting," Hansen said. "Getting the timing right…"

"Are you saying you can't do it?" I asked quickly.

The grizzled veteran's lip pulled back. "I can do it. But if I miss and we all die, don't say I didn't warn you."

"I won't say a word," I said, smiling tightly.

"But how are we going to get past that battle station?" Kwon asked suddenly, leaning his bulky body forward over the command displays. "I was thinking maybe we'd have to land troops on it—or something."

I could tell he was disappointed he wasn't going to get the chance to kick some Panda ass in person.

"Don't worry," I told him. "I'll have something for you and your marines to do, but before I get to that…" I brought up the holotank's planning function and started a script I'd written. "Once we accelerate to cruising speed, we'll launch our mini-missiles in a cloud toward the battle station."

"What about our regular missiles?" Hansen asked. "What about the Panda fleets? The logical thing to do is to hit both forces and send a full spread in behind the little ones."

The warrant officer was referring to our nuclear-tipped ship-killers. If enough of them got through, they could take down the battle station or at least tear it up badly.

"No," I said. "First off, we don't have a lot of them aboard and I don't want to use up our supply of radioactives—we're not home yet, and I want to hang on to critical materials. Secondly, I want to keep casualties between us and other biotics to a minimum, no matter how abhorrent their customs. Third, we don't know exactly what that battle station is defending the Pandas against, but I suspect something serious is on the far side of that ring. If we take down their fortress, whatever is on the other side of the ring might pour though and destroy the Pandas."

"Killing Pandas?" Kwon asked. "That sounds like a pretty good idea to me, sir."

"What if the enemy they fear is even worse?" I demanded.

Kwon snorted. "They ate our officers!"

"I know," I said. "But crazy as it sounds, that may be how they exchange ambassadors or receive visitors in their culture. No, we have to escape with minimum damage to either side and move on to locate more rings. That's the only way to get home."

Kwon fell silent. I glanced at Hansen, but he didn't offer anything new.

"On the other hand," I continued, "if some of our mini-missiles do strike home, I won't lose any sleep over it. Their job is primarily to provide a distraction. Hopefully, the battle station will use its weapons to take out the threat rather than trying to stop us from going through the ring. They'll have no way of knowing those missiles aren't nuclear-tipped."

"Okay, but what about the other things you did to my ship?" Hansen asked.

My expression hardened. I'd given the man a lot of leeway as the local expert, and I was a very junior officer, but I wasn't going to let him get away with thinking he was in charge. Divided command was a recipe for disaster. "It's not *your* ship, Hansen. It's *our* ship, or it's *my* ship. Forget that, and we're going to have a serious disagreement which will end badly." My eyes bored into him long enough to see him back down.

Then I threw him a bone, lowering my voice, as everyone else on the bridge was listening. I said, "We have to stick together on this, Chief, for everyone's sake."

He nodded, his lips drawn together in a thin line, and I resolved to keep a close eye on him.

"Now," I spoke more loudly, "the extra engine power is so we can goose it and speed through the ring faster than they think we can. The Pandas have seen this ship's performance as we ran from their squadron, so they will be calibrated for what they expect. Hopefully that will throw their aim off enough to allow us to zoom by."

"What about the new shield generators?" Hansen asked.

"We'll use them to double up on shield power. Two layers will cover most of the ship, and we'll drop the outer screen and be able to fire the main beams if we have to."

"So…what about my marines?" Kwon asked.

"How many do you have left?"

"Thirty-two," he replied.

I nodded. "That's good. Adrienne, get down to the troop pod and do a count on our serviceable skateboards. They'll each need a sensor package, a steerable repeller, a radio receiver and a tiny nuke. Use the minimum amount of radioactives, and make them out of solid steel so there is more mass to blast in all directions if they blow. We'll sync them up with the suits, and each marine will control one with his own HUD. We're going to send them out in front of us in space."

"What will that do?" Kwon asked. "Do you think maybe we're Centaurs? Am I getting the joy of blowing myself up?"

"I thought you wanted to get into this battle," I said.

Kwon grunted unhappily, but said nothing more. I was glad he didn't go up against me on this. I was having enough trouble with Hansen. I could see now why Dad had always liked Kwon—he followed orders.

"Get started on configuring those invasion systems," I said, "and get them slaved to the marine suits."

Once they'd left, I turned to Hansen and explained the other part of the plan. After some thought and a few tweaks, he agreed it was a good one. We started working on scripting the ship's brainboxes for as many contingencies as possible.

Murphy's Law, or "Sod's Law" as Adrienne said it was known in the UK, states that whatever can go wrong, will. Then there's the old adage about no battle plan surviving contact with the enemy. Both of them seemed to apply when it came to Marvin. Just a few minutes later, Hansen spoke up from the helm. "Sir, I'm having trouble getting confirmation of the script from *Greyhound*. The brainbox is not responding."

That annoyed me because the yacht and the missiles that were still mindlessly following it were an important addition to my plan. Not only that, I wanted to install that third shield generator on *Greyhound*. This far from home, the flexibility of having an extra, fast little ship might be critical.

"Try hailing Marvin directly," I said. Thinking about it, I realized several days had gone by since I had spoken to him. That couldn't be a good thing. Whenever he fell silent, I had to wonder if he wasn't cooking something up that he knew I wouldn't like. I probably should have had Kwon drag him aboard *Valiant* when I'd had the chance.

A video stream came to life on my console. Marvin appeared with only a few seconds delay.

"Hello, Captain Riggs," the robot said.

"I'm not a captain, Marvin. I'm just an ensign."

"By naval tradition, the officer in charge of any ship is given the courtesy title of Captain, no matter his rank. Therefore, you may call me 'Captain Marvin.'"

I paused, startled at this sudden conversational turn, and almost exploded in anger before realizing that I had to out-think and out-reason Marvin if I was going to regain control of the situation. Obviously he had somehow talked himself into seizing *Greyhound*. Given how far away he was and his ability to outrun us, I had no direct way to enforce my will upon him.

"I'll call you Captain," I said carefully, "if you can convince me your claim to that title is legitimate."

"Space salvage law says that any party may take possession of abandoned property."

"*Greyhound* is not abandoned property, Marvin."

"On the contrary, it became abandoned when Adrienne Turnbull, its owner's legal proxy, departed."

I crossed my arms, racking my brain for what I remembered of my classes on space law. "To be salvaged, a vessel must be abandoned by everyone, correct? Otherwise, a ship could be seized on a technicality if all the officers or owners happened to leave. In other words, it has to be empty and unattended to become salvage."

All Marvin's cameras, which seemed to have multiplied to at least a dozen, now focused on me, or at least on my image aboard *Greyhound*. "I believe that is correct," he said cautiously.

"But you are a citizen of Earth, as you have asserted before, and you were aboard the whole time. *Ergo*, the ship was not salvage and you're not the new owner, nor the Captain."

There was a certain degree of triumph in my voice as I finished my declaration. I knew I had him, and it had been rather neatly done at that.

His cameras drifted listlessly. "I'm experiencing immense disappointment. I think it is what you think of as—sadness. I've always wanted to be a ship captain."

"Marvin," I snapped, "Are you blocking our access to *Greyhound's* brainbox?"

"No." His tentacles began to fidget.

Not liking that one-word answer, I pressed him. "Then why can't we reach it?"

"Define 'it.'"

"By 'it,' I mean *Greyhound*'s brainbox!" I said, my voice rising. "Put me in contact with the ship!"

Marvin's many tentacles rustled and moved like a nest of nervous snakes. "Captain Riggs, you're already talking to it."

"What?" Then I got it. "Marvin, did you take over the brainbox? Did you incorporate it into yourself?"

"I believed I was Captain. It seemed irrational not to do so."

Finally, I realized how clever Marvin had been. Unless I wanted to manufacture and program a fresh brainbox in the middle of a combat situation, I was stuck with treating Marvin like *Greyhound*'s controller. So he ended up being the captain anyway. Now I had to find a way to make that work for me.

"Okay, Marvin. According to Star Force regulations and Earth space law, Fleet can commandeer civilian vessels at need by order of the senior officer on site. That's me, and *Greyhound* is hereby commandeered and placed under Fleet command. By my authority, I am appointing you a temporary warrant officer in Star Force with all the privileges and responsibilities thereto."

"Will I be paid?" Marvin asked.

"Of course, though it will be a while until any of us collects our paychecks."

"Then I accept." All of his cameras and tentacles rose up into a position I would have called "jaunty." I wondered if he had maneuvered me into this action or if it had just been an acceptable fallback plan of his.

I went on, "Because you're now an officer in charge of military property—that is, the ship and the contents of the brainbox you incorporated—you're clearly under my command. For now, you can be the sole crew member of *Greyhound* until I say differently."

"Then I'm Captain Marvin after all."

I sighed. "If it will make you happy yes, but don't get arrogant, or I'll bust you to enlisted rank and put one of my human warrant officers in charge. Or maybe I'll promote Kwon and he can be the captain."

Marvin squirmed. "That would be a grievous strategic error."

"And another thing, stop cannibalizing the ship for your own use. That's misappropriation of Star Force property."

"Aye, sir."

After that Marvin was very cooperative, which to me was a dead giveaway that he'd gotten most of what he'd wanted from me in the first place. I knew the robot had played me, but at the same time, I now had the backing of law behind me rather than just force and persuasion. It remained to be seen whether that would work to my advantage. I made a mental note to get Adrienne looking up all the regulations and laws in the ship's databases relating to Star Force military justice. After all, if I had to court-martial Marvin, I'd need an ironclad case.

We spent the final hours before we came within range of the Panda battle station getting a shield generator to *Greyhound*. To do it quickly, we fitted a repeller on the device and then launched it on a path where Marvin could overtake it and pick it up easily. Hansen and Marvin had to perform something of a dance to make sure the Panda missiles stayed focused on *Greyhound*, but in the end it worked out.

Once Marvin reported the generator had been installed, we were ready. I made sure my people rested and had a meal. I ate breakfast with Adrienne.

"Last meal?" she joked as I put my plate of food down on the table across from her.

"Not nearly as good as what's on *Greyhound*," I complained.

"The beds suck, too."

"We call them bunks. Welcome to Star Force." I raised an eyebrow and shoveled some form of reconstituted egg product into my mouth.

"Speaking of that…how come Marvin gets to be a captain and I'm still a civilian?" she asked me.

"He's just a warrant officer," I said without thinking, and then I realized what she was really asking. "Do you want to join Star Force?"

"It might make it easier to deal with the scientists and engineers. Right now I don't have the credentials to get respect that way, and I have no formal rank or status aboard this ship."

"Good point," I said as Adrienne forked some more breakfast sausage into her mouth. At least that stuff always tasted the same no matter what it was made of. "Okay, I'll appoint you as a warrant officer, too."

"With a date of rank preceding Marvin's."

"Deal." I could see she had thought this through. She was constantly proving to me she was smart as well as pretty. I felt a little guilty at such a stray thought. The sensitive and moral part of me shook its finger and told me sternly that not enough time had passed since Olivia's death to be thinking of her sister. But it was hard not to, after having been thrown together in this life or death kind of situation.

I smoothed my face, afraid my thoughts had shown on through. If she'd noticed, Adrienne didn't let on. I never knew with women. In the emotions department, they were much too deep for me. I wasn't a complete clod, but I'd always gravitated toward more outgoing girls, the ones that were comfortable with guys. Olivia had been like that. Adrienne was different. She was less boisterous, more feminine—but still intense and strong. There were a lot worse alternatives to have as my companion at meals.

Oblivious to my thoughts or faking it, Adrienne said, "I guess I'll need a uniform. In fact, you could use another set, and I believe others might need spare clothing as well. If we live through the next hour, we can have the factory make some new clothes."

I nodded, unsure what to make of her plan, but it seemed harmless. "That's a great idea."

"What about that Crustie?" Adrienne asked. "Is he being taken care of?"

"Yeah, he's fine," I said. "He has his own quarters, though he complains the compartment is too small."

"I'll check to see that we have scripts for his suit and food."

"Thanks," I said. "You know, you need some regular duties aboard ship if you're going to be a warrant officer. I think I'll put you in overall charge of all the civilians and the factory. That will relieve me of some worries and let me focus on operations."

She smiled like the sun coming out. "That's a wonderful idea. You're getting the hang of this command thing."

I realized I was smiling as much as she was. Her words and face had made me feel good. I had to wonder if I'd been played again. But even if I had, I figured in this case, it was all for the best. After all, I trusted Adrienne far more than I did Marvin.

-14-

Like most battles, this one started slowly and built up in intensity. I stood at the holotank, dividing my attention between it and the forward screens.

"Signal Marvin to start his script," I told Hansen.

I'd given Marvin a very precise plan and had explained exactly why I needed it done that way. He'd agreed without dissent. Like a kid who finally gets that new toy he's been wanting, Marvin wasn't yet bored with being the captain of his own ship. Maybe that had been a secondary intention of his all along. Maybe he had stowed away on the yacht so long ago in hopes that he could sneak aboard and "salvage" it.

Or maybe he'd planted the bomb himself. I turned that thought over in my mind and looked at it from all angles, not finding anything to prove or disprove it. I filed it away for later.

I watched as *Greyhound* accelerated smoothly in a long looping course, keeping the missiles close enough to continue their lemming behavior. They pointed their noses toward their mutual target, keeping separation from each other but otherwise acting mindlessly. Their programming was barely sophisticated enough to aim slightly ahead of the target, where it would be when they got there. Normally this would be an advantage, improving hit probability, but in this case, it also made them highly predictable.

I was depending on that predictability.

"Launching the mini-missiles," Hansen said as the time hack came up on the screen. From this point forward, everything was preplanned. In the holotank I saw the four hundred little powered darts cruise forward under maximum repeller power, which wasn't a whole lot. We were still an hour out from the ring and battle station. That hour would give our missiles time to build up enough velocity to be perceived as a threat.

"They're all activated," Hansen said a minute later.

Next, we launched the drones Adrienne had been putting together with skateboards and small warheads. Marines operated them by remote control from their suits, one per man. Normally, the skateboards would be carrying the marine pilot, but today they were providing me with extra tiny ships on the cheap.

"Make sure you don't enable the nukes on those drones," I reminded Hansen. We'd had the marines practicing with the slow-moving guided weapons, repeller missiles really. But if there was one thing every Fleet officer knew, it was that if something could be broken, misfired or made to malfunction, a marine could do it.

Hansen shot me one of his signature "get off my back" looks and went back to watching his board.

Instead of heading toward the battle station, the drones proceeded in front of us, toward the ring. I intended for them to lead us through. Maybe they wouldn't be needed, but if there was something waiting on the far side, they would give the unknown enemy thirty-two extra targets, and maybe a nuclear headache.

Over the following minutes, we played a waiting game. *Valiant*'s gunnery noncoms held the mini-missiles aimed at the Panda battle station while I watched a spider web of tracking lines in the holotank slowly converge. The marines kept themselves occupied by practicing with the repeller drones operated by their suit HUDs.

Greyhound's long loop came back to meet ours ten minutes before engagement—just outside of the predicted range of the battle station's biggest beam weapons. They hadn't fired missiles at us, for which I was grateful. Probably they figured there was no point in wasting ammo when their beams could do the job. The longer they waited, the easier this was going to be. Like a mechanical clock with many moving gears, my plan was coming together.

Crossing into range of the enemy introduced variables. I had no idea exactly when they would start firing. I fidgeted, but tried not to show that I was sweating underneath.

"Shields on," I said as we closed into range. "Keep all the capacitors at full. The weapons are last priority." If everything worked right, we wouldn't even need them on this side of the ring.

"They're firing," Hansen announced.

The holotank displayed fresh red lines representing the shots of dozens of huge antiproton turrets. They stabbed outward through space, slowly reaching for us. Fortunately, they weren't targeting *Valiant* yet. Instead, our green pinprick missiles began to wink out, turning into white flares of pixels that quickly faded to nothing.

"We're losing mini-missiles faster than expected," I said. "That's gonna be a problem later."

Greyhound, trailed by its flock of thirty-six Panda missiles, eased in alongside *Valiant*. As the weapons were still finishing up their curving course and were trying to aim ahead of their target, they actually flew a path that would take them, by our finely-tuned calculations, through a spot exactly twenty miles above the ring—precisely where the battle station was.

Unless the Pandas were able to regain control of their missiles, I had turned their weapons against them. Now, if we were really lucky, they would have proximity fuses with huge nuclear warheads and no ability to distinguish friend from foe. It wasn't so much that I hoped they would strike home and blow the snot out of the battle station—I just wanted the huge fortress to be desperately concerned with the threat to their existence and therefore, ignore us.

"Coming in range of their secondary beams," Hansen said. The battle station had hundreds of smaller antiproton beams, presumably used to knock down missiles, boarders, or fighter craft. They joined the bigger weapons in lashing out, trying to pick off the mini-missiles. In response, our controllers threw them into random repeller spins, trying to keep them alive as long as possible.

"We're still losing them too fast," I said aloud. "We should have made more of them." By my calculations, all of the mini-missiles would be picked off before the Panda missiles got within range, giving the battle station about thirty seconds to shoot at us, even with our extra speed.

"Hansen, arm all the drone warheads," I said, coming to a decision.

"About time!" he said, perking up.

I glanced at him then contacted Kwon. "Marine commander, divert half the repeller drones. Keep the other half aimed at the ring. Target the battle station and try to get them into detonation range. Go ahead and blow them up when they reach their maximum damage radius. I want to rattle the Pandas and keep them busy."

I heard a sigh come out of Hansen. He wasn't getting the Panda blood he dreamt of. That was too damned bad.

Diverting the drones had been one of my contingency plans. Better to risk going through the ring with fewer of them than suffer a pounding from all those Panda beams. I doubted *Valiant* could survive a concentrated barrage for long. Our surprise burst of speed might save us once, but I was reserving that for a last throw of the dice.

The drones filled in most of the time between when the last of the mini-missiles died and the Panda missiles arrived. "Ten seconds," I called. The holotank showed the sixteen remaining repeller drones had passed through the ring. The marines would pick up control of them when we followed.

"They're targeting us," Hansen barked as the battle station turrets slewed toward our ship.

"Flank speed, now!" I yelled, but Hansen had already put the pedal to the metal and punched us forward with all the power of our engines. *Greyhound* fell back slightly, then caught up again to ride in our shadow. Marvin was no fool. He was putting the bulk of *Valiant* between him and the threat.

The battle station fired a titanic salvo toward the ship instead of the last of the mini-missiles. Most of their shots missed sternward. *Valiant* rocked with one heavy blow and several near misses. Power surges ran through the ship, causing the fluctuating inertial fields and grav plates to bounce us around, but everyone had nanite arms holding onto their bodies by this time.

"Shields held," Hansen reported with relief. "We took a direct hit from one of their big guns, but we got lucky. It landed where we had a double screen."

"Yes," I said with a pointed look. "We were lucky."

He didn't look at me, but I figured he'd gotten my point. If he didn't, the crew had. My dad had always told me a commander has to convince his people he's always one or two steps ahead of the average officer. He didn't have to be the smartest guy in the fleet, or the bravest—but it helped. He just had to anticipate and keep winning, because everyone loves a winner.

More importantly, people follow winners.

The Panda guns turned to deal with their own traitorous missiles next, and we passed through the ring at high speed. We never did get to see what happened to the battle station, and within moments we were too busy to care.

When we exited the ring, the ship was buffeted with turbulence—at least that's what it felt like. The screens lost visuals. I looked at the holotank, which synthesized inputs from all our sensors, and shouted in alarm: "Full braking!"

Whatever attitudinal problems he had, Hansen was an excellent helmsman. He turned the ship end-for-end, throwing us into a full-powered deceleration. I noticed Marvin had done the same with *Greyhound*.

"What's going on?" Hansen asked, holding tightly to the controls as *Valiant* shook like an airliner in a thunderstorm.

"There's something big in front of us," I replied. On the holotank plot, it looked like an enormous curving wall. "Damage control," I called. "Get those repair nanites to the forward hull. I want my visuals back." We'd lost external cameras to whatever we were passing through. It must be gas or dust, something relatively thin. If it had been thicker, we'd be heating with friction as if entering a planet's atmosphere.

Then I noticed the drones that had been ahead of us weren't there anymore. The swarm of green contacts had vanished from the holotank.

"Kwon, are any of our marines in contact with their drones?"

"No, sir," Kwon replied in command chat.

I pulled up the radiation levels on my console. They were high for open space, though not dangerously so.

"I think I know what happened," I said aloud. "The drones detonated about a second before we flew through the ring. They vaporized a minefield or some kind of guard ship, clearing our path, but they left all this gas and dust."

"That fits," Hansen replied. "We're smoothing out." He was right. We were passing beyond the area of destruction. Then the visuals came back on as optical sensors were repaired or replaced, and the main screen showed what we were up against.

While it was difficult to get a good view directly ahead due to our engine exhaust, the curving wall was so large and so far away that it didn't matter. Looking from the main screen to the holotank and adjusting the scale, I finally recognized our situation.

"We're *inside* something," I said. "A huge sphere...or maybe a hollow planet."

We stared at the growing pool of data, trying to make sense of it all.

-15-

Once we had slowed enough to avoid slamming into the wall ahead, I had time to examine the situation. We cruised slowly inside an enormous globe. The ring was behind us, spinning in the middle of the globe. Floating with us were strange structures like snowflakes, thousands of them drifting around. They were between five and twenty feet in diameter.

"What are those made of?" I asked, relaying the question to the science lab below decks.

"Some kind of crystal," the answer came back from Hoon, who was leading the analysis team. "Spectral analysis indicates high levels of silicon."

"What keeps them floating around?" Logically, the gravity of the sphere must pull objects down toward the ground, so something must be countering it for the snowflakes to remain in space.

"I believe they have repellers, Captain Riggs." Marvin's voice came over the comm channel. I hadn't told anyone to include him in the discussions, but he'd somehow tapped into our communications. I probably should have included him, so I let it pass.

"Nonmetallic repellers?" I asked.

"Yes," he replied. "They're fascinating machines, using both mechanical and electrical processes but only trace amounts of metal. I am looking forward to examining them."

"Hold on, Marvin," I said. "That will have to wait. We need to find out where we are, and what's dangerous in this environment. That battle station was defending the Pandas against something."

"That's *Captain* Marvin—and I believe the situation is self-evident."

I growled in exasperation. "You're under my command, Marvin. I don't have to call you 'Captain.' Check your regs. Now, what's self-evident? We've been a bit busy planning and executing our escape from the last system. All you had to do was follow orders, so I'm sure you had plenty of time to take readings and form theories."

"The gas and dust we encountered as we came through is the remnant of structures blown apart by our drones."

Something didn't quite seem right about that. "Our drones were contact-fused," I said. "What are the odds all sixteen struck one of these crystalline snowflakes and detonated?"

Marvin said, "Snowflakes…? Ah, the structures. Perhaps there was a dense concentration guarding this side of the ring. As soon as one small nuke detonated, the shrapnel from the blast spread out and struck the remaining drones; and they were destroyed in a chain reaction."

I nodded. "That seems reasonable."

"Sir," Hansen broke in, "the snowflakes…they're heading toward us, converging on our position."

I looked at the holotank and saw that he was right. "They're not very fast. We have time. Take evasive action to stay away from them. Marvin, what do you think these things really are?"

"Automated Litho defense systems."

"What will they do if they catch us? Blow up?"

"I do not believe so. From my analysis of their structure, they will probably latch on to any foreign object they encounter."

"Latch on?" I looked up at the screen where one of the snowflakes spun slowly, looking harmless. "What's that supposed to do?"

"I don't know."

I paced around the holotank, watching Hansen pilot us away from the largest concentrations of the slowly converging structures. What could they do to us? Just attaching themselves like barnacles seemed a very ineffective tactic. Then I looked back at the holotank and told it to display the overall number of snowflakes detected.

"There's more of them now," I said.

"Correct," Marvin replied. "The number has risen from under two thousand to over ten thousand in less than five minutes."

Alarmed, I raised my voice. "Where the hell are they coming from?" I demanded.

"They're rising from the inner surface of the sphere that we're encapsulated within."

I realized he was correct. We were inside of a ball that was as big as a planet. It covered millions of square miles of area. How many of these snowflakes might there be?

"I know what they'll do," Adrienne said suddenly. She'd been pretty quiet during the running battle with the Pandas and our escape through the ring. But now she stepped up to my side and studied the holotank with me.

"It's simple," she said. "They're like antibodies. They float around until they detect alien objects like our ships, and then they'll just get thicker and thicker until we can't avoid them. They'll attach onto us, slow us down, and eventually overwhelm us. Maybe they'll crush us or rip us apart."

"It's getting harder to dodge them," Hansen said. "We may need to shoot our way out."

"Out? To where?" I asked. "There's nowhere to go."

"We can use nukes to clear them away for a while," Hansen suggested with a shrug.

I stared at the screens and the growing number of contacts depicted in the holotank. They were tiny points of dull orange light, meaning the brainbox wasn't completely sure if it should classify them as enemy systems or not.

I was certain, however. They were very dangerous and should be colored a bright red.

For a while. Hansen was right. Each of our small supply of precious nukes would probably buy us a few minutes, but that was a very temporary solution.

"All right, people, I can't be the only one thinking here. Start scanning and using your imaginations. What can we do?"

Adrienne spoke up again. "Maybe we can talk to them."

"Good idea. Marvin, you're our translator. Get working on any signals they're giving off—or any kind of language. They have to be coordinating among themselves somehow. You said they're just a kind of nano-machine, after all."

I turned to Hansen. "Is there any way out of here?" I asked.

He shook his head. "None that I can see."

"Can we shoot some of these out of the way?" I asked.

"The two main lasers should have no problem, and the midsized ones will be effective, but our point-defense beams don't have enough punch. It's easier to damage a machine—like a missile—than it is to destroy a smart rock."

"Maybe," I said. "Let's experiment. Start firing at the ones in front of us. Clear our path. See what it takes to kill them." I knew this was only a short-term answer, as we'd run out of energy before we destroyed tens of thousands of snowflakes. Glancing at the holotank, I saw the number of visible snowflakes had risen to more than thirty thousand and climbing.

My suspicions were right. Our big lasers each blew a snowflake to dust with one shot, but it took several hits with our smaller ones before a target was cut to pieces and no longer moving on its repeller. Whatever these things were, they seemed cheap, tough, and in endless supply.

"Where are they all coming from?" I demanded. "Were they waiting dormant, or are they being generated or manufactured as we watch?"

Marvin replied, "They seem to be calving from the rocky inner surface of the sphere."

"*Calving?* What does this have to do with cattle?"

"It's a specialized term for pieces breaking off glaciers or monoliths," Marvin said in a superior tone.

"Thank you, Captain Dictionary," I replied.

Adrienne touched my hand briefly. I glanced at her, and my anger and frustration faded a little. The situation was maddening, and she was trying to let me know I was exhibiting too much emotion in front of the crew.

I sucked in a breath, nodded to her, and forced a tight smile. When I continued speaking, it was in a level tone of voice.

"So…" I said, "If these snowflakes are like antibodies, do they function as cells or individual Litho creatures? Could the Lithos be completely communal entities able to break apart and reform at will for various tasks?"

"I was about to suggest that," Marvin said. He sounded a little annoyed that I'd come up with it first.

"Admit it, Marvin," I said. "I figured something out before you did."

"Your theory has yet to be proven."

"But it fits the facts," I said.

Marvin didn't reply. I imagined he was sulking, and that made me happy until I happened to look back at the holotank and see the number of snowflakes had grown to more than one hundred thousand. Given the inner surface area of the sphere we were trapped in, I didn't see any reason why it couldn't eventually reach a million—or even a billion.

"Now we know why the Pandas use antiproton beams despite their shorter range and high power consumption," I said. "They weren't trying to stop an invasion of Macros. They feared *these* things. And I'm willing to bet these formations are cousins with the living dirt we found on that dead world in the Panda system."

"An elementary deduction," Marvin said quickly. "That's been part of my operating theory for the last several minutes."

I knew then that he *had* been sulking, but I decided not to rub it in.

"And do you have any other tidbits of wisdom in your brainbox you'd like to share?" I asked.

"I believe the Pandas built their battle station and fleet to counter the Lithos, and that the Lithos built this facility to contain the Pandas."

"Excellent. But how about something more practical? Such as how to get out of this trap?"

"I'm working on that."

Since Marvin was in the same predicament we were, I believed him and let him alone for now.

"Cody," Adrienne said, "how thick is this shell we're in?"

I looked at Hansen, who shook his head. "Our sensors only penetrate rock about a hundred feet deep. After that, it could be a thousand miles for all we know."

"That's a good question, though," I said, shooting a smile at her. "What about other sensors? Infrared? Ultraviolet? Gamma? Neutron radiation? Neutrinos? Gravity?"

"We don't have gravitic sensors," Hansen replied. "The others show some variation—but nothing conclusive."

I programmed the holotank to consolidate all the readings to see if there were any patterns. Sometimes combining sensors revealed information that a single sensor would miss. "There's a hot spot here," I said, throwing the location up on the main screen. "All sorts of radiation and lots of neutrinos. What could that be?"

"Neutrinos usually come from stars," Hansen said after a moment. "And they pass right through almost everything, even planets."

I nodded. "So now we know the direction of this system's sun. From the number of neutrinos, we're less than one AU away from it. I have no idea how that helps us, but the more we find out about this place, the more likely we are to figure a way out of it," I said in a firm, confident voice. "Keep scanning. We need all the information we can get. Make sure you feed it to Marvin."

Hansen said, "Ensign Riggs, at a guess, I'd say we have about another half hour before I won't be able to avoid or shoot these things anymore. Then we'll have to slow down to avoid damaging ourselves, and that will be the beginning of the end."

I could see what he meant. Once they started sticking to us, the process would accelerate until they swallowed the ship. Maybe they would just entomb us and forget about us as a piece of grit encapsulated by an oyster. Well, I didn't want to become some kind of permanent cosmic pearl. "Use a nuke if you need to buy us time," I told him.

Desperately, I ran the holotank through many variations of sensor data, trying to find something to give us a chance. I wished I had gravitic sensors. Then I slapped my head, cursing myself for my stupidity. "Adrienne, go grab the nerds and the engineers and get them to the factory. I need a gravitic sensor, fast."

"But—"

"I don't care how you do it," I cut her off, "figure it out. Challenge the techies. Call the lobster an idiot and tell him the only way he can prove he's superior is by showing the stupid humans how to quickly design and make a gravitic sensor—preferably a sensitive device that can focus on one area at a range out to ten thousand miles. Make sure it can be controlled from the bridge. Now go!"

Adrienne shot me a reproachful look, but at this point I didn't care. Life and death hung in the balance, and I didn't have time for courtesy.

"Sure would be nice to have some of those antiproton beams," Hansen mumbled.

"Sure would have been nice to express that idea several days ago, when we had time to make modifications," I retorted. "Keep it on the list, though, because you're right. We should have taken a cue from the Pandas. *I* should have. Are we sure there aren't any openings in this sphere? Any tunnels?"

"Nope," Hansen said.

"Installations or structures, above or below ground? Anything that might be a command center?" I had a vague idea of nuking whatever mechanism controlled this killer trap, if we could only identify it.

Hansen shook his head after checking around with the other bridge crew. "Nothing big enough to be obvious, but there's a lot of surface area to search. If it was small, it could take weeks to find it."

He was right. Unless the nerve center I was hoping to find was as big as a city, we weren't going to find it in the next half hour. The rising snowflake count now exceeded one million and showed no signs of slowing down. In fact, the increase was accelerating. I felt like we were red-coated British soldiers facing a million Zulus: high-tech weapons with limited ammo against massive numbers. I paced back and forth, trying to figure a way out.

"Marvin, have you found anything?" I transmitted.

"I've located a low-power carrier wave in the gamma band, but it will take some time to decode."

"How long?"

"Days."

I slammed my fist on the holotank's pedestal. "Not good enough! We need to buy time." As that was a statement not a question, Marvin didn't reply. He must have been at full neural capacity trying to crack the Litho language and search for an exit at the same time. I believed he was doing his best. After all, his metal hide was in this with the rest of us.

I racked my brain for a solution. What would Dad do? I rifled through my memories of all the stories I'd heard him tell; all the news accounts, documentaries and war vids I'd seen.

Snapping my fingers, I said, "Marvin, keep trying to crack their language, but start sending pieces of it back at them. Try to break it down by words or strings or scripts. They're machines, so they should have a very rigid syntax. They don't seem very clever. Maybe they can be fooled into accepting our recorded commands."

Marvin did not acknowledge even though I could see the channel was open. I hoped that meant he was running his brainbox at maximum capacity, not that he was ignoring me. I hated to depend on the erratic robot, but I had to admit he could outperform a team of engineers if he was motivated. Dad had kept him around for a reason. He was a temperamental and dangerous—but highly effective—piece of equipment.

"We have roughly ten minutes until we'll have to use a nuke," Hansen called.

I contacted Adrienne who'd gone down to the factory deck. "What have we got?"

"It's coming together now," she reported. "They came up with a sensor box cannibalized from lab equipment. You would have thought we were chopping up their own kids. Once I told them it was life or death, they became a bit more cooperative. It should be hooked up to the control network in five minutes."

"Thanks. Good work." I closed the channel. "*Valiant*, notify me when the gravitic detector is hooked up. I'm inputting its first script now." While my computer skills were only average, this little program was simple.

"Command accepted," the ship's brainbox told me as it digested my instructions. Minutes later, the brainbox continued: "Gravitic detector is online."

"Execute the script."

Staring at the holotank, I watched as our two ships maneuvered as if in a video game, dodging clouds of snowflakes and shooting. I wondered if the Lithos had any more surprises for us if we did find a way out. Perhaps it would be something more dangerous than space-borne antibodies.

A thin fan on my display reached out from our ship and began scanning the surface starting with the hot spot. Unlike radar, a gravitic detector could map the mass density of just about anything, and gravity could not be blocked. That meant that with proper focus, we could look within the crust of this inside-out planet and see how thick and dense it was, giving us a crude picture of its structure.

"Five minutes," Hansen called.

With agonizing slowness, the holotank built up a picture of part of the sphere. Surveying the whole thing would take hours, but I hoped this globe would have some kind of structure that would give us an advantage. It couldn't be made of only raw dirt or it would deform and collapse. Something stronger than soil or even rock had to be holding its shape. I imagined a geodesic dome with its triangular struts supporting much thinner parts in between.

"There," I said, transferring what I saw to the main screen for everyone to see. "Form follows function. Only a few shapes will support a smooth sphere. I was right: these are geodesic triangles." I used a cursor to mark the shapes of huge struts beneath the soil, tens of miles long and half a mile thick. "They're extremely dense, most likely some form of crystal, as the Lithos don't seem to like large amounts of metal."

"How does that help us?" Adrienne asked from behind me. She'd come back onto the bridge and now stood at my side, gazing at the holotank.

"Great job with the detector, babe," I said, then I froze as I realized I'd accidentally spoken to her as if she were Olivia. I forced myself hurriedly onward, hoping no one had noticed. "These main struts hold everything in place. There are lesser ones filling in the sections and even smaller ones filling in those sections in a latticework."

"That means it has weak spots. How thick is the thinnest part?"

"Right here." I stabbed a finger downward. "Only about five miles of soil. Not even hard rock."

"Only?" Adrienne stared at me from close range.

I noticed her face was flushed. Had I embarrassed her with my slip-up or was her face pink from exertion? Still, she didn't look mad at me. It looked like I had gotten away with it—at least for now. It occurred to me that I was becoming a little too comfortable around her. I reminded myself to be more careful in the future. Then I got back to the situation at hand.

"Query the tech team fast," I said. "I need to know if we can blast through with the nukes we have aboard."

-16-

Adrienne turned and ran off the bridge, calling over her shoulder, "If I don't ride herd on them in person they'll debate until we're all dead."

Her drive and decisiveness really made me happy. I had to give Lord Grantham his due. The old man had raised two highly competent daughters, and I for one applauded the effort.

Less than a minute later, she contacted me. "Hoon says it's possible. I'm uploading the detonation parameters now."

I turned to my XO. "Hansen, get with your best missile controller and set up a firing plan to drill through the crust at that weak spot. Remember to take nuclear fratricide into account." That was the tendency of one nuke to blow up and destroy others nearby before they could detonate.

I knew we couldn't rig them to detonate on contact because flying debris would set them off in a chain reaction. The timing had to be perfect for each one to enter the hole the last one made and dig out some more soil. The farther they bored in, the harder it might be. Without more accurate data on the internal structure of this sphere, we just had to hope it would work. Many things could go wrong, from the tunnel collapsing to some clever Litho defense mechanism closing it up on us, or maybe they had the ability to harden or thicken the area in response to what we were doing.

"Firing a nuke now," Hansen said, far too soon for him to have set up the firing plan. The man was competent though, so I just watched as the first missile shot forward toward a high concentration of snowflakes. At ten miles out it detonated in front of us, clearing a pathway free of the weird rock-machines.

Normally nuclear blasts in space don't have much range of effect because there is no air or other medium to carry the shockwave, but this time there were thousands of snowflakes, each weighing five to twenty tons. As they vaporized, the plasma, hot gas and dust pushed outward, which damaged and shoved away even more of their dying mass. Every now and again something went even better than I expected, and this was one of those times.

Hansen bolted *Valiant* into the cleared area with *Greyhound* right alongside. The dust and gases buffeted us.

"Marvin," I called, "are you going to be all right?" The yacht's hull wasn't nearly as thick as the battlecruiser's.

"I have made modifications to this ship that should allow me a high probability of survival," he replied. It shouldn't have surprise me that Marvin would take good care of himself. I wondered what these "modifications" he had made were. The thought made me shudder. Then again, if it helped us survive, I knew I shouldn't worry about it too much. I did hope though, that he hadn't cannibalized all the food and beer. Military rations or even worse, bulk factory foodstuffs would get old quick.

Hansen piloted us through the hole and dove toward the planet's inner surface thousands of miles below. I could see most of the snowflakes were now behind us, forming up like a mob of preschoolers chasing a soccer ball.

Shooting stray snowflakes to clear the way, Hansen launched the first digging missile, which blasted straight for the weak spot on the surface at high speed. Everyone watched it on the display with anticipation.

The missile leaped forward, with Hansen following close behind. Our gunners targeted snowflakes to keep the nuke's path open, for we had to brake and stay back to let our missiles do their job of drilling through, without getting caught in the blasts. We also had to worry about the millions of snowflakes following us in a huge dark mass. The timing would be very tricky.

The nuke went off with a tremendous explosion on the surface, and our sensors dimmed automatically. By that time the second and third missiles were on their way, but now we couldn't help by shooting snowflakes. The visual and radioactive overload made our targeting too difficult. Less than a thousand miles above the surface and falling fast, nose down, we were committed. We couldn't even see directly whether the nukes were boring their way through or not.

"Slow down as much as possible," I told Hansen. "Fire a nuke backward to keep them off our asses if you have to, but we need to know we have a chance of making it through before we fly into that tunnel."

"Yes, sir," Hansen replied, grimly clutching his controls. The man had been yanking and banking for over an hour. Sweat poured from his face and down into his suit. I knew from experience that the stress of piloting was different from hard physical activity. Nanite treatments made people faster and tougher, but didn't do much to help hold a high level of mental concentration.

I watched as he followed orders, firing a missile backward to blow up behind us, temporarily driving the mob back, destroying tens of thousands of snowflakes.

Nuke after nuke went into the hole on the surface at carefully timed intervals. Dust and gas belched out of the tunnel.

"It's not going fast enough," I said. "Some of the snowflakes are going to catch us. We can't afford to use many more nukes and be sure we can still blast through this shell."

Hansen didn't answer. Piloting took all his concentration.

"Adrienne," I called on the com-link. She was working below in the production chambers. "Get the factory to modify the marine tactical grenades. I need a few extra nuclear charges. Just cheap quick ones like the drones—a booster, a warhead and a fuse."

"On it, Captain Riggs," she replied, sending a shiver through my veins. *Captain Riggs*. That did have a nice ring to it, even if it was just a courtesy. Still, if something was repeated often enough people would come to believe it. The crew needed to believe in me and my ability to get them home.

"Hansen, have your controllers start launching the new cheap missiles the second they're ready in order to keep us clear of snowflakes. Save the good ones for the drilling." Soon I saw a measured series of explosions taking place behind us, blasting the forefront of the mob and dispersing it for a minute or two at a time.

The millions out there kept coming though, and some slipped through.

The moment I had feared finally approached. We couldn't go forward into a tunnel full of nuclear bombs and shockwaves. We couldn't go sideways because we had to keep launching our missiles directly down the hole, and we needed a straight line of sight for the guidance signal. We couldn't back up because a million Lithos were on our butts, and we couldn't burn the hundreds of stray snowflakes that were coming at us from every other direction.

"Kwon," I said, "Get your marines out onto the hull with the heaviest beam weapons you can carry. Keep a good lookout and when a snowflake latches onto us, try to kill it or cut it away. I have no idea what they'll do to the hull, but it can't be good."

"Riggs' Pigs will get it done," Kwon replied eagerly, and I chuckled. There weren't many traditions in a service as young as Star Force, but everyone knew the name of my father's marines, and the crusty old noncom had carried it here so far from home. Little things like that could be big morale boosters or could even make the difference between winning and losing against a tough enemy. Anyway, I knew this kind of close combat was what Kwon lived for.

Everyone on the bridge was fully and desperately engaged now. Hansen was piloting the ship, gunners and missile controllers directed their weapons, and I oversaw it all. I was sure the rest of the crew was busy too—or if not yet, they would be soon.

I felt the first snowflake strike us.

The jolt wasn't big, but it was sharp—like a rock hitting a metal door. Then came two more impacts in rapid succession. The ship shook and everyone on the bridge eyed the hulls for buckling and their consoles for flashing red indicators.

The snowflakes continued to fall—about one every ten seconds. On the viewscreens, I could see marines firing their lasers by teams, burning the star-like points off the snowflakes. As Hansen kept the ship moving, every one of the living rocks that lost its grip flew off into space, but unless we also killed their repellers, they just came right back.

I focused a camera on one of the bigger ones and watched what it did. Its arms curved inward like a six-limbed starfish, and I realized that the snowflakes all had six appendages. That seemed more evidence that the Pandas had some hand in creating them. Once the arms touched the hull, they grabbed onto anything they could—struts, sensors, weapons, safety rings—and began to rip and tear like a clawed hand scrabbling at skin. Our armor was tough, but I could see that if we gave these things enough time, they would chew their way in like diamond-tipped drills.

Kwon's huge figure leaped past my camera, leading several battlesuits up close to the nearest snowflake. It didn't seem to have any defense or even awareness, and Kwon had obviously figured this out because he clomped over in his magnetic boots. At point-blank range he began cutting arms off the thing like a construction worker.

"Riggs, check the tank," Hansen barked, and I looked up to see a flashing alert in yellow: an unknown contact in the holotank. Whatever it was, it was big and had risen, or launched perhaps, from a kind of mountaintop off to the side about a hundred miles.

Or rather, I realized after a closer examination, the thing *was* the mountaintop and all. It moved toward us as if the entire monolith had lifted off and now flew within the enclosed space of the inside-out planet. If it had been more potato-shaped, I would have called it a powered asteroid, but it had remained conical like a rounded pyramid. Zooming in, I could see alien structures; jaggedly beautiful crystals that reminded me of geological formations in places like Death Valley. These were more regular, though. Purposeful, I would say—like the structures on a military spaceship.

"Oh, shit," I breathed. "I think that's a real Litho ship. It's too regular to be natural, and…" I fiddled with the sensor readings, "it's got a massive repeller signature."

"Fall back, fall back!" I heard Kwon yell on the general channel.

On the screen displaying the hull of the ship, I saw a marine being pulled apart by one of the snowflakes. Up close, the thing looked more like a six-armed octopus than a starfish. Its tentacles had sped up, and after tossing the bits of battlesuit away, it started to scramble after another. I realized with a sick feeling that the Lithos were now aware of the marine counterattack and something had instructed them to go after my men.

Kwon and his men beamed the monster down, but more were landing all the time; and I saw we'd already lost three of our precious marines. Soon, instead of surrounding and destroying the snowflakes, the troops were huddling against the airlocks and fighting to hold the snowflakes at bay.

"How long?" I asked Hansen.

"Ninety more seconds," he said.

"We may not have ninety more seconds. Can we move in closer to the breach?"

"I'll try."

Valiant descended farther, frantically defending herself with cheap nukes and overheating lasers. The marines clung to the hull holding off the enemy, but they couldn't last forever.

"Captain Riggs," came Marvin's voice, "the snowflakes are receiving signals from the Litho ships. Their level of cognition is improving and they're becoming more aggressive. Using the magnetic shield will block the signals, and I believe they'll go back into their previous mode."

Ships? There must be more around I hadn't seen. More bad news. Also, if we turned on the shields, our lasers couldn't fire effectively. Then I had an idea.

"Hansen, turn on the starboard secondary shield and have the starboard lasers stop firing. Kwon, fight your way over to the starboard side of the ship. The starfish will get stupid on that side, so clear them fast and dirty. Then we'll switch sides."

I don't know if it was Hansen or one of the other bridge crew, but I saw my orders being carried out and soon the starboard side had been cleared. I was just about to tell them to reverse field when Hansen shouted: "We're ready to enter the tunnel!"

"Kwon, get everyone back inside, now! We're moving and it's going to get hot out there." Turning back to Hansen, I said, "As soon as the marines are back in, punch it. That Litho ship is almost here."

I wasn't sure what to call it. The ship was bigger than a battleship, but outsized and crudely formed. I recalled a saying I'd heard somewhere: "Quantity has a quality all its own." The Lithos certainly had quantity.

"The Litho ship is firing missiles," I heard from someone. Looking at the holotank, I saw about forty big, slow spikes like broken stalactites accelerating toward us.

The spikes were being propelled by something that created exhaust plumes. Chemical rockets? It occurred to me that if the Lithos could make guided chemical rockets, they could probably make gas-powered lasers.

"Come on, Kwon, we have to go!" I yelled.

"We're in, sir!" he replied, and Hansen shoved the throttles forward without being told.

Valiant slewed from side to side, Hansen snarling and shouting profanity. "We're horribly unbalanced. Tons of snowflakes are stuck on the port side."

I could see he was right. Some had been knocked free by the acceleration, but most of them were digging in with the razor-sharp tips of their crystal claws and holding on.

"Will the explosions scrape them off?" I asked.

"I can try," Hansen said as he entered the blast zone near the surface, completely obscured from normal view by dust and debris. We flew on radar, aiming for the tunnel mouth. As we entered it, the ship rattled and shuddered from the gases and shrapnel forced out by the nuclear explosions. It seemed as if we flew into the mouth of a massive shotgun while it was firing, trusting our armor and piloting skills to keep us from taking a big rock on the nose.

"The shockwaves are tearing a lot of them off," Hansen said with satisfaction. "But we're losing sensors and some of the laser barrels from the turrets."

"We can fix those later," I yelled over the sound of the screaming artificial winds. "Just keep us going forward. It's our only chance to survive. We have to break through!"

The last two missiles had been launched in front of us and the gravitic reading said the bottom of the tunnel—what was really the outside of the sphere—was only a few hundred feet thick. The first nuke actually did it, breaking a hole through to the other side. Suddenly the outside pressure dropped and the noise and turbulence evaporated to almost nothing. The second missile sailed into empty space without detonating.

A cheer went up as *Valiant* shot through the hole, momentarily leaving *Greyhound* behind.

"How're you doing, Marvin?" I asked as I tried to bring up an optical view of the yacht. All the rear-facing optics seemed to be offline and I couldn't get a visual.

"I have survived with moderate damage to my ship. It will need repairs."

"When we can," I replied with relief.

Too soon, I realized we weren't out of the woods as the Litho missiles exited the hole behind us, still accelerating. Those didn't concern me too much, as these seemed even slower than the Panda missiles had been.

What had me worried was the massive, quarter-mile wide prow of the Litho mountain-ship. I watched as it nosed its way through the breach and followed us out into open space.

-17-

"Retarget that last missile on the Litho ship," I ordered, referring to the drilling warhead that had flown through and not exploded. No reason to waste it.

Moments later I watched it go arcing toward the huge flying rock that followed us. The Litho behemoth was at least a mile long and shaped like an unshelled brazil nut, or maybe a rough obelisk. I didn't expect the missile to hit—after all, the enemy had to have some kind of shielding—but I figured the attack would provide us information on their defensive capabilities.

"Light them up with our main lasers as the missile makes its final approach," I said. "Let's see what they counter with."

The dot in the holotank that represented our lone missile converged with the much larger red contact. When the two had almost come together, our main laser batteries began humming and rumbling. These familiar sounds indicated the gas chambers were being filled, ignited, and recycled. At this long range, we were really taking pot shots. It wasn't like we could miss with a target that size, but they landed with weakened impact due to the spreading of the beam at that range, reducing their effect.

Chunks of crystalline structure floated away from the hulking hull, but there was always more rock. Zooming the optics up close, I eyed their ship in detail. What looked like beam weapons of some sort crusted the side that was we could see. If they were in fact, weapons, they were huge, the size of skyscrapers jutting out like cannons. I hoped their power did not match their size.

When our lone missile came within a dozen miles of the Litho ship, we knew the huge spikes they were aiming toward us were indeed weapons. The "cannons" finally shot our lone missile. They did so almost lazily. The power of their weapons didn't seem to be much greater than our own, despite their bulk. Our sensors showed it was a cruder form of the Panda's antiproton weapons, further supporting my theory of their origins. It took them several shots to hit and destroy the missile, so their targeting wasn't that good either.

The best news was the big ship was slow. We were losing it, drawing further away with every passing minute. Satisfied that we were no longer in immediate danger of destruction, I ordered my bridge people to stand down and I turned my attention to our new environment.

We'd been in this star system for some time, but as we'd been encapsulated inside the Lithos spherical trap, this was the first chance we'd had to look around. As I had deduced, the hollow planet behind us was situated several AU out from a hot white star. If it had been a true planet, it would have been third in line from the star just as Earth was back home.

The abundant radiation pouring off the star wasn't comparable, however. This system burned hotter and brighter than Sol did back home. Four more planets were detected and displayed on our screens over the next half hour, making seven altogether. The closest-in two worlds were sun-blasted and dead. The hollow world we'd just escaped from was similar in size and surface composition to Mars—but much hotter. The next world in line, planet four, turned out to be an airless rock with small ice caps. The remaining three worlds were gas giants.

Out of all of them the only interesting planet was the sixth. It was the largest and appeared to be a beautiful green-banded world with a hydrogen-methane atmosphere. None of the planets in the system were what humans would have called life-bearing worlds though, given the existence of aliens like the Blues and the Lithos, that definition had been expanded.

The gas giants also sported many moons, some of which looked to be somewhat more Earthlike and habitable by biotics.

I turned my attention away from them for the moment and swung the optics toward the central star again. The closest two planets to the center, One and Two, showed some kind of activity. Their surfaces were too hot to get any good readings from infrared, and there wasn't much electrical power; but the radiation plotters showed the planets were crawling with...*something*.

Something that I suspected had taken notice of us.

"Looks like more Litho ships," Adrienne said as red icons popped into existence in the holotank. She'd come back to the bridge and now stood watching the data I'd been perusing.

"I agree," I said. "They're lifting off the rocky inner planets."

Dozens of markers had now appeared. They rose into space from the two airless worlds, all of them representing enormous ships similar to the one chasing us.

"This whole system is infested with Lithos," Adrienne said.

I glanced at her, not sure if the quaver in her voice was indicative of fear or disgust. Maybe it was a little of both. Either way, she didn't seem to be in a diplomatic frame of mind toward our newest alien hosts.

"Should I call back the bridge crew, Ensign?" Hansen asked. "They only just went on break, but..."

"They're pretty far off and moving slowly. I think we have a little time. No need to sound the alarm yet."

I wanted to give my people a moment to rest, to think we'd escaped—even if we hadn't yet. Hansen frowned back at his console. I could tell he didn't approve, but I didn't much care.

"What about those snowflakes?" Adrienne asked. "I don't see any."

"I doubt there will be many in open space," I replied. "They are only effective inside an enclosed area. They'd be too easy to run away from. And speaking of running..."

"I've set a course to orbit the central star in a long circle," Hansen said. He'd obviously been listening to us. "We can easily keep ahead of them."

"We need to do more than keep ahead of them," I said. "We need to find a place where we can lick our wounds and use our factory to improve our situation. Adrienne, could you go to the factory deck and set the system to manufacture more munitions? We're low."

"We're low on supplies, too," she said. "Do I have permission to cannibalize ship components?"

I glanced at her. Things were bad if we were down to that. "Yes. Start with the deck plates and the bulkheads between the smaller holds. And don't get carried away. I'll try to find new supplies for you soon."

When she'd gone, I stared at the system represented in the holotank. "Where can we go?" I asked myself quietly.

What do you do when surrounded by an implacable enemy? I felt uneasy as any new leader might. As long as we kept moving we were all right, but as soon as we stopped they would close in.

Marvin broke in on the ship-to-ship channel transmitting from *Greyhound*. He was still tagging behind us.

"There's a comet cloud at the fringe of this system," he said into my ear.

"Comet cloud?" I asked, frowning.

He'd obviously been listening in on our bridge chatter, but that was hardly unusual. After all, both our ships had just made a narrow escape and we were still linked up for tactical chat.

Marvin didn't explain further. I figured he was busy processing all the new data available and still working on the Litho translation, so I adjusted the holotank for an even wider, larger-scale view.

Most star systems had a comet cloud, a mass of hundreds of thousands, even millions of balls of slushy ice and rock orbiting far beyond the outermost planets. In Earth's solar system, we called this the Oort Cloud. You would think that so many would make for a dense group, but space was large enough that they remained thousands of miles from one another.

But why would Marvin mention the system's comet cloud? The Lithos could chase us out there as well as anywhere.

Of course, the farther out we went, the longer it would take them to catch us; and we could use comet material in our factory—but I figured there had to be more to Marvin's suggestion than that.

"Take us on a spiraling course away from the star, avoiding the Lithos," I said to Hansen. "Right now we need time to gather information and for Marvin to crack the Litho code."

And time for me to think of something to do next, I thought to myself.

"Done," said Hansen. With a few taps on the controls and verbal instructions to the brainbox, he set a course then took his hands off the console and stretched wearily in his chair.

"Return the crew to a normal watch schedule," I said, still staring at the holotank. The bridge was already half-empty, and within minutes Hansen was asleep in his crash chair. I shook my head. With such long duty shifts, I had to expect compromises between rest and readiness. I let him slumber. I could use some sleep myself, but I felt a need to figure out Marvin's interest in the comet cloud.

What might make the comet cloud a safe refuge? Did the Lithos avoid comet clouds? I mentally listed all the things that Lithos seemed to thrive on: dryness, check; vacuum, check; hot sunlight, check. On Tullax 6, where we'd originally encountered them, they were sluggish and primitive. They didn't fire rock missiles or crystal lasers at us; they just tried to grab us, and we'd gotten away. That was a cold world, a long way from the Panda sun.

The hollow planet we'd found on this side of the ring was hot and had a larger surface area than normal, as it had been blown up like a balloon, sucking in all that radiation and heat from its star. Here in this system, the Lithos had been much more dangerous and active.

There wasn't much metal in their structures either. Logic would suggest they could become much more efficient if they simply incorporated dense metallic material to perform the tasks it was suited to—carrying electricity, armoring, stiffening structures—all the things everyone else used it for. But maybe the metal would interfere with their bizarre metabolism. The

Lithos seemed to be stuck in a kind of high-tech stone age, unable or unwilling to change.

I turned the situation over in my mind. They liked hot, dry, airless, radiated places. Comets were mostly the opposite: wet, cold, full of outgassing and cryo-volcanic activity when exposed to the slightest heat. Some of them contained metallic ores, but there was rarely much in the way of heavy radiation. Marvin was right; they wouldn't like comets or any cold wet world with an atmosphere. But would that be enough to keep them away? Missiles could still chase us down, even if the ships were unwilling to venture so far. Still, if we had enough time we could devise defenses against those.

I looked for a likely candidate, and after hours of computerized searching, I found one. Then I felt a hand on my shoulder and turned to see Adrienne, looking freshly showered and smelling clean. She was out of her pressure suit—and I liked her that way. I realized I still had my suit on and a wave of fatigue reminded me how long I'd been on my feet.

"You need to rest," she said, dropping her hand. "The Lithos won't catch us for days at the earliest."

"I will, but—" I pointed at my target. "This is where we're going. It took me quite a while to find a suitable object."

"That's a big comet," she said, tapping on the controls to bring it in closer. "Forty miles wide?"

"We need it big," I replied. "I want to set down on the far side so if the Lithos send any missiles our way, they'll have to go all the way around it to hit us. Their missiles will have decelerated by the time they get to us. I also want a comet so large that we can find most of what we need there—water, ores, volatile gases. We need a lot of supplies."

"Why this one in particular?"

"Because it's also outbound in a long elliptical orbit. All we have to do is land on it and we'll keep on going away from the Lithos until we decide to come back. I don't think they like comets or the cold at the edges of star systems. They need heat and radiation." Once I explained my reasoning, and she tentatively agreed with me.

"I'll pass this on to the tech team and make sure they keep trying to figure these Lithos out."

"Thanks for handling the techies," I said with a warm smile. "That's a really important job."

"I still need that warrant."

I nodded, and then logged her official appointment as a warrant officer with a date of rank preceding Marvin's. "Now you can go clothes shopping. You need a proper uniform."

"You just made my day." Adrienne said. She smiled and touched me on the elbow with concern. "Now, it's time you went to get some sleep."

I stopped arguing and trudged down the passageway to my cabin. There I stripped out of my suit but didn't bother to go to the officers' showers. On a ship of war like this, only the captain's stateroom had its own facilities. I needed a beer, but I was too tired to go searching for one. I wasn't even sure if there were any real beers left aboard. Star Force had never been a dry service, not since my old man liked to knock back a few bottles between battles, but I had no idea of the arrangements aboard this ship. Then I had a thought. There might be a stash in the wardroom, which was the officers' mess and social space. With only a few warrant officers left, there ought to be plenty to drink.

That changed my mind. Wearing only boxer shorts, I padded down to the wardroom and rooted around in the small galley until I found a bottle of something German. It went down nicely, so I grabbed three more, downed them all, and then headed back to my cabin with the fifth and sixth in my hands. I was feeling fine again.

On the way I saw Adrienne, or maybe I should say she saw me. She'd caught me by surprise, but I didn't care. I was already feeling better than I had all day.

"I thought you were asleep," she said in a slightly scolding tone.

"I always have a drink before bed," I said. "Do you want to join me?" I waggled my beers at her and grinned.

Adrienne raised an eyebrow. "Nice look," she said, glancing down at my boxers.

"You too," I replied. I put a thumb into my waistband and snapped my shorts.

We stared at one another for another second then she suddenly blushed and pushed past me. I was left with her lingering scent and entirely too many distracting thoughts. I told myself it was just a natural reaction to the stress of combat, a well-known phenomenon. My body was thinking about procreation after facing death. Popping open and slugging down the fifth brew, I marched myself back to my room and collapsed onto my bunk. Fortunately, sleep came soon after.

The next morning I found a factory-fresh ensign's working uniform made of smart cloth hanging on my door handle. Once showered, I put it on. It fit perfectly after the smart cloth settled in. I liked the crisp high collar and it felt good to wear the symbols of my chosen profession. A military unit wears uniforms to promote cohesiveness, and it needs its leader to look the part.

I headed down the passage to Adrienne's cabin.

"Thanks, Miss Turnbull, for the uniform," I said, standing in her doorway.

"Not coming in?" she said, sitting in her spot at the tiny table across from the only chair. She looked sharp in a regulation warrant officer's uniform. It was the first time I'd seen her that way, and I found that I liked the look.

"We can eat in the wardroom," I replied. When confusion and hurt crossed her face, I shrugged apologetically. "It's nothing personal. You're a warrant officer under my command now. We can't be spending time much in our cabins together behind closed doors. Bad for morale and discipline. People will assume I favor you because of a special relationship."

Nodding sharply, she stood up to assume an approximate version of attention. "Thank you, *sir*. I understand, *sir*. Will that be all, *sir*?"

Great, just great. Unlike Olivia, she didn't understand military service. She thought she could just put a uniform on and it would all work out, but every organization had its rules and principles that were dangerous to violate. Dad seemed to be able to get away with such things back during the freewheeling Macro Wars, but that attitude had bit him in the butt from time to time, as well.

"I'm sorry. I hope you'll understand eventually," I said softly and shut the door. I ate by myself in the wardroom and felt lonely for the first time since this ordeal had started. Academy officers always talked about the weight of command, and now I felt it.

I'd started to rely on Adrienne as a friend and confidant. What's more, I'd given her what she wanted, the rank to go with the job she was doing. Despite all that, she was mad at me because—surprise!—with rank came responsibilities and rules. Thinking about that frustrated me. I couldn't favor her over others. In fact, I now had to keep her at a distance precisely to stave off any appearance of favoritism.

The whole thing might have been a rookie-commander mistake. I regretted giving her the rank. I considered going right back and talking her into giving it up—but I didn't. It wasn't going to make either of us any happier at this point.

Checking the holotank on the bridge, I could see about forty monster Litho ships slowly trailing after us. I wouldn't call it *chasing* as they were so slow, but they did have an air of determination about them. They headed in our direction, spreading out as if forming a loose guard. I could see they were attempting to prevent us from doubling back past them. They were trying to drive us away from their worlds. I eyed the outer gas giants and those cold moons full of materials I could use, but they were all too close to the angry, lumbering Lithos.

-18-

I spent the next hour looking over the star system, wishing I knew more about it. At some point I remembered I had more than one ship under my command.

"Marvin," I radioed. "Is *Greyhound* in good enough shape to go on a scouting mission?"

"Maybe," he said with evident reluctance.

"What do you need in order to turn that maybe into a yes?"

"Access to the factory for repairs."

"I think we can get you fixed up." It wasn't enough for everything the battlecruiser needed, but *Greyhound* was much smaller. "Go ahead and dock."

I met Marvin at the airlock connection. He had grown, now comprising modular segments of unknown purpose. He looked more like a segmented insect now, and he'd sprouted fresh appendages as well. New cameras of various sorts from microscope sized to large vid size dangled and wormed in the air at the end of snaking stalks. I spotted other input systems such as microphones and radiation detectors as well as more manipulative tentacles than I could easily count. He probably massed over a ton now, though most of his body was so flexible this did not impede him in his octopus-like crawling.

"Hello, Captain Riggs."

"Still trying to butter me up?"

Several cameras reoriented themselves and took up different positions. "No buttering. Now, please move aside."

I stepped sideways and slid around him into the airlock.

"What are you doing?" he asked, freezing in place.
"Going aboard *Greyhound*," I said pleasantly.
"Why?"
"Marvin, you're a Star Force officer now. *Greyhound* is a Star Force ship. I'm your commanding officer. You can ask 'why,' but I don't have to answer you. On the other hand, you do have to move out of my way."

All his cameras were focused on me now, and I realized that in these close quarters, he could probably rip me limb from limb before anyone could help me. I also realized that I was unarmed. Then again, maybe my enhancements would be enough. I'd never engaged a robot in hand-to-hand combat before.

"I will be happy to escort you around my ship, sir," Marvin said with sudden cheerfulness, his lumbering body reversing direction.

I was left with nagging suspicions. What might he be trying to hide?

"All right," I said. "Let's see what you've done with your first command."

My fears turned out to be well founded. Inside, I found the neat, luxurious passageways and rooms had been turned into chambers from a crazy technologist's hell. Even without a factory, Marvin had made more modifications than a dozen mad scientists might have thought of in their twisted minds. Cables and pieces of machinery squirmed, attached without apparent rhyme or reason to various surfaces—walls, ceilings, even decking where no human would put anything for fear of tripping.

I sighed loudly. "Marvin, was all this really necessary?"

"Are we speaking philosophically, or…?"

"Let me tell you what *is* necessary," I said. "As a Star Force officer, you must perform the minimum modifications in order to complete the mission. But this ship must remain serviceable for humans. And by the way, what happened to all our stuff?" I looked around for my cabin. I'd left some personal things there. I really could use a change of underwear, for instance. Even though the smart cloth I now wore was supposed to obviate the need for it, I liked my boxers.

"I have preserved your personal belongings intact," Marvin said in an injured tone.

"What about the food and drinks?"

I wanted to save our beer and liquor supply—for special occasions, I told myself virtuously. The factory could produce raw drinking alcohol and a low-quality beer, but I could see that an authentic Earth drink might become a real treat as our supply dwindled. Our predicament reminded me of an old sea story where a sailing ship was cut off and had to raid or scavenge for supplies. The most important item to keep in stock was the rum to keep the crew from mutinying. I didn't think we'd have that kind of discipline problem, but people in combat need an outlet.

"I have kept all consumables in pristine condition," Marvin replied. "I recall in particular how your father enjoyed fermented beverages. Would you like to inspect the ship's beer stores, sir?"

That impressed me. Even if Marvin's consideration was just a way to keep me happy, it had worked. I had to give him credit. "Thank you, I will check it when we're done. That was very thoughtful. But for now, let's take a look at the staterooms."

Marvin froze again, turning his cameras on me. "I would advise against that course of action."

"Why?"

"Because you're in an excellent mood, and I wouldn't wish to spoil it."

I sighed heavily.

"Just show me how to get to the staterooms," I said. "There are new crawlspaces and barriers—I can't even find the central lift."

"You will not be happy."

"Come on, Marvin."

Without another word, he led me through the maze he'd built. I could hardly recognize the inside of the ship anymore. After what seemed like several minutes of wriggling and climbing through passages that were clearly built for Marvin's new form, but not for mine, we stood before a cabin door.

Opening it, I saw something out of some weird vid. Everything had been scrunched together like a 3D puzzle. The ceiling had been lowered, and the various pieces of furniture now seemed to be stuck to the walls wherever they could fit. There was no room to stand, and even if I'd wanted to I could barely crawl inside to lie down on the bed. On the positive side, it looked like nothing had been damaged permanently.

"I needed the space so I did some...rearranging," Marvin said.

I shrugged. It wasn't so bad. "Fine, just as long as we can put it back the way it was sometime later. Are all four staterooms like this?"

Marvin squirmed some more. "I only preserved two this way, one for you and one for your woman. The others are—gone."

"What do you mean, gone? And she's not my woman," I said quickly.

Cameras stared at me. "I've been observing humanity longer than you have existed, Ensign Cody Riggs. I know the physiological and psychological signs of attachment."

"Attachment, maybe, as in friendship, but I think it takes a human to know whether another human is 'his' or 'hers.'"

Marvin performed a tentacle-ripple that passed for a shrug. "My empirical observations suggest otherwise."

Ignoring the stupid robot and his unwelcome empirical observations, I squirmed inside to retrieve my clothing, packing it into a pillowcase, then went and got Adrienne's stuff. I noticed a pair of skimpy underwear but forced myself to shove it all into another pillowcase without thinking about it too much. With the two makeshift sacks over my shoulder, I headed back to Marvin.

"What else have you done to this ship?" I asked. "Anything of operational usefulness?"

"I've thickened the ship's armor and improved the efficiency of the magnetic shield. I've also rearranged vital systems to be less vulnerable to damage. The ship's single laser mount has been upgraded with improved sensors, but without access to *Valiant's* factory I couldn't perform more significant alterations. I suspect I could at least triple *Greyhound's* usefulness as a combat auxiliary given full access to the factory deck."

Unrestricted access to the factory...? I considered the idea briefly, and came up with a resounding response which I didn't verbalize: *No.*

"Coordinate with Warrant Officer Adrienne Turnbull for anything you need from the factory," I said. "You're not to use it on your own except in the case of a true life and death emergency." I pointed my finger at him accusingly. "And don't go bending that principle. She's in charge of all production, and while I'm sure she can give you a few barrels of constructive nanites if you ask nicely enough, you're not getting full control. I don't want our only factory to be diverted toward some crazy experiment of yours."

"Command accepted," Marvin said. I now realized that when he felt insulted he deliberately talked like a brainbox, like a crewman who exaggerated his "yes, sir" and "no, sir." He was playing the good, cooperative robot. Well, I wasn't buying it. Right now he was probably trying to lull me into a false sense of security, building up a bank account of goodwill toward the inevitable time when he would go rogue again. I suspected that only the threat of the Lithos and his lack of a factory under his control had caused him to follow orders up to this point.

"Good," I said. "Thanks, Marvin. I have what I need. Good job with your ship. Just keep in mind that other Star Force personnel need to be able to use it if you're unavailable or incapacitated."

"Command accepted," Marvin repeated in a tone of quiet defiance.

Apparently, he was still sulking. I ignored him and went back aboard *Valiant*. Marvin followed at a distance.

The crew bustled about, and I nodded and smiled at them as I walked through *Valiant's* passageways. Morale seemed good. We'd gotten out of a tough situation, and under my command at least, we'd only lost a few people. I headed up to the bridge. After checking that everything was all right there, and that we continued to cruise toward our target comet, I spent some time touring the ship.

In the big factory space at the center of the battlecruiser, I saw Marvin talking to Adrienne. I waved, but she pretended not to notice. I shrugged, figuring she'd get over it.

Suddenly, I was confronted by Professor Hoon. As soon as the Crustacean saw me, he came scurrying over in his suit. For a moment I regretted not carrying a sidearm. Waving his lobster claws, he said, "You there. Offspring of Kyle Riggs. You still have not apologized for your offense against my person."

"And you have not apologized for assaulting me with your claw. And by the way, I now command this vessel and its occupants, so don't go getting all high and mighty toward me."

"I am not part of your military organization," Hoon replied arrogantly. "I have diplomatic immunity as a representative of the Crustacean government." In fact, "arrogant" seemed to be his only tone.

My voice climbed. "Your government and your entire race only exist because my father saved all your watery butts. I tolerate you because you're supposed to be smart, and we're going to need everyone to pull his weight. If you're so damned intelligent, why don't you come up with some ideas to improve our capabilities or find a way back home?"

I took a step forward, and despite the fact that Hoon massed several times what I did, he backed up.

Waving his claws, he spun around and scuttled away, burbling. I looked up to see the rest of the tech team watching and trying to suppress grins. Probably Hoon bugged them, too. I didn't see any point in them trying to hide their expressions unless Crustacean suits had software that translated our faces. Maybe they did. The lobsters *were* intelligent and intuitive.

The factory was churning out nanites and more complex equipment at full blast, but it was running low on critical supplies. Kwon and his marines were on this deck, wearing their battlesuits for extra strength. Adrienne had them carrying the last pieces of dead Macros and other junk to the maw, like a line of worker ants. I was happy to see everyone pitching in.

I walked up to her, and she looked me over coolly.

"Everything okay?" I asked. I could have meant with Marvin or with the general situation, but I figured I'd let her answer in her own way.

"Sure. Everything's perfect, Captain Riggs, sir."

"Excellent. Here are your personal effects," I said. I handed her the sack of undies I'd retrieved from *Greyhound*. She looked into the sack then closed it again suddenly. Maybe there was something embarrassing on top.

"Give Marvin whatever he needs from the factory, within reason, to get *Greyhound* in shape," I told her. "I have a new mission for his ship."

"Aye, aye, Captain, sir," she said, still not looking at me.

"Thank you, Warrant Officer Turnbull," I countered.

I thought I saw an eyebrow twitch. When Olivia had done that, she was trying not to laugh. That was good. If Adrienne finally decided the situation was amusing, maybe it meant she was getting tired of our little spat or whatever it was we were having. Quitting while I was ahead seemed like the best idea so I nodded at the technicians and left them to their manufacturing.

Back on the bridge, Hansen lounged at the helm with just one other noncom on watch. I nodded to him, and he nodded back warily.

"Fine job yesterday," I told him, and it was an honest compliment. The man was a crack pilot, and I was happy to have him. "I've never seen a better hand at the helm." That was true too, though possibly just because I had so little experience aboard warships until now. Still, it sounded good.

"Thanks," he replied, relaxing.

I stared at the holotank. "They're still chasing us," I said, looking at the forty-odd Litho ships that trailed us in slow motion. I wasn't sure what to call them. The size of small dreadnoughts, these flying mountains only had the firepower of cruisers or even destroyers. With their thick crystalline armor, however, I bet they could absorb an enormous pounding. Simply blowing one of them apart, even with fusion warheads, would take forever.

"Yes," Hansen agreed. "Once we land on the comet, we'll have about three days before they catch up, assuming they keep coming."

"I'm hoping they don't like the cold. They seem to prefer sunlight. Maybe part of their energy needs come from stellar radiation. It's clear to me they operate more effectively when they're warm. Maybe they'll reach some kind of limit and stop, like hunters who don't want to chase their prey too high into the snowy mountains."

"Very poetic, sir. I hope you're right." Hansen seemed to think for a moment, then he spoke again. "What's the plan, if you don't mind my asking?"

I looked at him in surprise. "Of course I don't mind. You're my XO. You can ask me anything you need to." Turning back to the holotank, I went on, "We're going to take as much time as we can to repair and prepare. If they let us, we'll use the factory and the comet materials to build more ships—a bigger force. We need to optimize our weapons against the Lithos."

"That could take months," Hansen objected.

"That's right. It might take quite a while."

His face darkened, but he said nothing. I wondered if the man had been hoping to be home for Christmas. I just wanted to see home at some point in the future. I still didn't know who had killed Olivia, and that was a driving force for me.

That thought gave me a pang of regret. I'd been so busy worrying about staying alive I hadn't had much time to think about my recent loss or how we'd gotten here. It was still possible there was a traitor aboard this ship. If so, they seemed to be lying low. But I hadn't forgotten the past. In time, I was sure I'd figure out how this whole "adventure" had started.

"While we build up," I said, "Marvin is going to go scouting for us. We haven't found the ring yet. We have to know how to escape this system if things go badly. It might be anywhere—even inside one of the Litho planets. We need to find it and eventually figure out a way to pass through it."

"Why?" Hansen asked. "We could build up and go back to the Panda system with big enough ships to clobber them. Then we can take all the time we need to figure out how to activate the first ring we came through to go home. As I see it, every move we make is taking us farther away into the unknown."

"Marvin said the ring only went one direction."

"And you trust the robot? I read up on it today. That ring did originally operate in both directions. Macros came through it and invaded the Crustacean world."

I thought about that for a moment. "I don't entirely trust Marvin," I admitted, "but the other scientists haven't contradicted him to my knowledge. I don't think we can beat the Lithos either, not head to head. How are we going to fight our way through that planet-sized defensive structure of theirs? The Pandas haven't been able to do it."

"Maybe they don't want to," Hansen said darkly.

"Why not?"

"You think the Pandas made the Lithos, right? And once they lost control of them, they turtled-up in their own system. If humans were in that situation we'd never rest until we were able to break out and explore, but maybe the Pandas are different. Maybe they're content to stay in their own little corner and let the Lithos form an impassible barrier keeping them safe. Maybe they don't care about what they unleashed down on the other side of their ring. They're beasts anyway, creatures that eat each other just to say hello."

I rubbed my neck, realizing I could use a haircut. "You may be right. But, we might have tried to hide if we had a way to beat the Macros without losing ships. Right now it's all speculation. Maybe once Marvin cracks their language, we'll find out more."

Hansen eyed me, until I found myself frowning at him.

"What is it now, Chief?" I asked, him.

"Do you even want to get back to Earth, Riggs? Maybe you and the robot want to stay out here and have a good time."

I almost laughed but realized he was serious. "Of course I want to get home."

"Are you sure? Maybe you like command so much you don't want to give it up just yet."

It was my turn to frown. "That's an unreasonable accusation, Hansen."

"Sorry sir. Please accept my apologies."

I could tell he didn't mean it, but I accepted his apologies anyway. I took a deep breath and told myself everyone was under a great deal of stress and that I couldn't expect them all to be happy with someone who was practically a kid in command.

Hansen lapsed into silence again, staring at his board. Space travel could be tedious in the great gulfs between planets, though less so than it used to be, with our upgraded engines and stabilizers. *Valiant* was five times as fast as one of my dad's old ships.

I kept quiet as well, playing with the holotank, examining everything the sensors had picked up and the brainbox had collated into one common picture. Data poured continuously into the ship, with everything represented in three dimensions.

The next few days dragged. We landed on the comet and began mining it. This wasn't as exciting as it sounded. The surface of a comet when far, far out in space, doesn't even have a tail. There was very little stellar wind out here to damage its icy surface in any way.

The comet was cold, dark and forbidding. The sounds of drilling vibrated through the ship night and day as drones worked with marines to chew up chunks of ice and minerals and then transport them into the battlecruiser's belly. During these days, which quickly stretched into weeks, we managed to make a lot of repairs and replenish our munitions.

Adrienne didn't seem to want to talk to me anymore except about work even though I'd made a few overtures to test the waters between us. She was all snap and pop, a veritable caricature of a military officer when near me, and it seemed obvious she was rubbing it in. I had no idea what to do except wait for her to get over it. Or maybe she never would. My heart, already heavily scarred, gained a few more stripes, but I couldn't allow myself to care. I had people depending on me for their lives.

Beer helped, fortunately. I'd brought over a sizeable ration from *Greyhound*, and I was hoarding them in my cabin. I shared a few with Kwon—no one else. It was different with him. He didn't care about protocol, and he'd known me all of my life. But I couldn't do that too often, especially not in front of the others. He was a subordinate too, after all. He seemed to be spending his off time with the largest woman in the crew, a petty officer by the name of Steiner who overtopped me by at least two inches. Well, more power to him.

I was returning to my cabin after drinking with the big man when a feminine figure rounded a corner and bumped into me. It was Doctor Kalu, one of the civilian scientists. She was West African with exotic eyes and dusky skin. I grabbed her to keep from falling over. I was more than a little "bevved up" as Adrienne liked to say.

Her arms went around me to hold herself up, and I suddenly became aware of her body pressed up against me. In one of those weird moments that only happen late at night when tired, drunk or both. We didn't let go of each other right away, so we just stood there.

"Mmm. Hello, Captain Riggs," she said, looking into my face.

Dr. Kalu was sleek and tall. She had curves I found unusual and...interesting. More than once I'd caught her staring at me—but then again, lots of women had done that throughout my life. I was semi-famous, after all. I'd gotten used to it.

She was so close and warm, and I'd denied myself so long... Without thinking, I kissed her—or maybe she kissed me. Soon we were full-blown making out, until a crewman crossed the end of the passageway. Fortunately he seemed not to notice us in the dimness of the night cycle. I broke the clinch.

"We can't do this out here," I said.

"Then let's go to your cabin." She ran her hand up under my tunic onto my naked back, surging my blood to all sorts of interesting places.

"Yeah, lets." Befuddled, I stumbled down the corridor toward my cabin holding the woman close to me. Unfortunately, as we passed Adrienne's door I guess our bumping along the wall was too loud.

The portal opened, and I heard Adrienne gasp. She stepped into the passage, staring at us.

Kalu smirked and kissed my ear.

"Come on, Cody," she said, tugging me toward my cabin.

Adrienne's face went white. I could see it even in the dim light. Abruptly, my higher functions took over and I pushed the sexy scientist away. "That will be all, Dr. Kalu. Thank you for your assistance." I straightened my uniform as Adrienne continued to stare at me. "Sorry. A bit tipsy. Bumped into her…" I said lamely. Hell, that excuse had gotten me out of some jams before.

Kalu looked from me to Adrienne and back again, snorted with disdain, and then turned to stalk away.

"You're piss-drunk again," Adrienne accused.

"It's not a crime. Neither is socializing with civilians. What do you care anyway, Miss 'yes, sir, no, sir'?"

"Socializing? Is that what you call it?" Her expression could have frozen fire.

"Whatever. I'm going to bed. Alone!" I turned my back on her, not wanting to deal with any more crap. It wasn't like she was my girlfriend or anything. She wasn't Olivia. When I reached my cabin, I fell into my bunk and slept.

From then on Adrienne took great pains to avoid me, and I didn't bother to force the issue. She'd have to learn to deal with me as I was, not as she wished me to be. I wasn't some plaster saint. If I wanted to knock back a few and have some fun with a civilian, what business was it of hers? She'd wanted to be in Star Force after all. It wasn't my fault that meant she had to follow the rules.

Only later when I had thought about it, did I realize it wasn't luck that Kalu had just happened to run into me there. The woman had been stalking me like prey. That realization cooled my desire for her. She made it clear on several later occasions that she would like to pick up where we'd left off, but my interest had soured. I didn't want to be anyone's trophy, the alpha male prize in a small sexual pool. I guess ol' Cody Riggs was destined to never get any. There just weren't many other civilian women aboard, and I'd declared that the Star Force females were out of bounds.

The crew repaired *Greyhound* and upgraded her more or less as Marvin wanted. I'd had most of the food and drink brought aboard *Valiant*. The liquor was well-packed in boxes and locked in the former captain's cabin with only me allowed inside. Then I sent the robot and his ship to find the other ring. He took the long way around, avoiding the inner planets.

First he paused near several of the largest asteroids in the system. These monster rocks were almost planets being hundreds of miles in diameter. I wanted to know whether the Lithos were everywhere or only on the larger bodies. Marvin didn't find any evidence of infestation. I'd been worried that the silico-nanites had been spread like dust throughout the star system, seeding and growing on the surface of every world.

The science team decided, after long study, that it was probable the Pandas had created the Lithos and seeded them here in this system. Once the Lithos had gained sentience, they'd spread themselves around deliberately. To the Lithos, the asteroids were cold, unpleasant islands, and so they hadn't colonized them.

Back in home space around Earth, the rings connecting our local systems had seemed to conform to a pattern. One ring would be near a star and one far away. In the Panda system, both were middling far, but that was the only anomaly we'd found. Well, that plus the third ring in the Thor system. Maybe there were more of the rings inside planets in other systems, and we simply hadn't found them yet.

In any case, here in the Litho system I thought the other ring would most likely be farther out, so I told Marvin to work his way from the outside sunward, starting with the farthest gas giant and its moons.

Once we'd had a chance to chart the stars, we figured out we were five hundred fifty light years from Earth at a star with nothing but a catalogue number. I declared a naming contest with the crew nominating and then voting on the ones they liked best. "Matterhorn" won out, I suppose because of the flying mountains.

I wondered if Hansen was right after all, since this star system was farther away than the last one was. Maybe we *should* turn and try to fight our way back to the Matterhorn ring where we'd arrived. Either way, I had to do what my father had done repeatedly during the Macro Wars: build a new fleet and use it to get the job done.

But before Marvin reached Matterhorn 7, the outermost planet in the system, the Lithos made their move.

-19-

We'd been in the Matterhorn system for weeks before the Lithos finally decided they'd had enough of their uninvited guests and decided to crush us once and for all.

"They're launching, sir," Hansen said, sitting bolt upright.

"Got it," I replied, staring at the red pinpricks that had appeared around the Litho ships. First, dozens sparked into existence, then hundreds, and then thousands. I could hardly believe my eyes. "How can they have so many missiles?"

"Maybe their ships are also their factories," Hansen suggested.

"That makes sense. If their silico-nanites permeate everything, then possibly they can manufacture things on the spot. Maybe they move materials around a bit, but they aren't like us, with everything in discrete packages and mechanisms. They're more like a massive substance with a collective mind. Maybe each flying mountain is some kind of single colony-creature."

"Or colony-planet."

"Right. Whatever silicon structure they invade, it becomes completely infected. Everything ends up as part of the Lithos except for the things they don't like—too much water, too cold, and no significant radiation."

Hansen nodded. "So they've been making missiles—or maybe I should say 'calving' them off of their substance."

We watched in growing tension despite our factual discussion. Hansen had already sounded the alarm, summoning personnel to their battle stations even though the threat was far away. I frowned briefly as I hadn't given him that order. It was a reasonable thing to do, however, so I let it go.

The Lithos continued launching. There were somewhere above twenty-five hundred missiles now. More than enough, but they weren't stopping.

"Forget about how they did it," I said. "Why did they choose to launch now?"

"Because they figure they have enough to beat us?"

"Maybe." I adjusted the holotank. "This shows intercept in ten hours. And look...the ships aren't following the missiles."

"Conserving energy?"

I stared, watching the clouds of missiles. It appeared every Litho ship had launched at least a hundred, meaning a total of over four thousand headed our way. What was more remarkable was that each one was hardly smaller than our battlecruiser. So big...my blood ran cold.

"Those can't be missiles."

Hansen stood up to join me at the holotank. "What are they then?"

"Small attack ships?"

"But the Lithos build everything to huge scale, even bigger than the Macros. How likely is it a ship of that size even has a ranged weapon?"

"I don't know. Get all the sensors you can on a couple of them." I turned to Hansen. "We have ten hours until they arrive. Get the analysts working on it."

For about ten seconds, I pondered what the Lithos could be up to. I didn't like anything my mind came up with.

"What are you weird bastards going to do?" I muttered. "Hansen, we're lifting off. Get all the mining equipment aboard and stowed. You have half an hour. And send Marvin a query to see if he has made any progress on their language."

Marvin didn't answer our messages. He seemed to be continuing the scouting mission I'd given him, but wouldn't respond. Maybe he was working on an unauthorized experiment and thought radio silence equated to invisibility. Or maybe he simply had nothing to say.

A few hours later we had good visuals and readings on the missile-ships. Shaped like triangular crystal arrowheads, they appeared to be symmetrical and have no weapon ports or sensors. We detected enough radioactives aboard to make atomic bombs, but they had chemical rockets for boosters and repellers for normal mobility. Maybe they were simply missiles after all, but I had a feeling the Lithos still had some surprises in store.

The missiles caught up to us with alarming speed. They were significantly faster than the battleships that had fired them. As an experiment, we flew away from the comet but without running at flank speed in a panic—not yet. I wanted to see if they simply adjusted to follow us like the snowflakes, or if they anticipated us, like the Panda missiles.

Surprisingly, they did neither. They stayed on course directly toward the comet we'd just left behind. Because of their huge size, the missiles could slam themselves into the floating iceball before detonating. Subsurface blasts would blow out great chunks, and the heat of the atomic fires would melt and crack the ice. That prediction of destruction bothered me because I didn't understand it. After all, if they broke the comet up, we could just go on to another comet and then another. Then I remembered the numbers and really considered them.

"*Valiant*," I said to the brainbox, "approximately how many Litho missiles will it take to break our target comet into pieces of less than one mile in diameter? Give me an estimate within ten percent accuracy."

I waited almost a full second before I got an answer. I presumed the brainbox was incorporating a lot of variables and running millions if not billions of modeling runs. Eventually it gave me its best guess. "Approximately fifty-nine."

Fifty-nine into four thousand...that meant the missile swarm could follow us and break up almost seventy comets before they were all expended.

The Lithos hadn't even needed to target us, I realized. They knew we could outrun their missiles. They just planned to dog our heels and take away all our materials. Like cavalry harrying a force they could not directly beat, they would raze our potential food supplies, the equivalent of burning barns and poisoning wells.

Long before they ran out of missiles we would run out of fuel if we merely kept searching near the edge of the Matterhorn system. If we were to have a chance of surviving their attack, I had to do something about those missiles.

Blowing them up with nukes would take materials to build missiles and warheads, but to get the materials, we needed missiles and warheads. It made for a conundrum. "How are we going to get rid of the missiles, or gain enough time to set down and mine more comets, or maybe mine an asteroid?" I asked out loud.

"Maybe we don't have to," Adrienne said coolly from my elbow. I started, not having heard her come up close to me because I was so deep in thought.

"What do you mean?" I asked without turning to look. I could see her face reflected in the polymers of the holotank, and I tried to determine what her expression might be. Distorted by curvature and the varying lights in the background as well as the glowing nanites inside the tank itself, I couldn't tell for sure.

"As long as we stay ahead of them, we have nothing to fear," she said. "I know you want to keep mining that big comet both for access to resources and for hiding behind it, but what if we think smaller?"

"Think smaller?"

"If the chunk was small, we could grab it and keep going. If it was the right size, we might even be able to push it along with us, staying ahead of the Lithos."

My mind broke free of its circular paralysis. Adrienne had given me a paradigm shift. I'd been thinking big, but she was right. Big comets were big targets. A lot of interesting things could be done with small ones.

That also gave me other ideas. "Hansen, do we know how they're targeting us? Is it active radar like the Panda missiles?"

Hansen shook his head. "Nothing active. If I had to guess, I'd say heat or radiation, probably the latter. With lots of mass, it becomes easier to detect radiation. The biggest ground-based detectors use hundreds or even thousands of tons of various materials."

"That much mass is a piece of cake to these flying mountains or even their huge missiles. Okay, Warrant Officer Turnbull, I want you to produce a radiation source that mimics our signature, put it on a simple drone, and soft-land it back on our comet. At the same time you launch it, take measures to reduce our own gamma and neutron output. Shield our reactors, our nuclear warheads—anything that radiates."

Adrienne turned to look at me, but I still didn't want to risk meeting her eyes. "That's a good idea, Captain," she said with some slight warmth in her voice. "You're making a decoy flare—something to draw off the missiles."

"Exactly. And have another one ready. If we're lucky, we'll disappear entirely to them in the explosions. They'll lose us and become confused by the fallout going in all directions. We'll just fade into the background like a diving submarine."

"And if not?"

I looked at her. "Then we'll do it again, and again, until they either lose us or they've run out of missiles."

"I'll get right on it, Captain," she said. Then she was gone, leaving an empty space beside me that I could feel.

"Hansen," I said, "find us a comet chunk out here between a fifth and a half the ship's mass and set up an intercept to take it aboard." I addressed the brainbox next, *"Valiant*, we need to reconfigure the ship to capture such a piece and bring it safely aboard, either whole or in stages." After almost an hour of discussion back and forth with the ship's brain, we worked out a modification that should do what I wanted.

Hansen found a target beyond the big comet, which was coming up quickly. An hour later Adrienne reported the drones were ready, just in time. "Launch one as soon as you can," I told her. Five minutes later, I saw a green dot in the holotank detach itself from us and decelerate at heavy Gs for a landing on the comet. We diverged by only the barest fraction of a degree, just enough to slide by the big ball of ice. As soon as we were past, we curved slightly again to put ourselves behind it, hidden from the Litho missiles. We also turned around and began to decelerate with repellers only. I wanted no engine flare to mark us.

We could still see most of the Litho missiles because they were spread out. Some of them had a line of sight on us, but hopefully they were fixed on the decoy. With our increased shielding, we hoped they would lose us among the pinpoint stars in the background.

Hours passed.

"Here they come," I said as the holotank showed the leading missiles reaching the big comet. The main screen flashed then darkened as the system compensated for the blasts whiting out our view.

"Full deceleration!" I ordered, knowing that for as long as the detonations went on, the Lithos wouldn't be able to see through to us. "Get us lined up on that small comet."

"On it," Hansen said, his hands gripping the controls as we shook under heavy deceleration. In the holotank, missile after missile slammed into the big comet, spreading billions of tons of irradiated and vaporized mass in all directions, the perfect screen for our activities. I wished we had a better view of the destruction of the ball of ice, but the explosions made that impossible.

Still, our sensors could count detonations and at forty, I ordered, "Reduce braking. Use only repellers." I wanted our engine signature to be gone by the time the Lithos stopped pounding the comet.

"Repellers only, aye," Hansen said. "Rendezvous with our chunk of junk in forty-seven minutes."

"Excellent. Miss Turnbull, pick out another big comet and send a drone to it." Soon another decoy was on its way.

The explosions ceased at fifty-one, which made me glad I'd stopped the braking early. On the other hand, that was fewer than we had predicted. Tricking the missiles into suiciding against decoys was going to take a long, long time. They could destroy eighty comets at that rate before running out.

Then the cloud of missiles continued by and through the debris of the comet. I held my breath as they passed the explosion zone, cruising straight forward in our general direction. Waiting, waiting...I breathed again as I saw them turn slightly to follow the decoy. My plan was working.

Half an hour later we pulled up quietly and carefully to the small comet drifting in the direction we were going. Tiny, really, it still massed a quarter of the size of my battlecruiser.

I had programmed the holotank for a close-up representation of our rendezvous. *Valiant* now sported a spidery scoop in front, a kind of basket on the prow that would half enclose the ball of ice and minerals. Nosing forward, Hansen scooped our target up and slowly applied repeller thrust to keep it pinned against the ship.

Unfortunately, the small comets weren't dense enough to hold much metal. They were mostly fluffy ice with just enough "dirt" inside to give our factory a diet meal after a lot of processing. It was like eating cotton candy—it was hard to get full.

While the ship digested tidbits, I ordered Kwon to take some marines out on the hull in battlesuits and start carefully cutting one-ton chunks free. That sped up the process. In their suits, the marines were strong enough to roll or carry these ice boulders into chutes. Grinders would break them up further. After that, they would be fed into the factory.

"Keep making decoy drones," I told Adrienne over the intercom. "Get eight or ten ready. After that, the priority is fuel, food and water. Then repairs and more drones."

Hours turned into days of routine. Adrienne and I began to eat together in the wardroom again, and tensions eased between us, but I still felt like she was holding something against me. I found that exasperating since I couldn't think of what I'd done that was improper. She couldn't have it both ways—being a warrant officer under my command and my close friend at the same time, and she didn't have any right to interfere with what little action I was likely to get from other women.

Despite all my misgivings, I found myself enjoying her company and seeking it out. I hoped she'd eventually start to understand how things had to work. My personal feelings, whatever they were or might be, had to be secondary to command and survival. Besides, I hadn't really sorted out how

I felt about her—or even how I should feel about her after her sister had died. Mostly, I tried not to think about it.

I told myself it had to be easier for her. If she liked me, she could hardly feel strange about it, as she'd barely known me before her sister died. To me, however, everything about her reminded me of Olivia. Every time I started to feel normal, I would suddenly be thrown off as Adrienne said or did something that caused a blurring echo in my mind. I knew it would be a long time before I would see only the living girl in front of me.

Now that we had the materials coming in from various comets, I made sure the enlisted mess was stocked with basic fake beer. It wasn't very good coming right out of the factory, but with Kwon in charge of rationing it and reining in any troublemakers, it provided a welcome diversion.

It also made me feel a lot less guilty about drinking the stores of the good stuff locked in the dead captain's cabin, which had become my own personal storeroom. Whenever I wanted some real privacy, I would shut myself in there, drink, and think, with only the brainbox able to get a hold of me directly. Many times I considered contacting Kalu and inviting her in, if she would still have me. But something always stopped me. In such a small, closed environment as this ship, some things couldn't be undone.

Greyhound and *Valiant* both kept radio silence to ensure the Lithos did not reacquire us on their sensors. Marvin was approaching Matterhorn 7, the outermost, many-mooned green gas giant, and he had done something to his ship to make it even harder to track than before. We only knew where he was because we'd kept a telescope automatically focused on him from the time he'd left with orders to *Valiant*'s brainbox to make sure we didn't lose the visual.

The Litho missiles didn't get any smarter, so we kept up our routine of decoys, their launches hidden by the explosions of each comet in turn. I thought about sending several decoys off at once just to simplify our lives, but that might have provided the enemy a clue that they weren't really following us out into deep space after all. I wanted them to see what they expected.

Hansen got good at grabbing chunks of materials. Some were icy like comets. Some contained more metals and rock, which we desperately needed. What we weren't finding were a lot of radioactives. The factory could manufacture enough for the decoys by bombarding metals with radiation, creating isotopes with short half-lives, but those were useless for making nuclear bombs. Nukes needed stable uranium or plutonium to trigger the reaction that gave them their explosive power.

We ended up with a completely repaired, fully stocked ship, except for the warheads for our missiles. Smaller ones could be substituted, made of overloaded fusion generators—simpler versions of a marine suit's suicide bomb—but I wanted the real thing, and I wasn't sure how to get it.

Forty or so Litho ships still waited between us and the system's sun, daring us to turn and come back. Their position was inside the stellar orbit of the gas giants so I hoped we could eventually swing around and approach through the most far-flung planets. Their moons should provide rich sources of everything.

If we did show ourselves, however, nothing would stop them from launching another few thousand missiles, driving us away again.

We were behind the power curve and needed a solution that allowed us to get ahead of it—or something to cleverly counter their tactics.

One night while I dozed in my cabin, thinking about who had planted that bomb and killed Olivia two months ago, an idea occurred to me.

-20-

"Cryo-what?" Adrienne asked.

For the first time since this whole adventure had started, I was doing something I hated: I was holding a formal meeting. We had the time, and I needed technical input, so it seemed like a good idea. Still, I kept it small. Nothing was worse than a meeting with too many participants and a bored audience encircling them.

Along with Adrienne, we had Hansen and the senior Star Force ship's engineer, a woman named Sakura. She was a computer specialist, but had a reputation of being excellent with all forms of equipment. Moon-faced and stocky with straight black hair and a classic Asian look, her appearance seemed to match her reputation. She was older, severe and never smiled, but I found her interesting nonetheless.

I'd also invited the lobster, Hoon. I figured it might be a good time to mend fences with the Crustacean as my idea involved solving a scientific and technical problem.

"Cryo-volcanoes," I replied. "As I understand it, if an icy moon orbits a planet quickly enough, tidal forces will create heat and pressure that liquefy frozen water and other fluids such as methane and ammonia. This creates pockets of liquid that form geysers as the stuff is forced upward through holes and cracks."

"Your verbiage is imprecise and unsophisticated," Hoon said.

I stared at him then leaned slightly forward in my chair until he went on.

"However," he continued, "your statement is generally accurate."

I wondered if he'd taken my stare as a threat. If so, it had worked. The arrogant lobster was starting to learn how to control his insulting manner, at least a little. That was all I wanted. Prickly and annoying—I could handle that. If I wanted more, sheer crazy obstinacy for example—well, I already had Marvin.

"Thanks. Now," I turned to Sakura, "can you reconfigure the ship for that kind of environment? Extreme cold?"

She drew together her shoulders as if she'd felt the temperature drop in the room. "I believe so. We'll need to manufacture some really effective insulation, and then there's the energy consumption to consider."

"But we can do it, right?"

Sakura nodded. "Yes, sir."

I liked that she didn't throw a bunch of technical bullshit at me. She'd simply told me what she thought.

"Then that's our next priority," I said as I turned to Adrienne. "Please help her, Adrienne. See if you can work together to turn this ship into a cryo-submarine. If the Lithos hate cold liquid, then we want to be where there's plenty of it. Of course, if we can find a place where the liquid is actually water, and it's only as cold as Earth's arctic, that would be a real plus."

"What's the point of this?" Hansen asked.

"If we can find the right environment, the water will shield us from all detection. It will also deter the Lithos from following us even if they know we're there. And if we can set up a cozy underwater hideaway, we should be able to mine the sea floor for what we want."

"But what do we want?" Adrienne asked. "Other than radioactives, we already have everything we need. Eventually, though, people are going to get antsy. Without an immediate crisis, this ship is going to seem smaller and smaller. Are you planning on setting up some kind of colony?" Her expression told me she didn't like the idea.

"Not a colony, no. But a temporary base would be very useful."

"How would it be useful? I still want to know," said Hansen.

"To do what Star Force always did back in the Macro Wars. Back when my father defended Earth even when the old nations tried to screw him at every turn. Back when he commanded expeditions into neighboring systems so that he could fight the Macros on their doorsteps instead of ours." I smiled confidently, knocking my knuckles on the table with a grin. "We're going to build a fleet."

The others chewed this over for a moment. I wondered from whom the first objection would come. I would have put my money on Hansen, but he looked interested—even eager. I supposed he figured he would end up in command of a ship and could thus get away from me.

Adrienne nodded thoughtfully, as if already planning how she would carry out the expansion of her responsibilities. Hoon, I couldn't read, but fortunately he spoke up. "I believe this idea has merit. Of course, it must be developed. Studies must be made and algorithms written. There is much work to do. For the first time you have favorably impressed me, Captain Cody Riggs. You have recognized the inherent superiority of the hydrological environment over the atmospheric. There is hope for you yet."

My first impulse was to boot him again, but I held my temper. In Hoon's stalked eyes, I'd just made a concession to his point of view. It was no big deal to me what he believed as long as he made himself useful. Now that I thought about it, I was sure he'd be extremely helpful. Crustaceans thrived in cold Earth waters. Maine and Newfoundland were famous for their lobster and Alaska for its crab. Hoon might even be able to take off his suit and enjoy the native environment directly.

And if he was too much a pain in the ass, I would have some leverage. As with Marvin, I only had to know how to get a lever on him to get him to work with me.

"I appreciate your point of view, Professor Hoon," Sakura said, "but if we make more ships, where are we going to get crews?"

"When my father first formed Star Force, there was only one crewman per ship. Did you know that, Warrant Officer Sakura?" When she shook her head no, I went on. "Later, the ships usually had three to six crewmembers, with everything else being handled by the brainbox. In fact, the squads or platoons of marines usually outnumbered the Fleet personnel. It's only in the last twenty years, with the rise of a typical military bureaucracy that we now have ships like this one, which started out with…what? Eighty-some people aboard?"

"Small crews sound good in theory," Sakura replied, "but we only have two real engineers, three scientists—plus Hoon, two trained helmsmen and a couple of pinnace pilots."

I wanted to roll my eyes, but smiled instead. She wasn't getting it.

"We'll have to cross-train crew and marines as pilots and gunners," I said. "Devise some aptitude tests. Clone brainboxes for every ship, turret and suit. Automate as many functions as possible. A warship may be more effective with lots of humans to direct the nano brains, but I think with crews of three or so, we can achieve enough efficiency to make building a fleet worthwhile. We need the firepower. We need the redundancy. Right now, all our eggs are in one basket—or two if you count *Greyhound*."

"That's not correct," Hoon snapped. "My eggs are not in any baskets but are instead—" He suddenly cut himself off, and continued, "Excuse me. My translator appears to have momentarily malfunctioned."

I couldn't help myself. I laughed. "So your technology isn't as perfect as you think it is?" Uncharacteristically, Hoon didn't answer but merely folded his large claws and settled back on his walking legs.

"We're going back to the roots of Fleet, huh?" Hansen asked, suddenly wistful. "I joined up near the end of the Macro Wars, you know. I was a helmsman in the Dead Sun action on a six-man ship. Things were different then."

"They'll be different now," I said, with more confidence than I felt. "We'll keep *Valiant* with a large crew by our new standards plus a couple dozen civilians and marines. It will be the flagship."

Sakura said, "Why not just expand this battlecruiser? Or convert it into an even bigger ship, a battleship? With enough time and materials, we can do it." I could see she still did not like the idea of breaking up the crew.

I spread my hands in a gesture meant to indicate a reasonable attitude. "I'll tell you what, you get all the scientists, engineers and representatives from the crew and come up with two proposals: big ship and small ships. Take your time. Figure out all the pros and cons, then I'll decide which is best."

They nodded and looked slightly happier. I hoped I'd taken the right course. It was my intention to delegate work and make the decisions, but I needed them to carry out my plans. I left the meeting very satisfied with the group.

* * *

It took more than two weeks, but we finally lured all the Litho missiles to their deaths by getting farther and farther beyond the edge of the system and incidentally curving around the star and back, close to the orbits of Matterhorn 6 and 7.

During this time, I watched as Marvin carefully scouted Matterhorn 7 and its several dozen moons. Looking for the ring to the next system was the top priority I'd given him, along with the secondary mission of gathering any information that might be useful. I hoped he hadn't gotten bogged down in exploring just for fun.

Once the Litho missiles were gone and I was fairly certain we hadn't been detected, I had Sakura set up a low-powered communications laser and sent Marvin a message, telling him the kind of place I was looking for and ordering him to report back to me using the same technique. *Greyhound* didn't have a ring-based communication system as it was a civilian ship. But as long as we were both in deep space with no enemy in the background, this method should be completely secure.

When the response came back, the news was a mixture of good and bad. Marvin had located another Litho enclave on an airless rocky moon circling Matterhorn 7, the greenish, outermost gas giant. By calculating its orbital velocity against its size, Marvin pointed out that this body had an extremely low density for its volume and a higher temperature than normal. Put another way, it was too big for the way its mass acted and too hot. This made a very good case for it being hollow and colonized by Lithos.

And unless the Lithos had a special love of building hollow planets, it likely contained the ring we were seeking. I stared carefully at the sensory reports coming from that moon for long hours but never got much information out of them. Still, I believed the ring was in there, like a prize stuck in the middle of a chocolate egg.

Building a containment sphere around a ring was a novel twist on a battle station, but the Lithos apparently had the power to reshape whole planets. Probably it took the Lithos decades or longer, but if their entire race consisted of hives or cooperatives of silico-nanites, terraforming was probably the equivalent of building roads and bridges for us: just something they did to improve their living space.

I had to assume the Lithos were smart enough to learn from our breakout at Matterhorn 3. In the weeks we'd been running and lurking, repairing and planning, they would have been preparing as well. The last time, we'd surprised them. They hadn't anticipated a new player entering their system from the Panda system. They had to expect we would make a play to get out via one of the rings.

This time, they would be ready.

There was no way we were going to make it through their defenses without reconnaissance, clever planning, and figuring out some way to surprise the Lithos. We also needed the fleet I envisioned. I didn't like the "one big ship" approach, but I was willing to listen to my people. Dad had told me that sometimes he had already made up his mind what to do, but he'd made a show of considering every viewpoint just to make the dissenters feel better. My old man was a cynical guy, I had to admit, but most of the time he was right.

Marvin had also located a place that looked to be tailor-made for us to hide within, a cold-water moon orbiting the gas giant Matterhorn 6, which was nearing its closest approach to Matterhorn 7 at the moment. Of course, that meant the two

Jovian planets were still several AU away from each other, hundreds of millions of miles, but relatively close in interplanetary terms.

Matterhorn 6 was enormous, larger even than Jupiter back home, and was therefore hotter. Its gravity was so great that some low-grade natural fusion was probably going on near its core. In other words, it was almost a sun by itself. Should it ever get close enough to one of its neighboring gas planets to collide, the resulting combination would probably be massive enough to ignite into a small companion star.

Because of this, the moons of Matterhorn 6 were warmer than one would expect this far out in the system. Rather than temperatures in the minus two hundreds, the moons had a surface temperature of around minus fifty Celsius on average, and one of the close-in icy bodies had enough tidal heating to average just below freezing. It had huge water-ice caps and a narrow band of freezing cold sea around its equator. Deep in the seas, the temperature was almost warm.

When Hoon saw the data, he declared it nearly perfect and even comfortable for his race, depending on what elements might be dissolved in the seawater. If the radiation levels weren't too high, it was a habitable world for Crustaceans.

Sakura was happy as well. From her point of view, freezing H2O was a lot easier to deal with than cryogenic liquid methane. Really, it would only be a little worse than what a deep-diving submarine had to deal with back home. Hoon actually *volunteered* to advise us on underwater matters, and I was feeling pretty optimistic.

The trick was going to be getting there.

-21-

We floated silently through interstellar space with all emanations shielded. Sakura had put the new insulation in place inside the hull, which reduced our heat signature. Aimed in a carefully calculated arc, we set our course for the icy inner moon of Matterhorn 6.

Like a reaver on a misted sea, we sailed on unpowered, hoping the Lithos could not see us even as we neared the planet. Their forty ships had spread out after they'd lost track of us but still patrolled in the orbital path of Matterhorn 7. They were smart enough to know how far we could have gotten and from what direction we would come if we decided to backtrack. Without the ability to use active sensors, we used the brainboxes combined with people working overtime on the telescopes, heat detectors and radiation monitors. My greatest fear was getting noticed too early, before we could make a mad dash for the cold water.

I rubbed my eyes constantly, as they itched from too many hours of staring into glowing screens. One of the many benefits to enhanced healing was the ability to cause yourself minor irritations and even damage—only to have the nanites in your blood dutifully fix the problem. I knew marines who'd gotten into bad habits, chewing nails and the like, depending on their nano 'friends' to heal them again and again before it became a problem.

I could tell Hansen felt like telling me to chill out, but I was as tense as a cat sneaking past a guard dog—make that forty guard dogs.

We almost made it to Matterhorn 6. The planet loomed large on every screen, dwarfing any planet I'd ever visited.

But three quarters of the way there, I saw a change in the status of the patrolling Litho fleet. First, the nearest Litho cruiser turned ponderously in our direction. Soon others followed suit as the word of our presence spread across the system.

"We've been spotted," I said to Hansen. "Punch it." He didn't bother to reply, he just pushed the throttles smoothly to the stops. I felt my weight shift as the Gs leaked through our stabilizers, the big modified engines shoving us forward.

Valiant really wasn't too much faster now than she had been because we'd fattened up with stored supplies and spare parts, not to mention extra shield generators, gravity plates and processing gear for raw materials. Now I wondered if that would come back to haunt us.

Our estimated time of arrival on the moon dropped from six hours to two. We couldn't make it faster because for every minute we spent accelerating, we'd have to decelerate at the end.

"It's all right," Hansen said confidently. "Those tubs of theirs are way too slow to catch us. Spread out as they are, not many of their missiles will, either."

"If I was superstitious, I'd say you just jinxed us," I replied.

"*Shit*. What's this?" Hansen said not a minute later.

His exclamation drew my eyes to the holotank. The nearest Litho ships seemed to be coming apart. I'd expected missile launch, but this looked like something different. Instead of calving off their usual spearhead-shaped repeller projectiles, they seemed to be dividing themselves into pieces of approximately equal size. They were smaller than we were, but bigger than a Star Force missile—I'd call them fighters.

"*Shit*," Hansen barked again as he saw how quickly they were speeding up. "They're faster than we are!"

"I guess we underestimated them," I said, sounding calm—only I knew I was faking it. "What would we have done in their place? Faced with an enemy that can outrun and outmaneuver us, we would have tried to match them in capabilities, right?"

"Right." Hansen grimly tapped at his console, probably trying to squeeze out some extra speed. "They built faster weapons. They're going to reach us just short of the moon, and we'll be decelerating. This isn't going to be fun."

"That might work to our advantage. It depends on whether they're going to take one pass and fly by or decelerate along with us. Can we get more speed?"

"If we shed some mass," he replied.

Much as I hated to do it, he was right. We had to lighten the ship, allowing our engine power to push less ship and thus do it faster.

"Sakura," I called on the command channel, "we have to dump some mass. Get Kwon and his marines to help you jettison anything we can spare. Water, metals, other raw materials, anything we'll be able to mine out of the sea floor."

"If we're going to fire any missiles," Hansen said, "we might as well do it early. That's mass, too."

"Good point, but..." I stared at the holotank. "Each of those forty ships has broken up into at least forty fighters. That means we have sixteen hundred of them on our asses." I vacillated a moment, and then said, "Go ahead and target the two nearest clusters. They haven't spread out too much. Let's see how they deal with nukes."

"Firing." Two tracks curved away from us and headed back toward the pursuing fighter squadrons. I paced for the tense minutes it took the missiles to reach their targets.

"Detonate them short of the Lithos' predicted antiproton beam range." I set the holotank to show me that distance and watched as the first missile approached the leading fighter group.

Suddenly, beams from the fighters lanced out all together, spearing the missile from much farther away than I'd expected. I stared at the readout for a moment, querying the sensor data. "Those weren't antiproton beams. They were lasers." No wonder they could reach much farther. "Send a signal to blow the second missile beyond the new range!"

"Done," Hansen said. This time our nuke detonated with a spectacular explosion, but from much farther away. When the blast cleared, I saw that three of the fighters looked like they had been knocked out, but the rest came on.

"At least we know we can hurt them," he said.

"One of our few missiles for three fighters is a losing ratio. It's also bad news that they have adapted their weaponry to make it more effective against us."

"They're fast learners," Hansen said.

"Apparently. That means we have to be even faster. How's the ship's mass looking?"

"We've dropped a thousand tons, but I'd like to see at least two hundred tons more. With those new lasers, we'll be in range before we can splash down. I'd rather not have to land in the water under fire."

"Agreed." I contacted Sakura again. "How much more mass can we dump?"

"Everything easy is already gone," she replied. "Now all we have are manufactured goods."

"We need to shed two hundred more tons and the sooner the better. Start with the extra shield generators and any drones we have left. We won't need those."

"There's no way we have two hundred tons more to dump!" Sakura protested.

"Do the best you can. Rip out nonessential lab equipment, half the toilets, the mess tables, bunks, whatever. Riggs out."

"Yes, Captain," Sakura said woodenly.

Had there been a hint of resentment in her voice? It seemed like such a minor thing. Maybe she really valued her lab equipment.

I turned back to Hansen. "Fire off the rest of the missiles except one. Target the nearest group and have the controllers try to get at least one in close before detonation to wipe out that group. That will get rid of tonnage and buy us a few more minutes."

My mind quickly moved onto bigger concerns. All but one of our nine remaining full-up nuclear missiles soon left the rails, curving back around to come in all at once at the nearest enemy fighter group. With several minutes to see our weapons coming, the enemy spread out, which made their point defense less effective but also reduced the number of fighters we could catch in one blast. Still, we got three of our missiles into effective range, sacrificing the others to do it, and nearly wiped out that squadron, leaving only two operational Litho fighters. Those didn't worry me, because our heavy lasers far outranged them. Even our secondary batteries hit harder and reached farther. Only in great numbers could they beat us.

"Are we going to make it?" I asked.

"Not quite, but a lot fewer of them will get shots at us before we get there." Hansen furrowed his eyebrows. "It's going to be rough."

"Rough we can handle. This ship will make it through." I really did believe that—even though I was speaking for the sake of the bridge crew and anyone else who might hear my words.

For a crewman, one of the perks of standing watch on the bridge was to be the bearer of rumor, known in Fleet as "scuttlebutt." When off shift, most headed for the mess to eat where they invariably found a ready audience to tell what was happening in the ship's nerve center. Smart noncoms kept their fingers on the pulse of a crew by taking their meals there. I figured Kwon would alert me to anything I needed to know—if we lived long enough to care.

Updating the calculations, the holotank told me that three more Litho squadrons would catch us before we got under cover beneath the cold waves. This was assuming they did not try to match velocities with us but only braked when they had come into range.

The first group came closer and closer. Hansen held off on flipping the ship around to begin his braking maneuver until the last possible moment. Just before they came into range of our two heavy lasers, I told him to flip the ship so we pointed back the way we came. This not only set us up for deceleration, it aimed our best shielding and firepower directly at the enemy. I let them come a little closer, knowing that the nearer they were, the harder our weapons would hit.

"Fire," I said, and our laser gunners started picking them off. Unfortunately, it turned out that several shots were needed to fully slag one of their fighters because they were so big compared to a comparable craft of Star Force design. They were actually as large as the original Nano ships, like our gunships or frigates. At least a hundred feet long and made of stone, it took hard hits from our main batteries to knock them out. Since the Litho fighters seemed to be mostly made up of crystal, they were also hugely massive and could obviously take a pounding.

"Combine the two shots on one," I ordered. "Target the nearest fighter in each case." Steadily the Litho fighter numbers dropped as we blasted each in turn as fast as our heavy beams could recharge. By the time they came within range of our secondaries, we'd destroyed a third of them.

"Use half the standard lasers on one fighter at a time," I said. "If one blast kills a fighter, split them up again. I want to find the minimum number of guns it takes to kill in one salvo." It turned out we needed six to kill in one shot.

We killed about fifty of them before they started firing back.

Nineteen of their lasers lanced out, aiming at one spot on *Valiant*. These were weaker, and apparently fired at extreme range, because they failed to destroy their target, Heavy Laser Number Two.

"Overheating in HL2!" one of the laser gunners reported.

"Evasive maneuvers, Mister Hansen. We can't let them gang up and fire everything at one spot like that again." Hansen used side repellers to jink us slightly in random directions. It wouldn't make them miss completely, but it would complicate their targeting and spread out their hit pattern. It would also reduce the time they had to strike at a particular spot.

By the time the attacking squadron was down to eight fighters, we'd taken a bunch of minor hits, losing sensors and pieces of armor. It was then that the Lithos sprung their next surprise.

I saw pinpoints of red bloom in the holotank as the eight turned into eighty. "Multiple targets, missile launch!" I snapped. "Priority to individual point defense fire." If they had nukes onboard, we had to shoot them down.

The new swarm jumped toward us with startling speed. Sensors showed they were smaller, tinier even than our own missiles. In the Lithos' usual scale, they must seem like mere bullets rather than missiles.

Bullets... "Give me a radiation reading on those missiles," I barked.

"No radiation," the word came back.

"Okay, they're not nukes," I thought out loud. "Conventional warheads of that size can hardly hurt us. They aren't going to hit hard enough to damage us much by impact. What are they trying to do?"

And then I remembered the snowflakes.

"Kwon, prepare to repel boarders! Get some men on the hull, and station reaction teams at key points inside."

I was guessing, but nothing else made sense. They had built, or modified, these new missiles for one purpose: to be fast enough to chase us down and deliver *something* to damage us. All their radioactives had probably gone into their engines.

At the end of the chase, the only method these Litho weapons had left to attack us was manually with claws grown out of their own odd bodies.

-22-

"Give me a visual on one of those projectiles," I said.

As I suspected, it turned out to be a snowflake. Closer and closer the cloud came, leaving the shrunken fighters behind. I pulled up one of those for a moment, and noticed it wasn't firing anymore. In fact, the fighter had lost its arrow shape and now looked like just a chunk of rock.

"They used the remnants of their fighters to push against, and abandoned them, like marines jumping off ships," I said. "How are we doing on shooting them down?"

"Not so well," Hansen said. "They're small targets and have turned edge-on. They're evading as much as they can. But I got a little surprise for them." He laughed.

"Does anyone else need to know about this trick of yours?" I asked.

Hansen blinked then reached over to key his communications. "Sergeant Major Kwon, tell your men to get below and brace for hard deceleration. I'm about to hit the brakes in fifteen seconds." He held up a hand and slowly counted to zero, watching the chronometer. Then he ran the engine power up to maximum.

Valiant shuddered and bucked in response.

"We're off-balance," Hansen said though gritted teeth. "All that mass we dumped changed our center of gravity." Fighting the controls, he soon steadied the ship.

As he did so, I watched the falling snowflakes leap toward us like mad things. As we were pointed prow-backward with our engines braking our speed, we were letting them catch up to us that much faster. At first I thought Hansen had made a mistake, but then I figured out his surprise. If I was right about these snowflakes, they could only do us serious damage if they were able to latch on and try to dig in. Now our combined closing speeds had increased so much I doubted they could attach before bouncing off.

"Hang on," Hansen muttered just before some of the snowflakes hit us. *Valiant* shook, and I heard clangs and groans as we were struck at high velocity. Then all was quiet again.

"Oh, crap," I said as I watched more snowflakes fall toward us. This time they had linked arms and turned into a kind of super-snowflake, a latticework of crystal. "This is going to hurt."

Now Hansen's maneuver hardly mattered, as the hexagon of joined Lithos acted as a net, not to be thrown off. At least forty of them, linked together, smashed against the hull. A few got knocked off into space, but the rest let go of each other and began to dig their sharp crystal claws into the ship.

"Keep it together, Hansen. I'm getting into armor. And tell the crew to grab their self-defense weapons!" I bolted out the door and down to the marine deck.

My battlesuit stood humming in its niche, an extra I'd had built for me but never used in combat, only in battle sims. I threw off my pressure suit and jumped into the monstrosity. My biometrics turned it on, and its primitive brain announced, "Armored Combat Suit System: Active. Welcome, Cody Riggs."

"Thanks, suit. Now give me a HUD view of the ship with all friendlies and enemies." Examining the situation, I saw several breaches already imminent. Kwon and his troops were back out on the hull, fighting to keep the snowflakes from getting in. Only a few marines had stayed inside. I cursed my decision to send so many out onto the hull. The real danger would be if one of those things started rampaging around within the ship.

Grabbing a laser rifle, I plugged its thick cable into my suit. Then I looked over the other auxiliary weapons, trying to figure out what would be most effective—I couldn't really use heavy explosives inside the ship. Finally I grabbed a breaching cutter and slung it on my back. It was like an old-fashioned chainsaw with a monomolecular band.

The HUD led me to the nearest breach. I saw a crystal spike coming up through the floor, sawing and probing even as smart metal tried to close around it. The thing had already gotten past the hull and the maintenance crawlspace.

Turning the laser rifle to its closest focus and highest setting, I blasted the reaching arm. Refracted green light washed everywhere, darkening my visor to almost black, like a welder's mask. The Litho limb shattered, sending shards rattling into my suit. When I could see again, though, I saw smoking gashes in the walls where my beam had touched, and several painted surfaces had ignited from the heat. Alarms blared and automatic suppression systems blew in halon gas. I had to switch to short-range sonar to see.

I approached the hole in the floor and the blackened limb cautiously. The limb was still moving, so I fired another shot through its stump and into its central body mass. It took several shots, and by the time it was dead, the fire system was working overtime. Obviously, lasers were not optimal inside the hull— too much collateral damage.

I stowed my laser rifle in its cradle on my back and pulled out the cutter. It had a two-handed grip, like a huge sword, with a protected blade and a moving belt. The cutting band had an edge one molecule thick, the sharpest thing possible to materials science.

Starting it up, I ran down the passageway toward the next incursion, where I saw a group of crew faced off against one of the things. Fortunately I came into the fight from the other side.

"Cease fire!" I yelled over the close-range com as I rounded the corner. Despite my order, a bolt from a laser pistol scored my armor, narrowly missing the cutter. "Cease fire, dammit, unless I'm out of the way!"

The snowflake loomed in front of me, a juggernaut twenty feet across. Its jagged arms ripped and tore into the deck, overhead and bulkheads, a slow-motion wrecking machine. Thumbing the button that pulled back the safety guard, I set the cutter against the nearest arm and pulled the trigger that made the flexible blade whirl at high speed.

I *felt* more than heard the supersonic whine as the device sliced into the crystal like it was made of cardboard. In a second, I'd severed one arm and set to work on another.

The monster turned on me like a giant double-jointed hand that could fold itself backward. I jumped away, holding the cutter up like some two-handed sword-wielding warrior or a chainsaw killer from an old slasher vid. Fencing with it for a moment, I managed to cut off a third arm. At that point it was doomed as it was not able to balance well enough on two appendages to use the third offensively.

"Kwon," I gasped as I carved the thing to bits, "as soon as you get the hull clear, get to the armory and grab breaching cutters. They work better than lasers inside."

"Now you tell me!" he grunted, still in his own fight. "We got most of them, sir. Second Squad, finish clearing the hull. First squad, follow me!"

On my HUD I could see his icon move to the airlock. He was moving in my direction and that sounded fine to me.

I knocked out another snowflake with my cutter before marines surrounded me and fanned out in all directions. Clearly my work felling crystal timber was over. I handed the device to Kwon as didn't have one.

"Use one of these cutters instead of your laser," I told him. "Beams do almost as much damage to our own ship as to them. As soon as you've finished them, start damage control!"

"Yes, sir!" Kwon took the cutter from me and headed for the nearest snowflake. Kwon had it under control, so instead of forcing my way to the new front lines, I headed back up to the bridge.

Everyone looked at me with surprise as I stomped over to the holotank in my heavy armor. Opening my faceplate, I talked to *Valiant*. "Lower gravity on the bridge to point three G."

That would lighten me up a bit. Then I retracted my gauntlets and helmet into the suit and reduced the servo boost. I didn't want to accidentally smash a console with an ill-timed sweep of my hand.

Right then the holotank told me that we had to keep decelerating hard if we were going to make our landing. Unfortunately, this braking allowed the next two Litho squadrons to catch up to us with frightening rapidity. Furthermore, instead of coming at us one at a time, they cleverly formed up into a mass of more than eighty fighters—which were much harder to deal with.

"Engage them at maximum range," I said. "Divide up your fire into smaller groups this time. We have to kill or disable as many of those things as we can. If we're lucky, we will force them to launch their snowflakes early."

We were only able to knock them down to sixty-six fighters this time before they began calving. Over five hundred additional snowflakes blossomed in the holotank, all heading directly toward us.

"Ready that last nuke," I called. "Set it to detonate as near as we can stand. I want them to be as densely packed as possible." I hadn't been entirely sure of why I had saved the last missile, but there was an old battle saying about the winner usually being the commander who kept something in reserve for the right moment.

This seemed to be that moment.

The missile flashed out of the tube and, seconds later, detonated close, right where I wanted it to. It vaporized at least half the snowflakes and only gave our ship a good sunburn. Two hundred and fifty was still too many for my comfort, but it was a hell of a lot fewer than five hundred. "Keep engaging. Run the lasers as hot as you can." It didn't matter how hot they got or if they had to shut down, because I figured this would be the Lithos' last chance at us for a while.

"It's too many," I whispered as I saw the count fall to two hundred. We weren't killing them fast enough. The snowflakes were matching course and speed with us, and we couldn't maneuver much if we wanted to splash down where we needed to. I tried to come up with options, but any delay in landing would allow even more Lithos to catch up. Furiously, I worked solutions in the holotank, and came up with only one possibility.

"We can't handle that many," I announced. "Hansen, turn us over and accelerate again. Put us in a planetary orbit around Matterhorn 6, along the track I've plotted. We'll swing back and try again."

"What?" he demanded. "You're crazy. If we do that, we'll have to face a thousand fighters and ten thousand snowflakes instead of just a hundred and fifty!"

"I don't have time to argue. Do it or we're all dead!" I snarled, taking a heavy step toward him.

Hansen let out a stream of profanity and slammed the controls hard over, spinning the ship around and changing course away from the ice moon we'd nearly reached. Snowflakes that had almost latched onto us now fell back as we pulled away and blasted some of them with our naked engine exhaust. In this form, the Lithos didn't have the speed to catch us, and a few moments later, we'd made it out of immediate danger.

As we curved away from the snowflakes, I saw that my choice had been the right one—at least in the short term. While the Litho fighters probably could have kept up with us, the snowflakes couldn't. They were the equivalent of our marines, who could move around in space but couldn't match a warship's speed and maneuverability. In either case, boarders had to get close, and I'd goaded them into deploying too early. Unable to divert their course, they were soon falling into the freezing ocean of the icy moon below us.

"Hug the planet," I told Hansen. "As huge and high-grav as it is, you should be able to keep our speed up in a tightly powered orbit, just skimming the edge of its atmosphere. We'll make a complete circuit out of their view, altering course so we'll come back at an unexpected angle. The Lithos won't be able to see us until we crest the horizon."

"We've lost a lot of speed," Hansen said. "An orbit will take two hours. By that time they'll all be waiting for us at the ice moon. We'll have to run a gauntlet that might kill us."

"I don't think so." I quickly set up a holotank replay of the last several hours using a handheld cursor to point at the relevant items as I spoke. "Look here. Those that didn't splash down into the icy waters are following us. Whenever we turn, they keep dogging our tails. If they knew we were heading for the moon, they would have cut us off here." I drew a glowing line along the shortest path. "But they didn't. Whatever they know, they aren't acting like they're anticipating us. They don't understand our plans. I think they just saw an opportunity and took it. If we'd been in open space, those fighters would have caught us one squadron at a time, and eventually worn us down. But as soon as they broke up into snowflakes, they lost their high mobility."

Hansen rubbed his bare head with one hand. "All right—that seems to make sense. But the Lithos *don't* make sense. Why give up their fighter maneuverability so early?"

"Because I suckered them, and they made a mistake. They're too predictable. Present them with what looks like an optimum solution based on all the variables, and they'll seize it. They don't necessarily take second and third order possibilities into account. So when we slowed down and started killing them with our lasers, they calculated that they could do us more damage by launching the snowflakes."

Hansen cocked his head as if finding this hard to believe. "But they've been so smart up until now. How could they be so stupid all of a sudden?"

"Don't make the classic mistake of overestimating the enemy. Everyone makes mistakes. The Macros did during the wars. I studied all my father's campaigns. Every race we've run into had its blind spots, strengths and weaknesses. The Lithos are no different."

Hansen grunted, turning away and minding his helm in silence. I wondered what was going on in his head. Did he think I was cocky, a know-it-all, or a gambler?

My father had said that most military leaders grow risk-averse during peacetime. They were used to protecting their careers rather than sticking their necks out to attain their goals. He'd had to deal with that mindset during the Macro Wars. Now, twenty quiet years later, it seemed the same malaise had set in to Star Force.

The current crop of Fleet personnel played not to lose. Not me. I played to win. If we played it safe, we'd just get whittled down. I hoped Hansen see that my way was the right way.

"If the brainbox can fly the ship for a while, take a break," I told him. "Rotate the watches, but be ready to fly again when we come over the horizon. You're one shit-hot pilot, the best we have. If we're lucky, you won't have to prove it again." With that, I walked off the bridge and back to the marine deck to get out of my armor.

Once I was back in utilities, I swung by the factory room. Every Star Force officer learned how to program a factory, but I had been relying on Adrienne and Sakura. I waved away the technician and sat down at the control console. I felt like doing a little work myself.

I spoke aloud. "Unit One, this is Cody Riggs." All factories by convention were named "Unit" and then a number. It was something Dad had started and it had stuck.

"*Command personnel recognized*," it replied. Factories, like most brainboxes, would reply in the manner in which they were addressed – voice or keyboard. "*Unit One working*."

"Bring up the template on a breaching cutter."

"*Displayed*." It showed on the console screen.

I studied it for a moment. "Customization mode. Increase blade size by fifty percent."

"*Increased*."

"Add a second, opposing blade, like a pair scissors."

"*Specifics required*."

I worked with the factory brainbox on the template for a half hour until I had a device more suited to fighting snowflakes. With two blades, the wielder could use it as a double-bladed cutter or could configure it like huge chainsaw-snips. In that mode, all the user had to do was stick a crystal arm between the two, squeeze and sever the arm. I told the factory to make forty of them, left a message for Kwon to distribute them to the defense teams, then went for a meal.

I ran into Adrienne alone in the wardroom. Ravenous, I heated up a ration pack, opened a plastic envelope of fake fruit salad and sat down across from her. No one ever seemed to occupy that seat whenever I saw her eating, though that fact only just occurred to me. Was it because no one wanted to risk my wrath if I wanted to sit there or did she wave everyone else off?

"Great job with the weight dumping," I said by way of an opener.

She nodded her thanks, gazing at me under hooded eyes that were not smiling.

I continued, "We're going to loop around the planet and make another run at it. I'm hoping they haven't figured out our goal, and we can shoot by them this time."

"Sounds good," she said, looking down at her food.

I sighed, overloud, without meaning to. I'd been trying to put on a cheerful, positive face, but I felt like Adrienne had shut me out completely. It wasn't fair. I was only trying to maintain crew morale and discipline, and I didn't understand why she couldn't see that. Every manual, every textbook, every case study I'd read in the Academy had clearly shown how corrosive fraternization and personal favoritism was to a military organization. My father had experienced it firsthand. That didn't mean we couldn't be cordial and friendly. She'd remained more distant than Hansen or Sakura, and I barely even knew those two. It just made no sense to me.

"Adrienne, can we clear the air between us? I don't understand what the problem is."

Her face tightened and she looked at me. "Of course you don't. You're a typical male. No, strike that. You're a spoiled male that's never had to learn to deal with a real woman."

My jaw tightened. "Oh, I'm *spoiled*, Countess Turnbull? I didn't grow up on an estate. I worked on a farm getting my hands dirty."

"Not spoiled by money. Emotionally spoiled. You've never had to consider any girl's feelings before. They've all thrown themselves at you since you hit puberty."

"Is that what this is about? Kalu? Nothing happened between us, but even if it had, what business is it of yours? I'm your commanding officer, which is what *you* asked for. You wanted to join Star Force. She's a civilian."

"That's no excuse. I didn't ask for you to turn into such a jackass."

That felt like she'd stabbed me in the gut, and I stood up. "Jackass or not, I have a job to do, and so do you." Too bad she couldn't see that, and just get over whatever was upsetting her.

I sure couldn't read her mind. Picking up my food, I carried it toward another table, fighting back unexpected fury.

As I moved, I noticed Sakura was in the wardroom with us. She was eating alone and quietly. I hadn't even noticed her, but I felt a little embarrassed now. She had to have overheard my conversation. I glanced at her, but the woman remained expressionless and didn't meet my eyes.

The embarrassment stung. What was wrong with me? I was *Cody Riggs*, dammit. I should be able to handle Adrienne. Dad had kept a lid on that crazy woman Sandra before Mom, and she was a hundred times more trouble than Adrienne.

I watched Adrienne while pretending not to and chewed my meal. I couldn't figure her out. Olivia had been so much easier to get along with. Once again I found the devastation of her loss threatening to break through my professional demeanor.

Adrienne left less than a minute later. Apparently, she couldn't take the pressure either. I glanced over at Sakura, who chewed robotically.

"Engineer Sakura," I said, attempting to sound cheerful. "Mind if I join you?"

She looked startled, but nodded.

I moved to her side and sat down. "As I understand it, you're a computer expert. Is that correct?"

Sakura studied me for a moment before replying. "My original studies were in computer engineering. But I've since become a generalist as is appropriate for a ship's engineer."

I nodded. "I see. Could I have you look into something for me?"

"Certainly, Captain."

"Could you examine the software installation records in the ship's database?"

She chewed mechanically for a moment. "To a point, yes."

I frowned. "What do you mean?"

"They were erased at some point during our voyage."

Staring at her, I felt a cold sensation. Could this be significant? Marvin had said that someone must have taken his programming for the Yale ring and engaged it. If that had been done purposefully, the instigator might have wanted to cover their tracks by erasing the registry and logs. And that person might well have been the one who'd killed Olivia and marooned this ship on the wrong side of the Yale ring.

"We need to get that information," I said. "I want to know who had access and how the data could have been altered."

Sakura put down her fork with a tiny clicking sound. "Difficult," she said thoughtfully. "But not impossible. It sounds as if you believe this act was performed deliberately."

"I do."

She cocked her head slightly and gave me a quizzical squint. "But why? I'd assumed there was a system fault of some kind. This ship has taken a beating—several of them, in fact."

Nodding, I had to admit she was right. Could it be that I was grasping at straws?

"See what you can do—and report back to me soon."

"I will do as you ask, Captain."

I dumped my plate and left her then. Disturbed, I was glad to leave the wardroom. I went down the hall to the captain's cabin and raided the liquor cabinet, brooding over a triple Scotch.

I couldn't let the crew see me in this mood. My job was to get these people home, and to do that, they had to believe in me. It was a commander's duty to bear more than his fair share of the load. If Adrienne wasn't going to help out with that, then I'd have to ignore her. I'd forget her as a woman or a friend and just treat her like any other member of the crew.

Eyeing the empty glass, I capped the bottle and put it back in its padded slot. Then I went and armored up. This time I picked up one of the new cutters but no laser rifle. Soon, we would have to face the Lithos again.

Back on the bridge, I found Hansen had gotten there ahead of me. I'd taken an hour and a half so I knew he'd had an even shorter break. Still, he looked like he'd cleaned up and eaten and had a spill-proof cup of coffee in the holder at his elbow. He was a grownup. I wasn't going to micromanage him.

"I have the watch, Hansen," I said, announcing my presence.

"Yes, sir," he said, keeping his eyes on his instruments. "There was a low-power laser transmission from Marvin. It's encrypted text."

"He's taking every precaution he can," I replied. "Pass it here."

Hansen made a flicking motion, transferring the file from his screen to mine. I brought it up on one of the auxiliary screens beneath the holotank rather than displaying it for everyone.

99%+ probability #11 moon Matterhorn 7 contains ring. Holding at long range and studying Lithos. Good luck on ice moon.

Except for the sensor data on the ring moon, that was it. He could easily have sent pages of text coded in a burst with little additional risk, so I knew there was a lot Marvin wasn't telling us. Still, I couldn't see any way he could possibly sneak his way through either ring and leave us behind now, no matter how long he was left alone. He'd disappeared for months at a time back in the Macro Wars, but he'd always come back to stir the pot. Maybe if he had the time to study the Lithos, he could come up with valuable insights, learn their language, and collect important intelligence.

I hoped he didn't start communicating with the Lithos on his own the way he had with the Macros. That had led to near-disastrous results. In fact, in the much longer and more detailed message I sent back to him via tight-beam laser, I forbade him from contacting the Lithos of this system or cutting deals of any kind with them.

By that time we had reached the point where the ice moon appeared above the horizon of the enormous gas giant we orbited. The planet was so big that, as we skimmed its atmosphere, we could hardly see its curvature on the forward viewscreen. Instead, my mind tried to trick me into believing we cruised much lower, as if we flew an airplane just above the clouds of an Earthlike planet, except these clouds glowed blue and shimmered with hidden, silent lightning strikes. That got me wondering if there might not be some kind of life below us.

Perhaps there was something similar to the Blues that lived down there in that soupy gas. We hadn't detected anything, but then again, we hadn't looked very hard. Even if we had, Matterhorn 6 possessed the surface area of a thousand Earths, and it would have been easy to miss quiet life forms.

I turned deliberately away from that awesome view and stared at the holotank and its small auxiliary screens, which were much better for commanding the ship.

"Crew to battle stations," I said calmly. They were probably all there anyway, but making sure never hurt.

"Moonrise in ten minutes," Hansen said.

"If the holotank is up to date, I see only one squadron of Litho fighters and they haven't noticed us yet." Against the hot background of the planet and clouds, we were just a speck. As long as we did not light off our engines or transmit, picking us out of the clutter would be next to impossible until we got close. I'd counted on that as well.

"Make that two squadrons," I said, as more Lithos broke the horizon. Running intercept numbers, I said, "Whether they'll be able to catch us depends on when they see us. Do you have a least-time solution on the splashdown?"

"Yep," Hansen replied tersely, and I realized I was giving in to my nerves. Plotting and flying our course was the man's number one priority, and it had been stupid to ask.

"Two more squadrons," I called as they came into view. The four groups seemed to be holding in widely separated geosynchronous orbits around the gas giant, which made sense. They were in perfect spots to observe. I presumed other squadrons were even now moving into positions ringing the planet, looking for us. The only better formation for them would have been to break up the squadrons into flights of two to four allowing them to cover more area.

Maybe with their Macro-like hive mind, they got smarter and worked better with more of them near each other passing signals. That could be another explanation for why they liked to build everything so big. Probably there was a threshold of intelligence below which they became almost animals, simple beings with simple goals, like the snowflakes.

"Moonrise," Hansen said as the ice moon came into view. We were overtaking it in its orbit and coming in from a slightly oblique angle. Had I been the Lithos hunting a ship, I might have anticipated this move and waited to pounce, but they hadn't. As I had told Hansen, they simply didn't think the way we did, and vice versa.

Probably what we were doing didn't make much sense to them, either. From a Litho point of view, our ship must be like a dangerous bandit running madly in and out of their peaceful landscape, circling and dashing here and there to strike while they, the villagers, formed militia units and tried to drive us off.

That's what the Litho warships reminded me of, I realized. Militia. They didn't seem to have a professional fleet or military the way humanity did. I theorized that, in Litho society, every Litho was a potential warrior with little specialization. Like militias everywhere, they tended to focus on the immediate threat and not look ahead and think strategically. If fortifying their rings and sitting tight had bought them peace and prosperity until now, then why should they have developed heavier weapons and better ships?

In that way they did resemble humanity. Without an imminent threat, they'd turned to other pursuits, neglecting war.

Sadly, and unintentionally, I'd brought war to them. Maybe if we built up enough, we could get them to yield long enough to start a dialog. Every race Dad had confronted, from the Macros to the Blues who had created them, respected strength.

The holotank flashed red as the Lithos began to move.

"Here we go, people," I said. "They've seen us."

-23-

I watched four fresh Litho squadrons creep toward us on the display.

"They're leading us this time," I said. "Just a bit. Hedging. They haven't figured out yet that the moon is our goal."

"Can I pre-plot a firing solution?" Hansen asked.

I stared at the holotank until my eyes stung, and I had to blink. Their squadrons were almost in long range of our heaviest two lasers.

"Do you need much power for maneuvering?" I asked.

"It's not possible to answer that, really. Flank speed with full repeller assistance will draw down our capacitors quickly, but the plots say we'll beat them there if we push hard now. One thing to keep in mind is that the faster we go, the harder we'll have to brake at the end. We can't hit those oceans unless we're moving dead slow."

I wanted to pace back and forth on the deck, but in armor, I'd probably break something. "It all depends on what weapons they employ." Speaking that thought aloud decided it for me. "Start firing at long range. We need to make them commit to their chosen tactic and reveal their plans to us."

"Aye, sir. Mains, fire as they range," Hansen told the beam gunners. Soon, the big lasers *thrummed* bolts of energy at the nearest fighters, knocking one out right away.

In response, the Litho fighters shot forward and began evading wildly, buying themselves precious minutes. At the longest range, the seconds or even fractions of seconds it took for sensors to see evading targets and the light of lasers to reach them meant a likely miss. The closer they got, however, the more accurate our fire would be.

The nearest squadron took a beating. It wasn't until we'd destroyed twenty of them that the Lithos sprung their ploy on us. The squadron split into two. A group of the ships continued to evade violently like mad hornets but still headed in our direction. The rest of the ships seemed to tear themselves apart, with one chunk of each ship accelerating at breakneck speed toward us while the other portion stopped nearly dead in space and drifted. The sensors identified these threats as a new type of faster, nuclear missile. Because they were leading us and coming in at an angle, the brainbox calculations said they would intercept us if we let them.

"Target the missiles!" I said. "They'll hit us first, and if they have nukes, they'll kill us."

Our gunners frantically plied their lasers, the two big mains and the twelve secondaries, and then finally the dozens of point-defense turrets. Unlike in previous engagements, these missiles were not slowly approaching us from behind, providing easy targets. Instead, they were on a head-to-head collision course. They corkscrewed and pinwheeled to dodge our beams, coming closer every second.

The group of fighters that had split apart from the missile-firing types had moved directly between us and the moon. Maybe they'd figured out that was our goal, even if they didn't understand it. These enemy craft burst into a cloud of snowflakes, which formed a cloud between us and our goal. They were in position to cut us off, but they were now slow and avoidable.

"Five...four..." I counted down the strikes as we knocked out incoming missiles. "Down to three..."

They crossed into nuclear detonation range, and I knew then we were going to get hurt.

"Two..."

The world whited out and I was thrown into the side of the holotank. My helmet shattered the glass, but the material would heal itself eventually. In fact, the holotank would probably heal faster than my bleeding forehead. I felt the gravity shift under my feet as stabilizers and repellers strove to compensate for the turbulence of the blast. Half the control boards on the bridge flickered out.

I shook my head and pulled myself to my feet. The holotank had gone dark, leaving me without situational awareness. I dragged myself over to another console. Sakura, my chief engineer, had been manning this station. She'd been on the bridge checking something—but whatever her mission was she was incapable of finishing it. She was sprawled out on the floor. She must not have told the nanite arms to secure her well enough. Her external monitors said she was still breathing so I didn't fuss over her. I had no time for her now.

The console in front of me showed we were still more or less on course for the icy moon. *Valiant* had taken the proximity blast on her heavily armored nose, and it looked like only one of the enemy nukes had gone off. Maybe the first had cannibalized the second, destroying the atomic warhead before it completed its detonation sequence.

Their nuke had been relatively dirty. I noticed our radiation meters were all showing red. Anyone not nanotized would have taken a lethal dose, but all the humans aboard had been treated. I wondered about Hoon and how much he could take. Then I remembered that water was pretty good shielding material and hoped he was huddling in his cabin.

Hansen's bald head had a gash across it, but he was still in the game. Stoically, he wiped his eyes and fought the controls until the ship stopped pitching and yawing. Once I saw he was on the job, I stopped worrying about the piloting and checked for new threats.

"Here come the snowflakes," I rasped, my throat suddenly hurting. I think the helmet ring around my neck had been smashed into my larynx when I hit the holotank, but if that was my only significant injury, I was in good shape. "The nuke blast slowed us down, and it was perfectly timed to avoid killing the snowflakes."

"Another squadron is closing, staying in their fighter form," Hansen said. "It's a one-two-three punch."

Hansen was right. They'd set up a relatively sophisticated attack—missiles, snowflakes, and more fighters with lasers following behind. "Gunners, prepare to switch targets," I ordered. "Knock out those flakes before they reach the hull."

Half our secondary turrets had been knocked out. The mains were still operating at full capacity as they were heavily armored.

"Hansen, spin the ship around its axis," I said. "Make it hard for them to latch on."

"That's going to ruin our gunnery," he replied but initiated the maneuver anyway.

I guess he was starting to trust my tactical intuitions. I didn't mind his objections as long as he followed my orders immediately.

"We can't shoot down more than a fraction of them before they get here," I told him, "but they're coming too fast to really match speeds. They're going to get one chance each to land on us, and I want the hull to look like a mad merry-go-round, knocking them off."

"Kwon here," the marine broke in. "Permission to exit the hull, sir?"

"Not yet, Kwon," I said. "We're spinning. I don't want to throw marines off into space with the snowflakes."

"Sir," he said with a voice full of eagerness, "Give us a chance. We can handle a spin. We'll lock double safety lines and fight from the airlocks if we have to, but we need to get them on the hull, before they get in."

"All right, Kwon," I said, "but this time keep at least half your people in reserve for interior defense, with cutters ready. Kill any intruders and seal off any breaches. And remember, we're coming in for a water landing at the end of this."

"Yes sir! We're on our way."

I shook my head with a grim smile. I'd drawn an ace when fate had dealt me Kwon as my chief of marines.

With the holotank knocked out and the ship spinning, the sensors had trouble keeping the viewscreens stable. To stave off motion sickness, I had to stop watching them. Hansen, like most pilots, didn't seem to have a problem with it, and it looked like he was flying by instruments anyway. One crewman wasn't so fortunate and retched onto the floor, which I knew the ship would soon absorb and recycle. Not the most pleasant of thoughts, but with nanites, everything could be reprocessed, given time.

"Here they come," Hansen muttered.

"Everyone button up your suits," I called over the all-hands channel.

Impacts shuddered throughout the ship as snowflakes struck us. Our overloaded stabilizers leaked kinetic energy, and I belatedly slammed my visor shut and told the bridge restraint system to grab me with its tentacles. I brought up a systems schematic and found scattered damage, but nothing critical until one of the empty forward water tanks lost pressure. The brainbox sealed it off, but I figured I knew what it meant.

"Kwon, we have a breach in tank three. Send a team."

"On it," he replied.

I hated just sitting here giving orders; I'd much rather go charging into the hand-to-hand fight, but right now I was the only Academy-trained officer aboard. The warrants weren't trained to command a ship; they were specialists. Most of them were older and set in their ways. I didn't want to be too arrogant, but I believed I was irreplaceable right now. Maybe later, if we were still lost in this seemingly endless series of rings and planets, I could promote the best noncoms or warrants to Ensign. I guess at that point I'd have to promote myself.

Returning my full attention to the battle, I continued directing marines to hull breaches as I noted them. Some crew got caught in depressurized compartments near the hull, unable to defend themselves against the monsters before the reinforcing marines came. Snowflakes grabbed crewmen and marines alike when they could and tore them up. Our battle armor turned out to be like tinfoil to them if they got their appendages into us. While slow, their strength was inexorable. Fortunately the cutters worked well for close-in defense.

A panicked cry came over my battlesuit comm. "Sir, sir, this is Corporal Lopez. The SMAJ is down, and we're cut off!"

I checked, and he was right. Sergeant Major Kwon's icon flashed yellow on my HUD. Lopez and two others had holed up in one of the laser turrets. Two of the big twenty-foot snowflakes had flanked them and were even now ripping through the surrounding armor. In a moment, they would be squashing the marines like metal cockroaches.

"You've got the watch, Hansen!" I yelled as I pounded off the bridge, tearing a chunk out of the doorway as I went barreling through in three tons of powered armor. "*Valiant*," I called, "I need an opening above me to the next deck. Do it now. Then open all the doors between me and Kwon."

Over my head, smart metal thinned then spread apart. Objects dropped onto me as I rose on repellers. Books, a hand mirror, and even a pair of shoes fell into my upraised faceplate. I'd come through into someone's quarters but had no time for delicacy. I charged through the open door then bolted to the starboard side of the ship where the nearest snowflake shook and made grinding sounds with every movement. I raised my cutter as I charged. I'd just begun to shove it forward in scissors mode when the crystal arm whipped around and pinned me against the bulkhead.

How did these things see me coming? I'd yet to identify their sensory organs—if I had, I would have cut them out as an opening move.

The cutter in my gauntlets whined as it twisted out of alignment, and then one blade disintegrated as it tore itself to bits with its own belt. I shut that off, roaring with effort as I tried to bench-press a twenty-ton monster.

Instead of shoving it away from me, I pushed myself through the bulkhead behind me, because that was the weakest of the three involved objects—me, the Litho, and the wall. I fell awkwardly to the floor on the far side of the interior wall, then used the power of my legs to somersault backward and roll to my feet.

I could see the Litho had lost me for the moment and the hole I'd made in the bulkhead was trying to close itself. I used my HUD to pinpoint the marines I was trying to reach and punched my way through the wall.

We were inside the mechanical room beneath a laser turret. I could see the servomechanisms that rotated the laser, and I made sure I didn't damage them as I pressed myself inside.

Lopez was there as was another man. They slashed at the snowflake that was trying to tear its way into the turret to get them. They stood over a fallen, legless battlesuit that was noticeably larger than the norm.

Legs could regrow, so I wasn't worried about that. I widened the hole and addressed Lopez, who looked at me in surprise.

"Corporal!" I shouted. "Help me drag Kwon out of here. We're falling back!"

Stepping through, I readied myself in case the Litho I'd been dueling followed me through the bulkheads.

The corporal grabbed Kwon with me, and his comrade covered our retreat. The last man out was too slow, and the point of the monster's crystal appendage stabbed downward into his body, spitting him like a man spearing a fish. Blood sprayed, and I saw the HUD icon wink out as his life signs faded.

Leaping forward, Lopez carried Kwon through the hole I'd made. I'd taken a moment to take hold of Kwon's cutter. I used it to chop off the Litho's arm, then exited the turret. "Lopez, get Kwon to a med bay."

I followed them as they withdrew along the same route I'd advanced. When they were clear, I turned around and made for another knot of marines who were converging on the two big Lithos.

My HUD said that these invaders were the last to have made it into the ship. Two of the marines lost limbs during the fight that followed, but no one died as we made a concerted assault on first one invader and then the other. As soon as I was sure the ship was clear, I withdrew to the bridge and let Gunnery Sergeant Taksin, the next marine noncom in line, take over.

I'd just opened my faceplate to look at the holotank when Hansen said, "Braking in five seconds," over the general address system. "Prepare for turnover." As soon as he counted down, he rotated the ship to put the big engines in back for maximum deceleration. That brought up our final deadly problem.

"The fighters are catching up," I said.

"I have to fly the ship," said Hansen, his eyes fixed on his instruments.

I realized he was fully occupied. "Understood," I said, then let him be. Calling the gunnery stations, I said, "Fire at will at your nearest targets."

I noticed that Sakura's body was no longer sprawled on the floor of the bridge. I switched to the engineering channel and contacted her. "Sakura, are you alive? How are you doing?"

"I'm awake and back at my post, sir. Effecting damage control."

"Good," I said with relief. "Can you perform your duties, or are you still injured?"

"The nanites were very effective, sir."

I blinked and frowned. "Why were you on bridge when that strike came in?"

There was a moment of quiet, then: "I was looking for an entry in the software installation logs."

Thinking about that, I almost let it pass. I had plenty of other things to worry about. But I still wasn't sure why my Engineer hadn't been in Engineering during a critical phase of the battle. What she'd said had brought back thoughts of how this entire fiasco had started. Could it be she'd made headway in that investigation?

"An entry?" I asked. "Are you talking about the change that activated the ring and flung us out here into unknown hostile space?"

"Yes. You asked me to investigate."

"Well, what did you find?"

"Nothing of significance, unfortunately. The server maintaining the logs was damaged during the attack."

Her story was a little vague and odd, but then so was Sakura herself. "All right," I said. "Give me a report on your damage control efforts."

"We're sealing off breaches, Captain, but we won't have a smooth hull for days. We'd better land pretty gently or we'll burst some internal bulkheads and hatches from the impact and pressure."

"We'll try. Anything you need?"

"More people," she said without hesitation.

"I can get you that," I said, then switched channels. "Gunny Taksin. Get to Sakura in engineering. Your marines are now on damage control. We've got about seventeen minutes before we land, and we need as many of those breaches patched as possible."

"Will do, sir," he said. "Taksin out."

I contacted Adrienne next. "Adrienne, how are you and the scientists doing?"

"We're fine, Cody," she returned, sounding calm. "We'd like to do something to help."

She'd called me Cody, I realized. I felt pleased, forgetting momentarily that using my first name in a combat zone was an inappropriate familiarity from a subordinate. Right now, I didn't care about the rules.

"If the crew asks for help," I told her, "do whatever they need. If you go wandering around you'll probably just slow them down. Unless you have an idea? I'm open to suggestions."

"We can run the factory directly and free up Sakura," she said.

I imagined them feeding broken pieces of machinery into the maw and frantically remanufacturing spare parts or constructive nanites. They could do that kind of work.

"Good idea," I said. "Do it. Just stick to what you know, Adrienne, and you'll do fine."

"Thanks. Turnbull out."

It was only after she'd closed the channel that I realized I'd called her by her first name as well, and she hadn't objected. The exchange had formed a strange little moment of intimacy in the middle of a serious situation, and my morale was strangely buoyed by the exchange.

I didn't care if it was against regulations. She'd called me Cody, and I felt charged with energy.

Energy.

Valiant shuddered again as a Litho laser tapped at us from long range, and I slapped my helmeted forehead.

"Cease fire, all weapons switch to standby," I said, checking my board for the control subroutine I wanted. When I found it and made sure all the lasers were silent, I powered up the shield.

Immediately the shuddering ceased as the magnetic field absorbed and dispersed the enemy lasers.

"We don't have to shoot them down," I said. "They aren't going to catch us. All we have to do is avoid any more damage, and we'll be home free." I wasn't entirely sure I was telling the truth, but what else could I say?

"We're running low on energy," Hansen said, his hands still gripped the controls tightly. "The shield is a power hog."

I looked at the graphs and saw he was right.

"Will we have enough?" I asked.

"Not if we keep the shield up."

I hesitated for a moment, unwilling to open *Valiant* up to any more damage. "Adrienne," I called, "can the marine battlesuits be plugged in to the ship's power grid?"

"We can't spare the energy right now," she replied.

"No, no, I mean, can we *draw* power from their suit generators? They must still be fairly well-charged."

"I think so. Just have the marines put their suits back into their receptacles and I'll try to set it up."

"Will do. Ask Sakura for help if you have to," I said. "We need that power or we'll have to turn off the shield, and if we do that, we'll start taking laser fire again."

"Okay, Cody, I'm on it."

"Thanks, Adie. Cody out." A warm glow suffused me. Here I was in the middle of a battle and the most important thing to me was that I was back in her good graces, and using first names. Funny, but that very feeling prevented me from thinking what a hypocrite I was.

I called Gunnery Sergeant Taksin and told him to put the battlesuits back into their charging stations and to wait for instructions from the engineers in case reversing the energy flow needed some kind of manual override. Then I slipped down to Medical to check on Kwon. The idiot was arguing with the med bay, trying to get it to let him out, even with both legs gone above the knees. I had to order him twice to stay put, yelling at him. Finally, I told the med bay brainbox to sedate him for at least eight hours. Then I returned to the bridge.

"We're getting close to bingo," Hansen said. "Bingo" was pilot talk for just enough fuel—or in this case energy—to get home and land.

"I'll shut off the shield if I have to," I said, finger on the control. I was just about to power it down and suffer the laser fire when the energy reserves stabilized and then began to slowly climb.

"Yes!" I cheered. "The suits did the trick. The generators are small, but there are twenty of them in the charging docks." I realized several bridge crew were looking at me with something like shock. I didn't think it was any big deal, but then again, it *had* been a clever idea.

Hansen shot me a raised-eyebrow look, the only attention he was willing to spare. Somehow I had the feeling he didn't share the crew's enthusiasm.

The ice moon started to loom on the screen as seen through a rear camera and partially obscured by the blazing flare of the main engines that braked us. I tried to set up a landing calculation but I wasn't familiar enough with the standard controls. I'd gotten spoiled by the holotank, and resolved to refresh my training on the backups ASAP.

So this time, I cheated.

"*Valiant*, what is our landing profile?"

"Landing profile is within safety parameters," the brainbox replied. "Landing surface is liquid. Liquid landing protocols have been implemented."

That eased my mind somewhat. Of course, Star Force ships had standardized protocols for water landings. Some planets had almost no land, and since any spaceship was sealed against vacuum anyway, it wasn't that hard to design a hull to keep water out as well as air in.

"Will we have hull integrity?" I asked the ship.

"Hull integrity safety protocols have been overridden by the chief engineer."

That didn't sound good, but I had to trust that Sakura knew what she was doing. "Given current damage, how much pressure can we take?" I asked.

"Approximately 10.34 bar," said the ship.

"About 150 PSI," I mused. "How deep is that in feet?"

"Approximately five hundred and four."

I was pretty good at quick calculations in my head, and that didn't sound right. Then I remembered that the lower gravity of the moon meant the water pressure would increase much more slowly as we descended. "How deep is the sea floor?"

"Unknown."

"Use active radar to try to get a reading."

"Not recommended. Magnetic shield is in place."

Damn. I remembered we hadn't been able to ping the moon, and I hadn't thought to do it on the way in. Marvin would have done it, I was sure, and then I laughed at myself for missing the crazy robot. He did have his uses. I guessed we would just have to hope the sea was deep enough to hide us, and the sea floor not so far down we couldn't take the pressure. Otherwise, we might have to cruise around like a submarine, looking for a shallower spot.

"How long until splashdown?" I asked *Valiant*.

"Two minutes ten seconds at the mark: *Mark*."

"Okay. Count down the last ten seconds."

"Command accepted."

We sweated the last two minutes. The Litho fighters broke off about ninety seconds from impact, rocketing sideways to skim above the moon's surface, a rather brave act for them, considering their apparent hatred for cold and wet. Once they had turned away, I shut off the shield and was pleased to see the capacitors refilling fast.

One minute from impact, I told the crew to cease repair activities and brace themselves—despite the readouts that said we would land rather than crash onto the surface. *Whatever can go wrong, will,* was a good maxim to live by, and we'd already lost several people today despite our desperate efforts. I'd feel pretty damned stupid if someone else died because I became complacent now.

Everyone held on and wrapped up in restraints as the brainbox droned the countdown. When we reached zero, I expected to feel something significant, but almost nothing occurred. Hansen had shut down the main engines and now lowered us gently on repellers. Moments later we sank slowly below the ripples of the frigid ocean.

I breathed a sigh of relief, which was echoed by everyone within earshot.

We were down in an ocean full of icebergs—safe, for the moment.

-24-

The hull groaned around us as we descended to one hundred feet. The frigid waters of the moon's ocean closed overhead, and the external view transitioned from slate gray to black. It was an odd feeling, sinking into an alien sea. I doubted that any living creature had ever done so in these waters before. One could not help but wonder what we'd find in the inky depths.

"Take us obliquely northward," I told Hansen while we all stared at the gurgling black seas outside. "I want to get under the ice. The Lithos may be able to track us until we get deep enough."

Navigating with sonar that Sakura had cleverly rigged up, *Valiant* slid slowly and carefully northward. I knew that we still had some danger with hull breaches and that water had flooded some outer compartments, but our nanite-thickened pressure doors and bulkheads had held most of it back.

I contacted Sakura. "Report any pressure problems to the bridge," I told her. "I'd rather not surface, but I like the idea of drowning even less. Oh, and send a technician up here to get the holotank working."

"I'll do that," she replied. "We should be good down to four or five hundred feet, sir."

"Thanks." I closed the channel. "Hansen, take us down slowly, pausing every hundred. I'm not as confident about our hull integrity as our chief engineer."

A tech showed up and within half an hour she had the holotank functioning again, which was a great relief for me. Soon the display built a three-dimensional picture of our surroundings.

"The sea floor is down around two thousand feet," I said. "Too deep."

Hansen grunted. His manner was ambiguous.

"Something bothering you?" I asked.

"How well do lasers work under water?"

That stumped me, so I called Sakura again and put the question to her.

"The mechanisms will function fine," she told me, "but the range will be very short—a hundred yards or less unless the water is exceptionally clear. Even then, the range will be a quarter mile at most. And the effects will be different. If there is a lot of particulate matter in the water, most of the heat will dump into the liquid itself, flash-boiling it. In that case, our laser batteries will be steam-throwers."

"Thanks," I told her.

I turned back to Hansen, who'd been listening to the exchange. "Does that answer your question?" I asked him.

He tossed me a wry glance. "You might want to check your holotank."

I raised an eyebrow and turned to look. Well in front of us, perhaps twenty miles away at the limit of sonar range, I could see a group of contacts. As we got closer, I saw they were shaped like most swimming sea creatures. They resembled whales in size, ranging from fifty to two hundred feet long. Now I wished we had worked harder on a full set of undersea sensors.

"So there's life on this moon," I said. "Fairly complex life, too. I wonder how intelligent they are?"

The whales sped toward us at thirty miles per hour. As our own rate of travel was about the same, every minute brought us a mile closer together. About ten miles away, they stopped advancing and turned to their left, circling us and keeping their distance.

Suddenly the door to the bridge opened and Hoon barged in, wearing his pressure suit, of course. His low-slung, oversized body made the area feel suddenly crowded, and his claws waved in the air showing he was agitated.

"Step aside, Captain. I must have direct access to the best sensors available to observe these creatures."

I stared at the lobster. "How did you even know we'd seen anything?"

"The previous captain provided my quarters with a continuous feed of ship sensors, but I cannot control them," he replied. "Now please, let me see."

As he'd said "please," I got out of his way and let him access one of the unused sensor stations. He kept one eyestalk pointed at the holotank and one at the console, reminding me of Marvin. With surprisingly deft fingerlike digits on his mandible, he tapped at the controls, bringing up a bunch of data incomprehensible to me.

As I watched him, I realized I should have thought to bring Hoon to the bridge right away. As a scientist and a water creature, he would naturally know how to get the most out of our systems in this environment.

"These sensors are pathetic," Hoon said. "We must manufacture and configure a better suite."

"I agree wholeheartedly," I said. "Just as soon as we find a safe spot on the sea floor to set down and begin mining for raw materials, you can start working with Adrienne and Sakura on that." I figured that should motivate him.

"I will find such a place. You air-breathers will doubtlessly perform sub-optimally and will require a great deal of assistance."

"Absolutely. I expect you to humble us with your display of knowledge and undersea expertise. In fact, I bet you could write a paper on this moon for your colleagues to marvel over when we get back to known space."

"You continue to impress me, young Riggs, with your perspicacity and insight, if not your raw intellect. For a child, you show promise."

"Thanks, Grandpa." I rolled my eyes and noticed Hansen smiling. "Now, what do you think about these whales?"

"If you mean the swimmers circling us, I believe we could find out more if you reduced the power on the active sonar. If they can detect sounds, the pings are probably extremely loud, thus keeping them at bay."

"Good idea." I cut the sonar power in half. Immediately, the whales began edging inward as they circled around to our starboard. "It looks like you were right."

"Of course I'm right," Hoon snapped. "Please further reduce the sonar emissions."

I cut the strength of the sonar to minimum, giving us a mere quarter mile of range, enough to see the sea floor and avoid hitting anything. The whales continued to approach until they got within two hundred yards.

"Give me visuals," I said.

"It's too dark," Hansen replied.

"Then turn on the lights."

Hoon said, "Your lasers can be used in low-power diffused mode to provide illumination."

"Let's see, then."

On the main screen, a murky picture emerged. We were encircled by stately swimming shapes. I was already calling them whales, and in this case form followed function. They looked like whales for the most part, except for having four eyes equally spaced around their heads. This optical arrangement allowed them to see forward and probably well to the side. They displayed a cluster of tentacles near what looked like a mouth in front.

"These are not true hunting creatures," Hoon said, "but this sea clearly contains predators."

"How do you know?" I asked, genuinely interested.

"It is elementary. The tentacles are too small to grasp large prey, but are similar to many creatures of your planet and ours, serving to sweep plankton, krill or plant matter into the maw for digestion. This indicates these creatures aren't predators. However, their optical organs are placed in an optimal arrangement to see attackers. Swimming predators tend to have closer, more forward-set eyes for binocular vision, the better to hunt and strike. Since these creatures have banded together for mutual protection, they're displaying classic physical and behavioral traits which indicate predators must be present in the ecosystem."

Hoon was now in his element, and he proceeded to lecture us on sea life in general. The most important thing I gleaned from him was that this moon must contain a thriving ecosystem to support something as large as these whales. He inferred a whole pyramid of species based merely on his observations of this one. Despite myself, I was impressed.

I stopped listening to Hoon after a while and began thinking of the implications. We were going to have to deal with a living world we barely understood. It could be fraught with dangers, even if none of the local life was sentient. These whales seemed to be bigger than the largest Earth species. Maybe there were larger creatures still to be discovered. Perhaps the predators Hoon predicted were leviathans. I suspected my marines might get a workout on this moon after all.

As we proceeded northward, the whales paced us like dolphins following a seafaring ship on Earth. I took this as a good sign: if the local herd-creatures were calm, no dangerous beasts were likely to be near.

"We really need more sonar power if we're going to search much of the area," Hansen said when Hoon finally paused.

"An excellent suggestion," Hoon responded. "Give me control of the sonar and I will gradually increase its power and attempt to tune its frequency to minimally impact the local life."

I saw no reason to deny Hoon his toys, so I instructed Hansen to turn over all sensor control to the lobster and to take search suggestions from him. I needed to take a look at the damage below decks and show my face among the crew.

My first stop was the medical bay. I made sure Kwon was still sedated. Next I stopped by the cramped marine spaces with their triple bunks, battlesuits standing in alcoves. Some people were working on damage control, but many were off duty. I was glad to see Gunnery Sergeant Taksin resting his troops in rotation and not just burning them out. I told them Kwon would be fine. It would take more than losing a few limbs to keep him down. I also gave them my condolences for the marines we'd lost today.

I shook hands and praised them for their work, calling them "Riggs' Pigs" whenever I could. Napoleon once said, "The moral," —from which we got our word *morale*— "is to the physical as three is to one," so I dispensed as much morale as I could, promising them lots of hard work and beer as soon as we got the factory working on soft goods again. I also mentioned that this sea held life, probably dangerous life, and the marines' contribution to our survival would continue to be vital. My visit seemed to cheer them up.

Next I toured the perimeter, looking in on the crew while they worked hard with tools and nanite guides to fix the hull. Employing a combination of constructive nanites and manufactured parts, the repairs were progressing, albeit slowly. We'd dumped so much of the ship's mass there wasn't enough metal and raw materials to utilize for repairing bulkheads. We were short many vital resources, but the crew was on the job and I did as much back-patting and praising as I could stand. Leadership by wandering around, Dad had called it, getting out and being seen to care.

My real destination was Engineering, which resided near the center and stern of the ship, mostly comprising the big factory space and the engine room. There I found Adrienne sitting at the factory console with a frown of concentration on her face while Sakura stood across the room in front of the big control wall. On-duty marines in battlesuits, their helmets off, carried chunks of debris and fed them into the factory intake.

I noticed one marine carrying a boulder-sized crystal in his hands, and I moved to stop him.

"Is that a piece of Litho?" I asked.

"Yes, sir!" he said.

"Is that safe?"

"Warrant Officer Sakura said so, sir!"

I frowned, finding it odd that we should be grinding up dead enemies to build our own ship components. Wasn't this akin to using the bones of a dead man to build a house? The thought was troubling, but we did need the raw materials. The situation made me realize how difficult coming to some kind of peaceful coexistence with the Lithos was going to be. We were so utterly different; we were going to find it hard to find common ground and understanding.

"Carry on," I said, letting the marine work. I moved over to Adrienne's post. "How's it going?"

"Fine, but we don't have enough materials."

"You'll have all you can handle as soon as we set down. Are you quite sure it's appropriate—or even safe—to feed Litho bodies into the factory?"

Adrienne frowned. "Safe? Yes, it's safe. Don't trust me?"

"*Trust but verify* is something commanders have to do," I said. "You're in charge here, and I bet you don't just assume everyone thinks of everything, do you?"

She laughed. "Okay. Fair point. I check on everyone all the time to the point where they become annoyed with me. About the Lithos, Sakura and the scientists ran some tests when we first got samples back in the hollow planet, and she determined that our metal nanites could easily process the silico-nanites inside the material. They are only a little more virulent than living fungus or bacteria. They're not some super-germ. In fact, our own metal nanites are far more dangerous. I've always wondered what would happen if they became self-aware. They'd be hard to stop."

"Electromagnetic pulse, or any magnetic field, can control our nanites," I replied. "What controls these?"

"I don't know yet. The scientists are working on it."

I watched a crystal claw go into the factory's maw. It was disturbing how much the claw looked like the grasping hand of a stone statue. The outstretched fingers went into the grinder last, and the screeching sounded like that of a wood-chipper working on bone.

"We might regret doing this," I said.

Adrienne eyed me. "You lamented about using Lithos as raw material, and I can understand that. We wouldn't like it if they built ships out of dead marines."

"No, we wouldn't. We shouldn't make a habit of this process, either. They might be able to detect the fact that we've recycled their dead and take offense."

Adrienne looked at the factory maw thoughtfully. "You're holding out hope that we can come to terms with these creatures someday, aren't you?"

"Certainly," I said. "Think of the alternatives. Eventually, either we have to wipe them out or they have to wipe us out. That is—unless we can achieve some form of peace."

She looked troubled, so I changed the topic.

"You said something about scientists working on Litho anatomy," I prompted her.

"Yes. I assigned them to study the Lithos because having them help run the factory caused more problems than it solved. The scientists work better as a think tank, so I gave them their own laboratory and enough work until we set down." Adrienne pointed at a door nearby.

When I entered the think tank I saw the three human scientists with their eyes glued to instruments—microscopes, scanners and the like. Hoon was absent. He preferred to work in his own watery quarters where he was more comfortable. I also suspected he didn't get along well with the human science team.

On a high-magnification screen I could see nanites moving, performing their incomprehensible tasks. I'd seen such things before, of course. Everyone had, at least on documentary vids, but these looked a bit different. Where *our* nanites, descendants of the original Nano ships, looked like spidery construction machines that scurried here and there, the Lithos appeared to be crystals that mostly stayed interlocked with each other. They would slide and move without ever really losing touch with each other.

Doctor Benson, the most senior of the scientists, noticed me and jumped up to rush over. "Hello, Captain Riggs, Good to see you again. You remember Doctors Chang and Kalu."

"Doctor," I greeted him, and then the other two: "Doctor; Doctor. I thought I'd drop by and check on your research."

Kalu looked at me with her big eyes for a moment then turned away.

Benson gushed about his findings, oblivious to his colleague's unease. "Oh, it's absolutely fascinating, Captain.

The intermodal tendencies of these silico-nanites are unmatched. We—"

I put on my best smile. "Doctor Benson? Could you please summarize—for a layman?"

The man cleared his throat and wiped his hands on the front of his white lab coat. "Yes, of course. The Lithos are a silicon-based life form that seems to be infinitely reconfigurable and scalable."

I held up my hand again. "You mean, they're communal and can form structures of any size?"

"Yes. And, the larger the network they form, the more intelligent they become. They—"

Again, my hand rose to get the man to pause. "How large must a colony be before they become collectively sentient?"

"That's a hard question to answer because of the variable threshold of true intelligence. I—"

"How large," I asked, breaking in again, "to be of average adult human intelligence? Just an approximation."

Benson squirmed, but eventually told me twenty tons and up seemed to be about right. That was an interesting number to me because the snowflakes varied from about five to twenty tons at the largest. Apparently the Lithos wanted their suicide troops to be just smart enough to do their jobs, but not enough to have much instinct for self-preservation. Maybe the larger snowflakes were the assault commanders. "So how smart is one of their cruisers—a mountain-sized ship?"

Throwing up his hands, Benson said, "I can't answer that. Intelligence isn't linear. Dolphins have far larger brains than we do but aren't as conventionally intelligent. A brainbox, even a big one, can store far more data and calculate faster than a biotic but still lacks all imagination. Then there is an anomaly like the Marvin robot." Seeing my brows furrow, he went on hastily, "The best test of intelligence is to observe behavior. I don't think the Litho ships are any smarter than one of our ships with its captain and crew. That's probably the best comparison: the larger the Litho, the more it acts like a community rather than one unitary individual."

"So where does one Litho end and another begin?"

"I can't answer that right now. It could take years or decades to come to even the most basic understanding of the Litho anatomy and culture."

I sighed unhappily. "Doctor, that's all very interesting, and I'm sure it's valuable in the long run. But right now, I need insights that will help us survive their attacks and to fight back."

Benson drew himself up in a huff. "I am a scientist. I am not *military* nor am I interested in developing ways to kill another sentient species." His voice dripped contempt.

Irritated, I put my index finger on the man's chest and prodded him with it. "The Macros were sentient and bent on the destruction of all biotic life. I assume you have no problem killing those "sentient" beings. These Lithos have chased us all over the system repeatedly attacking us even when we posed them no threat. I'm not looking for a way to commit genocide, but I would like to stay alive and get home. What about you, Doctor? Got a wife and kids at home, or a mother, father?"

Benson turned red and sputtered.

I turned to take in the other two, who were staring at us.

"Listen to me," I said. "This isn't a scientific expedition. *Valiant* is a Star Force warship. Our most important mission is to make it back to known space and report our findings. I don't want anyone to commit some kind of atrocity, but we need intel. Study the aliens all you want. Discover everything you can. But if I *ever* find out you've withheld anything that might increase our chances of survival, anything that we can use in a fight, I will consider you traitors to the human race and to our allied biotics. You'll be tried and punished on that basis. The standard punishment for conviction is immediate spacing of the perpetrator, I must remind you."

I took an angry breath and eyed them. They looked alarmed. None of them said a word.

"These Lithos were apparently built to kill Macros," I told them. "If they can beat the Macros, they can probably beat us, too. Who knows how far they've spread? They might be on Earth's doorstep even now with an armada, waiting to burst through a ring we don't know about. The Lithos we found here might represent their weakest rear guard. They may own a hundred systems." I slammed my fist into the wall, deforming the smart metal for a moment and making the scientists jump. "You three may hold the fate of humanity in your hands. Don't fall in love with your subjects and forget you're human."

With that, I stalked out, containing myself. I'd given in to my temper, but I hadn't lost control. Hopefully, the eggheads in their lab had gotten my message. I doubted whether the crew or the marines would be so understanding if they thought the scientists were sympathetic to the enemy.

Back in the big room, I saw that Adrienne sat idly tapping at her touchscreen. The factory that occupied the center squatted silently, and no lines of marines brought their chunks of materials to feed it. Seeing me, she waved.

"Run out of spare parts?" I asked as I moved to her side.

"Yes. There's nothing left to reprocess." She tilted her head and looked at me. "You can't fool me, Cody Riggs. That smile is pasted on."

I sighed and shook my head. "I'm pissed off. Those big brains in the lab…all they care about is studying the Lithos over the next few years or possibly decades. When I told them I needed ways to fight them *now*, Benson as much as accused me of being a baby killer. Here they are, grinding up the enemy dead and dissecting them, and somehow I'm the bad guy for trying to find a more efficient way to kill them. I told Benson he'd better get with the program, or else."

"Or else what?" she asked.

I wasn't sure what she was thinking, but I decided to try to make her understand my position.

"Adrienne, I'm the captain. It's my responsibility to get us home and get the information we've collected back to Star Force. To do that, everyone under my command, civilian or military, alien, human or robot, has to pull his weight. I can't have them holding back because they sympathize with the enemy."

"We did draw first blood, remember," she said. "That's something to keep in mind if you want to make peace with them eventually."

"Huh?"

"Inside the hollow planet. When the snowflakes were coming our direction, we shot first. Maybe they were just trying to establish contact."

"Have you forgotten the dirt-creatures trying to grab you on Tullax 6?"

Adrienne crossed her arms, cradling her breasts as if she was cold.

"No," she admitted, "but those were probably wild Lithos, out of touch with their society and programmed to attack anything made of metal. I bet they mistook our suits for Macros. Or maybe they wouldn't have hurt me. Maybe they would have tried to form a connection, nanite to nanite."

I shook my head. "They would have detected the metallic nanites in your bloodstream and tried to kill you. Has everyone started to feel sorry for these creatures? They don't have to keep attacking us, you know. They could try to talk to us by some other method. The Pandas use radio, and the Lithos are smart enough to figure out how to use it too, but they haven't tried to talk to us."

That seemed to give her pause. We'd searched for signals on every conceivable frequency and beamed some of our own before going radio silent, but had found only that one gamma carrier wave. We needed Marvin to decode it, and he wasn't talking.

"Look," I said, "I'd love to call a truce and open negotiations with the Lithos, but until then, we have to be ready to fight. That's just a fact, unless you want to give up and die. I'm not going to do that or let anyone on this ship consider it." I grabbed her by her shoulders, wanting to shake some sense into her, but I gentled my touch. "I'm going to get us home, Adrienne. I swear it. But I need everyone to help. I need them to do their best, and I need you. To convince them, I mean," I hastened to say, letting go and dropping my eyes.

"I understand, Cody," she said gently, reaching out to touch my arm briefly. "You've got a tough job, and you've been…I can't imagine anyone else doing it better. I'm sorry. I was trying to be helpful in my own way. I didn't realize how it was coming across. We're all under so much stress right now."

I touched her wrist and then ran my fingers up her arm to rest my hand on her shoulder.

"That's okay," I told her. "Everyone's on edge. As soon as we find a place to set down, we can all relax." I lingered, touching her a moment longer. I was elated that I'd avoided some kind of blow-up. "I have to get back to the bridge."

With a smile, Adrienne gently removed my hand from her shoulder.

"Go on, then," she said. "Be the captain, Cody Riggs."

-25-

Hoon found a likely spot to set down a few hours later, but I vetoed it. I wanted to be farther away from our splashdown point in case the Lithos had something up their non-existent sleeves. They'd proven creative and tricky up until now and slipping silently away like a submarine of old seemed like a cheap and easy way to avoid trouble.

I was glad I did. We'd gone about five hundred miles northward, a tenth of the way toward the pole and barely under the permanent ice, when shockwaves reached us.

"What the hell was that?" Hansen snarled as he fought with his controls.

"The Lithos, taking another shot at us," I replied.

"They're bombing the ocean?"

"If I were in their place, I would grab the nearest asteroids in planetary orbit and give them the right push to fall onto the moon, aiming where we splashed down and working outward. That's why I wanted to get farther away and keep our signature low."

The realization that we'd all be dead if we'd gone to ground where we'd splashed down raised my stock in the eyes of the crew. I reminded myself that I couldn't always be right. Even my legendary father had screwed up now and again. I just hoped when it came to be my turn it wouldn't be a critical error.

The bombardment continued for another day, but as we traveled farther and farther away, the shocks lessened.

The Lithos had tried again, but failed to kill us.

Had Hoon possessed hair, he would have been pulling it out. As it was, he complained bitterly about the huge amounts of sea life that was undoubtedly dying in our wake. If he hadn't hated the Lithos before, he surely did now, which was fine by me. As my oceanic expert, I needed him at maximum motivation.

We turned eastward and circumnavigated most of the way around the moon before turning north again. After ten long days, we found a perfect spot. With two hundred feet of permanent ice pack above us and a sea floor at a depth of three hundred feet, I couldn't imagine anything detecting us. The only thing that could penetrate our cover was gravity and neutrinos. The ship didn't have particle weapons, so there was no worry of neutrino emissions. We had nothing aboard like stardust, nothing dense enough to bend gravity. To be certain, we even kept all our gravity plates turned off. We effectively became ghosts.

Conceivably, if the Lithos wanted us badly enough, they might be able to grab a really big asteroid, get it going fast and drop it on the moon. But we were now over six thousand miles from where we'd started. Unless the bombardment cracked the crust of the moon itself, I figured we'd survive.

In the beginning, our construction plans were frustratingly slow. We used marines for short jaunts out onto the sea floor to grab boulders and nets full of what looked like coral along with all the animal and plant life that went with it. Hoon eagerly sorted through the loads, seizing specimens and popping them into buckets full of native seawater. The rest went into the factory to build specialized sea mining vehicles.

For example, gills attachments for the battle armor extended their range a lot. The marines' lasers had to be re-tuned to optimize them for water use, because they'd already encountered a few predators. We needed lots of high-pressure sealant to stop leaks. The list seemed endless, and Adrienne proved worth her weight in rare earths, coordinating all the things we needed as my logistics manager.

I gave her two days to find her sea legs, so to speak, and then broached the topic I'd been thinking about over breakfast.

I'd found that the first meal of the day when she was well rested and after she'd had her coffee was a good time to bring up risky subjects.

"Looks like we're doing all right on the mining efforts," I opened.

"The major things are done, and our raw materials are flowing in faster and faster. Why?"

"It's time to start making something we really need."

She stopped chewing, and then swallowed her bite of fake eggs. "Which is?"

I heard a hint of challenge in her voice, which I found I liked, in small doses. "Parts for another factory. Getting two factories working will pay off big in the long run."

Adrienne put down her utensils to place her hands flat on the table and lean toward me. "That would take months. We're running at capacity now. Half the production is going to extract fuel, crack oxygen, purify water, and make food for the crew. The other half is going to making special items for the sea environment. And, what about the rare elements? Those are hard to find, and we can't make another factory without them. Astatine, lanthanum, erbium, neodymium…"

"I can see you're skeptical—"

"No, Cody, I'm not skeptical. I'm telling you it isn't practical. Not unless you plan to camp down here for a year or more altogether. I have a whole plan to get things done and you're talking about disrupting it."

"How long would your current plan keep us here?" I asked.

"A minimum of three weeks will set us up with a smooth-running operation."

"Too long," I said, shaking my head. "If the Lithos are as single-minded as I believe they are, every day is precious. We have to push harder."

I knew I'd let the crew slack off for several days. Everyone needed a rest and some good sleep. But right now, I wanted to step things up a notch. "We're going to have to go back to extended shifts," I said.

Her eyes widened. "Sixteen hours? That will burn people out. They'll make mistakes."

"No, I was thinking twelve hours. Two shifts per day, rather than three."

She nodded, thinking it over.

"I can do more," she said. "I'll get Hoon looking for the rare elements we need. Then we'll streamline the raw material collection to something better than marines or loaders carrying in chunks. There's too much down time in the process while stuff is loaded in, broken up, and so on."

I could see the wheels were turning in her head so I waited for her thoughts to finish.

She leaned forward as if waking up. "What we need is some sort of sluice. A continuous feed, a conveyor belt that brings in material as fast as the factory can eat it. That way the labor and equipment stay outside, gathering, not wasting time carrying, hefting and shoving stuff into the processor."

I nodded. "That's a good idea."

Sipping her tea, her eyes unfocused as she thought about it. "A day to set up the conveyor belt. It will help if we enforce conservation measures on water and food."

I shook my head. "No way. Work the crew for longer hours if you have to, but they need hot showers, lots of food, and at least one beer a day on average. You're in charge of this, Warrant Officer Turnbull. Don't ask: give orders, kick ass. We may not be getting shot at, but time is life right now. We can sleep after we're dead."

"Slave driver." Her lips quirked upward.

A hundred dangerous responses to that quip suggested themselves to me, but I just smiled in return. We finished the meal in a more relaxed silence, and then I went back to work.

I kept on my feet constantly trying to be everywhere at once. I gave directions when I needed to, but mostly I resolved disputes among tired, irritable people, keeping a smile plastered on my face.

I put on undersea armor and worked alongside the marines for a shift at a time. It felt good to do something physical. Sometimes I stood guard with a laser rifle and beamed down the occasional native shark. There were a lot of aggressive species here—far worse than back home on Earth. Most of the time I spent loading shovels full of sea floor into the hopper, which took it to the conveyer that carried the endless tons up the ship's ramp and into the factory room.

Hoon proved to be invaluable when it came to locating the rare elements we needed. He took a sea-scooter we built for him and scoured the seafloor. I sent marines along with him as he seemed to have no fear of the local life. He insisted they wouldn't like his flavor, but some of the big predators might have swallowed him by the time they realized he wasn't tasty.

Another conveyor belt, more underwater loaders, and the next phase got underway. First I directed a series of enormous domes be built, each a hundred yards across. We made them from constructive nanites, inflating them with air pressure and fitting structural supports as they expanded. One of them surrounded *Valiant* to make it much easier to repair and refit the battlecruiser.

Our single factory never stopped operating and never broke down. It was a marvel of engineering, combining the best of the Macro and Nano technologies. Because we had templates for every conceivable naval system, all Adrienne had to do was make sure the factory stayed full of materials and out came the goodies in a steady stream. Substitutions had to be made for lack of certain exotic elements, but we were able to procure almost everything we needed by digging deep into the sea floor.

The ships I was planning to build weren't Star Force regulation-standard, naturally. They were thin-walled tin cans that lacked all but the most critical systems. Anyone who piloted one of these flying crates wasn't going to enjoy it since the only pressurized living space would be inside their own spacesuits.

We moved the ship factory outside *Valiant* into one of the domes for ease of access. The dome was really a geodesic structure of construction nanites mixed with calcium and other deposits scooped right off the floor of the cold ocean. The nanites were programmed to seal up if a dome sprung a leak, but I wouldn't want to be inside one if the Lithos came back and bombed anywhere near this position.

"All right," I said to Adrienne and Sakura as we sat at the boards that controlled our factory. Rather than leaving them separate, I'd suggested they be placed facing each other, like a piano player with two keyboards. That way one person could monitor both. "One small item would help before we make our next move. I need an ultra-stealthy directional laser transceiver that we can get on the surface in order to talk to Marvin. It needs to be undetectable. I figure he's painting the moon with a coded signal from time to time, and we need to be able to find and return it."

"We can do that," Sakura said, pushing her black hair behind her ears.

"Good. After that, our next project is to build antiproton beams. That's what the Pandas used, and that's what our think-tank people say is the fastest way to kill Lithos." That admission had been dragged from the scientists, and I'd had to intimidate them a bit. They probably thought I was a tyrant, but I couldn't let misguided ethics stand in the way of my plan.

"The mechanisms are completely different, so we'll have to replace the guts on everything," Sakura said. "I don't want to give up lasers completely, though. What if we run into something new?"

"Is there a way to keep both options, other than just splitting them half and half?" I asked.

"I was thinking about that," Sakura said. "There's no perfect solution, but the limiting factor is not usually the number of turrets. There's enough hull space to place twice as many weapons. The problem is a lack of power and human operators. Especially with these antiproton beams."

"So what you mean is, we can just make and install the APs," I said, coining a term for the antiproton weapons, "and hook them up alongside the lasers?"

"More or less. We'll have to make sure they don't interfere with each other, and—"

I waved. "I know there will be tradeoffs. I trust you to figure out the details. Consider the project approved. Set up an equivalent AP for each laser. Let the gunners switch between them at will but not use both at the same time. Also, since we'll be keeping fewer crewmen aboard *Valiant*, use the extra space for more generators and capacitors. This ship needs to be optimized for three functions only: command, control, and combat."

Adrienne nodded. "I assume we'll want AP weapons for the marines, but they can only carry one thing at a time."

"They can leave their lasers in the armory or squads can carry a mix. Once the weapons are done, start making improved missiles optimized against the Lithos. Throw in whatever else you can think of. I also want some smart mines with repellers on them that we can drop out and fly into position. Stealthy ones, if you can, with nukes." I paused to let them catch up in their note-taking and then went on. "What about anti-snowflake defense? Maybe a tall turret that can depress a small AP weapon enough to shoot them off of our hulls? Or is there anything else that you've thought of?"

"I have a few ideas," Sakura said. "What next?"

Now she was getting it. I wasn't interested in a long technical discussion. Those were fun, but I didn't have time to indulge myself as the commander.

"Once you've got *Valiant* into shape, we'll need more ships. What will a Litho-killer look like?" Both of the women gazed at me, puzzled. "I mean, if you could design a ship of any size—specifically to fight the Lithos—how would you make it?"

They didn't answer, except to look thoughtful. I could see my question had seeded their fertile imaginations. "Okay, let me give you a few parameters and you can get to work. I want the new ships to be operable by at least one and no more than six crewmen—whatever works best. They have to be able to keep up with *Valiant*, and operate with her. Our people have to know they can survive contact with the enemy. They each need an escape pod in case they get swarmed by snowflakes." I took a breath. "They also each need a powerful self-destruct if all else fails. Better a clean death than being crushed and digested by Lithos."

I could see that last requirement bothered them somewhat, but they would get over it. I wasn't looking for kamikazes, but just like every marine could overload his power pack, these ships would be able to self-destruct.

"The new ships can be any size, by the way. Don't think that because the crews are small, the ships have to be small too, unless that's the best solution. My goal is to have the most combat power per *person*, not per ton. People are our limitation. Hell," I revised my own instructions, "if you think a fully automated, pilotless ship is the way to go, I'll consider that too. Now get to work on all those things. We'll meet once a day talk about your progress. Feel free to call me whenever you need to."

Getting up, I smiled encouragingly at them both and then took my leave. I turned at the door to see them with their heads together over the design screens, already deep in planning their production runs. That was what I wanted. Give them a goal and let them come up with solutions.

I had another dozen items I wanted them to produce, refit or add, and was thinking of more all the time, but we had only so much time so I had to prioritize. While I had no clue what kind of timetable the Lithos would impose on us—would they gather all their forces and blockade or bombard the moon, lose interest and go home, or something in between?—I had my own idea of how long we could wait.

I remembered reading studies on submarine crews done by the US Navy back in the twentieth century. While a nuclear sub itself could theoretically stay submerged for as long as the food held out, crew performance started to degrade rapidly after about ninety days without a significant stand-down.

We'd been more or less locked aboard one battlecruiser with each other for more than two months. We now had some living improvements—the big domes where people could jog or play sports, the ability to manufacture alcohol and other supplies and the mixed nature of the crew allowing pairing up. But I still figured that the three-month time limit was a rule of thumb. I wanted to stay down here no more than another month before breaking out and giving everyone something to think about other than how annoyed they were with each other.

Already we'd had a few brawls. As everyone was nanotized, these weren't terribly dangerous, as long as noncoms were around to step in and keep anyone from getting killed, but disciplinary problems represented a danger sign for me.

Kwon was back on his feet now, with a supporting lower body exoskeleton to help him walk around. Legs didn't grow back that fast, not even with the help of nanites, and we didn't have any Microbe bath facilities. The good news was that he could still knock heads and keep order. Gunny Taksin was relieved about that, I could tell. The man was a good noncom, but he was no Kwon. Nobody was.

To relieve some tension, especially among the marines, I suggested Kwon set up one-on-one bouts with rules—boxing or cage-fighting, whatever he thought was appropriate. He took the idea and ran with it, and soon we had our own ultimate fighting championships. You'd think marines would have no energy after working long sea-floor mining shifts, but a few always felt like beating the crap out of their fellows while the rest got to watch.

-26-

After a week went by and the weapons work was underway, I insisted on seeing the draft of the new ship design. It turned out they had two.

Sakura wanted a blizzard of small, simple, automated combat drones the size of Fleet fighters. They would be directed by crewmen aboard *Valiant* with local control systems located in a half-bright brainbox on board. Each would have one AP and two missiles in external racks. It would be highly maneuverable but would need refueling fairly often. In essence, it would turn *Valiant* into a carrier or mothership, with half our fighting power in our combat drones.

Sakura's plan also had the advantage of being able to kamikaze these small ships without loss of life. It would be simple enough to replace ships even if *Valiant* was in space, as long as we had the raw materials.

The other design, Adrienne's, was for a three-man frigate. A tenth the size of a battlecruiser, these ships would be more independent and capable of long-range missions. The frigates could also carry significant firepower, not needing much space for people. The ships would be built for maximum power, weapons and engines. Lightly armored, it would be sort of a gunboat with multiple missiles and beams. Adrienne had taken my suggestion about anti-snowflake turrets to heart and there were special APs at strategic spots that could sweep along the skin to burn off any snowflakes before they cracked the hull.

I debated with myself for a whole day before splitting the difference and telling them to make both. First we'd build several manned battle frigates and then as many unmanned combat drones as we thought we could control. This added some complexity to our operations—but also a lot of flexibility.

At my direction, Hansen and our noncoms took the design specs and set up a training program for the new positions. The battle frigates each needed a pilot and a gunner. The third position was for a marine, and he or she needed basic competency to take over either of the other two spots. I could have gone with just two seats, but I wanted these little ships to be able to repel a boarding snowflake or two and keep fighting in space. Somehow, marines always seemed to save the day, so I insisted on them as part of the package.

Hansen had wanted separate training simulators, but I vetoed that idea as too complex. The ships would have a power-down simulation mode, and as each came off the assembly line he could use it as a training device. I made sure their engines and generators were to be installed last. I didn't want any new gunners accidentally blazing away with real weapons inside our domes.

Valiant's gunners also needed to learn new procedures with the APs, and we trained every remaining crewman and marine to direct the combat drones. These would fight in flights of two like old-style atmospheric jets: a lead and a wingman—or wingbrain—per ship. Each director could be assigned as many flights as he or she could handle. In a pinch, I could direct all of them through *Valiant*'s brainbox since the humans weren't really flying them but merely giving orders to their brains.

In the end, we were able to manufacture fifty of the little unmanned craft, an amazing accomplishment born of a lot of hard work and an abundance of raw materials. With the squadron of battle frigates surrounding *Valiant*, we'd have a tough little task force.

During all this time, the whales watched us. Hoon did his best to communicate with them. He eventually declared them highly intelligent animals, almost sentient, like Earthly apes or dolphins. If there was a fully sentient race on this moon, they hadn't come near enough for us to notice, and we weren't wasting any effort on scouting.

We'd constructed a separate dome for Hoon filled with seawater, filtered and conditioned to his liking. He said the native fluid contained an excess of certain minerals and was slightly low in oxygen, but otherwise he seemed comfortable. I supposed the conditions were analogous to humans on a world with thin air that stank. The resources we diverted were actually quite minimal, and I wanted to make sure we didn't get blindsided by some kind of native kraken or waterborne parasite. I considered Hoon's dome a form of insurance as well as good diplomatic relations.

One day I took the time to inspect his operation. Inside his enclosure, he had a whole zoo—a menagerie of local creatures which looked more or less like Earthly sea life, but I was far from an expert. To me, the fish looked like fish, the crustaceans like crustaceans, with all sorts of variants filling the many ecological niches.

In one pen, it appeared that he'd cultivated hundreds of lobsters closely resembling his own species, except they were much smaller.

"Your evolutionary equivalents?" I asked him, leaning on the slick retaining wall that ensured none of the critters climbed out of the pen.

My smart suit performed well underwater and I'd become accustomed to operating in a liquid medium. I leaned close and eyed the lobsters, and they eyed me. What seemed odd to me was the universal fixation of their focus. They stared as if I was the one being studied in a cage instead of the other way around.

"Don't be ridiculous," Hoon said. "Even if these *were* native life, the likelihood of such a close equivalent evolving would be infinitesimal."

"Uh huh," I said, wondering if Hoon had ever met up with a terrestrial lobster. Staring at the crawly things mesmerized me for a moment, and my mind was distracted enough that I almost missed Hoon's meaning.

"*Wait* a minute," I said. "What do you mean 'even if these were native life'? What else could they be?"

Hoon's motions became agitated, reminding me of Marvin when he wasn't certain of my reaction to something. I guess every species has a fight-or-flight response that manifests itself similarly. Hoon was easier to read without a suit. Unlike Marvin, he didn't try to dodge or dissemble.

"They're my offspring, of course," he admitted.

"Ah...." That was a stunner. "Congratulations. Um...are you female?"

"Don't be ridiculous. If I were female I would have programmed my translator to sound to you like a female of your species. In my species, the male carries the eggs after the female lays them, and they are fertilized in a proper ceremony. I've had them itching and aching in my under-pouches for months. Some of the eggs quickened and hatched when they sensed the presence of a large volume of water."

"Some of... How many of them are there?"

"In total? Over two hundred."

I realized by now that the little Crusties had lined themselves up in semicircular rows and seemed to be intently listening to my conversation with Hoon...with their father, I should say.

"Cute little buggers," I said.

"Do not patronize me. I know how your people see our form—we resembled a food delicacy on Earth. Disgusting. Do not for one moment think my children are available for your consumption."

"I wouldn't ever consider *eating* them, Professor Hoon," I said. "But I bet they're going to eat us out of house and home, and we don't really have room for them on the ship. So...what's your plan here? Are you planting a colony?"

"Exactly. A wild colony, to be sure, but one that will be compatible with the local ecosystem. I will educate these children as much as possible and leave brainboxes to teach them of their people and their storied history."

Appalled, I said, "You're just leaving them? Half-grown children, with machines to raise them?"

"Our people aren't like yours," Hoon said with an air of one giving a lecture. "Our young are turned out into the wild and the fittest survive. Those that return full-grown receive an extensive education. This is only logical. How else can the race improve?"

"Why not protect and educate them yourself, so they all grow up to contribute?"

"Ah, you are a revolutionary!" he said with amusement. "You should understand that in my society these infants would have already been released into the wilderness. Not one in a hundred would survive to adulthood. For years I have longed to conduct an experiment doing as you suggest. I hope that by letting them grow bigger and giving them some skills, at least one in ten will survive. Perhaps even one in five! If I tried this among others of my kind, I would become a pariah—possibly losing my status entirely."

That put a different perspective on things. To Hoon, leaving the children here, protected by the dome and educated by automated systems, was already a radical improvement on the norm. I had no doubt his "experiment," as he put it, was just that: a test of a new way of doing things and not a concession to fatherly feeling. Ever the scientist, the main emotion Hoon felt was curiosity. In human terms, he was practicing a form of eugenics: experimentation on children and their development.

Part of me was horrified, but I found the larger part of myself in agreement with Hoon. What could possibly be wrong with giving each and every one of these weird little kids staring at me a better chance at life? And who was I to judge another sentient race's procreative customs?

"Hoon, there are depths to you I never imagined. Congratulations on the birth of your many children. You have my blessing to plant a colony here."

Actually, I rather liked the idea of leaving a part of our alliance here on this moon even with the danger from the Lithos. In a few generations, there should be so many lobsters running around this planetoid that some would survive no matter what the Lithos did. The ruthless part of me also thought that anything that made long-term trouble for the rocky bastards was all right by me.

"Captain Riggs, your single-minded dedication to our mission of getting home almost makes up for your deficient intellect and education—no, do not thank me for this compliment: it is well deserved. I do appreciate your tacit approval of my plan and hope you can come visit my laboratory again next month. Goodbye."

With that, he turned his tail to me and scuttled nimbly over to another enclosure. I had been dismissed.

To Hoon, I was nothing more than the flunky in charge of the ship that carried him. I could have gotten irritated, but I chose to laugh instead. He was what he was and wasn't likely to change. The most I could hope for was to get some use out of him, and to that end, keeping him more or less happy seemed like a good investment.

My next order of business was to take a look at a stealthy sensor package I had ordered prepared. Soon it was ready to go up through the ice. Using a mechanical drill to limit any heat signature, it tunneled its way slowly upward through two hundred feet of frozen water, trailing a cable of smart metal connecting it to *Valiant*'s brainbox.

If I hadn't known better, I'd have thought the ship was getting bored, although it may have been merely an excess of processing capacity that made it seem excited at the prospect of seeing the outside world. After all, it had plenty to look at on the sea bed and in the water. Still, it was programmed for space, not oceans, and even a computer might be said to have a comfort zone.

Once the sensor package poked its pickups and cameras above the endless ice, some hours passed before we learned anything. Nothing seemed close in the sky. No Lithos lurked in orbit as far as we could see. Without active sensors, though, we couldn't be sure. The Lithos had little in the way of heat or radiation signatures that we could detect with this minimal package. Their bigger ships would give off some gamma, but mostly I knew we would have to spot them optically as they crossed in front of bright stars or perhaps flew between us and the glowing gas giant below.

Eventually we were able to see several Litho cruisers in far planetary orbit. Once we'd worked out their patterns, it became clear that enough of them were patrolling to keep our ice moon under close surveillance at all times.

This fact relieved my mind quite a lot. Sure, it was possible they were preparing some kind of massive response, maybe a fleet hiding in a counter-orbit on the opposite side of Matterhorn 6. Had it been me setting the trap, I'd have made it look like no one was watching. I doubted they were trying to trap us. However, I warned myself against thinking of them as humans. They weren't, and I had to remember that.

Half a day later we heard what I had been waiting and hoping for: a low-power encrypted laser transmission from Marvin. While the Lithos might detect this, the chance seemed minimal, even though the laser spot was probably hundreds of miles wide. Of course, Marvin had no idea where we were on the moon, so he had to spread the beam out. He was risking detection, but knowing the crazy robot I figured he'd built that into his calculations. Maybe he was using a small laser relay drone, or a mirror, to hide his real location.

Once the duty noncom called me to *Valiant*'s bridge, I read:

Greetings, Captain Riggs. I've cracked Litho codes and can interpret their language now, though intercepting transmissions has proven difficult. They use point-to-point packets of moderated gamma rays, not broadcasts. I also believe they primarily "see" in the gamma and X-ray bands. I will forego more detailed data to minimize detection risk. Also, I have observed an important development: the Lithos are massing a fleet near the Matterhorn 7 ring-world. From my limited signals intelligence, I believe their purpose involves the ring, and not Valiant*. Beyond that, I do not know.*

-Aboard Greyhound, *Captain Marvin out.*

While fascinating, there was a lot Marvin had left unsaid, but at least it appeared he'd managed to report the most critical fact about the Litho fleet. But I wished he'd given me a basic idea of how many ships they had. I also noticed he hadn't asked me to acknowledge the signal or to send him further instructions.

The time stamp on the message said it had been recorded less than a day earlier. Clearly, the time had come to make our move. I put myself on the base-wide PA and made an announcement.

"This is Captain Riggs. We've just received word that the Lithos are massing a fleet near this system's outer ring at Matterhorn 7. We're now on watch-and-watch. Mothball the base and prepare the squadron for departure. I want us ready in twelve hours, people, so get your asses in gear. Riggs out."

-27-

"What is it, Hoon?" I asked. "I'm very busy right now."

I hurried down a passageway. The lobster kept up with me easily, churning and scratching the deck with his many legs.

"I came to protest our departure," Hoon said. "There's far more we need to learn about the life forms on this moon."

"Sorry, Professor. We've got to go. If we stay, we may never get another chance to leave the system."

"But why not simply remain here and build a civilization? In a generation, we will be able to rise up with a thousand ships and destroy these dirt-bound marauders."

"We humans can't have five thousand children at one time. Besides, this world isn't our kind of place. It's your kind of habitat. Stay and build a colony yourself, and good luck." I turned to walk away.

"I will consider your offer," Hoon said.

With a backward wave of my hand I departed, dismissing him as he had earlier dismissed me. In the end, he didn't exit the ship. When *Valiant* lifted off, he was still aboard. Maybe he didn't want to be marooned here with hundreds of infant Hoons any more than I did.

We left one dome in place with an expanded brainbox and educational system that Hoon programmed. It would form the core of the new Crustacean base, and his children would be raised with all the knowledge and traditions the professor could cram into it.

I'd given my crew a deadline of twelve hours, but I was secretly happy to be ready in twenty. I ordered everyone to battle stations the moment we fired up the engines. I knew we might have to fight as soon as we rose up out of the cold ocean.

The domes opened behind us to let the seawater in, and the tiny flotilla of ships we'd built proceeded like submarines in our wake. As a group, we traveled toward the open waters of the equator. Above us the ice slowly thinned, and I directed everyone to minimize their use of sonar. Now wasn't the time to alert the enemy that lurked overhead.

A vast gathering of whales soon escorted us, arriving from all directions. They had been summoned first by our pings, and then more came after hearing the low-frequency songs of the creatures themselves. When we finally broke the surface, thousands watched us go. I wondered what they thought of us. Maybe, if their intelligence was high enough, they believed us to be godlike beings descended from the sky. Perhaps we'd accidentally started a primitive religion, and they would worship the colonizing Lobsters. I mentally waved goodbye and put them and the undersea world out of my mind.

I turned my thoughts to the Lithos as I took my place on the bridge. Now that production had been suspended, I'd installed Adrienne as my ops officer and made her responsible for passing commands to the frigates. The combat drone directors now sat at the outer ring of stations on the expanded bridge. Hansen had stayed on as my helmsman and XO, his own decision. I'd offered him his own ship, but after thinking it over for a day, he had decided to stay put. I hadn't asked specifically why he'd chosen that option, but I was glad to have him, despite his attitude.

"Go active on all sensors," I instructed the bridge crew. "Give me maximum squadron acceleration, directly away from the gas giant."

My tiny fleet rose in formation with *Valiant* at the center. The frigates spread out in a sphere around her and the combat drones dispersed farther out, pairing up and patrolling our flanks. This was a flexible, general-purpose formation.

Soon the holotank built a picture of the area around us. Several Litho cruisers still hung in the skies. The nearest moved to intercept us. Our combined speeds would put us in beam range within minutes.

"Parabolic formation, focus on the cruiser," I ordered.

"Parabolic formation," Adrienne echoed, and she sent orders to the frigates while the crew at the controller stations sent instructions to the combat drones.

On the holotank, I saw the squadron formation change shape into a concave dish with its inward curve toward the Lithos. Against a single enemy or small formation, this gave us maximum firepower while ensuring none of us got in each other's way.

"Pass the word, use lasers only. I say again, *lasers only*. Begin firing at extreme range."

"But sir," Hansen protested, "APs will be much more effective. We could get close enough to hit them with dozens of beams and probably take them down."

"Precisely, Mister Hansen: *probably*. I'd rather not clue them in to our real power. I'm following Sun Tzu's advice: 'When strong, appear weak. When weak, appear strong.'"

Adrienne passed along my orders, and soon our heavy main lasers peppered the Litho cruiser with long-range shots. Blasts blew chunks of rock and dirt off the enemy ship as the beams impacted and converted themselves to heat, causing far less damage than the APs would. We might be killing Litho-nanites by the trillions, but crystal and dirt took a lot of energy to vaporize with lasers.

Even so, each of the twelve frigates carried one such main laser, and *Valiant* had two. With fourteen beams slamming into the cruiser, we quickly tore it apart, and then it did what I expected. The big ship began to disintegrate and break up into fighters.

By this time, our medium lasers were in optimal range as well as the heavy APs, but no APs fired. Only our medium lasers joined the chorus, and we quickly shredded the enemy small craft despite their attempts to evade.

Moments later, the few surviving Litho fighters broke up into snowflakes, aiming at us.

"All ships brake," I said. "Combat drones engage. Frigates, pull up close around *Valiant*. Take your time and burn them all, using lasers only."

Hansen shook his head at my orders, but said nothing. I didn't bother to explain it to him. I wanted to exterminate every Litho fighter launched by that cruiser, and to do that, I couldn't have our two formations flashing through each other. If they did, we'd miss some of the snowflakes.

I'd thought long and hard about this tactic—or perhaps it could have been called a policy. Adrienne had argued against it, but eventually I'd convinced her mind, if not her heart, that I was right. At first she'd thought it was too much like burning escaping crewmen who'd abandoned ship. But after I explained that I believed the snowflakes were their marines, not their crew, she understood. In actuality, I wasn't sure if they differentiated between the two before breakup, or if these snowflakes were even distinct individuals until they had been calved. Certainly, the Lithos regarded them as completely expendable, unlike our feelings for our own marines.

Therefore, I wanted to hunt them all down. My theory was that by doing so, we might deny the enemy whatever intel they might have gained by fighting us—by getting close to us. I hoped that the cruiser we killed couldn't make a detailed report in the heat of battle. By exterminating all trace of them, I hoped we would leave the other Lithos believing all we had done was build up our numbers and not improved our weaponry and defenses.

Another cruiser moved to intercept us, but I ordered my ships to turn away, and we easily outdistanced it. Once it became obvious they couldn't catch up, their ship broke up into fighters as I'd expected it would. That was their fastest form, and the only one that could catch us other than their missiles.

"Combat drones keep retreating, the rest move into a convex parabolic pattern," I ordered, setting us up for rearward fire. "Continue with lasers only. Pick off the fighters at long range, and expect them to become missiles or snowflakes." With overwhelming firepower and a lot of time to shoot, we easily knocked out all of this next cruiser's military capability.

Another reason to use lasers and take our time with longer ranged shots was to train our many green gunners who'd only fired in simulation mode. Even though the exercise looked the same as live fire, anyone who has ever been in actual combat will tell you the experience is far, far different with real targets. This way when the chips were down, the gunners would be less likely to miss or screw up. This was especially true with the cross-trained marines, who had a tendency to get a little…*excitable* with the bigger guns.

Once I was certain the Lithos would be polished off or outrun, I reset the holotank so half of it showed me the situation around the greenish gas giant, Matterhorn 7, where Marvin had reported the ring moon and the other half showed me the Litho fleet. I still couldn't make out much detail because we had nothing but passive sensor readings to go on. It would take about a half hour for our radar pulses to reach them and the same time to return. This would lessen rapidly as we accelerated hard toward our destination.

On passive sensors I could see the modest gas giant and its moons, including what we were sure was the hollow ring moon. In orbit around that moon circled a cloud of ships. They were impossible to count at this distance, but there were certainly over a hundred; and all were cruisers or larger.

"Damn," I muttered. "I'd hoped the forty they sent after us was the bulk of their forces."

"That's too many for us to go up against," Hansen said, looking worriedly at me.

I ignored him, trying to think. He shook his head and muttered as I continued to stare at the holotank.

"We've got almost a day before we get there," I said at last, "even at normal speed. Cut acceleration by half, and divert our course a bit so that we can more easily curve away if we have to. Keep us outside their engagement envelope. I need to see what the active sensors say, and I want to get Marvin's report before we commit to anything." I was sure my unstable mechanical officer had observed a lot in the last three months, and I needed that intel.

Unfortunately Marvin wasn't responding to our radio broadcasts or wide-beam com-laser pointed in his general direction. Hopefully he would get in contact when he felt safe.

Within the hour our radar returns from Matterhorn 7 outlined the situation, though I wasn't certain it clarified the picture. Roughly two hundred forty Litho ships orbited the moon we believed contained a ring. About half matched the cruisers we had encountered before. The others ranged in power from destroyers to battleships, in Litho terms, not ours.

"Looks like there's an asteroid with them," Hansen said as he came up beside me to view the holotank. With so far to go and no immediate threats, he was doing the right thing by shifting to XO mode and discussing tactics with his boss.

"I doubt it's an asteroid, at least, not anymore. These are Lithos, remember? Given what we know about how they operate, what useful things could they do with an asteroid?"

Hansen put his nose to the holotank glass. "I guess they could seed it, infect it, or whatever they do to turn it into a ship."

I clapped the older man on the back, drawing an annoyed look. "That's what I was thinking. It's a ready-made dreadnought, five miles long and two wide."

"Too big for us to handle."

It was my turn to be annoyed. "Hansen, we're not going to *handle* it. I didn't build this fleet to wage pitched battles with dreadnoughts. I didn't even build it to exterminate Lithos. I built it first and foremost as a show of strength, to try to get the Lithos to deal with us. If that doesn't work, it's fast enough to run, strong enough to fight, and flexible enough to get us home."

"Then I have to ask, *sir*, why we're heading for that fleet!"

"We're not heading for the Lithos' fleet, Mr. Hansen. We're heading for the ring, and their fleet happens to be in the way."

"Same difference, isn't it?"

Exasperated, my voice became harsh, but I spoke quietly enough that no one other than Hansen and Adrienne could hear.

"Hansen, you've been a pilot too long," I said. "You need to get your head out of your ass and look at the big picture. Stop looking at the obstacles and start looking at the goals. Tell me, when you're doing a tricky piece of manual flying, where do your eyes go? To the thing you might hit?"

Hansen frowned fiercely, and for a second I didn't think he would answer. Finally, he shook his head. "I look where I'm going, not at the obstacle."

"Exactly. When it's time to fight, killing enemy ships is our objective. But until then, our goal is to get through that ring. Firepower is just a means to that end."

Hansen slowly nodded. "Okay. I get it. So...how are we going to get through the ring?"

"I wish I knew. But," I held up my index finger and raised my voice to normal again, "I do see an opportunity here."

"Opportunity?" he echoed.

"Look at Matterhorn 3 with the ring that goes to the Pandas." I gestured to the half of the holotank that showed the rest of the system.

"There aren't any ships there."

"Exactly."

"But..." he rubbed his face. "Okay, how is it an opportunity when the entire enemy strength seems to be blocking our way out?"

"*Seems to be* is the key. To figure out what the enemy will do, you have to put yourself in his place. If you were the Lithos, would you just park your whole fleet at that exit if the goal was to kill us?"

"I guess not. So what are they doing?"

"I'm not sure yet, but I don't believe it has much to do with us. What does it look like to you?"

Hansen rubbed his jaw. "Guarding the ring...from someone getting ready to invade them?"

"That's one possibility I thought of. The other is that they're getting ready to invade someone else."

"Someone else? But who?"

"That's what we're going to find out. But now do you understand what I meant when I said this is an opportunity? Either way, there's going to be a fight." I rubbed my hands together. "Hansen, did you ever play strategy games when you were a kid?"

"You mean those online multiplayer things, where you build up and fight everyone until one guy is left?"

"Sure, like that. If you're the weakest guy in a three-way game, what's your strategy?"

Turning to look at me then back to the holotank, he said, "You get the two bigger guys to fight it out, and then you come in to finish off the winner."

"Exactly!" I slapped my fist with my palm. "Except the situation is even better for us. If the Lithos win, we might be able to wipe out their remaining strength and save the day for the other guys, in which case we'll be heroes to them. If the other guys look like they're winning, we can swoop in and contribute, showing that we're a potential ally or at least, anti-Litho."

"What if they're fighting the Macros?" Hansen asked.

That stopped me for a moment. "That's a smart question, something I hadn't thought of. Hmm. In that case, my instinct would be to make sure the Lithos don't lose, and I'll tell you why. If we'd been facing forty Macro cruisers and all the resources of a Macro-owned system, we'd be dead by now. If the next system is Macro-owned, and the Lithos are making a push, we need to slip through behind them. We'll shadow them like jackals following lions as they hunt."

"You seem to have everything figured out, sir."

I looked sharply at Hansen, trying to tell if he was being honest, sarcastic, or a kiss-ass. "I'm sure I don't. It's part of your job as XO to ask me hard questions so keep it up."

"No problem."

I wondered if Hansen was going to work out as my Exec in the long term. I'd hoped he'd either be a compliant, steady hand on the tiller, or a workhorse like Sakura. But right now he seemed to be too upset about having an inexperienced captain to focus on his job. Unfortunately, I didn't know of anyone better, unless I pulled Sakura out of engineering, which I wasn't prepared to do.

If only Olivia were here instead of Adrienne, she would be my perfect XO. My heart clenched once more within my chest, and I took a deep breath to shake off the threatening melancholy. I always seemed to think about Olivia at the damnedest moments. I reassured myself I would find my way back to Earth and discover who her killer was eventually. Marvin's suggestion that one of the crewmen aboard *Valiant* might have been involved was an idea I'd shelved for now. I couldn't afford to second-guess everything my crew did.

To stave off my feelings, I ran tactical simulations against imaginary Litho forces, and then against simulated Macro forces too, trying to prepare for anything. Hansen watched closely as did Adrienne. Before long, we were immersed in our work. Once we'd fought through several scenarios, I went on a quick tour of the ship and saw that everything was running smoothly. The crew seemed eager, focused, and in good spirits.

Marvin still hadn't responded so I sent a message to Adrienne's console, letting her know I was going to the wardroom for a meal. We still had a larder from the ice moon full of seafood, plants, and animals the science team had identified as safe to eat. Some of it was quite good, and unlike our dwindling Earth stocks, it was fresh.

Given Murphy's law, I figured sitting down to a meal with Adrienne was a surefire way for fate to prompt Marvin to call and interrupt us. If that didn't work, I'd take a nap. Actually, it was only after she'd met me and we'd eaten a leisurely lunch of ice scallops with a purple anemone salad that the expected call came.

We gulped our coffee and hurried up to the bridge.

-28-

Marvin finally contacted me, though only on audio. I suspected he didn't want me to see him. Who knew what kind of monstrosity he had built of himself by now? "Greetings, Captain Riggs. How did you find the ice moon?"

"Cold and wet. Let's skip the pleasantries, shall we?"

"I was merely attempting to conform to human behavioral norms." The reply came back with only a fifteen to twenty second delay, indicating *Greyhound* was reasonably close, but I still hadn't located him on sensors. Marvin was one sneaky robot.

I snorted. "When have you ever done that? Never mind. What have you learned about the Lithos?"

"I've begun transmitting an encrypted data package."

"Give me the most important stuff first," I said.

"The Lithos have opened a tunnel through the crust of the hollow moon orbiting Matterhorn 6."

Marvin sounded puzzled but eager, so I played along. "That surprises you?" I asked.

"From my experiments on the Litho nanites, I would have expected that they would simply land on the outer surface of the planetoid and transfer their templates through to the other side, reforming on the interior of the hollow shell."

"Whoa, slow down, Marvin," I said. "They can transfer themselves through a planet?"

"Only their templates, not their actual mass."

"Explain that."

"Litho templates are what make them something more than a collection of silico-nanites, by organizing them into functioning clusters of nanomachines. The template is analogous to software, while the nanites are infinitely configurable hardware, not so different from our own nanite constructs."

"Maybe transferring through takes time and energy," I said thoughtfully. "Or maybe it's disruptive. Once they form ship templates, it has to be more efficient to remain that way rather than to go—uh—downloading themselves through the dirt or whatever you'd call such a process."

Marvin's voice brightened. "Perhaps you're right."

"Back to the tunnel…how big is it?"

"About ten miles in diameter and one hundred in length."

I zoomed the holotank's display in on the hollow moon and rotated it until I found the hole. Small compared to the size of the moon, I only found it because I was looking for it specifically. "That will make quite a gauntlet to run."

"I believe I have a solution," Marvin said, sounding smug. Then he stopped talking. Obviously he wanted me to bargain for the knowledge he would dispense.

I almost took the bait, but remembered all those stories Dad and Kwon used to tell about how to keep the upper hand with the robot. "That's all right, Marvin. We'll figure something out."

"Aren't you curious about what I intend to do?"

"Hmm. Not terribly. Most of the time the things you want to do are too risky anyway."

"I'll tell you if you want to know." Now Marvin had begun to sound worried.

I injected boredom into my voice. "All right. If you really want to."

"What follows are the most critical elements of my report. I've cultivated and trained my own silico-nanite variant to operate independently of the Lithos, but in their own medium."

"You mean you have altered nanites that will fight for our side in the dirt?" I asked.

"That's what I just said."

"Yes, but I said it a lot more simply. Marvin, are you saying you can infect the Lithos with the altered version and kill them? Like a disease?"

"Unlikely. They're far too numerous and adaptive. My nanites can, however, perform certain specific actions beneficial to us."

"Like nanite commandos? Okay…"

"An apt analogy."

"So what will they do?"

"The possibilities are endless. For example—"

I made a sound of annoyance. "What will they do for us to help us get through the ring?"

"Ah. Such specificity," he said, sounding disappointed. "I believe I can seed the inside of the tunnel with a silico-nanite mist dispensed from missiles, sufficiently virulent to temporarily block its inner surface from complying with Litho control mechanisms."

"So that will hold the tunnel open and keep any defense mechanisms from stopping us?"

"Theoretically. The effect should operate for a limited time—perhaps thirty minutes."

"That should be long enough," I said. "Wait…you said *missiles*? Where did you get missiles?"

"I may have misspoken. These vehicles are more like delivery drones for silico-nanites."

I looked left and right where Hansen and Adrienne manned their stations. Adrienne shrugged and Hansen held up his palms as if to say, *who knows?*

"Marvin, what did you make these drones out of? You didn't dismantle more of *Greyhound*, did you?"

"Absolutely not. *Greyhound* is in excellent condition, and I have in fact improved its effectiveness for my purposes by several hundred percent."

Pacing up and down in front of the holotank, I began to worry. "And just *how* did you do that?"

There was nothing on the channel but silence for ten or fifteen seconds.

"I'm sorry, Captain Riggs, your transmission is fading. If you can hear this, please try to reestablish contact at a later time."

I tried to reopen the channel, but he'd gone silent.

"What the hell is he up to?" I asked no one in particular, throwing my hands up in frustration.

Adrienne cleared her throat. "I might know," she said. "Back when you told me to use *Valiant*'s factory to give him parts and materials to repair himself, he asked for some unusual things. I was so busy…well, I didn't question the requests. But now that I think about it, he may have been able to cobble together a very small factory."

"*What?*" I stared in shock at Adrienne. "That crazy robot has a factory? How big a factory?"

She shrugged. "I don't know. Not bigger than a microwave oven."

"Big enough then. He's had the time, certainly. He's been wandering around for a month or more. There's no end to the trouble he could make. Good God, he could have made fusion weapons!"

"I don't remember you telling me not to give him things," she said stiffly. "In fact, you said to supply him whatever he needed."

After the last months my memory of exactly what I'd said was a bit hazy, and I knew how Marvin could find the slightest loophole in any semantic construct. It wasn't fair to take it out on her, and it was doubly stupid since she was one of my very few friends aboard.

"Right, not your fault," I grumbled. "Marvin pulled another fast one, that's all."

"He wouldn't hurt us anyway," Adrienne said. "He may look all weird and scary, but he's really a pussycat."

"A robotic pussycat with a ship, a factory—maybe missiles, modified nanites, and fusion warheads," I replied. "Don't let him sucker you again. He can be one damned dangerous machine."

"Okay, but we still need his help."

"Let's make sure he needs ours, too," I said. "*Valiant*, thoroughly scan Marvin's data package for malware, clean or quarantine anything questionable, and then upload the data to the holotank. Make sure you keep your own neural circuits isolated."

The brainbox replied, "Command accepted. Processing. Processing complete. Malware detected. Malware quarantined. Data uploaded."

"What was the malware supposed to do?" I asked the ship.

"The intended function is to gather basic ship data and periodically broadcast an encrypted burst."

"That's all? Just gather data, not interfere with anything?"

"Correct."

I thought for a moment. "*Valiant*, create and execute a program that replicates the effects of the malware, but remains under your control. Transmit the data Marvin expects until command personnel say otherwise. Then delete the malware."

This way, I figured Marvin would think he'd slipped a Trojan into our system, but I could feed him false information any time I wanted, just in case he did betray us somehow.

"Program created and running. Malware deleted."

I turned back to the holotank and watched as Marvin's data poured in, dramatically refining details of what we'd known about the system, especially concerning the hollow moon. He must have been watching that small world for most of the last two months using every passive sensor he had—or that he could construct. Hopefully that would work in our favor.

"Hansen, take a close look at this and plot a course to give us the best view you can of that tunnel."

The helmsman nodded. "The signal is emanating from the southern pole, so that should be easy. We'll just park far out in space but in line with the tunnel. What then?"

"Then," I said, "We wait to see what happens."

* * *

The main Litho fleet paid us no attention as we maneuvered well away from them, watching. The several cruisers we had outrun while escaping the ice moon had followed us, but they were now hours behind. As long as they didn't calve into fighters or missiles, we were safe.

"I hope something happens soon," Hansen said, "or we'll have to turn and deal with the cruisers following us."

"You don't like the idea of more target practice?" I asked.

"Why poke the hornet's nest?"

"Because we aren't getting home by playing it safe. And speaking of poking...*Valiant*, have you integrated Marvin's translation program?"

"Program ready."

"Good. Put it online and get ready to transmit on the gamma bands they seem to use."

"But sir!" Hansen interjected.

I turned to give him a hard look. "You wanted to talk to the Lithos before. Have you changed your mind?"

Hansen glanced at the holotank and the hundreds of ships orbiting the moon enclosing the ring ahead of us. "Sir, you laid out a whole tactical plan. We wargamed it, refined it and we're all ready. Talking to them now may change the equation."

"Talking to them was always my first goal. Conflict 101, Hansen. Politics must drive military strategy as strategy drives tactics. Only when politics fail do we fight. Before, we couldn't talk to them. Now we can try, coming from a position of strength. If we don't try diplomacy now, we'll have no choice *but* to fight. Even if we fail, we may gain some useful information." I was talking as much for the crew as for Hansen. People work harder and fight better when they know why they're doing things, as long as explaining doesn't make the leader look weak or defensive.

Hansen subsided, and I noticed Adrienne smiling at me. At least she was with me on this one, which gave me a warm glow of confidence.

"*Valiant*, begin translating and broadcasting to the Lithos."

I paused, gathered my thoughts, and began speaking.

"People of this star system, I greet you in the name of the planet Earth and its people. Despite our recent clashes, we're interested in a peaceful resolution to this conflict. Please reply."

Minutes later words returned. The translation brainbox rendered in flat machine tones to avoid imposing meaning they might not possess. "*Intrusion destruction pain loss cold metal object threat maker imposition anger resolve.*"

I mulled that over then turned to my staff. "Ideas?"

"Nouns and adjectives, no verbs," Adrienne said.

"Not even adjectives, if you count *cold* and *metal* as nouns, not descriptions," I said thoughtfully. "Maybe they think only in terms of concrete objects or concepts. *Intrusion destruction pain loss* could describe our arrival in their system. *Cold metal object* could be our ship. *Threat maker imposition*…that's ambiguous. *Anger resolve* could mean their state of mind toward us."

"Doesn't sound promising," Hansen said.

"At least they're talking." I tapped my fingertips on the armrest of my chair. "Send: *allow*—no, that's a verb. Send: *permission escape negation destruction desire peace*. Make sure they're all translated into noun forms."

"Message sent."

Pacing in front of the holotank, I watched carefully for any sign of a physical reaction from the Lithos, whether favorable or not. Nothing happened immediately.

"Where are the transmissions coming from?" I asked.

One of the cruisers chasing us blinked in the holotank. "The vessel has been marked," *Valiant* said.

I turned back to the display in surprise. I'd expected to be talking to their asteroid-dreadnought, or at least one of the battleships. Based on our theories and Marvin's analysis of their template forms, I thought that larger would equal smarter, or at least more important, as with the Macros. Yet it was a chasing cruiser that replied to our broadcast.

"Strange…" I said.

"Maybe they have a divided command structure, and we're not the main fleet's responsibility," Hansen ventured.

"Maybe. Try hailing Marvin. Tell him I know he has a factory, and I'm not angry."

"Message sent." We waited, but heard nothing from Marvin.

The Lithos replied in the meantime. *"Negation escape peace destruction."*

"Crap. I think they just told us to go to Hell," I said. "Anyone catch anything different from that message?" I looked at Adrienne. She rubbed her face with her palms then left her eyes covered as if that would help her think. The mannerism sent a knife into my gut as I remembered that Olivia used to do that. I wondered how long it would be before I could get back to Earth and find her killer.

A moment later, I scolded myself for my thoughts. Thirty people had lost their lives in the ring mishap that started this whole thing. Why was Olivia so much more important to me than thirty random humans? Maybe it shouldn't be true, but that was just the way I felt. Probably most people were the same even if they wouldn't admit it.

"I can't make that phrase mean anything good," Adrienne finally admitted.

"*Valiant*, transmit the following: *peace desire* then a distinct pause then *truce.*"

We waited for several minutes with only the murmuring of the watch-standers passing reports and coordinating among the crew, breaking the silence. No message returned.

Finally, Adrienne couldn't stand it anymore. "Are they still coming after us?" she asked.

I looked at the holotank. "Yes, no change. Maybe these Lithos are just too alien to converse with on our terms. You'd think the ones following, the ones we're talking to, would care that we're going to kill them all when they arrive. They can't win, and if the main fleet comes toward us, we can run."

Everyone was silent for ten seconds, checking and rechecking the data. Nothing changed.

"They're crazy," I said, breaking the quiet spell. "Four cruisers coming after us and they aren't even joining up to form one squadron. We'll pick them off one by one if they come in separately."

"Sounds good to me," Hansen said.

"Yeah. I guess it *is* good news…but I wish we could at least call a truce."

"Perhaps killing those four ships will put an end to it," Adrienne said. "If they do have a divided command, perhaps each force is like a feudal warlord's vassals. By weakening one, the other feels stronger. We might be doing the main fleet's dirty work for it, while providing them with valuable intelligence on our capabilities."

"Dammit, I feel like I'm in Oz and I can't see behind the curtain. Our only option is a military one."

"So much for your 'show of strength' theory." Hansen said, putting real sarcasm into his voice.

That crossed a line for me. I couldn't let it pass. He was undermining my authority. However, there's a saying in the military: pulling rank means you've lost the argument. Putting a subordinate in his place while neither looking like a bully nor sinking to his level was an art I hadn't yet mastered. I didn't yet have my father's near-absolute command position, his raw physical power, nor his experienced crews. I was just one ensign thrust into the spotlight. Still, I had to try.

Turning a steely stare on Hansen, I eyed him for a moment.

"It's easy to take cheap shots, Helmsman." I locked eyes with him until he lowered his. "Very well."

I turned my back on him, but I wasn't finished yet.

"Pass the word to rotate the watch. *Valiant*, notify me of any significant change in the Lithos' disposition. Mister Hansen, take a walk with me, would you?"

-29-

I led him without comment through the corridors to the ship's pool room. By tradition every ship had one, though it was often officially designated something else like "auxiliary storage," or "recreational spaces." The game was called "pool," but was more like jai-alai with baseball bats.

The object was not to put balls into pockets but to hit the other player with them. The sport combined skill, agility, and hand-eye coordination—as well as requiring a healthy tolerance for pain. While the nanites kept the resulting injuries from maiming the participants, they didn't stop them from hurting.

"Pool?" Hansen looked at me sideways as I palmed open the door.

"An excellent stress relief, don't you think?"

"Yes, I do." He stepped inside, looking around casually at the bumpers, which amounted to small repellers built into the walls. The bumpers allowed for adjustable difficulty, a modern improvement on the plain walls of the past.

Back in the old days, these rooms had been made of hard steel so the balls simply bounced off purely by physics. There was always significant energy loss that way. Modern pool rooms had adjustable repellers that could be set in any way the players wanted, from damping shots up to sending a ball back at exactly the same speed no matter how hard it was hit. On the control pad I changed the settings to "marine," the highest level. Now I could fire a bullet in here and it would ricochet back just as hard.

"What's this really about, Ensign?" Hansen asked.

He was within his rights to call me that, but constantly omitting the courtesy title of *Captain* by definition implied disrespect.

"We need to clear the air," I told him. "A little talk, a little game." I grabbed a ball and bounced it off the nearest wall, catching it again, and then picked up a bat.

"Sounds fine to me."

"Hansen, I don't want you to be a yes man, but you're straying into a disrespectful zone in front of the crew. There's a way to disagree with your commander and a way not to, and you've been around long enough to know the difference. If you have such a hard time with me, why didn't you accept command of your own frigate?"

"Maybe I should have," he said.

"You didn't answer the question."

"You really want to know? *Sir?*" This last came out in a sneer.

"Talk."

"Because I want to be on the bridge when one of your reckless decisions backfires. I want to be there to take over command when you run into something you can't handle and fall apart. I owe that to this crew and this ship. And the way I see it, those frigates are just expendable screens for *Valiant*. I didn't live through the Macro Wars just to become a sacrificial pawn to your ego, and I pity those poor suckers who are."

By this time he'd come up to me and pushed his chest almost into my face. I'm an average-sized guy, a shade under six feet, but Hansen was four inches taller and fifty pounds heavier.

With two nanotized men, size differences mattered. The bigger guy generally had the advantage. I say *generally*, because other factors came into the equation. Skill, experience and so on. In my case, I had my father's DNA, which had been rewritten in Marvin's special baths, as well as the nanites in my blood. I wasn't as strong as my dad, but I was still considerably tougher than the average marine.

I gave him a confident smile. "Sounds like you *want* me to fail. Why is that, Hansen? I've never sacrificed anyone. In fact, I've done my damnedest to bring everyone through alive. There has to be something more. Did your pet turtle die due to one of my father's decisions?"

"You're a smartass, Riggs, just like everyone says. You're so full of yourself you think it's all about you or your heroic daddy. You want to know what's bothering me? I have more time in Star Force than you've been alive. You're fresh out of the Academy and six experienced officers died so you could take command in front of me on a technicality. That's bullshit, and you know it. I should be in charge."

My smile widened into a grin. "At least you're being honest now. You want to be the boss. And you know what? If I was certain you'd be the better captain, I'd turn it over to you." I wasn't actually so sure about that, but the line sounded good. "But clearly, you're not."

"Clearly? How is that clear?"

"After the captain got eaten, you wanted to punish the Pandas. That would have been suicide."

"It was a natural impulse to attack the Pandas."

"Could you have gotten us through that ring?"

"I would never have gone through the ring. That was your first crazy move. I would've stayed in the Panda system, outrunning them until we found a safe place to repair and rebuild. Now look at us! We're more screwed than ever, in the middle of a battle with fleets ten times our strength and an enemy worse than the Pandas. You know what I think?"

"Now's the time to tell me," I prompted him.

"You're still a boy. I think you want to hunt aliens, get some trophies, and prove you're just as good as your old man. And you want to do it all with your highborn princess by your side. If you want to get home, it's only because you're trying to live up to your father's reputation for fighting and screwing everything in sight. It doesn't matter to you how many people you kill to do it."

I stared at him for a second. "You think quite a lot of yourself, don't you?" I asked him.

He snorted at me and shook his head.

"You know," I said thoughtfully, "I have no problem with you pulling me aside and arguing your position, but by regulation—and frankly, by suitability—I'm the captain of this ship. You're the best man I have for XO but this habit of undercutting me in front of the crew is going to stop today, one way or another."

"It's going to stop? Why? Because you say so?" He looked at me in disbelief.

"No. Because I'm going to prove to you I'm the better man."

"You're not going to do that," he said, laughing.

I gave him an unblinking stare. "I'm going to make your day, Hansen. We'll have a contest of your choice. Pool? A fistfight? Lasers at fifty paces? Whatever you want. If I win, you lose the baggage, straighten up, and accept my right to command. If you win, I'll turn over command to you."

Hansen eyed me with a hungry expression. I could tell he wanted what I was offering, but he was a little wary. His eyes searched my face. "A duel, huh? Is that the only option?"

"Are you scared?" I asked him, smiling a little.

He smiled back. "Hardly. You're cocky—and kind of skinny."

"Then choose," I said.

He took a step toward me. I stood my ground.

"You'll really give up command?" he asked. "Why?"

"Because I'm not going to have an XO I can't trust to back me up one hundred percent. So, make your choice or wet yourself and back down. We only have about ten hours until the first Litho cruiser comes into range."

His face darkened. "Let's play pool," he said.

I felt relieved. A fistfight would have been more iffy and lasers would have risked serious injury or death—but pool allowed for a gentlemanly contest. I congratulated myself on manipulating his choice. I'd deliberately led him here, thereby planting the suggestion of playing pool in his mind. What he also didn't know was that I'd been the star of one of the Academy intramural pool teams and even then I'd held back my full capability.

"Here," I threw him the one-ball. "You first."

Hansen rolled his shoulders and warmed up a bit, tossing the ball from hand to hand. "Ready?"

I nodded, standing relaxed.

Winding up, he batted a hard two-bank shot aimed center mass, a standard ploy. It came in fast and it looked like he was quite good—for a ship's crewman. I stood there and took it in the chest.

"Good shot," I said, coughing only twice. I wanted to run my fingers over my ribs and determine if he'd cracked them, but I resisted the urge. I forced a confident grin and waited for his next swing.

When he batted again, a two-banker, I stepped aside and caught the ball as it went past. Without pausing, I let the momentum carry me around and fired a straight one-bank off the far wall. The pitch resembled an old-fashioned fastball. The hard sphere bounced into his back almost as fast as I had thrown it, which was very fast indeed. It slammed into his left kidney before he could more than begin to dodge. He staggered, grunting.

"What the hell...?" he muttered, eyeing me in shock.

"My shot again," I said, locating the three-ball and this time using the bat.

Crack! The ball streaked to the floor and bounced up at a wicked angle, but missed his hastily covered testicles. Instead, I nailed him in the thigh. He hunched then straightened determinedly. His eyes were already bloodshot, and he watched me with bared teeth.

"Four-ball in two," I announced. This shot banked twice and nailed him in the buttocks. He almost dodged it, but I was cranking up the velocity of my strikes each time.

Most marines could bat a ball at about a hundred fifty miles an hour, which meant the heavier ball carried much more kinetic energy than an average baseball. I could nearly double that speed with my inherited Microbe physique, meaning my shots hurt more than a baseball batted right into a bystander.

By the time I made my final shot, I almost felt sorry for him. It struck him in the shoulder, and I heard a bone snap as he was knocked to the floor. After picking up the nine-ball, I bounced it in my hand and looked at him expectantly where he lay. To his credit, he'd taken eight shots in a row without conceding.

"That's game," I said, putting my hands on my knees and staring at him.

"You cheated," he gasped, rolling painfully onto his back. "That's impossible for a normal human, even nanotized. You've got some kind of enhancements."

I shrugged. "I used every advantage I had to win the game within the rules, just as I always do. So no, I didn't cheat. You chose the contest. You didn't have all the intel you needed, and you made a poor choice."

"And I was going to take it easy on you," he said ruefully, rubbing his broken shoulder. "Okay, Riggs, I'll live up to my part of the bargain, but that doesn't mean I believe you're the better commander."

"I hope for all our sakes you're wrong."

I held out a hand for him to take. He hesitated, but finally did so. I lifted him to his feet by his good arm, letting him feel the effortless strength I kept leashed inside.

"Eventually you'll change your mind," I told him. "If not, you can always have a frigate to command. And for your information, I don't intend to sacrifice ships with crews in them. That's what the combat drones are for. Now, let's go get a beer."

After splitting two of my hoarded Earth beers with Hansen, I sent him to the medical bay. I knew he'd be feeling better in an hour, and almost one hundred percent by morning. Nanites were wonderful things.

I didn't return to the bridge immediately. Instead, still feeling the adrenaline from the confrontation, I grabbed a couple of cold cases of factory beer from stores and went down to marine country in the ship's belly-pods. Handing three bottles per man or woman, I shared a drink with the troops, slapped backs, and traded dirty jokes. Marines tended to be coarser than Fleet, but that was because their duties were harder, their job descriptions more dangerous, and their life expectancies shorter than the crewmen. They were the ones that engaged enemies personally, hand-to-hand and face-to-face, and I loved and respected them for that.

"Hey," I said to Corporal Lopez, whom I'd just beaten arm-wrestling, "you want to play something you can win?" Showing the marines I was better than they were at something was good leadership.

"Sure, sir," he said.

"I need some suit practice. Force on force sim, what do you say?" The battlesuits could be occupied in simulation mode, and though they would never leave their niches, from the point of view of those inside, they would be running around fighting through any scenario in memory.

"Oo-rah, sir!" he said, with the others around joining in the cheer. Oddly enough, letting them show *they* were better at something was also good leadership. Mutual respect.

We suited up enthusiastically and soon were crawling, running, and jumping through blasted landscapes, "shooting" each other with realistic enthusiasm. I insisted we set the suits on hurt mode, so we would feel some of the pain of being shot via feedback circuits.

I got hurt a lot. I didn't care. In a way, it felt good. Maybe I was punishing myself a little bit for my own arrogance, because inside the suit's VR world, my extra strength and speed didn't mean squat. It was set to do what an average marine could do, no more, no less, and I was happy to see these troops were good at their jobs. They kicked my ass all over the battlefields of a dozen planets, moons, and spaceships.

Roman emperors used to have a guy that followed them around saying, "Remember, you are mortal," at intervals, just to remind them they weren't really the gods they claimed to be. I figured this could be my version.

Some people might wonder how I could be doing all this while hovering off a hostile planet in a war zone, but throughout history, naval combat has always involved long stretches of waiting punctuated by short periods of blazing hell. The British of the wooden ships era didn't beat to quarters until a half hour or less before engagement, and always made sure the men were fed a hot meal first.

That's why I took the time to decompress when I could, and insisted the people under my command did the same.

Permanent vigilance just meant that no one was on his best game when the crap hit the airfoils.

Also, on the sea, with the sole exception of the pre-sonar U-boat era, ships could always see threats coming from a long distance. In space, that's even more true. If your sensors are good enough, you can spot planets circling in a nearby star system light years away, so it's hard to sneak up on anyone. Between our active sensors from thirteen warships banging away, the eyeballs of the watch-standers, and the brainboxes of the combat drones spread out around us, we should have plenty of warning.

Checking in at the bridge after the morale-building exercise, I found out nothing had happened yet, and Marvin hadn't answered, so I decided to take a shower and a nap. Afterward, I dropped by the wardroom.

There, I saw Adrienne in her usual seat, three computer tablets neatly lined up in front of her. Rivulets of smart metal like mercury threads connected them to each other and the table and then on to the ship's network. An empty cup sat off to one side, and some of her hair had escaped from its pins to fall over her face as she stared downward, so she didn't see me come in.

Pouring two cups of coffee and doctoring hers the way she liked it, white with no sugar, I placed one in front of the tablets as she tapped at their screens. It looked like she was working on some kind of technical schematic.

"Thanks," she said, looking up and brushing her hair back. It slid forward again to frame her face, and for a moment I was back at the Academy, sitting across from her sister. She must have seen it in my eyes, because she dropped her head to hide behind the cornsilk cascade again. I didn't know whether she was upset, sad or something else. Women are hard to read at the best of times.

Part of me wished I could move on, but part of me wanted to cling to Olivia forever. What were those stages of grief? I'd moved quickly through denial and anger. Bargaining didn't seem to come into play, so Adrienne and I orbited each other between depression and acceptance. The only remedy I knew was to keep busy, focusing on the problems at hand and those of the future.

"So, what're you working on?" I asked.

"The eggheads' theoretical model of Litho ship structure based on Marvin's data and their own researches."

"What have they found?" I craned forward to get a better view, and she turned one tablet around to face me.

"It's the weirdest form of life I've ever encountered. The closest analogy I can come up with is computers and software, or maybe demonic possession of rocks."

"Those are two wildly different metaphors."

"I know. Let me explain by starting from the beginning—when Lithos first infect a world. Let's say it's one that's part hot dry desert and part wet with plants and oceans. Drop some silico-nanites in the desert and they start replicating, organizing the rocks, and soil. They absorb and store sunlight and all sorts of radiation, anything that can provide energy, including oxidizing petrocarbons like oil, natural gas, and coal. They use that energy to live, reproduce and spread. Where they find pockets of wetness, they heat the surrounding rocks and boil the water away, as we would drain swamps to make dry land. That kills all the biotic life, of course."

"Sounds like an infection all right." I sipped my bad factory-synthesized coffee, wishing I could invite Adrienne to the captain's cabin to brew some real cappuccino on the machine there.

"It is. When it gets deep enough and finds geothermal heat, it spreads even faster. When it finds metallic ores, it goes around them, like we treat rugged badlands. It's not that they can't deal with them, but to them, it's impassable, inhospitable territory. Eventually, in a matter of only a decade or two, they will render most of the planet uninhabitable by biotic life. Of course, if the world started as a hot waterless rock, it could take only months, while an ice-covered moon might be an impossibility."

I drummed my fingers on the table. "Remember Tullax 6?"

"How could I forget?" Adrienne unconsciously rubbed her arm where the dirt—the Litho—had grabbed her.

"Your uncle said the scientists believed that world had once been life-bearing. I think that was the Pandas' homeworld. The Macros had conquered it at some point, or nearly so. Some Pandas escaped, or maybe they had already colonized Tullax 4. When the Macros clobbered them, they created, or perhaps found and modified, the Litho nanites and used them as an anti-Macro weapon. Unlike conventional weapons, the Lithos turned out to be wildly successful, but they couldn't be stopped once they got deep into the planet. Eventually, the Lithos terraformed Tullax 6 into their kind of place, destroying its usefulness for the Pandas."

Adrienne nodded enthusiastically. "Then the Pandas rebuilt their society on Tullax 4, which is too wet for Lithos. They used the Lithos to kill off the Macros on their moon, and the moon of Tullax 5 where the other ring is. The remaining Macros went through that ring to escape."

"Then either the Pandas went through and seeded more Lithos, or the Lithos had achieved sentience by that time and followed the Macros through, taking over the Matterhorn system." I chuckled. "The Pandas must have crapped their shorts when the Lithos developed intelligence enough to build spaceships."

"So the Macros must have escaped through the Matterhorn 7 ring, if they escaped at all. That's the same ring we're trying to go through."

I nodded. "It all seems to make sense, though without confirmation it's all just speculation."

At that moment *Valiant*'s voice reverberated from the walls. "Captain to the bridge. Captain to the bridge."

"On my way," I called. I looked into Adrienne's worried eyes as she stood up with me, grabbing her tablets. "Maybe we'll find out soon. I just hope the answers don't kill us."

-30-

When I reached the bridge, I took a look at Hansen. He looked a little glum, but I could tell he had fully recovered from our pool game. With the medical bay to assist, his injuries had already healed enough for him to sit comfortably. He gave me a cool nod from the helm.

"I've got the watch, Hansen," I announced.

"Captain has the watch."

"What have you got, helmsman?" I asked as I stepped up to the holotank.

"The first of the four Litho cruisers is coming into long range in one minute."

"We've been hailing them in their language?"

Hansen shrugged. "I'm flying the ship."

Adrienne left the ops section and came to my side.

"We've been transmitting friendly packets periodically," she said, "but so far, there's been no response."

I examined the holotank. We were in the same lens formation again, perfectly set up to annihilate the enemy with at least a thirteen to one advantage in firepower.

"They still haven't moved to counter our formation. They're acting senselessly, throwing themselves away. I don't get it."

"Maybe they don't really want to kill us," Adrienne said as she took a seat. "Maybe our diplomacy has had some effect. Could it be an honor thing?"

"I don't know…they're coming straight for us." I frowned. "Try one more time. Transmit: *peace desire, truce, confirmation insistence*."

We waited and waited.

"In range," Hansen announced.

"Stand by," I said.

Several more tense minutes passed as they advanced into the teeth of our waiting guns.

Hansen said, "Sir, the Litho cruiser is entering range of our medium lasers and our heavy APs, and we're in theirs. We have to fire or we're giving them the first punch."

I gripped the ring of metal around the hototank tightly, feeling my fingers create indentations.

"Dammit. Why can't they just be reasonable? We're going to have to slaughter them. Gunners, shift to APs but hold your fire. Main lasers, defocus and fire several low-powered shots into them. Let's light them up with a few spot-welds first."

"Main lasers fired. No effect. Sir, they've opened fire. Number five laser damaged."

Frustrated, I finally decided I had to give the order.

"Full coordinated salvo, open fire on my mark. *Mark*." Lights dimmed as the entire power output of the generators plus a chunk of the capacitors pumped through our antiproton beams, reaching out to strike the enemy in one hammer blow.

On the main screen the optical view whited out, while the synthesized radar picture showed the front half of the mountain-sized ship vaporizing. It simply disappeared, leaving the ragged back half spinning through space like a rogue comet.

The hope monkey had gotten to me, I realized. Dad used to talk about the psychological phenomenon he'd often battled. We humans have a flaw in our minds that seduces us into believing what we want to believe, instead of what the hard evidence indicates. Now and again hope came through, but more often than not, it resulted in disaster and despair. Hardening my heart, I substituted anger for sympathy.

"We tried to make peace," I said. "We did our part. They had every chance. Now, it's war."

I could feel Adrienne's eyes on me, but I ignored her. Now was not the time for recriminations or second thoughts. Somehow, even when enemies are trying to kill you, it's hard to burn them down when you know they have no chance. Machine gunners in World War One and Coalition bomber pilots in the Gulf War all reported struggling with shame at killing helpless fighters. But if you spent too much time worrying about it, you wouldn't be worth a damn.

I suppose I should've been happy that I struggled at all. Anyone who kills without a shred of remorse is likely a monster. But remorse or not, more killing was inevitable, and if I had to be the guy to give the orders, so be it. The only other choice was to keep running and lose the opportunity. Besides, I told myself, the Lithos were death machines, just like Macros. It didn't make any sense to mourn a machine.

"Second cruiser coming into range."

"Switch to lasers. Fire as they enter extreme ranges." I wanted to save power and give the capacitors time to recharge, as well as let the gunners have more practice. There was always the chance that the Lithos would veer off from disaster and decide to talk. The Crustaceans had to face annihilation before finally accepting an alliance. Maybe if the Lithos got pummeled badly enough…

No dice. We mowed them down like grass on a golf green. The lasers hit lightly at long range, and the Lithos broke apart into smaller ships in response. All that did was provide us with more target practice. I was glad to see that my crew seemed steady and competent, not jubilant like they'd been during our earlier narrow escapes. To me, that meant the fires of combat were forging them into professionals.

I realized that applied to me, too.

At some point during the battle, Adrienne must have slipped out. I didn't like it, but I understood. Still, I had to at least contemplate reprimanding my friend who was also my ops officer for abandoning her post. I reminded myself that she hadn't gone through the rigorous training required to handle a situation like this. At least she wasn't really needed in a static beat-down, but it set a bad example.

Fortunately, Adrienne came back in to stand beside me as we destroyed the last Litho ship, which had broken itself down into snowflakes. Not one of them reached our hull. Face set, Adrienne was all business as we mopped up the last of them.

As if on cue, the main Litho fleet began to move the moment we'd destroyed the task force. The first of many ships disappeared into the tunnel that served as the entrance into the hollow moon.

"That answers our question," I said, "they're going to turtle-up inside their planetoid."

The second ship arrowed down and vanished inside the sphere.

"Like bees ducking into their hive," Adrienne said, staring raptly at the holotank's display. "Are we really going to follow them in?"

"Maybe," I said, then shrugged. "Probably. I'm not sure yet, to tell the truth. *Valiant*, hail Marvin. Tell him Captain Riggs wants to talk with Captain Marvin." If we were to follow the Lithos inside the hollow moon, we would need everything going for us.

"Hello, Captain Riggs," Marvin's voice came a few seconds later. "I'm on my way."

"Crawling out of the woodwork now that the threat has gone, eh?"

"As would any sensible being in my situation," he replied. "I don't have the combat capability of even one of your frigates, so I must remain circumspect."

"Fine, fine. You're here now. By the way, where were you hiding?"

"I clad myself in comet ice and drifted into a position of passive observation."

I had to admit—to myself, not to Marvin—that had been a clever idea.

"We may need your silico-nanite commando drones soon," I told him. "I'm inclined to follow the Lithos in, but it's going to be tricky. Do you have any advice based on your observations?"

"The tunnel through the crust took fifty-seven minutes to form. I suggest you make your move quickly once the last Litho enters. They may decide to close it behind them."

"Fine," I said. "Fire your drones as soon as the last one enters, and we'll follow closely."

"Agreed."

Over a hundred ships disappeared into the hole as the minutes crawled by like a chain of beads pulled along by an invisible string. Human ships would never leave so little buffer space between them, but I imagined Lithos didn't worry too much about crashing into one another.

"Marvin, what else can you tell us about the situation?"

"I'm almost certain they're entering a ring at the center of the artificial planetoid. Based on readings from certain instruments I've fashioned, I'm detecting quantum vibrations that are consistent with local variations of collapsed matter."

I clapped my hands together, startling the bridge crew. "Good news, then! There *is* a ring inside that rock, and they're using it to invade another system."

Adrienne gave me a reproachful look. "Spoiling for another fight?" she asked.

"For a fight? No. I'm hoping for momentum, for progress toward getting home. Sometimes those are the same thing."

"Are we going to destroy their entire fleet, sir?"

I frowned at her then looked back at the holotank.

"Remember, I tried to talk to them. Besides, they're machines, just like the Macros, devoid of mercy and feeling. They aren't biotics like us."

"You don't sound completely convinced," she said.

"Maybe not," I admitted.

I turned and leaned toward her, speaking quietly. "Right now I'm about to lead this expedition into danger, hoping it gets us closer to home. They have to have confidence in me, and they need to believe they're doing the right thing. Now's not the time to undermine me or cause them to doubt themselves. If I'm wrong, it's on my head."

Adrienne nodded, her hair touching my cheek as she turned away. Her nearness affected me in an unexpected way. I waited until I was sure she had stepped away then turned back to the crewmen. Some of them had been watching us quietly.

"Pass this on to all ships and crews," I said. "General quarters! Battle stations! Marine commander, suit up your troops."

In the holotank, I noticed a flashing yellow contact appear and move quickly toward us. Zooming in, I saw it looked like a comet with an engine flare and designated it as *Greyhound* for the confused brainbox. Marvin was on course to join us just as the last Litho ship entered the sphere.

Minutes later, Marvin flipped the *Greyhound* and decelerated, throwing the last of the ice cladding off. As the hull of the ship was revealed, I noticed that in place of its former smooth porpoise shape, suitable for space and atmospheric travel, it had been transformed into a bigger version of Marvin himself. A dozen large tentacles and many smaller ones had been constructed and attached. Some of these new limbs had claws and manipulators at their termination. Others seemed to be holding instrument packages or weapons. All of them were attached to the original fuselage, which now functioned as a central hub. The strange-looking craft's bullet nose and drifting tubular limbs reminded me strongly of a squid, except the arms ringed the waist instead of the back end.

"That's the ugliest damn yacht I've ever seen, Marvin," I transmitted on the ship-to-ship channel. "Now, please launch your drones."

"Your visual descriptors are unhelpful, *Ensign* Riggs," Marvin responded.

I wondered if I'd hurt his feelings. If that was even possible.

As the last Litho ship disappeared into the artificial moon, the Marvin-ship launched a dozen drones one after another, which flew quickly down toward the pole below us.

"I suggest we follow as closely as possible in order to utilize every moment," he said. "My silico-nanites will only last so long.

I nodded. "Combat drones first. Send down eight of them, well spaced, and keep them lined up on the tunnel. I want some readings before we fly in there. Hansen, start our descent."

Five minutes later Marvin's drones dropped into the tunnel, their exhaust plumes glowing like tiny fireballs. Rather than shooting through after the retreating enemy fleet, they adhered to the walls of the tunnel. According to my sensors, the ploy worked—Marvin's drones full of silicon nanites had stopped the aperture from closing.

Valiant's own combat drones entered the hole at high speed a minute later, with the mothership following ten minutes behind. If Marvin's estimate on how long it would take the Lithos to close up the path was accurate, that gave us a short time window.

I'd already set up the holotank to receive and synthesize the data from the combat drones, so I watched them in what was nearly real-time. With their active radar pinging madly, a high-res picture formed quite quickly once they reached the hollow interior.

The expected ring floated in the center of the artificial globe, but that was not my greatest concern. If the Lithos had left a rearguard in any strength, we might have to turn around. I wasn't going to let us be ambushed at the bottleneck.

I knew disaster still might await us if the Lithos had planted nukes around the inner edge of the tunnel or floating mines like we used, but our active sensors detected nothing, not even snowflakes. The hollow inside was oddly devoid of any Litho presence. This actually worried me more than having to fight something as it implied I had missed something.

"Okay, I'm not seeing any Lithos. Why might that be?"

"I would think that would be obvious," Marvin's voice came over the radio.

"Save the guessing games for downtime, Captain Marvin," I said.

"My silico-nanites are holding the tunnel open. The Lithos expected it to close; therefore, they believed they had no need of defenses."

"Why isn't the inner surface of the tunnel calving snowflakes or ships? You can't tell me that every Litho or template or whatever already made it through." Silence greeted this question. "Work on that one, Marvin," I said. "We still have a couple minutes before we commit."

"Maybe it's the same reason that their main fleet didn't seem to coordinate with the cruisers that ran into our fire," Hansen said. "What if this moon is part of a different—uh, call it a collective? Like Litho nations. Maybe they had permission to pass through another Litho nation's territory, but they aren't really allied."

"You'd think the local moon-Lithos would defend their own home, in that case," Adrienne countered.

"They might have had an agreement not to launch anything for a certain period of time," I said. "For example, until the tunnel closed. Lithos appear to have a machine intelligence in that they use concrete words, just nouns, which indicates inflexibility. They didn't even negotiate when we had the upper hand. Possibly, when they have agreed to something—for example with another Litho collective or nation—they like to stick to it as long as they're not provoked into a change of plan. We're not attacking the moon so they aren't attacking us."

"Kind of like the Macros except the Macros didn't divide themselves into groups," Hansen said.

"Not as far as we know." I cracked my knuckles. "There's *so* little we do know about these beings."

"Right now," Hansen said, "I know you have to make a decision, sir."

He was right. Within two minutes we would zoom through.

"Do you have enough room to brake?" I asked.

"I've kept our speed down enough with the forward repellers. No problem."

"Then let's go through. Put two-thirds of the combat drones in front, then eight frigates, then us, then the rest. Turnbull, ensure everyone spreads out when they enter the sphere."

"We're not going straight into the ring?" Adrienne asked.

"I want to scout around first. If something happens inside the moon we can escape through the ring, but until then, let's be a bit cautious. Once we brake, apply the formation we've had so much success with. Point your weapons at the ring and be ready to blast anything coming though—on my confirmation, of course."

The transit through the rabbit hole was quick and painless. Marvin's trick with the silicon-nanite drones seemed to have worked. In fact, when I looked for Marvin on the holotank, I saw him right behind *Valiant*. I had figured it was a fifty-fifty shot whether he would come along with us, but I guess his neural circuitry had come down on the side of loyalty to Star Force. Or perhaps he was curious about what was on the other side of the ring.

Once we'd positioned ourselves in front of the ring, far enough out to react to a surprise, but near enough to enter it ourselves within a minute, I ordered a pair of combat drones through. They had orders for one to return after five seconds and the other to return after thirty. When they disappeared into the ring, I crossed my fingers.

After one anxious minute had gone by with no sign of the little ships, I spoke a few choice epithets.

"Prep four this time, with orders to return in one, two, three and four seconds respectively. Send them through backward so they don't even have to turn around." I hoped this approach would be fast enough for one of them to make it back, but I was beginning to doubt the ring was safe.

"Why not just send a nuke through, first?" Hansen asked.

"I thought of that," I admitted. "But what if it's a biotic species fighting the Lithos that knocked the combat drones out? I don't want to start off by killing potential allies. Still, it may come to that if we can't get any data."

The next flight of four went through, tail-first as I'd directed. One second later the first one that had entered returned, spinning and partially slagged. The other three never came back. I stared at the holotank, waiting for the vital data but saw nothing.

"Marvin, go retrieve that combat drone and see if you can recover any data from its brainbox. Share it with *Valiant's* brainbox immediately. No delays for curiosity's sake—but feel free to examine what's left of it after you've transmitted your report."

Greyhound swooped forward to pick up the combat drone in its tentacles. I figured it should keep Marvin busy for a little while. He always liked a puzzle.

Long minutes passed hanging in front of the ring. I could imagine a battle raging on the other side, and I itched to find out what was going on. That must have been how Marvin felt when he desperately wanted to tinker with something but couldn't.

Finally, the robot uploaded some data to our system. I made a smaller, separate space for the synthetic 3D model the holotank brain was trying to fill. Setting it for one-tenth slow motion, I watched.

First, it showed the four combat drones and the ring around them on the other side. Half a second later all of them registered incoming beam fire of some sort, causing extreme heating of the small hulls. At the same time, their radar pulses revealed hundreds of ships battling one another nearby.

The Litho fleet seemed to be fighting its way out of the kill zone in front of the ring. It was impossible to tell what condition they were in for along with the many large Litho craft, the holotank displayed thousands of smaller ones—fighters, missiles, and snowflakes.

Other shapes were unfamiliar. These ships resembled deadly raptors, birds of prey with folded wings and outstretched talons. I had no idea whether their appearance was utilitarian or purely aesthetic, but at least they were distinctly non-Litho and non-Macro.

"They're beautiful," Adrienne said from beside me, reaching out with one slim-fingered hand to touch the glass. "There's no question those ships were built by biotic creatures, and they must be a sensitive people. We have to help them, Cody."

"Sensitive people who are taking a pounding," I said, examining the slow-motion snippet of battle with a tactician's eye. "Yes, they need help, but they're also the ones that are shooting our combat drones."

I wondered if Adrienne was being hypocritical, but I didn't think now would be a good time to bring it up. Previously, she'd been upset at me for crushing the Lithos, but now that more familiar creatures were endangered by them, she had changed her mind. I restrained the impulse to point this out, especially as I agreed with her for more practical reasons: The enemy of my enemy was a potential friend.

Using a handheld cursor, I traced a circle around a group of eight alien craft that were the size of gunships.

"These ships are picking off our combat drones as they come through. Marvin," I said into the air, trusting that he was listening in. "What did they hit us with? Lasers?"

"Grasers, actually," came his reply. "Gamma-ray lasers. Not particularly effective against our ships, but an interesting optimization versus Lithos. Rather than attacking Litho ship material directly the way antiproton weapons do, the gamma rays should theoretically reach into the Lithos to disrupt their templates. However, this approach will obviously fail against large enough Litho ships, with sufficient mass as armor."

"Are our magnetic shields effective against grasers?"

"They can be adjusted, but doing so will increase vulnerability in the more common laser wavelengths."

"Do it. Pass the word to adjust all the magnetic shields for grasers, but be ready to reset them again as soon as we have formed an alliance with these, ah, raptor people. Report when ready." I wondered whether there were sentient birds inside those ships. Eagles, maybe?

"All frigates report ready," Adrienne said after a moment.

Unfortunately, our combat drones didn't carry shields. Especially with craft that small, every bit of mass and power involved tradeoffs. Now I wished I had equipped a few of them as scouts, recon drones with no weapons but more survivability. One more thing for the list.

"Marvin, will the frigates' shields hold against those grasers?"

"They will hold against the gunboat grasers, but there are other, larger Raptor warships in the vicinity."

"Sounds like you just coined our name for these people. All right, Hansen, when I give the word put your shields up. Set the combat drones to follow, but do not engage the Raptors until one of our manned ships does. Set them in free-fire mode against the Lithos. Can we do that?"

"It will take a moment to program," Hansen said.

"Take that moment. We won't be able to direct the combat drones with the shields blocking our transmissions, so we'll have to hope their brainboxes are smart enough to do what they're told. Frigates will do the same: only fire at the Raptors if it's life or death, until we do. For *Valiant*'s gunners, hold fire. Remember, with the shields up, we can't shoot or even communicate easily."

"What's the overall plan, Captain Riggs?" Marvin asked.

I stared intently at my short 3D holo-vid, mindful of the fact that the longer we waited, the further reality would diverge from the only snapshot of the battle I had.

"We'll enter at full acceleration along this curve." I drew an arc with my cursor. It curved out the other side of the ring and toward a region full of Lithos. "*Valiant* first, then the frigates, then the combat drones. If the Raptors are cocked and locked to shoot, we've got the heaviest shields–double shields, in fact. As soon as the frigates and combat drones come through, they will speed up and spread out to precede us in standard attack formation. You'll have to use your best judgment from there, but my intent is to begin firing at Lithos as soon as they come into AP range. Hopefully as soon as the Raptors see we're on their side, they'll leave us alone."

"What if we can't win?" Hansen asked.

"I've heard enough what-ifs, people. You have your orders. Frigate crews, Godspeed—and go kick some ass."

I took a breath as people went into motion all around me. Boards lit up, weapons and engines thrummed into intense life.

"Restraints on. Shields up...Let's fly."

We slid into the ring and everything vanished.

-31-

"Graser impacts registered," *Valiant* reported the moment we exited the ring. "No significant damage."

The main screen whited out and then dimmed as nearby nuclear blasts flared into life and quickly faded to a dull bluish radioactive glow.

"Punch it, Hansen," I said as I watched the rest of my small fleet follow us through. As ordered, the frigates and combat drones went to flank speed and overtook my battlecruiser, spreading out in a shotgun pattern in front of us.

We swiftly passed the eight small Raptor gunships guarding the ring. They kept firing at our stern, but they'd been waiting in a slow holding pattern. Their engines glowed white as they began to follow us, but we pulled away easily, leaving them in the dust. That made me happy. I didn't want to have to kill my potential allies, or vice versa.

As we slipped beyond the range of the ships guarding the ring, we were free to concentrate on the main battle ahead. *Valiant* displayed input flowing from her sensors revealing a nearby knot of ships. I stared at a force of about twenty Litho ships locked in combat with six Raptors. They were mopping up the badly outnumbered handful of bird-shaped vessels.

More data came in to be displayed as soon as the ship could make sense of it all. I saw the battle swell in scope. Squadron versus squadron engagements were taking place all around us. In most of these small fights the Lithos were winning, but the Raptors had the upper hand in a few cases.

We sailed forward, bearing down on the closest fight. With our weight added to the Raptors' side, the numbers would become even, but our beams and missiles were Litho-killers and could change the outcome of the fights. Until we ran out of juice, I estimated we had at least a four to one advantage in firepower—and I intended to use it.

"Turn off the shields," I said. "Save the power for weapons."

Watching in satisfaction as the capacitors topped off again, I waited for the frigates to notice and drop theirs as well. That allowed us to communicate again. "I want a high-speed pass along the edge of the Litho formation, targeting their ships with our APs," I said. I marked four of them with cursors. "Drop as many powered mines as you can in our wake and set them to seek nearby ships. That will keep them busy."

Adrienne passed on my orders and the combat drone directors maneuvered their flights. My squadron of drones spread into a plane formation, angled so we would strafe the huge Litho ships.

In the holotank, pixels fell out of our vessels and drifted behind us. The repeller mines immediately decelerated, steering for their targets. We'd optimized these warheads for Lithos as well, creating enhanced-gamma warheads that would disrupt their templates. As they were area-effect weapons, they should kill snowflakes and missiles with their gamma pulse on detonation even if their blasts could not reach the enemy directly. If they got close enough, they should give the bigger vessels a bad sunburn as well. If they actually impacted a Litho ship, their small nuclear warheads would take chunks out of them.

Our ships' main batteries were already firing as we'd entered the battle well within medium range. Swaths of rocky Litho-armor boiled away under our AP weapons; hulls annihilated as the antiprotons found their normal-matter counterparts and converted all the mass of both into energy. This effectively split most atoms, creating local fission, which released neutrons in a chain reaction that split even more atoms. These tiny impacts multiplied as trillions of particles struck their targets. Whole sections of the Lithos turned into low-grade atomic piles, going instantly critical and igniting. The cascade reactions were not quite bomb-grade yield, but they were close.

We closed in and made our pass, raking the enemy stern. At point-blank range the devastation was spectacular. The enemy was soon obscured. Our active sensors couldn't even penetrate the cloud of plasma we generated as the Litho ships transformed into blowtorches. They were flying mountains, and we'd just turned them into volcanoes.

Before the first pass ended, the enemy cruisers met their doom. We left the four ships smoldering with hulls that resembled molten lava.

"Shields up!" I ordered. "Casualty report, Turnbull?"

"One combat drone impacted—a stray snowflake," Adrienne said. "We pretty much creamed them."

It was less than a professional estimate, but it made me smile.

"A more than fair trade," I said. "Well done, everyone. Continue until we're out of their effective range then drop the shields and bring us about smartly."

I felt the shudders of beam impacts as we executed this maneuver. The other sixteen or so Litho ships had now taken note of us and were firing with a mix of APs and lasers. A group broke off and charged our flank. I watched with grim pleasure as the two dozen mines we'd dropped began to explode in their faces.

Most of the mines blew up before they reached their targets or were taken out by Litho point-defense beams, but two reached the largest ship-mountain among the enemy squadron. The mines detonated against its hull in sequence, spaced well apart. They left twin glowing pits a hundred yards deep and destroyed several of the huge weapon structures. The large ship—a battleship by the look of it—came on, damaged but still intent on catching us.

After a minute of evasion, we drew ourselves out to extreme range. In space almost nothing is truly out of range but beams eventually attenuate and missiles can be picked off. Everything gets harder to hit the farther away it is. Thus, range was a judgment call, but we'd set up parameters beforehand in our extensive practice runs.

Hansen shut down the shields without me ordering the action—and correctly so. As the guy really flying the ship, he remained hypersensitive to our energy reserves. Without fuel, the big fusion engines weren't much use. Without energy reserves, our repellers and beams were useless as well. Sakura and the engineering team were supposed to keep it all running and in balance, but no ship ever designed has enough power to do everything.

I glanced over and saw *Valiant* was at three-quarters capacitance or so, not bad after taking out four Lithos, but we had hundreds of targets remaining on our scopes. Hansen flew the squadron in a smooth turn that made us hard to hit and kept the G forces down—heavy inertial stabilization sucked juice as well.

While he executed this maneuver, I tried to get a sense of the overall battle. Broadly speaking, the Raptors were fighting on the outside of an expanding hemisphere of Litho ships, as if the rock fleet had pushed outward from the ring in the shape of a mushroom cap. This made sense as it spread them out of the bottleneck as fast as possible without wasting the effort that turning around completely would require. A high radiation count and the amount of debris in front of the ring was evidence the Raptors had hit the attackers with a nuclear bombardment or mines and had done some damage, but the situation was still too confused for a ship count. The Lithos might have lost up to seventy ships, but our sensors may have missed some, and others had apparently broken up into fighters, snowflakes, and missiles.

As the squadron commander, my main concern was where to apply my firepower. We resembled cavalry on this battlefield, a mobile but fragile mailed fist. We were a force that could hit hard, but which couldn't afford to slow down and get swamped by the enemy's slower, more powerful forces. We had to strike suddenly, drive through, and keep going to set up another strike. I couldn't see any other way to help the Raptors achieve victory.

"Here," I said, shoving aside an overeager restraint-tentacle to mark a course that cut behind the ring and across to the other side of the mushroom cap. "Push us along that line as fast as you can while keeping formation. Have a dozen combat drones fall back to knock off those missiles chasing us."

"This wastes a lot of time," Adrienne said. "The Raptors are fighting and dying."

"And more will die, but I'm not going to throw away this force. Ops, pass the damned orders!"

Adrienne looked away with a tight face to do as I'd instructed. Once she'd done so, I explained the situation to her matter-of-factly, keeping my voice low.

"This tactic does three things: One, it allows us time to fill up our capacitors. Two, it keeps our speed up, and speed is life in air or space." I noticed Hansen nodding unconsciously, a pilot's response. He was listening in without looking at either of us.

"And lastly," I said, "the Raptors are losing the particular fight we're heading for because of this." I pointed at the Lithos' one dreadnought. "We're going to take the Lithos from behind and help our new allies win, saving some of their lives."

"Fucking-A right," Hansen murmured, and I realized I'd scored big points with him, though I had lost some with Adrienne. The ship and crew had to come first though, and I couldn't have her delaying the execution of my orders until I handled her every objection. Maybe I should have recruited and trained an ops officer from among the available noncoms. Had my judgment been affected by a pretty, familiar face? A more senior officer would probably shake his head and tell me I'd made a rookie mistake putting Adrienne on my bridge, but it was too late to worry about it now.

The combat drones covering our tail took out the missiles following us, losing several of their number when one of the Litho nukes detonated too close. I remembered something then. Our combat drones carried two external missiles each, and naturally fought better after they were fired because they didn't have to drag around the extra weight. It occurred to me that I should have designated a combat drone coordinator, a kind of CAG, "Commander, Aerospace Group" in military jargon, to direct them more tightly. As it was, I'd thought it would be easy to pass orders to the controllers directly, but I couldn't run the squadron and multiple combat drone missions at the same time.

Checking, I noticed we had about five minutes until we entered the effective AP range of our targets, so I told the restraints to release me and clomped over to the arc of director stations across the front of the circular bridge.

"You, Chief..." I said, tugging on the striped sleeve of a beefy Fleet noncom.

"Bradley, sir," he said, turning to look at me.

"Pass your combat drones to your best director. You're my new CAG. Stand up and run the combat drone group for me. I'll talk to you, and you talk to them, got it?"

The man looked anxious but did as I told him. "Got it, sir."

I looked him in the eye. "Can you do this? If not, tell me who can."

"I can do it, sir," he said more firmly.

"Good man." I slapped him on the shoulder, forgetting to restrain myself and rocking his fireplug body. He touched his shoulder, surprised that it hurt, then, with his headset on, he turned to walk up and down behind his people.

"CAG, when I tell you to launch missiles, fire them ship by ship, and then employ the clean birds first, understand? They'll fight better."

"Roger, sir."

"Okay. Give me ninety-six missiles in a spread pattern, twelve on each of these eight ships." I marked them in the holotank, a group on one side of the fight, then sent the update to the combat drone stations. That would give us forty-eight clean combat drones, each with a close-range AP beam for counter-fighter or counter-missile use.

Turning away to let Bradley coordinate that strike, I said to Adrienne, "Turnbull, give me a lens formation focused here." This time I marked the enormous Litho dreadnought, the largest in their fleet, five miles long and two miles wide. Our ships were tiny compared to it, and I had to keep telling myself that it wasn't as scary as it looked. "Release half our remaining mobile mines right now, and make sure they only target Lithos.

Once that's done, Hansen, begin gentle braking to let the mines fly out ahead of us." This tactic turned the guided mines into crude missiles, effective only because the enemy was large, slow, and directly in front of us.

First, the ninety-six missiles shot out in front of us on trails of hot blue plasma, then more than a hundred repeller mines were deployed, immediately pulling away from us as we braked. These two salvos represented half our remaining ordnance, but I didn't see any point in holding onto it if I could kill Lithos and save Raptors.

Stepping around to the other side of the holotank, I looked at our formation from the point of view of the Raptors. They swooped and fired on the Lithos at close range, going toe-to-toe with their enemies, who right now were caught between two formations.

"Make sure any missiles that miss the Lithos," I said, "don't retarget on the Raptors. That goes for the repeller mines too."

The weapons people worked to implement my instructions. I turned back to the helmsman who waved for my attention.

"The mines have contact fuses," Hansen reminded me. "We can't control them. If they fly past and a Raptor gets in the way…well…" He shrugged.

"Good point," I said, frowning. "Let's make sure that doesn't happen. *Valiant*, send a signal to the mines to detonate themselves as they reach the Litho line, regardless of proximity to target." That would limit their effectiveness as they might blow in space rather than continuing to seek their targets, but it would also eliminate friendly-fire problems.

"Command acknowledged."

"Here we go," I said as our first salvo entered the Lithos' engagement envelopes. As I had hoped, the enemy had been fully entangled with the Raptors and now had to pick their poison. They chose to turn and present their angled, more heavily armored front faces to the greater threat, my nukes.

Litho beams blazed, picking several Star Force missiles out of space at maximum effective range. At the same time, counter-missiles calved off from their big ships, accelerating fast toward our swarm. I'd ordered a spread, but the groups naturally tightened up as they arrowed inward toward their eight targets.

"*Valiant!*" I barked, realizing what was going to happen. "Switch targets! Retarget all missiles toward any other Litho ship!"

I'd made a rookie mistake, and my green crew hadn't caught it. Each missile group had pointed itself at its target for too long, and all it would take was a nuke or three in the right spot to catch the tight cluster in a blast.

After a moment much longer than I liked, *Valiant's* brainbox responded, "Retargeting. Signal sent."

Our missiles had just begun to change their courses, groups looking like forward-bursting fireworks as they turned and blasted laterally as hard as they could, when the Lithos' defensive nukes detonated. More than three-quarters of our weapons disappeared in the blasts, and I let loose a few choice vulgarities. I'd been too late.

A moment later I had cause to feel better. Behind the wall of nuclear blasts the Lithos had thrown up, the holotank displayed more than a dozen heavy thermonuclear blasts—caused by our weapons according to the radioactive signature. When the overload cleared, I saw two Litho ships heavily damaged and two others hit.

"They took out most of our missiles, but the ones that made it past couldn't be shot down due to all the interference," I said. "*Valiant*, in the future, randomize the maneuvering of similarly targeted missiles in each salvo to hide their destinations for as long as possible."

"Protocols updated."

I hoped that would improve our missile performance, but nothing was guaranteed. Every protocol had its weaknesses. Space combat was often as much art as science with so many possibilities of move and countermove involving differing weapons, all played out in three dimensions.

Our next blow came from the repeller mines we'd thrown forward. They'd been called poor man's missiles since mines didn't have the maneuverability to do more than adjust their trajectory slightly toward their targets. If our normal missiles were space-sharks, mines were paddling dogs. I hoped the Lithos didn't see them coming until too late, as they were smaller and heavily stealthed.

"Entering our long laser range," Hansen announced.

"Begin long-range laser fire. Switch to APs as they reach. Don't spare the juice," I said.

"That may cause them to break up."

"All the better. The radiation from the gamma-enhanced nukes will hurt their small craft more than their big ships," I replied. I'd been expecting that objection. At least Hansen had delivered his complaint in a neutral, matter-of-fact tone.

Valiant hummed with resonance as our two big lasers began to fire, as did the corresponding mains on our frigates. Given our number of combat drones, I'd mandated the frigates have the heaviest weapons possible, but they were short on point defense. Because of the Lithos' size and toughness, I did not see small, highly accurate lasers as the best use of limited space and power. Besides, the combat drones could provide that function in a pinch.

The Lithos now fought back-to-back, less than ten miles apart from each other. That was a very tight range in space. A half-dozen ships plus fighters and snowflakes battled ten or so Raptors on the far side, while eight Lithos had turned toward us, two of which were heavily damaged. Unfortunately for us, this group included their biggest ship.

The cruiser we were pummeling began to calve into fighters just as our mine barrage reached their line. As I had hoped, they hadn't seen our weapons, and over a hundred explosions rippled among the enemy. While none of the mines contact-detonated, their area of effect caught all eight Lithos within.

The new fighter group that had recently been a cruiser now disintegrated. The arrowheads still existed, but instead of moving purposefully, they spun like glitter through the void.

"Excellent!" I shouted. "Their fighters are too small to shield against the enhanced gamma."

Unfortunately the barrage didn't seem to have a great effect on the large ships. Perhaps it killed off a few templates near their surfaces, but if I were a Litho fighting against the

Raptors, I'd keep my "people" deep within, behind effective shielding. We'd exploded the equivalent of a neutron bomb and fried the fighter pilots, but their battleships had thick armor.

"Hansen, optimize our speed so we get time for a heavy pass through the Lithos along the side here." I drew a line in the holotank. "That will bring us up next to the Raptors if we decelerate hard. Try to give them room, though. I don't want them to feel we're a threat to them."

"Got it, boss," Hansen replied. "*Valiant*, patch my course plan to the frigate pilots in realtime."

Hansen informed the other pilots things were about to get rough. I privately agreed with his assessment.

-32-

Hansen was right. The radioactive dust had cleared somewhat, revealing the mountainous prows of the five remaining Litho effectives. They were aiming toward us now, and they began to fire.

"Keep us evading, Hansen," I said as *Valiant* shuddered with beam hits and near-misses. "Concentrated, continuous AP fire on the nose of that dreadnought, now!"

The helmsman was already ahead of me as I saw our formation slide sideways to cut past the edge of the enemy. Tentacles grasped me tighter as the ship rocked with hard G-forces, and I watched as our power reserves dropped by half within thirty seconds.

Fountains of fire bloomed all around the pointed bow of the Litho dreadnought. It looked as if a hundred small volcanoes had erupted all at once. Our antiproton beams converted matter into exotic elements and isotopes, tearing the ship apart. In the holotank I could see the beams lash out from our side, briefly connecting our ships to the enemy with razor-straight lines.

But answering lines were coming back at us. The four enemy cruisers sent their beams slashing across my formation, and I felt the punch in the gut as they intersected two of my frigates. The first wobbled and began to tumble, continuing in a straight line even as we curved on our attack run. The other simply disappeared, blown apart by the heavy concentration. I slammed my fist down on the nearest hard surface, causing it to buckle before it began to reform, but otherwise showed no emotion. Now was not the time to call attention to our losses.

And then we'd passed them, still firing with all the beams that we could bring to bear. Staring at the Litho dreadnought we'd punched in the nose.

"Come on, come on," I muttered, but the enemy commander didn't cooperate. I'd hoped to hit him hard enough to cause him to break up. I considered the smaller Litho forms to be a lesser threat, even *en masse*. Our gamma bombs had turned out to be highly effective fighter-killers.

Hansen brought us hard about, decelerating to join what I hoped were our allies.

"Bradley," I said, addressing my newly appointed CAG, "send two clean combat drones after that frigate. Their director's only job right now is to get it stabilized and try to bring it to somewhere safe outside the battle zone."

I couldn't spare a manned rescue mission yet. Two combat drones more or less wouldn't win or lose this battle, but by doing this, I showed I cared about every individual under my command. Calculated? Sure, but it was no lie. I *did* care.

My CAG seemed to be holding up all right, shuffling the combat drones around to screen our force. I'd hardly noticed their presence like a cloud of gnats in the holotank, but they'd kept several missiles and at least a dozen fighters off our backs as we made our run, so they were proving their worth. "CAG, how's the drone fuel holding up?"

"Below half on most birds, sir," Bradley replied. "It will help if we can launch the rest of the missiles and start rotating some aboard for refueling."

"Not in the middle of a fight, Bradley," I said.

Valiant had the capability to service the combat drones, but she was no carrier. Only two at a time could be brought in. At least no personnel needed to be involved since small brainboxes controlled the refueling and rearming bays.

I moved to Bradley's side to examine his boards. "Be as conservative as you can with your shots, but keep them with us. Weapons fire is the biggest drain on the combat drones, not simply flying around."

"Yes, sir."

"In fact," I continued, "launch a full strike with the remaining combat drone missiles at the nearest cruiser. That will clean them up and save some fuel." It wasn't the best use of the weapons, but I was still feeling my way through my squadron's capabilities and tactics, and had to balance pros and cons of everything.

The nearest cruiser was one of the six—now five—which engaged with our supposed allies.

"Divert a quarter of those missiles toward that fighter swarm," I said, watching the cloud we had launched fighting to overcome inertia and line up on the enemy. Firing missiles sideways or backward had its drawbacks as they did not have the benefit of the launching ship's velocity.

Another minute brought us around in a loop that flanked the five Lithos engaged with the Raptors, who were down to four ships of their own. All of the Lithos were damaged. "Long range fire," I said, wanting to distract the enemy from our allies. Our power reserves had risen to sixty percent, so I figured we had one more monster firing pass in us before we had to pull back and recharge.

The back line of Lithos had turned around and sought to reinforce their five ships as we had swung wide. Their other three crippled ships, the two cruisers and the dreadnought, looked to be withdrawing in a small group toward the ring. "Look, they're running," I pointed out mainly to keep our people's morale up. "That's good news. They're not impossible to break."

Now four Raptor heavy cruisers flew with us. Together, we faced ten Lithos and a fighter squadron. All of the enemy ships had sustained significant damage, but none so badly that they were running or breaking up. I watched as our barrage of sixty missiles neared their targets, fifteen toward the Litho fighters, forty-five at one cruiser.

Only one of the first group made it through to detonate near the Litho small craft. It knocked out all but a couple of them in one blow. At least a dozen of the other group ran the gauntlet to pummel the Litho cruiser, three detonating on contact, the best result we could hope for. No battleship, it began to calve at the last moment, but then broke apart into several ugly chunks bearing no resemblance to spacegoing vessels. The blasts flung them off in various directions.

My crew cheered.

"Lens formation. Stay tight," I reminded them as our grouping became sloppy. "Hansen, point us at the nearest ship. Everyone else cue off *Valiant* and fire when ready."

We accelerated toward the melee again. The Lithos turned five of their nine ships to face us in a ragged slanting line. I could feel our heavy and medium APs firing. Unlike lasers, they accelerated actual particles to near light speed and thus generated recoil almost like guns. Hansen muttered profanities and wrestled with his controls, keeping *Valiant* aligned like a race car fishtailing down a wet track.

"Missiles, full spread, now. Target the third cruiser in line." A moment later my battlecruiser's six missile tubes and the two on each remaining frigate spat more than two dozen guided nukes. The barrage seemed puny compared to the two earlier off our combat drones, but it was all I had. Even as they leaped away from us, our APs turned the lead cruiser into an inferno.

In return, a swarm of missiles calved off our opponents and beams of their own came questing for our lives. Unwilling to give up the offense, I did not order shields raised.

"Combat drones forward," I snapped. "Get their missiles or force them to detonate."

In the wake of our missile strike, all sixty-some remaining combat drones accelerated, putting their mechanical bodies between us and the Lithos. This made me doubly glad they were unmanned. Even if we had enough pilots, I would never have been able to use them as such a sacrificial screen.

Frigate six fell back, main engines knocked out, curved away from the fight and heading for deep space and possible safety. The pilots had named the ships, but I hadn't memorized them yet so I just left them numbered in the holotank. Maybe I knew some would be lost in this fight and thought the pain would be lessened if I didn't get to know them too well. I was starting to regret not building, say, two cruisers rather than twelve frigates, but this had provided us maximum speed and firepower. Unfortunately I had to accept the casualties.

"Number six has taken heavy damage," Adrienne reported, confirming what I already knew. "They still have repellers and life support."

"Tell them to play dead. We'll pick them up later. Target the next cruiser."

As we shifted the APs to the cruiser second in line, our missile salvo reached the third. Four made it through to explode near the enemy, but that didn't take him out. Instead, he broke up into two dozen fighters.

Then our sensors overloaded again as a massive number of Litho nukes detonated between us in a rippling wave, wiping out two thirds of our attacking combat drones in one fell swoop. Whether that was the Lithos' intention or just a programmed reaction to our birds' presence near their missiles, I didn't know, but the effect was the same.

"CAG, divert what's left against their fighters," I said. "Use their suicide bombs if you have to. I'd rather face their slow cruisers than anything speedy."

"Yes, sir." Our score of remaining combat drones angled over to engage their Litho counterparts in mutual annihilation. At that point I ceased to concern myself with them.

Splitting my attention between the holotank and the forward viewscreens, I saw our APs hammering our target. It took longer to finish this cruiser off because we had lost three frigates and several of our own weapons, and our capacitors had dropped below ten percent reserves. The Litho cracked in half just as we swept by at close range, pouring fire into him. Molten magma churned on all the nearer surfaces. One chunk shot into our path, and I thought for a moment we had breathed our last, but in the deceptive vastness of space, we slipped by.

Unfortunately, frigate eleven did not. I watched a rear screen as the ship was obliterated. We curved away in a path that would put us behind the Raptors. More curses escaped my lips, things that should have made Adrienne's ears turn red, but she remained stoic. Four frigates knocked out with two, maybe three dead crews. I tried not to let my face show my concern.

Where before this battle had seemed like a sterile tactical problem, one where we would swoop in and out slashing our enemies to ribbons, now the load of it came crashing down on me. I hadn't really been prepared for the gut-punch of having people under my command killed like this, as a direct result of my decisions. It felt like losing, and I told myself Cody Riggs wasn't going to lose.

Never.

Fortunately, no one appeared to notice my turmoil as Hansen led the remaining ships around in a wide circle aimed at coming in behind the Raptors and making another run. Forcing my mind back to the problem at hand, I checked the energy reserves. Twelve percent and climbing slowly—too slowly. Suddenly I felt gun-shy, unwilling to risk any more lives with these brutal close AP runs.

"Switch to lasers," I ordered. "Use targeted long-range fire, heavy guns only. Back up the Raptors and coast in. We need to recharge."

Hansen grunted in agreement, trimming out *Valiant* so the restraint tentacles relaxed a bit.

Unfortunately, every shot we fired meant that much less juice in the batteries, but power management was always a zero-sum game. We already had the battlesuits in their niches as auxiliary generators, and I'd turned most of the marines into gunners and combat drone directors anyway. Another thing I realized was that I'd rather have marines running the combat drones as losing the little craft would naturally free up my grunts for other duties as the battle progressed.

I was finding I had a lot to learn after all. Every battle showed the book was just a baseline and each situation played out differently.

"Lay one missile on each remaining enemy ship or cluster," I ordered. We were running low on missiles, but I still wanted to add to the Lithos' complications, and maybe we would get lucky.

Another Raptor went out in a blaze of beam fire, but not before he turned and slammed into a Litho cruiser, detonating in a flash of fusion overload. That seemed to inflict just enough damage to trigger its calving. "Two more missiles at that fighter swarm," I said.

Our lasers pushed one more cruiser over the edge, and we launched another pair of missiles at that group. Checking the power reserves, I saw we had recharged to over thirty percent. "Switch the heavies to AP fire. We need to break up the rest of the Lithos. It seems like they'd rather stay intact, so we want them to calve." I wasn't certain why, but my instincts said that anything an enemy desired, I would try to frustrate.

It became apparent a moment later. The missiles targeted on the first Litho fighter swarm got picked off even as it closed with the three remaining Raptors. Those turned tail suddenly and ran, extending the Lithos' time needed to engage. The enemy second fighter group followed in the wake of the first, the whole mess heading roughly in our direction, as we had been firing over the Raptors' shoulders before.

"Shift fire to the fighters," I said, but it turned out to be unnecessary. The three Raptors formed up closely and, as the Litho fighters overtook them, an astonishing storm of point-defense grasers lashed out. The enemy ran into a wall of unseen fire for gamma rays, like X-rays, were invisible to the naked eye. It was only by second-order effects such as impacts and firing tube leakage that our sensors could determine what ensued.

In this case, as the enemy fighters ran into this tornado of pinpricks, they simply lost all power and began to drift, some tumbling. Their templates—their "pilots"—must have been killed, scrambled by the lethal Raptor wavelengths. Even though the Lithos were nano-machines, this still made me shudder. Something about invisible death reaching through the walls and destroying the intelligence within seemed more horrifying than ordinary destruction.

I now realized why the Raptors' tactics made sense, at least more than they had to me before. Rather than trying to clobber Litho warships in turn, destroying them utterly as we'd tried to do, they were merely breaking them up into fighters or missiles. That would render them nearly ineffective because of the Raptors' extraordinary rear-facing point defense. It was a horse archers' tactic to sting the enemy and get him to chase, then fire the Parthian shot to the rear.

Against the Lithos—hell, against anyone that generated a lot of fast craft like fighters or missiles, it was smart, damn smart. We'd have to seriously consider beefing up our own point defense in the same way.

However, it didn't make for ships that could hold a line, or a ring, any more than horse archers could go nose to nose with heavy infantry. Once the enemy had enough mass, they would be inevitably pushed back.

The three extraordinarily maneuverable Raptor heavy cruisers, looking vaguely like birds with forward-swept wings and taloned feet, finished off the fighters and then came about in elegant curves to take positions off our port side, a bit ahead.

"Interesting spot they picked," Hansen said. "If we turned toward them or fired missiles, we'd be facing that phalanx of point-defense beams."

"Makes sense. They see we're anti-Litho, but in their position I'd be careful too." With our combined squadron, I was confident we could finish off the rest of the local Lithos. "Hansen, full braking. Hold the range open. Let's go back to lasers and fire another salvo of missiles, spread among the rest of the enemy. Our goal is now to provoke them to calve."

"We'll let the Raptors pick off the resulting small craft, aye," Hansen said.

When our ships slowed, the Raptors slowed with us. I had thought they preferred to close with the enemy, but now they were showing some discretion and tactical flexibility. "Let's hope we never have to fight them. Our missiles and fighters would be useless."

As the remaining several Lithos had all taken damage, it took only a few moments to pummel the first into splitting up, and the Raptors took care of the resulting mixed swarm of missiles and fighters by presenting their tails.

"Maybe we should call them Skunks," I remarked, "or Porcupines. I wonder what they'll look like in the flesh?"

"Just as long as they don't try to eat us or kill us, I don't care if they *are* skunks," Hansen replied.

We destroyed the rest of the Litho squadron similarly without a loss on our side, for which I was very grateful. What followed was a lull in the fighting. It gave me much-needed time to take a look at the overall situation.

It wasn't good.

-33-

After telling Hansen to follow the Raptors we accompanied, I widened the perspective in the holotank to examine the rest of the star system.

Two stars occupied the center of this system, a binary pair composed of a young hot yellow star like Earth's sun and an older red dwarf. The ring we had just gone through orbited these stars with no planet nearby. It was about half an AU out. That meant it was hot around here, with an average of four times the stellar radiation of something at one AU. The Lithos must be happy about that. I wondered if this was one factor in the Raptor's difficulty in holding them back. The Lithos performed better when close to a star.

The nearest planet appeared to be a green, Earthlike world about one AU out. I labeled this Prime, both because it was first in line counting outward from the central stars, and because our sensors said it was heavily inhabited and industrialized. The green world was offset from the ring's orbital position, but it was getting closer all the time because the ring orbited faster and was overtaking it.

The battle between the Lithos and the Raptors wasn't over, but it had definitely entered a quieter stage. We'd done our part to turn the tide, and I felt good about that.

The Lithos still had over half their fleet intact. At least a hundred fifty bulky ships now stood in a rough spherical formation ten thousand miles out from the ring. The Raptors had interposed themselves between the enemy fleet and their green homeworld. They were holding their own but numbered about half of the Lithos in strength. They were backing up and breaking off. As they ran, they continued to snipe with long-range beams while the Lithos glided slowly forward, chasing them.

I told Adrienne to send two pairs of frigates after each of our damaged ships with orders to get the crew off and self-destruct the vessels if the engines couldn't be restored. I didn't want anyone, not even our new allies, to be able to examine our tech without permission.

As we watched, the Raptor fleet continued to fall back toward Prime. Given the slower Litho acceleration, the enemy should take days to arrive there, assuming they did not calve into smaller ships. Against the Raptor point defense that would be suicide, so we had some time before the next major battle that seemed likely to decide the fate of their homeworld.

Farther out in the star system, the holotank showed two more Earthlike planets with both water and industry, although there was much less evidence of civilization than on Prime. I figured these were Raptor colonies. A bluish planet I called Two, the second from the central stars, actually seemed to be hospitable to humans by its temperature. Prime registered as too hot and dry. Farther away still was Three, a rather cold, wet and gray planet that was sparsely inhabited. The fourth planet was a smallish red gas giant, and then came two Mars-sized icy worlds of white and black. All of the planets and their moons had orbital installations chirping with radio traffic. The chorus of emissions, radiation and heat sources made it impossible to be certain which of these worlds might hold another ring.

Something occurred to me as we swung wide around the ponderous Litho fleet heading toward our rendezvous with the Raptors who were retreating toward Prime.

"Where the hell is Marvin?" I asked the ship.

"Last known location of Marvin is shown here," *Valiant* said, causing an icon in the holotank to flash.

"That time stamp is almost an hour old, right after we came through!" I complained. The ship didn't respond as I'd made a truthful statement that required neither a correction nor an answer.

Running my finger over a slidebar on a touch-screen, I ran recorded events backward to the moment we exited the local ring. Then I let go of the slidebar and allowed the recording to advance.

The results were interesting—and irritating. I watched as *Greyhound* curved away from my squadron immediately after coming through the ring into the battle zone. Marvin's rebuilt ship accelerated at an astonishing rate.

"Marvin sure gave her some legs," I said. The yacht dodged past the eight Raptor gunships that had fired on us before losing itself in the glare of the twin suns.

"*Valiant*, hail Marvin. Make sure our transponder is working, and maintain active sensor sweeps. We have no need to hide right now."

"Hello, Captain Riggs," said Marvin's voice a moment later.

"Where are you, Marvin?"

In response, *Greyhound's* icon appeared, paralleling our course at a million miles out. He'd turned on a transponder and my system had automatically placed him.

"I haven't abandoned you, *Captain* Riggs."

"Thank you, *Captain* Marvin. I need you to work on talking to the Raptors—the biotic species that appears to be dominant in this system. As you can see, we're tentatively operating as allies with them against the Lithos."

"Raptors—nomenclature stored. I congratulate you on your tactical prowess and on your ability to form friendships quickly, Captain Riggs. I've already begun recording and processing signals from the Raptor ships and their homeworld, which is your apparent destination."

"Excellent. I need some other things from you when you're free. First, find the other ring or rings in this system. Second, see what you can do to assist in the rescue of Star Force personnel aboard the damaged frigates. I've already dispatched ships, but with your little factory and repair capabilities you may be able to do more for them than our people can. Oh, and if you can spare the neural chains, start analyzing the Raptors' combat systems to identify any weaknesses."

A perceptible pause followed. "Is that all?" he asked finally.

I detected a hint of sarcasm in Marvin's voice. "The correct response would be 'is that all, *sir*.' Remember, Marvin, you're under my command and you're on Star Force's payroll. If these challenges bore you, or are beyond your capabilities, I could consider a change of assignment. I believe the food service system aboard *Valiant* is inefficient. Have you ever wanted to be a cook?"

"No, Captain Riggs. I'll execute your lengthy list of demands without delay."

"Smartass," I said, but he'd already closed the channel.

"Maybe you should invite him to the pool room," Hansen suggested.

I chuckled, then turned to my new CAG. "Bradley, do we have any combat drones left?"

"Just one left, sir. I've already taken it aboard for servicing."

"Make sure you upload its experience to the factory so the new combat drone brains won't be complete blanks. Sakura?" I said over ship's command channel, "what's our status?"

"We'll have most of our damage repaired within a day," her voice replied.

"What about building more combat drones?"

"We have materials for about six more. After that we'll need to do some mining."

"Go ahead and build one to give our remaining combat drone a wingman, but hold off on the rest. I have about a dozen ideas for improvements."

I heard Sakura sigh over the intercom, which meant she wasn't making any effort to hide her feelings. "Sir, as soon as we can, we need to have another production meeting to discuss our current and future equipment."

"Couldn't agree more, Chief. For now, do your best."

"Skipper," Hansen called, "the group of Raptors we're following isn't moving to rejoin the Raptor fleet. If they were, we'd be changing course by now. I've also noted that our escorts have been accelerating."

"Where are we going?"

"Directly to Prime, I believe." Hansen punched up a projection of our track, which came very near Prime. "We'll be there in about a day if we maintain these parameters. We could get there faster on our own if you give the order."

"Hmm," I mused. "We're probably being escorted to meet their leaders. If I were in their position and outside help suddenly showed up, I'd be eager to find out more about us. Unless Prime has some heavy defenses, they're going to go down fighting, but they will go down. Seventy ships won't stop the Lithos even with our help."

"Captain," Adrienne said suddenly, "it's worse than that. Look at the ring."

I manipulated the holotank with careful touches. The perspective swung around sickeningly, then paused. Another squadron of a dozen or so Lithos was just coming through the ring behind us. Among them was a big ship—a dreadnought. They must have rapidly repaired these vessels or calved them from the hollow moon itself.

"Well, that's unfortunate," I said, staring for a moment at the situation. "I really don't want to abandon these people, but we aren't responsible for their predicament, and I'm not going to get us all killed in some futile gesture. Once we locate the other ring make sure we lay a course to get us there fast, just in case."

"What if there's something worse on the far side of the next one?" Hansen asked.

"Always the optimist, aren't you?" I asked. "We'll do what we can and what we have to, XO. We survived and prospered in the Lithos' own system so let's not give up just yet. Did you say we could go faster?"

"Yes."

"Do it. Increase our acceleration gradually but continuously until the Raptors can't keep up. I want to reach Prime as soon as we can. We may need every minute before the Lithos arrive."

"Understood." Hansen programmed in the parameters, then took his hands off the controls. In open space, there was no need for fine-tuning. He shook his head and stretched. "Permission to rotate the watch?"

"Granted."

"I'll stay here until 1600 then continue the normal rotation," Hansen said. "I'll call you if something comes up, sir."

Because he was in charge of the schedule, I didn't argue with him. I liked to have one of us on the bridge at all times.

"Sounds good. Oh, and start having Chief Bradley shadow you as officer of the deck. If he works out, he'll be warranted to stand command watch." Right now all I had in the way of commanders was Hansen, Sakura, Adrienne and me—with Kwon in a pinch. We'd lost the gunnery and medical warrant officers in the original ring mishap.

"Aye aye, sir. I have the watch."

When I left the bridge, Adrienne followed. I glanced at her, trying to gauge her mood. She appeared to be all business. She didn't look at me, and I decided not to look at her. She'd followed me without asking, so it was up to her to tell me what she wanted.

A stop at the wardroom gave her an excuse to speak as I pulled a plastic beer bottle out of the chiller and popped it open. When I dropped my eyes from the first long pull, I found Adrienne holding an open one herself, finishing a swallow. Unusual, that. She detested the factory-brewed stuff. I waited to see what all this meant.

Adrienne cleared her throat and then tipped the bottle's neck to clunk against mine with the distinctly unsatisfying non-clink of plastic.

"Cheers," she said.

"You too," I responded. "Are we cool?"

"If by that peculiar Americanism you're wondering if I'm still in a snit...then no, I am not. Yes, we're cool. Let's talk, shall we?" While her words might have been light, her expression seemed somber.

Encouraged, I slid into a chair. "I'm sorry if—" I began, but she cut me off.

She held up a firm hand, still frowning. "No, sir, it was I who was out of line. I'm not really Star Force—or at least I'm very new to everything." She searched my face with concern. "How are you holding up?"

I took another drink to avoid looking into those deep, blue eyes. "Well enough, I guess. Professionally I'm satisfied, but I can't say I'm happy."

"We lost people today. People—" Her voice hitched and then came back after she sipped from her beer. "People I knew—at least some of them. Petty officer Sultan, for example. She and I used to play handball at the ice moon base…"

"I'm sorry," I said again. "It's hit me hard, too. Probably we haven't fully felt it."

"What I mean is," she went on, "I just now truly realized how serious our jobs are, especially yours. This isn't a lark, and there's no place out here for personal concerns. Our heads have to be clear. I know now why you kept me at arm's length, and I have to agree. You can't have me second-guessing your orders, and I can't expect to share every meal with you when others can't."

"Well, people can sit at our table whenever they want," I protested weakly.

"They won't though, so I've decided that we can't do this anymore."

I held my teeth together to keep my jaw from sagging in disappointment. "Can't share a meal?"

"Not alone." Adrienne paused, idly smoothing a napkin on the table. "You know, I've done some reading on the topic of old Royal Navy customs. The captain would dine by himself or he might invite officers in rotation to share a meal in his cabin. His steward and perhaps a midshipman served even then so he was never really alone with any officer. Once a week, or as often as his personal supplies held out, he would invite all the officers to a real dinner party. Also, he would only eat in the wardroom when invited by the other officers as the captain's presence was deemed inhibiting to their comfort."

I slammed my bottle down causing the cheap beer to foam. "This isn't the Royal Navy, Adrienne, and I'm not a sea captain. I'm not going to set up some kind of weird formality based on nineteenth-century customs."

"I'm just trying to point out that there are other ways to do things that might help mitigate morale problems. You want it both ways, Captain Riggs. You want me all to yourself socially at meals, but you also want to be chaste and innocent of any deeper relationship in the eyes of the crew. You don't sit down socially with Hansen or Sakura or even Kwon, and yet you expect instant respect and obedience from me on the bridge."

"Oh, so now you know more about command than I do?" I knew I was being unprofessional, but the words sprang out of their own accord.

Adrienne lifted her eyes to meet mine. "I know about class and hierarchy because I was brought up with wealth and social standing. I grew up with servants who were valued members of the household but nevertheless were *not* family. There were boundaries not to be crossed, but within those boundaries there was kindness and respect. That's why I've come to realize you were right. However, you've got all this theory from books and from the oddity of four years at the Academy. My understanding comes from a lifetime of experience."

"So," I said, "let's hear it. Tell me what I'm doing wrong."

Refusing to be baited, Adrienne remained thoughtful. "This ship is like my father's estate. Without economic incentives, status and the favor of the powerful means everything, because there's no outlet beyond this ship. No one has a family to go home to or a bar in which to carouse. These seventy-odd remaining souls are it. For example, you just handed Bradley a plum—if he can handle it. With a word, you elevated him to the aristocracy in your kingdom."

"Is there a point here?" Part of me knew I shouldn't be, but I was getting irritated at this alternate version of Olivia lecturing me about my job.

Patiently, Adrienne continued. "Everything else on this ship runs on a system. Back at the undersea base, we'd started working out our social system naturally. It helped a great deal that no one was shooting at us for a while. However, the training program and the twelve three-person frigate crews broke that up. Now you need to start implementing some kind of social system or it will form naturally, but it will be warped under the pressure of combat."

I rolled my eyes. "So all I need to do is invite people to dinner once a week?"

"Now you're being deliberately obtuse. How can someone so smart with tactics be so stupid with people?"

I paused, realizing I'd finally pissed her off. Was that what I wanted? I told myself it wasn't, and that I should listen with an open mind. It was hard because I really did want her company—alone.

Adrienne dumped her beer on the smart metal deck and wiped her mouth with a napkin. "That's the last time I drink this swill in comradeship with you, Ensign Riggs, and from now on our meals together will be only in the company of others. Good day."

She stood up and marched out of the wardroom.

Once the door had shut I hurled my bottle against the wall and tossed hers next for good measure. Who did she think she was, trying to run my command? Telling me who I could and couldn't eat with? Modern people didn't need all that social rigmarole to maintain discipline. I had four years of leadership studies behind me and all the stories from my old man packed into my brain, and that was all I needed. After two more beers I was even more convinced I was right, especially when Sakura and Hansen came to the wardroom and got some food from the auto-galley.

One step above packaged rations, food produced by the galley took the form of factory-made pastes combined with available spices. After it cooked them in various ways—anything fried tended to be popular—it dispensed meals to order. I sat down with the two warrant officers. They both greeted me respectfully and made small talk, but neither seemed comfortable.

Maybe they had a thing going and I was the third wheel. Sakura was wearing makeup, which was unusual, and maybe even perfume. With a little help even her stocky figure looked pretty decent, and a guy couldn't fault her straightforward personality. Maybe she'd settle Hansen down a bit if they got together.

As soon as I politely could, I finished and left, grabbing a six-pack on the way out. I was feeling pretty good by that time but once alone and in my quarters my mood turned dark, and I headed for the dead Captain's cabin. What the hell, Sir William didn't need his booze anymore. He was Panda droppings by now. I shook my head grimly and muttered to myself. A crewman passing me in the passageway threw me an odd glance.

In the captain's stateroom I finished off what I had brought, and then found a couple of Belgian bottles aptly decorated with a horned devil on them. I polished them off while the high-resolution wall-screen displayed random views of Earth's wonders. Punching up the Yosemite program, my favorite, I passed out on the sofa looking at Half Dome beneath a blazing sunset.

I wondered if I'd ever see it again with my own eyes.

-34-

Waking up was unpleasant, but I'd been hung over worse. *Valiant*'s voice insisted I get up and start my shift in fifteen minutes, enough time to run a hot shower and change underwear. Checking my chrono, I cursed.

"*Valiant*, why wasn't I awakened at the start of my shift?"

"You didn't respond to the alarm. Warrant Officer Hansen rescheduled your watch one rotation later."

Damn. I felt like a fool getting drunk and sleeping through my duty. I never should have added those Devil-brand beers on top of the others. They packed a punch. Well, as I worked as hard or harder than anyone else, I decided to forgive myself and forget about it.

When I stepped onto the bridge, I acted like nothing was wrong. I nodded to Kwon, who was officer of the deck right then. That in itself was a rebuke. Kwon was utterly trustworthy and reliable within his comfort zone but was completely out of his depth commanding ships.

Fortunately *Valiant* was capable of following a course on its own until I reached the bridge…assuming I was sober.

Thinking about the empty bridge depressed me. Obviously, I wasn't as good a commander as I'd been telling myself I was. I'd missed my shift and gotten nearly a dozen people killed so far on this mission.

Kicking myself into gear, I checked on the two damaged frigates. I felt relieved to see that one had been restored to mobility. On the other the crew had been rescued, and the ship destroyed as I'd ordered.

"Go below, Kwon, you're relieved," I said.

The big man grinned and saluted as he hastened away, probably on his way to have a beer and a date with Steiner. I could tell he'd been uncomfortable standing watch on the bridge.

Hansen had given me some extra sleep, but he'd also cleverly paid me back. We were about six hours from arrival at Prime, which meant I really had a shift and a half, as I wasn't about to leave the bridge during the approach. I mentally saluted him. Subtle rebukes didn't bother me as long as he didn't do it publicly. Anyway, I deserved some punishment for my sins, and everyone else could use the time off. I expected them all here during any emergency no matter whether it was their watch or not. How could I expect any less of myself?

The holotank now showed a highly detailed representation of the system as *Valiant* had ample time to gather sensor readings as we flew. The Lithos still barreled ponderously toward Prime, and the damaged Raptor fleet was just behind us also hurrying home for repairs.

On the outward side of the planet and far beyond it, I saw a group of Raptor ships still under hard acceleration. Zooming in, I counted about a hundred vessels similar to the ones we accompanied: warships. These must be their reinforcements, their relief fleet, hurrying to get home in time to fight the Lithos. They weren't going to make it, though. They would be several hours late.

Tracking their course backward, I saw they'd originated at Six, the farthest, Mars-like world at the edge of the system. While I couldn't be sure, I could think of only one reason a fleet that large should be stationed there.

The second ring.

"*Valiant*, hail Marvin." Once he'd acknowledged, I said, "Good job with the two frigates, Captain Marvin. How are you doing with the translation?"

"Ready when you are, Captain Riggs."

"You seem in a good mood, Marvin."

"I'm in an excellent mood. With so much to do, I've finally approached full utilization of my neural capacities."

"Too much brainpower can be a curse, eh, Marvin?"

Marvin didn't reply for a moment, as if he was parsing my meaning. "I never thought of that, but you're correct. With increased neural circuitry comes increased room for boredom. Perhaps I should consider dumbing myself down to a near-human level."

"Funny robot. Did you notice the ring at the sixth planet?" By risking an educated guess, I wanted to impress Marvin with my own brainpower. Too often he seemed to forget he didn't know everything.

"You have confirmation?"

"Just keep looking, Marvin," I said airily. "You'll find it. In the meantime, give me a briefing on these Raptors. I presume you have decoded imagery?"

A moment later a graphic appeared in the forward viewscreen and the watch-standers there started to chatter.

"So, this is a Raptor?" I asked, examining the picture. "I thought they'd be hawks. These look like ostriches—giant, mean ostriches."

A large, flightless, predatory bird was the closest analogue I could think of. The picture was a sort of group portrait. They had long necks, two thick legs and deadly claws. Unlike earthly birds, they had leathery skin and tails, rather than feathers. The mottle-brown creatures posed and stood in a formal line. They were all at least partially clothed, and I couldn't determine their genders. Each displayed needle-pointed teeth in a long flat snout—or maybe it was a beak. They stood upright and dragged thick tails on the ground behind them like kangaroos. The tails ended in a ball of spikes. In fact, the more I looked at them, the more they looked like a cross between a prehistoric bird and a kangaroo—minus the fur.

"Are those freaky tail spikes natural?" I asked.

"Yes, they are. In fact, that is the species' greatest natural weapon. I've gathered from their transmissions that although their society uses tools and is quite technologically advanced—nearly equal to our own—they maintain primitive social traditions."

"Our modern tech level isn't all that advanced, Marvin. There was a massive intervention by the Nanos and Macros. Our technology and culture are still trying to absorb it all. If these people developed these ships all on their own—they are quite impressive no matter how their social structure operates."

"I believe there was a similar technological intervention here. Certain design elements of their ships and machinery suggest Nano technology has been used as opposed to indigenous nanotechnology, if you can comprehend the difference."

"Got it, Marvin." I put my feet up on the console in front of me, staring at the critter. "The spikes in their tails seem to correspond to their ship tactics," I observed. "I can imagine these things in their primitive past running up to some meat critter, poking it with a stick, and then running away and whacking it with their tails when it charges them until it is dinner. Do you have images of these beings in their normal society, in an urban or military setting?"

On the screen appeared four pictures of Raptors in a sampling of locales that could almost have been Earth. One showed a warrior with a firearm of some type and utilitarian clothing. The warrior had devices draped about it, walking down a trail. On others I saw scenes probably captured from their version of netvids—a parent with offspring in a jungle setting, a family in a ground vehicle, and a group playing some kind of sport with a spherical ball.

"Do the clothing styles indicate gender?" I asked.

"Yes, the bright clothing is worn by the males who, by the way, have retractable display ruffs around their necks. The females wear muted colors. Of course, this tendency is subordinate to their professional attire though it still shows through for one sufficiently observant to pick out the subtleties. In fact, you can see…"

I let Marvin ramble on, briefing me on Raptor society as I tried to retain as much as I could. Any detail might be useful. However, after a certain point my mind rebelled with information overload. I felt like I'd been transported back to the Academy and it was time for class to end.

"Thanks, Marvin. Please package all that up into a briefing. Try to be concise, no more than half an hour, and transmit it to every duty station for the crew to observe. Keep the content at a level anyone can understand, all right? And emphasize that these people are to be our allies, not our enemies."

"Gladly, Captain Riggs." Marvin really did sound delighted. "Packaging data for consumption by unsophisticated persons is a challenging and worthwhile endeavor."

"Great. Now bring *Greyhound* in to join our squadron. I don't want our new friends getting the wrong idea with you lurking out there."

"I think lurking is a pejorative term, sir. I prefer 'distant reconnaissance.'"

"'Keeping a safe distance' is another descriptive possibility. I'll tell you what, robot, I'll send a frigate out and escort you back in so it's clear you're with us. God knows they could mistake that monstrosity you've turned *Greyhound* into for something hostile."

"I still think—"

"Marvin, do it. At the first sign of hostility you can bug out, but for now I want you nearby and firmly identified as one of us."

Marvin dropped the channel then. As soon as the frigate neared him he rendezvoused with us without incident. The Raptors didn't even twitch although we detected they had active sensors pinging away at *Greyhound*.

Once his ship had rejoined our formation, Marvin made words form in the holotank, which only I was near. *Captain Riggs, please go to your stateroom for a private captains' conference.*

Interesting. So there was something Marvin didn't want the rest of the crew to hear. Or at least, he wanted me to choose to tell them. I typed back, *Captain's cabin,* then announced, "I'll be in the old captain's quarters for a few minutes. *Valiant*, call Kwon to the bridge." Once he relieved me, I took the call at Sir William's old desk.

"Now what's this secret?" I demanded.

"Not secret—unless you make it so—but unusual. Possibly sensitive. I'm still stymied by the nuances of human social interactions, but this information seems potentially controversial."

"Thanks for not blurting it out, Captain Marvin," I said, "but please tell me what the hell you're talking about."

"I'll show you." On the big viewscreen Marvin caused several pictures to appear.

It took a minute before I started to realize what it was I was seeing. "Are those Pandas?"

"Yes, Captain Riggs."

"It looks like they're laboring for the Raptors…" The bird-like guards were unmistakable in their role with weapons, uniforms, and watchful demeanors. Nearby, Pandas carried stones, tilled the soil, or performed other manual jobs.

"Slaves," I said.

"Captain Riggs, are you angry?"

"I'm getting that way. Sentients should not be enslaved. It's evil."

"How angry are you?"

I stared at the pictures on the screen. "I don't know, Marvin. Does it matter?"

"Would it be a good or bad thing if you were to become much angrier?"

Then I got it. Marvin was withholding something worse, but as usual he sought to manipulate or manage me just as he'd tried with my father or anyone else who had power over him. "If I get angrier, Marvin, I promise not to shoot the messenger."

"I am not aware of any messenger."

"An idiom, Marvin. Look it up. You're the messenger in this case."

"Idiom noted. Do I have your word you will not 'shoot the messenger'?"

Marvin didn't usually push this hard for assurances unless he was bargaining for something he wanted. In this case, he seemed worried that I would do something rash. Unless the crazy robot had misjudged the situation, the information must be explosive. If he really turned his neural processors on a problem though, he wasn't usually too far off.

"Marvin, I give you my word I will not hold you responsible for what you merely report—as long as you didn't have a hand in creating the situation in the first place."

"Good. I believe you. Here is, as the idiom goes, 'the real kicker.'" He must have looked that one up. A moment later a new set of images appeared in high-resolution detail, and for the second time in the last few months I felt my stomach roil uncomfortably. I went to the head and chugged some of Sir William's orphaned antacids.

Once my stomach had settled down, I sat back down in front of the screen and forced myself to look.

On it were images apparently lifted from a documentary with Marvin's translations alongside Raptor verbal symbols: *Pandas separated into cows and bulls. Pandas in holding pens. Pandas enticed to the slaughter rooms. Processing of Pandas. The choicest Panda cuts are selected. Panda steaks and chops are packaged. The whole Panda is used: nothing wasted!*

"Holy crap," I breathed. "This is *sick*. They're not just slaves, they're *meat*. No wonder the Panda society is twisted."

"Or possibly," Marvin replied, "vice versa. We don't know the full history of these two races. Did they develop in separate star systems? In that case, the Raptors apparently captured a Panda breeding population. Possibly both races arose on the same planet, and the Tullax Pandas are escaped slaves. Perhaps this influenced Panda development, causing them to begin the tradition of consuming enemies. Or, perhaps the Raptors were the ones who adopted a Panda custom. And then there's my tertiary theory, one which I'm sure you'll find fascinating. Did—"

"Okay, Marvin, you've made your point. We can't fully understand their behavior until we understand their past. But I can sure as hell judge their culture as it stands today."

I clenched my jaw until my teeth hurt as Marvin showed me more and more damning imagery.

"What are you going to do about it?" Marvin asked brightly, as if he was questioning me which of several tasty dishes I would enjoy sampling first.

I choked back a rash answer, breathing heavily as my mind slowly encompassed the brutal, bloody images in front of me.

"I'm not going to do anything until I know more. Marvin, I need you to start sorting through their documentaries along with any other source materials you can collect. Build me a summarized history of these two races—three races, really, if you include the Lithos."

"That may take some time. Days, at least."

"Give me a daily report on your preliminary findings. Go over the data with a fine-toothed comb."

"I fail to see how that form of grooming would be appropriate."

I sighed. "It's another idiom, Marvin, an idiom. Now get to work. Don't tell anyone about the Raptors eating Pandas—that's a secret for now."

"A secret? Excellent."

The channel closed, but I was left staring at the console, disturbed. Why was this particular secret 'excellent'? That was one of the key problems with Marvin. You never knew if his odd behaviors were just that—odd—or indicative of some deeper, darker meaning.

-35-

We entered high orbit without incident although our escort seemed to want to lead us closer to the planet. Marvin had done a decent job of coming up with a translation program, but I ignored them and didn't try to contact them yet. As soon as we showed we could speak their language, the Raptors might try to have us do something we didn't want to do. The lesson of the Panda dinner party was foremost in my mind.

I decided the time had come to name the system. I didn't feel like holding a naming contest again, so I declared that system would be called "Orn" short for "Ornithology," the study of birds. It seemed appropriate.

For over an hour, we orbited far above Orn Prime where I hoped the Raptors' ground-based defenses would be less effective. Our preliminary analysis showed eight orbital battle stations circling the green world, each the size of a super-battleship. That would help during the coming fight. Even those stations weren't enough to make it an even contest, however, since only two or perhaps three would be positioned to fire at any one time. On the other hand, if the battle went on long enough they might all revolve into range, following their orbital paths.

Radar imagery showed several missile installations were pinging us from the ground, but we found no evidence of beam-based defensive batteries. The planet's atmosphere appeared perpetually cloudy, and we calculated beam defensive systems would be less effective due to particulate interference.

The heavy water vapor alone would absorb and scatter laser fire.

Orn Prime had no natural moon, which gave it no easy platform to build a large ground-based defense without atmospheric interference. I didn't see more than a handful of ships awaiting us in orbit, and those looked to be vessels that had limped home from previous battles. Most of them hung in space around the orbital shipyards, which were hives of frenzied activity.

Taking a cue from the Raptors, I brought in our own drones and frigates to effect repairs aboard *Valiant*. It was a slow process as the ship wasn't designed or equipped to serve as a true mothership.

In preparation for initial contact with these newly met aliens, I made sure all my officers were on the bridge—Hansen, Adrienne, Sakura were on hand with Kwon and Bradley representing the enlisted marines and crew. For an hour or so the Raptors ignored us, but the expected call finally came.

"Incoming transmission from Orn Prime," *Valiant* announced.

I could see the source of the signal was a military base near one of the planet's largest cities.

"Marvin, are you on the line?" I asked.

"Ready, Captain Riggs. It's a combined audio-video transmission. Shall I return the same?"

"Yes, go ahead open a channel and use their language."

On the main screen I saw nine Raptors sitting at a table facing the video pickup. The Raptor in the center wore rich but dull clothing, as did the four to her right. I inferred they were female by their manner of dress, and none wore military accoutrements. The other four were, if I had to guess, two military males in brilliantly colored uniforms and two male civilians. I wondered if we were dealing with a matriarchy.

The female in the center of the group spoke for the rest. "Greetings, fellow biotic beings. I am called Ralda, Eldest of Raptors." I presumed Marvin had assigned certain words like 'Raptors' to otherwise untranslatable names and sounds. I mean, what did our word "human" signify anyway?

"I'm called Riggs," I replied, lifting a hand in greeting. "I'm the commander of this squadron of warships, and we come from the planet we call Earth. We entered your system hoping to find allies against the Lithos, your enemies. I hope we've proven ourselves worthy to be your comrades in battle."

Ralda waved a desultory hand as if shooing flies, and I had the impression of great age. I recalled she'd introduced herself as "the Eldest." Perhaps they chose leaders based mainly on longevity.

"Who is your Elder, Riggs?" Ralda said. "I would speak with she who is in charge."

"I—"

Adrienne put a hand on my arm, digging in her fingernails and leaning over to whisper in my ear. "If they have females for leaders, it might not be wise for a male to claim to be the boss."

I considered that for about two seconds then gently removed her hand.

"Eldest Ralda, we do not separate leadership by gender. I happen to be male, and I am in charge, no other."

"That is inappropriate. I cannot treat with a male of such minimal rank." Ralda stood up as did the rest of her entourage. Then she walked out leading all the females with her. The males stared after them, the video pickup shook as if it had been jostled, and then they began to whisper among themselves.

Unfortunately for them, the audio was good and Marvin was able to translate much of what they discussed. Apparently they were completely confused and at a loss until finally one of the military men stepped forward. "We apologize for the Eldest's abrupt manner. I am Lomm, Senior Staff Director. Perhaps we can establish relations on a purely military level."

"The military is only for males?" I asked.

"Of course."

"For your information, we have females in our military."

This caused another huddled conference, and then Lomm spoke again. "As long as we're not forced to speak with your females, I do not believe this will be a problem. Your internal perversions are your own concern."

"Perversions?"

Marvin broke in and said, "Perhaps that's not the best English equivalent. Maybe 'oddities' would be better."

"Just keep things simple and inoffensive, Marvin. I hate to think what nuances of meaning they're getting from us. Commander Lomm—"

Lomm's ruff came up suddenly and he hissed like an animal defending its territory. Just as quickly, this display subsided.

"Apologies, again, Commander Riggs. There must be some error in your translation software. I am not a mere commander. I am the Senior Staff Director."

"Fine. I meant no offense. Can I just say Senior Lomm?"

"That will not be excessively insulting."

All this fine diplomacy with effete snobs was giving me a headache. I could tell already this was going to be a long meeting.

"Okay, Senior Lomm, you may have to get used to our informal ways. Anything offensive is probably our translator's fault. Let me start by pointing out that all the politeness in the world won't matter in about three days when those Lithos show up and wipe your race off this planet."

"Your words are harsh but true. We are facing a disaster. But what can be done?"

"You have a relief fleet on the way from your outer colonies. Combined with your main force and mine it may be enough to defeat the Lithos."

The old warrior looked around, found a chair, and sat down heavily. "The relief fleet will not arrive until a day too late. That is unfortunate, as by that time the deaths of billions will have occurred. The Lithos are not here to conquer us. They will bombard our world then infect it with their templates. We will make our stand in orbit and pray to our ancestors we win."

"I disagree with your strategy. You have no chance. You'll lose your main fleet, then your homeworld, and then your relief fleet will follow in without support and be taken out as well. The rest of your worlds will then die, undefended.

While I spoke, Lomm's ruff deflated steadily as did those of his fellows.

"If, however," I continued, "you were to pull your home fleet back you may lose this single planet, but you may spare your race from extinction. It's a hard choice, but extinction would be permanent."

I knew it was easy for me to give the Raptors such sage advice. We weren't talking about Earth. I'd hate to have to face that kind of choice. It helped me to remember that my own father had made similarly dramatic command decisions in his day especially when the Macros were assaulting Earth. For example, he'd once bombarded and killed millions of Chinese in order to temporarily placate the Macros and save billions more civilians.

"Your words are dust in my ears but no more than I deserve," Lomm said at last. "We warriors have failed our mothers and our sisters. We reject your solution, however. It's better to die with honor than live to see our females turned to ash."

"Senior Lomm, please give me a few minutes while I confer with my officers." I made a cutting motion toward the main vid pickup knowing Marvin would be watching, and the audio went silent.

I turned to the others. "I need options, people. I don't think they'll pull back. I can't say that I blame them. How can we beat this Litho fleet before they wipe out Orn Prime?"

Adrienne tapped furiously on her console. "If they gave us all the materials we asked for we could churn out more than a thousand nuclear repeller mines in the next three days."

"Good idea," I said, "but that's not enough to blanket so much territory. The mines are very effective against the smallest enemy craft, but then, so are the Raptor point-defenses. The big Litho ships are the primary threat, especially their dreadnought. That must be why they've resisted the temptation to break up their ships against the Raptors—they know doing so is tantamount to losing the ship. No, we need something that will take down their flying mountains."

"Why are we doing all this thinking for them?" Hansen asked. "They have the resources of a whole planet to draw on. They must have thousands of factories."

"If I may interrupt," Marvin said over the ship-to-ship com-link, "I don't believe the Raptors have Nano-factories like ours. I base this conclusion on my scans of Prime, which show large complexes both on the ground and in orbit. These structures are consistent with more conventional industrial construction methods. Putting anything new into production would take them days, if not weeks."

I nodded. "So even if they were visited at some point in the past by Nano ships, they didn't acquire the factory technology. Maybe they exhausted most of their munitions trying to hold the gate. They probably have only a couple of days' production of missiles and mines to reload on their ships."

"That means our one single factory might be able to out-produce this entire planet in the short term," Adrienne said.

"All this is beside the point," I said. "Mines and missiles aren't going to save this world. Remember, the Lithos don't have to be alive to cripple this planet. Just one of their flying mountains falling onto a major city will kill millions and devastate the environment. We need something that will hit them so hard they can't help but break up."

Hansen leaned forward, "And if they don't? What if they just plunge past us and suicide? The Macros did that at times, preferring to die in order to kill as many biotics as possible."

"I doubt they'll do that," I said thoughtfully. "So far the big ships have tended to break up when stressed, trying to survive as well as kill the enemy. If they do as you suggest, Hansen, the planet is lost anyway. I can't see any way to divert them—especially that dreadnought."

"Captain," Sakura spoke up hesitantly. "If we had inexhaustible power we could do a lot more damage with our antiproton weapons. The Raptors don't use them much, favoring grasers. But in this case, the APs are needed to take down big ships."

"Makes me wonder why the Raptors don't make more APs and fewer grasers," Adrienne said.

Marvin's voice broke in. "Their antiproton weapons are more primitive than ours by at least one order of magnitude.

They likely consume much more power and must be significantly larger in order to do comparable damage."

"Then their ships would run out of energy even faster than ours," I said. "Pound for pound the Raptors' grasers are more efficient, but by keeping their big ships together as long as possible the Lithos have partially countered this advantage. Sakura, what if we had more heavy APs and that unlimited power you want?"

Sakura's brows furrowed in thought. "There's no way to actually do that."

"Indulge me. What if?"

"We could deal out a lot of damage, at least until overheating became a problem."

My mind was racing now with an idea forming that might buy the time the Raptors needed.

"Adrienne, Sakura," I said, "get the factory set up to build super-heavy APs, larger than the two we already have. The bigger the better. I want all the range and punch possible. Assume you have all the materials you need and optimize for fast production."

"Where is all this material and power coming from?" Adrienne asked.

"From the Raptors."

"What about sensors, brainboxes, mountings, everything else that goes into a weapon system?" Sakura asked. She was always the hardnosed, practical engineer.

"Just the AP beam projector, for now, thank you."

"But—" Sakura began.

I pointed at the door. "No time for further discussions. Turnbull can help you with the operational side. Please get down to the factory and start writing scripts. I'll feed you more information as I get it."

Frowning, Sakura and Adrienne left the bridge, but I knew they would get to work. Now that I had the beginnings of a plan, I had to get as many parts of it working in parallel as possible. "Unmute the audio and let me talk to Lomm."

Marvin did as I asked, and I turned to face the main viewscreen. Senior Lomm appeared as crestfallen as before.

"Senior Lomm," I said, "I have an idea, but I need someone high enough in your military and industrial hierarchy to be able to make decisions without others contradicting him—or her. I have no real idea as to the nature of your governing structure, and I don't have time to learn about it. I need one person who can get things done, *fast*. Is that you?"

I suspected it would not be as Lomm seemed uncertain. This council before us was probably akin to the World Joint Chiefs back home—ponderous and prone to inaction. I needed the field officer in charge of the fleet, but I'd already seen that "commander" wasn't necessarily a complimentary term—or at least not prestigious enough.

"No, Commander Riggs. I have no energy for such matters. The one you want is called Klak. He is Senior Field Director, and he commands the home fleet."

"Thank you for your time, Senior Lomm. I'll confer with Klak."

"It does not matter. We are doomed." The channel with Lomm closed.

"Makes you wonder if they're worth saving, eh?" Hansen remarked.

"Yes," I admitted, "but it helps me to think of this effort as sticking it to the Lithos and saving ourselves, not just helping these killer birds."

"We could always run," Hansen suggested. "We already helped them a lot. It's their fight."

I thought it over for a moment. Hansen had a point. Did we want to die for these people?

"I think we can give them a chance to win and still come out intact. You're right, it is their fight. But it's ours, too."

Hansen shoved his chair over to mine, the smart metal of the floor obliging him with a weird undulating movement.

"Riggs," he whispered, "we lost six good people in the last battle, and we don't have many to lose. Okay, we had to get through the ring, and you wanted to get resupplied from these people, I get it. But if we fight again, more frigates will probably be destroyed and even *Valiant*. If we lose this battlecruiser and the factory, we're all screwed. Now's not the time to play hero!"

"You want to let this whole system fall to the Lithos when we might be able to tip the scales?"

Hansen hissed in exasperation. "You wanted me to think big picture, right? Here it is: we have to get home and tell Earth, no matter what."

"Even if we all die, I bet Marvin can get home with all the intelligence. In fact, I'll tell him to do that at my next opportunity."

"I heard you, Captain Riggs," Marvin said from the console in front of me. Apparently he'd still been listening in. He probably eavesdropped whenever he could. "As a member of Star Force, I pledge to do my utmost to return the intelligence I have gathered to Earth—assuming my personal safety is not compromised."

"There you have it," Hansen said sarcastically, his voice rising again. "The robot will save the day as long as there's no risk involved."

"Hansen, you seem to be arguing both sides. You want to run from risk, and then you mock Marvin for wanting to do the same. Maybe the robot is braver than you are."

Hansen turned angrily back to the helm, but I didn't care. I was getting fed up with his whining.

"Listen up, everyone," I said to the bridge watch, knowing they would pass on my words to their buddies. "I want to help these people, but I'm not leading us to some stupid heroic suicide. We have to take a few chances to make it home, and the Raptors may provide valuable assistance if we earn their gratitude. So do your jobs the best you can. I have a plan."

-36-

After several abortive tries, the Raptors finally connected me to Senior Field Director Klak. An impressive specimen of Raptorhood, his multicolored uniform had numerous decorative threads and dangling metallic beads hanging off it. I guess military organizations were the same everywhere.

I expected another frustrating conversation, but Klak immediately suggested we meet aboard *Valiant*. I agreed after making sure there was to be no feasting involved.

Klak arrived half an hour later on a fast courier shuttle accompanied by two aides. I met him with Kwon and six marines as an honor guard—a fully armed and armored honor guard, just in case—and greeted the Raptors on the launch bay deck.

In the flesh, the Raptors were impressive. Running around four hundred pounds each, they displayed about a zillion teeth and their heavily spiked tails were just as vicious-looking. I could see they would make formidable ground troops though I wasn't sure how they could easily construct battle armor to fit.

These three Raptors hadn't bothered with suits. They came through the airlock with lightweight breathing masks that fit over their nostrils but not their snouts. They breathed in through these, and when they exhaled from their mouths I smelled ripe meat. I wondered if it was Panda meat, and I curled my lips in disgust.

Forcing myself to show no fear, I stepped up to Klak and saluted. In turn, he lifted both of his four-digit hands and thumped the floor with his tail, bringing it forward between his feet to do so. That seemed rather awkward, but thinking about the origins of saluting back in Greek and Roman days—showing the hand held no weapons—putting the tail in a nonthreatening position might hold similar meaning.

"Welcome, Senior Klak. I am Commodore Riggs." I'd decided to give myself this title, meaning a captain that commanded a squadron. It was true and should more nearly equal his position as what we would call an admiral.

"I greet you, Commodore Riggs," Marvin's running translation buzzed in my earbuds. The actual words sounded like sibilant hissing. Our words were beamed to the three via directional microphones on nano-tentacles here and there.

"Let's sit down, shall we?" I led them to a nearby conference room where Hansen waited. Despite his annoying manner, I wanted him to play devil's advocate and judge our new allies firsthand if necessary.

"May we examine your impressive ship first?" Klak asked.

There was no way I was going to give them free intel before talking. I thought a moment before formulating an answer.

"I'm sure there will be time for such pleasantries in the near future," I said. "But first we must come to an understanding."

I waved them to Raptor-style seats. Those had been easy to program from their many public broadcast videos we had. I sat down and looked at my counterpart across the table. "I command and lead this squadron of Star Force ships from Earth. Do you command and lead the fleets of your people?"

Klak hissed and withdrew slightly as if my question bothered him...but it was hard to read brand-new aliens. I might be misinterpreting his body language entirely. "I'm Senior Field Director of the fleet we attend. When the relief fleet arrives, I will be Subordinate Field Director to another, who is named Kleed."

"But the relief fleet is smaller than yours."

Klak hissed again. "You see the injustice, then! It is I who fought the Lithos, I who have spilled the blood of my warriors. Kleed is older but less deserving."

My eyebrows went up. "Your system gives command merely on the basis of age?"

"Within a locality, of course. Yours does not?"

Cautiously, I said, "Not always. It is only one of several factors. So...any agreement we reach might be countermanded by Kleed?"

Klak cocked his head at me. "It might, at his whim. His honor is...questionable. But it will not matter. We will all be dead by that time."

"Maybe. What if you could avert that fate? What if I showed you a way to win?"

The ruffs on all three of them flapped, and they hissed to each other too quickly to follow. At last Klak spoke urgently. "Tell us how."

I placed my hands on the table between us and leaned forward slightly. They didn't back away but leaned forward as if to listen more intently.

"I know of two ways to win," I said. "One is more certain but carries a grim price. The other is risky but may yield a great victory and save Orn Prime's people."

"Tell me both."

"The first is simple. Fall back to the relief fleet before the Lithos arrive. Do what you can before that—use mines, long-range fire, and your orbital fortresses—but preserve your fleet. Then, when your ships join into one massive force, come back and defeat the Lithos. We will help you achieve a decisive victory."

Klak shook his head in a rolling motion, like a dog flapping wet ears. "I cannot. I would eat my tail first! Billions of our females would die. Not only that, it would dishonor me, and I would have to turn over my fleet to Kleed. To him would go the glory. If this is the only way there is to win...I would prefer to eat my tail immediately."

I frowned in confusion for a moment. What was all of this about eating tails? I figured it must be some kind of idiom, perhaps referring to suicide. He was saying he would rather die than retreat. I guess he really valued his honor and reputation.

"There is another way," I said, meeting Klak's flinty eyes. "In fact, I would prefer this other way. But as I said, we might be risking your entire race because if we lose, your system will soon be overrun."

"Tell me. I will judge."

I brought up a display of planetary space on the conference table. The image encompassed both the Litho and relief fleets.

"How far does your authority extend?" I asked him.

"I direct this fleet only." Klak tapped the seventy-odd ships grouped near the planet.

"How about the orbital fortresses?" I caused those eight to light up.

"No. They are commanded by another."

"What about the shipyards?" There were four of these where many vessels of his fleet waited for their turn at repair.

"No. The Ministry of Production supervises them."

"The second strategy requires cooperation among these forces," I said, straightening my spine. "You'll have to convince or command those agencies to take unorthodox actions."

I proceeded to lay out my plan, describing the levels of energy I'd need fed into *Valiant* and what our weapons could do with an entire world powering them.

Klak stared into my eyes, and I wondered what was going on inside his strangely shaped head. Now it was time to see what value this guy placed on his honor. In my opinion, a real hero would do whatever was needed regardless of personal cost as my dad had often done. Not only had he killed millions to save the human race, he'd risked his own life countless times. He'd never worried about what people thought of him.

These Raptors reminded me a bit of the medieval Japanese culture. If a samurai found he was in an intolerable conflict between something he absolutely had to do and his own honor, the usual solution was to do it anyway and then commit ritual suicide—seppuku—to atone for it. If a samurai couldn't bring himself to commit seppuku, he was branded an outlaw and killed on sight.

If Klak was a truly honorable being, he would take one of my two offered solutions. If he was more pragmatic, he would probably try to convince the commanders of the orbital fortresses and the shipyards to go along with the plan and then bug out to join the relief fleet.

"All right, Senior Klak. Which will it be?"

Klak looked at me with those beady eyes for a long moment. "I will do what is necessary to implement your second plan. If that means discarding my honor…so be it."

The other two with Klak drew back for a moment as if astonished. He looked at each in turn. One of the subordinates lowered his head, apparently a sign of acquiescence. The other gave the Raptor head-shake and began to stand.

Suddenly, Klak's tail flew high in a vicious arc, crashing into the neck and head of the dissenter. The long spikes penetrated the back of his skull instantly killing the creature. When the dead Raptor sank down and sprawled on the deck, Klak turned his eyes upon the other and shook his bloody tail free of the corpse. The one who had agreed kept his head down still saying nothing. After a moment, the Senior grunted in approval and turned back to me. "As I said, I will do what is necessary."

For my part, I'd sat frozen with my arms and legs tensed to spring away. I'd managed not to appear outwardly fearful.

I could not help but glance down at the dead creature on my deck. Had that one been the more honorable of the two? It was hard to say. I reminded myself that their ways were not ours. Maybe summarily executing subordinates was common practice here.

"Excellent," I said, turning my attention back to Klak. "Let me explain exactly what I need."

Klak listened.

* * *

Minutes later we'd exchanged secure communications protocols, and the Raptors left, abandoning their dead comrade on the floor.

Hansen turned toward Kwon and his marines. "Get out," he said.

Kwon looked at me, and I nodded. "Take the dead Raptor with you and put it somewhere cool and safe. Preserve it, Kwon."

"You sure you don't want some Raptor steaks?" Kwon guffawed. Then he and his marines lifted the dead creature onto their shoulders.

When they'd filed out, Hansen turned to me and glowered. His expression was a mixture of disbelief and anger.

"Are you insane, Riggs? You're backing a military coup? We only just got here!"

"It's hardly a coup. All action will take place in orbit. It's not like Klak is deposing the government on the ground. He's only willing to do what's necessary."

"You say that so smoothly as if it wasn't all your idea. Your daddy would be proud."

"Hey, Klak made his choice. I didn't tell him which plan to choose, and I sure didn't tell him to kill his buddy. We can't judge them by our standards."

Hansen's hands worked as if he wanted to grab me. "You're one ruthless son of a bitch, you know that, Captain?"

"Just like my old man," I said. I banged my open hand on the table in front of him. "If this is what it's going to take to get us home, then we're doing it. And admit it: did you really want to see the Lithos bomb Orn Prime back to the Stone Age just to win the battle? Wouldn't you rather put it all on the line for the whole stack?"

I kept a wide grin on my face. Slowly, Hansen began to return it.

He chuckled ruefully, without real humor. "I'm just glad it's not up to me…sir. So what happens afterward?"

"Afterward?" I hadn't really thought about it, so I faked a casual lack of concern. "Either way, we're covered. Klak will take the fall for any wrongdoing, and we save the planet. If he comes out on top, he's our buddy. I'm sure they will be happy to send us on our way with goodie baskets running over."

"And if we lose the battle?"

"Then we meet up with the relief fleet and make a deal with them. We have technology they need, and we'll make sure to transmit evidence of all our efforts to help them to the other planets."

"Got it all figured out, have you?"

"Yup," I retorted.

"Remember Murphy's law."

"I know what it is."

"But you're too young to feel it in your gut, kid." Hansen poked his reversed thumb into his belly. "In here. You're playing with our lives and millions more on the world below. Billions, maybe."

I let my happy-face drop. "Yeah, Nels," I said, using his first name purposefully. "I get it. I really do. Between you and me, I'm as worried as you are, but we can't let the crew know that. I've been in enough poker games to know the best way to play a hand is without fear. Otherwise, you might as well fold."

We returned to the bridge, and twenty minutes later a secure call came through from Klak. "The director of the orbital fortresses has accepted my usurpation of his authority, but the civilian in charge of the shipyards refuses. I will therefore depose him by force." Klak shuddered as if this action was almost unthinkable. "We will implement the plan."

"Very well, Senior Klak. We await your word." I pumped my fist with jubilation after the channel closed. "Yes! Hansen, bring us down into a lower orbit."

I stood to pace around the holotank watching for Klak's moves. Soon enough, I detected them.

The orbital fortresses began to gradually speed and slowly rise. They also maneuvered toward each other for rendezvous. They were slow, never having been designed to do more than adjust their orbits. They weren't really ships, but if we got them into the right place at the right time…

Then I saw several of Klak's ships move in on each of the orbital shipyards. Zooming in, I could see a platoon of Raptor marines from each ship leaping the short distance to the space docks and taking positions all over their spidery structures. Combined with the troops from the vessels under repair, Klak reported he had seized the structures within the hour.

"Incoming call from Senior Staff Director Lomm," Marvin announced.

"Put him through, with video."

"What have you done, Commander Riggs?" Lomm demanded. He appeared to be all alone in a room, and he looked even older and more defeated than before. This time, however, his defeat was tinged with outrage.

"*Commodore* Riggs, please," I replied. "There was an error in the previous translation. To what are you referring?"

"Commodore Riggs, then. We observed that you met with Klak aboard your vessel. Now he has rebelled against lawful authority! Somehow you have done this."

"Senior Lomm, do you really think I could force Klak to do anything? I merely pointed out some hard facts and let him decide what to do. However," I smiled slightly, "what will *you* and your government do about it?"

"At another time I would have ordered our ground-based installations to fire on Klak's fleet. Then Kleed could arrest him when he arrived…but I'm not blind. With the Lithos soon to come, I cannot further weaken our defenses." The old Raptor drew himself up. "Honor demands I must eat my tail."

"Stop!"

I held up a hand, and he paused.

"Senior Lomm, if you do that, whoever takes your place may make a rash decision to fire on Klak. Eat your tail if you must, but not until the battle has been fought. If your valiant forces are defeated, it will not matter as your homeworld will be wiped clean of life. If you win, then you can decide to display your honor."

Lomm lowered his head. "I'm reduced to listening to the twisted wisdom of aliens…but for my people, I will swallow dung if I must. Commodore Riggs, all I ask is that you help us live."

"I'll do my best." I raised my hands in the best Raptor salute I could manage, though without a tail it wasn't quite the same. "Good luck, sir. Call me again if I can assist you in any way."

"You're getting pretty good at this diplomacy stuff, sir," Hansen said after the channel closed.

"Thanks…I think." I didn't point out that the more scruples people had, the easier they were to manipulate.

Turning back to the holotank, I saw the shipyards had been secured and now at least a dozen tugs had launched. Eight speeded to the orbital fortresses, one per sphere, and the others pushed barges toward one particular globe.

"It's working," I said to nobody in particular. Then I called down to Engineering, contacting Adrienne and Sakura. "Pretty soon you'll have all the materials you need," I assured them. "Did you get the specs on the Raptor power systems?"

"Yes, Captain," Adrienne replied. "We've already created adaptive transformers and modified the mega-AP plans to use their power grid."

"Excellent." I switched channels. "Marvin, I'm going to need your help."

"I am very busy, *Captain* Riggs."

"Sorry, *Captain* Marvin. But that's *Commodore* Riggs now."

"I'm not certain that it's legal for you to promote yourself that way."

"As I'm the only Star Force authority within hundreds of lightyears, I'm making it legal. It's only an acting rank anyway, subject to ratification." I hadn't forgotten that Marvin recorded everything and sometimes used blackmail to get what he wanted, so I was trying to keep my eventual court-martial clean and simple. "Anyway, Captain Marvin, I need your help with a rush project. Get the plans from Sakura, and start work on melding the frigates into the hull of *Valiant*."

"I already have plans for such an operation, but managing the actual process will require most of my mental and physical capacity for the next day."

"I could order you to do it, but I'd rather have your full and enthusiastic cooperation. I do have something you might like to examine…"

After a pregnant pause, he couldn't stand it any longer. "Yes, Commodore Riggs? What is it?"

"A dead Raptor."

"Oh," he said in a disappointed tone. "I already have several. I retrieved them from the aftermath of the battle."

"Really?" There went my leverage. Maybe. "In what condition?"

"Poor, unfortunately. Nothing but irradiated and burned fragments, to be honest."

"This one was freshly killed hours ago, and then flash-frozen. Wouldn't you like to have the corpse? Surely it would be better than your burnt, broken and freeze-dried specimens."

Clicks and pops came over the com-link as some kind of nervous sounds from Marvin, and I knew I had his interest. "All right, Commodore. Please have the corpse waiting in the launch bay."

"Not until we're done with the battle, Marvin. I can't have you distracted."

"When the battle is over, there'll be ample Raptor bodies to recover even some in good condition." He complained. "Your offer hardly seems fair."

"All right. I'll give you the body when you get the ships connected together, but you also have to be available to help with anything else that may come up. If we don't win this battle, all the scientific knowledge in the world won't matter much."

"To you, perhaps. I do not intend to sacrifice myself in a hopeless conflict."

"You think it's hopeless?"

"Perhaps hopeless is too strong a term. Let us say that your chances are less than optimal."

By that, I assumed Marvin figured he would fly like a bat out of Hell before a beam or missile got anywhere near him. Well, I couldn't really blame him. He wasn't inhabiting a warship, though I suspected *Greyhound* was now far more capable than he let on.

"Optimal or not, you are part of Star Force, so I need your maximum effort. Deal?"

"I always put forth my maximum effort." Sounding huffy, he closed the channel.

"Sure you do," I muttered. "But maximum effort for who?"

-37-

Like any good engineer, Marvin had overestimated the time he would need to complete the process of joining the frigates to *Valiant*. Working madly with *Greyhound's* many external arms, he quickly dismounted smaller beams and other external fixtures then smart-welded the frigates to the outside of the battlecruiser. The result was a Frankenstein's monster of a ship—or maybe it should be called a small mobile battle station.

Inside the new *Valiant*, Sakura and her people frantically connected all the power systems together, building everything so that the ship could take all the juice possible and feed it to every antiproton weapon we had.

"I need more raw materials," she told me partway through the process. "We've cannibalized everything we could. You promised me enough to build what we needed—not to mention these monster weapons we haven't even started on."

"I know, Sakura," I assured her. "The materials should be coming aboard very soon."

In the holotank I could see the first of a chain of Raptor tugs. It dragged an enormous barge and struggled to counter the inertia as it was already decelerating and maneuvering to dock with us. If Klak's people had done their work, the container should be filled with everything the Raptor shipyards hadn't specifically needed to repair their own ships—batteries, structural steel, foodstuffs, water, spare parts, whatever could be found. Of course, many of the parts couldn't be used in their current form. The tolerances were all wrong, and design of the couplings was hopelessly alien. But that didn't really matter. If we couldn't use something in its present state, we planned to feed it to the factory and turn it into whatever we needed.

Kwon and his marines were put to work as laborers again with the usual grumbling. I reminded him of the old saying: "The troops ain't happy unless they're bitching," and he laughed. The marines in their battle armor carried huge loads though widened portals, slowly emptying the cavernous barge. Three other supply vessels lined up behind the first.

All of this activity was matched on the Raptor side as the big orbital fortresses, each larger than a Star Force battleship, were pushed into place by the tugs as soon as they'd delivered their cargo to us. Soon, the eight spheres formed around us like eight balls glued together as closely as possible. *Valiant* began to resemble a molecular model, like a cube with rounded corners. If Klak's people were following the plan, they would be connecting and reinforcing their power systems, removing sixteen of their own beam weapons and preparing their mounts and targeting systems to adapt to the ones we were constructing with the factory. As our APs were at least a hundred times as powerful and ten times as efficient as theirs, this would create a super-fortress with long-range firepower.

Once we had produced the APs for the Raptors, I had the engineering people make more armor and refine the control systems for the shields so we could cover a number of different sections of *Valiant*. If we lost weapons in an area, I wanted to be able to screen there to improve our survivability. This would be a set-piece battle anyway, and we had given up a lot of mobility to turn our battlecruiser into an ugly, cobbled-together battleship.

At the end of a long, exhausting day, most of the work had been done. I handed over the Raptor corpse to Marvin as I'd promised him and ordered an eight-hour stand-down. A ration of two alcoholic beverages per person was issued. I made a quick round of the ship with a drink in my hand, a sure-fire way to show I was no longer in command mode, and I praised everyone's effort. Then I headed to my cabin.

My door had barely closed before I heard it chime. "Come in."

Adrienne entered, looking worn out.

"What happened to all that stuff about never socializing with me again?" I asked. I regretted the words the moment they'd popped out of my mouth. I kicked myself mentally, wondering what I was trying to accomplish. Dad used to tell me no man ever really won an argument with a woman—even if he got his way—because such victories were Pyrrhic. The win always cost more than it was worth.

Her neutral expression froze, and she turned around to walk out.

"Adrienne, I'm sorry. I...I'm tired, and that was a stupid thing to say. Please don't go."

Stopping with her back to me, she put a hand on the door frame. "I stopped by to apologize—for the last time we talked. I shouldn't have lectured you on how to command."

"Well, you had some good points," I said, walking slowly toward her but stopping at arm's length. With Adrienne's back turned, I had the strongest feeling of déjà vu, as if I was looking at Olivia. The shape, the size—everything about her was the same. She even had some of the same *presence*, I guess that's what you would call it.

This brought a confusing wave of thoughts and memories to my mind. A few months ago I'd seen Olivia lying in her coffin—but I could hardly recall her face. I struggled to push such thoughts aside and focus on the here and now. I raised a hand to touch her shoulder—but thought the better of it and pulled my hand back.

"You were right," I said. "You're still right. Just as soon as we're not in immediate danger I'll put some thought into setting up a better structure and a new routine. Something that will help people function over the long term under these unusual stresses. You can advise me."

"Hansen's your XO."

"But he's not my friend." Even as I said it, I no longer felt it was completely true. He and I had been getting along reasonably well since we had our little chat in the pool room.

"Is that all I am?"

Both of us fell silent. I didn't even breathe for a moment. Adrienne didn't turn around.

My world whirled and I felt as if yawning pits had opened up before and behind me, emotional crevasses where one misstep would send me plunging to my doom. What did she mean? Had she been Olivia, the question would have been coy, playful, and teasing. Adrienne didn't tease and bait the way her sister loved to do. Her lighter side was deeper down and muted. Maybe that was because of her sister's death—I just didn't know, as I hadn't really known what she was like before the tragedy.

"No, that's not all," I finally admitted, but I had no idea where this was going to go. Was she inviting me to make a move or just letting me know she was open to future possibilities? And how could I reconcile her with the images of her sister that still haunted me? "But…"

Before I could say any more, she palmed the portal open and slipped out into the passageway. She didn't even look back. She left me staring at the closed door.

Slowly, I made my way to my bunk and fell into it. I grumbled about crazy women giving mixed signals and sipped a beer. I was grateful when sleep finally came.

* * *

Valiant came to life again when the Lithos were only a few hours out of range. I drummed on the arm of my chair as I looked from the holotank to various screens and back again, weighing the situation.

Ensconced at the core of a cluster of Raptor battle stations, *Valiant* was effectively sixty times its original tonnage with the attached orbital stations counted in. I didn't like the lack of mobility they represented, but I savored our increased range. According to my plan, Klak had placed us squarely between the approaching Lithos and his homeworld.

I wondered at the sanity of my gamble. Sure, we might save a world, but was it our job to do so? Maybe in the future these sentient-eating Raptors would come to Earth and dine on my kin. If that did happen at some point, would they laugh about the fool of an ensign who saved their race a century before?

I spent the final minutes going over our new technical specs. The power cable which the Raptor space workers had attached to us was fully six feet in diameter. It should be able to provide us with all the energy we needed and more. In fact, I hoped Sakura had made sure our fuses and breaker systems were robust and ready. An overload could do us serious damage.

Similar connections linked the stations to one another. As only the forward facing four spheres contained the new APs, the back four could pump masses of current through the conduits to help power everything.

Our battlesuited marines, under the supervision of a couple of bosun's mates, had dragged and pushed the heavy cables until they mated up with the giant plugs Sakura had designed for them. Behind the plugs squatted a transformer-converter, and then the smaller cables carried the juice to our weapons. *Valiant* was now a mobile pillbox, though dwarfed by the gargantuan spheres attached to her hull.

If only the Lithos didn't make us all look tiny in comparison. My only hope was in our superior reach and firepower. Unfortunately, they had a lot more targets and each of them could take a huge amount of punishment.

Klak's fleet hung in space behind the reimagined *Valiant*, ringing us like a bull's-eye. I stood up to more closely examine the holotank and then zoomed in on the approaching Litho fleet.

"They're closing up their formations," I said. The enemy ships were drawing closer and closer together, but they were still aimed directly at Orn Prime. I was happy they were as predictable and direct as always. After studying them for a full minute more, I came to another conclusion.

"I think they're imitating us," I said.

Hansen let *Valiant* hold station and joined me. "Kinda looks that way, huh? What will that do for their position?"

I found myself rubbing my neck. "I'm not sure, but I have an ugly suspicion. Nothing can be done now, anyway."

A dozen latecomers to the Litho fleet drifted close to the central mass and joined the formation. The enemy had wisely slowed down enough to join up its ships. They planned to hit us with one fist. They'd all grouped themselves around the repaired dreadnought. We now faced over one hundred sixty ships, none of which massed less than the mega-station itself.

I mused that I now understood how pikemen must have felt in the distant past when facing armored cavalry on a medieval battlefield. Intellectually I knew our weapons would reach out farther and kill the enemy before they could kill us, but that didn't keep the pit of my stomach from believing we'd be crushed under the charging wave in the end.

Charging wave...if I remembered right, massed knights would destroy infantry as much by crushing and riding them under as with their lances and swords. Suddenly, I realized what the enemy was going to do, and there seemed to be no way to stop them.

"Get me Klak," I ordered. A moment later the connection was made. "Senior Klak, are your people on the planet below as ready as they can be? In shelters, evacuated from cities, and in the hills?"

"Some are, Commodore Riggs. Others refused to leave. Oddly, many will not believe in the severity of the danger."

These Raptors seemed more human to me all the time. "Klak, I want to tell you something, but it's for your ears alone." I waited until he moved to a private booth aboard his flagship.

"What is it?" he asked.

"I believe I know what the Lithos will do." Then I told him.

Klak took it well. "We can only do what we can do. At least your plan may yet save billions below us, and if we're defeated, so too will be the Lithos. Senior Kleed will succeed me and, with his last hundred ships, he will defend our star system. If I'm fortunate, I'll be remembered as one who sacrificed everything for his people—even my honor."

"Don't give up yet, Klak. I might be wrong. No matter what, half a planet is better than nothing."

"I agree." Klak said. He saluted me, and I returned it. "Now let's see to our forces," he said, "and may the One Above All grant us victory!"

"Yeah. Include me in your prayers," I said, cutting the channel. If there were gods, like my mother believed, I wasn't above accepting a little help from them. "Hey, where's Marvin?"

Scanning the holotank, I couldn't see *Greyhound*. A few seconds later a familiar voice emanated from the console in front of me.

"I took your suggestion and moved well away from the zone of battle," Marvin said.

"I didn't suggest—never mind. Fine. Just be ready to help if we need it."

Again a perceptible time lag of about six or seven seconds passed indicating Marvin was already a million or so miles away and probably retreating further even now. Beams could strike out to about a million miles, though not well or with much hit probability. I bet myself he would continue his withdrawal until he was outside that range.

"Riggs to Klak. I suggest you open fire now. I do not believe the Lithos will do much dodging, and with unlimited energy, the more we shoot the better."

No verbal acknowledgement returned, but a moment later the mega-fortress began a rolling barrage. I'd wanted Klak to have his gunners test the system, but he'd been concerned that would telegraph our new capabilities. His people were going to get to practice on live targets—if Lithos were really alive.

The first few shots missed even the enormous target the Lithos had become. The flying mountains had physically joined up with their dreadnought, turning themselves into a stupendous arrowhead pointed at Orn Prime. In the vastness of space they were only the size of an average asteroid, but any object that size with a mind of its own was frightening. Soon though, the mega-APs were scoring every time causing volcanic eruptions of magma flash-heated on the surface of the Litho titan. Hundred-meter divots appeared as the lava bursts threw flowing rock into space as if each one was an unstoppable fusion warhead. With the huge power generation capacity of the fortresses, sixteen shots slammed home every ten seconds or so. This meant a hundred shots a minute, six thousand an hour.

The Lithos were almost two hours outside of their own effective range, which meant over ten thousand mega-AP shots would boil away the surface of the combined enemy before they could strike back. As beam impacts tore deeper and deeper into their guts, I hoped the Lithos would yield to the urge to break up and race toward us as fighters or missiles—or better yet, as snowflakes. I watched eagerly, hoping to see them break like barbarians and lose their formation. I wanted to see them attack in a wild mass.

Unfortunately, their discipline held. An hour passed during which time we'd boiled off the first mile of armor, but we had at least four more to go—perhaps five. "Open fire," I told Hansen as the Lithos were finally coming into *Valiant*'s effective range.

Valiant rang and hummed with the vibrations of power, and I watched the capacitors empty and then almost immediately refill. We were like a beached naval vessel with truckloads of ammunition delivered from the land. We couldn't use all the juice we could access. What I couldn't do with generators like this!

But that was a false dream because the reactors that provided us so much power were as large as our ship itself, and they would gulp more fuel than we could carry if we tried to make them a permanent part of the ship. In ship design, nothing comes for free.

"Aim at areas that have been hit before," I told Hansen, who passed on my instructions to the front-line gunners. As we were locked into place and no longer needed a pilot, I'd turned him into my gunnery officer. "Try to keep digging deeper."

"Yes, sir. But at this rate, I don't think we're going to destroy them before they get here."

"Concentrate fire," I said.

"It's not working," Hansen said. "We're reaching the edge of their effective range now. Incoming fire expected."

I watched grimly as the enemy mass of ships came closer to our station. As large as this fortress I'd built was, we were vastly outmatched in mass if not in firepower.

"Hansen," I said. "It's time to start taking chances. Begin the shield-rotation protocol we talked about. Switch on the sectional shields between shots. We've got the power to spare. Power down each shield just before the AP behind it fires."

"Script is in and locked," he said, tapping at his console rapidly.

"Cancel the script if and when we disconnect from external power."

"Exception list updated, Captain."

Now the various indicators on the console really started to flash. They changed state every time one of our eleven heavy APs fired, recharged, or its associated shield switched off or on. I could have let the gunners control the shields, but as they were performing static, repetitive firing, I didn't want one of them to accidentally fire an AP into the back of an active shield. I wasn't entirely sure what would happen, but I doubted the result would be pleasant.

I activated the intercom. "Sakura, how are we doing below decks?"

"Five by five, sir," Sakura responded. "I'm keeping the firing rate down enough to cool between shots and not overload the system."

"Hmm. I need you to push this system to its limits now, Chief. We're going to start taking return fire, but the enemy is coming into close range where we can hit them harder as well. Put more power into the weapons. Push their tolerances and shorten up on the heat-recycle times."

"How hard should I push the guns, sir?"

"That's for you to judge."

Sakura sighed. "Yes sir."

I spoke to *Valiant's* com system. "Connect me with Adrienne—Turnbull, I mean." When Adrienne came on the line, I said, "How are we doing with the repeller mines?"

"Over six hundred are finished and ready to be deployed." This had been the factory's primary occupation during the final hours. Once the APs and other systems had been finished, mines were the only munitions I figured we could use to defend the station from close-combat attackers. With all the materials from the Raptors and the enemy coming on like an unswerving freight train, the simple little nukes seemed like the best use of factory time.

"Six hundred is enough," I said. "Switch to producing constructive nanites and smart metal. We may have to do emergency repairs. Riggs out."

I turned to Hansen, who seemed less than confident with his job as gunnery officer. "Have the missile launching systems take control of the stealth repeller mines we've deployed. Spread them out and start them on their way, but not at full speed."

I reflected that I could get used to this business of having unlimited power and materials at my fingertips.

"Why not throw them out there at full speed?" Hansen asked.

"Trust me," I said.

Hansen gave his head a shake then shrugged and followed orders. I liked that. He'd changed, no longer questioning my every decision. I wanted feedback and helpful objections, but Hansen had been a contrarian from the start. I was glad to see he did trust me to some degree now.

-38-

The repeller mines were ten minutes out when we began taking some hits from the Lithos. Then I got the word I was waiting for.

"Ground-based missile launch alert," *Valiant* said. In the holotank, I could see over a hundred contacts lifting from bases all around the planet beneath us.

"That's all they have?" I wondered aloud. "They must have fired everything they had into the ring battle. These missiles probably represent their reserves, or what they produced in the final days."

I stood to peer in the holotank. A few minutes went by as I watched the barrage climb out of the atmosphere and accelerate toward the Lithos. "They aren't even fast-moving. But they are a threat…"

Lights blinked all around me, and my frown changed into a slight smile as almost a hundred more missiles joined those flocking up from the surface. The Raptors had fired another barrage from their orbital fortresses and Klak's ships. Together, the bright exhaust flares made easy targets as they accelerated at high Gs toward the enemy.

"Increase the repeller power on the mines," I said, zooming in close to observe and working some quick calculations. I estimated the Raptor missiles would overtake and pass our mines three quarters of the way to the enemy.

"Launch our salvoes," I ordered. "We might as well gut-punch them now."

From *Valiant*'s tubes we fired thirty-two missiles in two waves of sixteen. I watched as Hansen flew the birds. They glided up to the mass of Raptor missiles and joined the flock.

"No," I said, shaking my head. "Send ours in first. Get them up to max acceleration, pass the Raptor missiles, and detonate ours early. But make sure they don't take out any friendly weapons."

"Detonate ours early?" Hansen asked. "Why, sir?"

"They aren't going to damage the Lithos, but they'll overload their sensors with flash, plasma and EMP. That will allow the main mass of the barrage to get closer."

"You're the boss."

Imitating a man who's completely calm and in charge, I watched the battle unfold. In my gut, I knew it wasn't working. It was a simple case of mathematical tyranny. They had too much mass, and we weren't going to be able to reduce them to zero before they reached us and overwhelmed us.

We continued to boil away their substance. Our blowtorch shots struck ever more heavily as they got closer, but we were taking losses as well. While *Valiant* had received minimal damage due to her shields, the Raptor fortresses that formed most of our composite structure had no such advantage. They took the brunt of the return fire and had already lost four mega-APs—whether that was due to Litho fire or overheating I didn't know—and I barely cared. Either way, the guns had been lost.

Time grew short as the minutes ticked down. I considered ordering my crew to decouple and run. In fact, as the clock kept going the urge became almost overwhelming. Why die fighting a hopeless battle for ungrateful, unpleasant aliens? I'd made a huge mistake, and my mind was racing to resolve it.

To my credit, I kept my outward mask rigid. I don't think anyone aboard suspected. They had faith in me. They believed in me—and as a reward, I was leading them into a slaughter.

"Missiles detonating in three…two…one," *Valiant's* voice droned. Our thirty large warheads created flashes of light, radiation and plasma in the void directly before the Litho arrowhead. Green Litho laser beams and antiproton weapons abruptly became visible, hundreds of them probing through the temporary dust cloud. They were searching for more incoming targets—the Raptor missiles.

In the end, the sacrificial smokescreen allowed many Raptor missiles to detonate much closer. Some even reached the enemy hull, carving huge pieces out of the rocky cladding with thermonuclear blasts. But the total tonnage lost was still small compared to the vast weight of the combined enemy fleet.

"I think we've stripped away close to half their mass," I said, looking closely at the readings. "Now, the mines…"

The missile blasts and the beams flashing in both directions had served to obscure our six hundred tiny repeller-powered mines. More than three quarters of them made it through the miasma to detonate against the enemy hull. Our viewscreens whited out as *Valiant* shut down the video pickups to protect them from overload.

When our vision cleared, I could see that only about a third of the mass of the Litho rock-fleet remained. The smoldering hulk was perhaps four miles in diameter. It still continued to fire hundreds of short-range beams, which probed forward looking for targets.

"There must have been successive layers, with more weapons beneath," I said. "Instead of structuring the super-ship to break up, they created a defense in depth like an onion."

"That onion is still putting out a lot of firepower," Hansen remarked.

It was true. The Lithos continued hitting us almost as hard as they had from the start. That was probably because we'd been killing armor and redundant beam weapons up until now. Every time we peeled off a layer of this ship, we exposed another weapon beneath it. We weren't getting through to the generators or the engines.

"Keep firing. Pass the word to allow as much overload as we can. We only have about five minutes left to win this."

"Klak's making his move," Hansen said, noticing before I did that the seventy-odd Raptor ships had begun advancing like a squadron of hawks. Much more graceful than the now-ugly *Valiant*, they made a fine sight, but I knew that this would be the final glory for many of them. They were simply not built to go up against the thing that lumbered toward us.

"Cease fire," I said as soon as our allies' ships threatened to obscure our lines of sight. "Top off our power supplies and cast loose the cable."

An audible groan issued from the gunners who'd been reveling in the endless ammunition provided by the abundant power. Now we were back on our own.

"Shut down the shields," I ordered. "We need to conserve power now. Hansen, take the helm. Maneuver us out into the clear and let's take up a flanking position opposite the Raptor fleet. As they engage, we'll try to come around to the stern of that flying mountain and hit its engines. *Valiant*, pass a message to the Raptors suggesting they swing around on their side and hit the engines as well."

What I didn't mention to my crew was my reserve plan, but I thought Hansen suspected. As he laid in a circuitous course, he gave me a small nod.

I was almost thankful for his quiet approval. If this battle went as badly as I now suspected it would, we could slip out the back and run. There was no reason we should die for our new allies in a hopeless battle. I told myself we'd do the Raptors more good alive than dead. We could warn other systems and maybe even get this news back to Earth where the intel people would be grateful for our deep scouting.

The Raptor ships either took my suggestion or had already been planning to do as I'd hoped. They swung around in a wide path to the flank and then the stern of the Litho mass. Now we had it surrounded on three sides. The Raptors began to make swooping, strafing passes on the enemy stern, blasting in with their forward weapons and then turning tail to dump a storm of point-defense shots at dead close range before zooming off.

We took our own shots as well, making sure not to cause any fratricide. We tried to target the crystalline beam weapons poking out of the soil. Unfortunately, it simply wasn't going to be enough to save Orn Prime. The Lithos stubbornly refused to break up. By the time they reached the location of the brave Raptor super-fortresses, they were down to a mere mile in diameter and very few functioning weapons. But despite all our efforts, there was simply no way to turn that much mass away from landfall.

The Litho monster plowed right into the clustered super-fortress. I winced as I watched the Raptors I'd abandoned die to the last man. The eight spheres popped like light bulbs. The Raptors fired to the end, but the civilian tugs, less brave or perhaps wiser, fled in their powerful little ships just before impact.

The Litho ship went into a spin with us and the swarm of Raptor ships still dive-bombing like hornets. The burning mass of rock and crushed metal fell inexorably into the planet's gravity well. We'd knocked out her engines, but momentum and gravitational forces did the rest.

This is what I'd feared. The joined Litho ships themselves became the final killing weapon. They refused to break up, and even though they'd lost their guns we simply did not have the time or firepower to stop them. The Litho juggernaut didn't try to save itself. I was sure there were thousands of individual templates involved, but to their credit none fled the central mass.

Winning this battle hadn't been their objective. Instead, like the Macros before them, they'd made a decision in their machine minds to do horrendous damage to their enemies, trusting that their sacrifice would tip the future scales.

As we watched the massed Litho structure turn into a glowing meteor, I consoled myself with the fact that it was much smaller than it would have been had Klak not implemented my plan. I had no doubt we'd saved millions—perhaps even billions—of lives. But now we sat and watched in sick horror as the population we'd sought to protect was devastated.

The kinetic missile made landfall at the edge of one of the planet's major continents. It would have been worse if it had landed in one of the torpid seas. The holotank showed a hundred-mile-wide mushroom cloud that formed gracefully, rising up through the atmospheric layers. The energy equivalent of at least a thousand megatons of TNT had been released all at once. The shockwave traveled in a perfect circle scouring the land clean of all life for a thousand miles. When it reached the ocean, it continued in the form of a tsunami that looked like it would eventually strike the opposite coast in a wall of water miles high, reaching inland for a hundred miles.

Fires broke out in Raptor cities as the planet-quake, estimated at between nine and ten on the Richter scale, reached them. Every building and structure was leveled, and I could imagine the millions trapped within the rubble. It was a disaster of Biblical proportions, a near-extinction event much like the asteroid thought to have wiped out Earth's dinosaurs long, long ago.

Even so, our estimates showed that up to half the people would survive the initial damage. With the other colonies to provide relief, the Raptor civilization had not been extinguished, and I doubted whether the Lithos would be able to make another push like this any time soon.

Even better, at least forty ships of the main fleet and the hundred ships of the relief fleet remained intact. Four orbital shipyards and the entire Raptor space infrastructure stood ready to rebuild. With these assets, I thought they should be able to hold the ring against the Lithos for years to come.

* * *

My crew and I stood in good order on the flight deck of *Valiant's* launch bay the largest open space left inside. Hansen, Adrienne, Sakura and Bradley stood beside me, with the rest in ranks behind.

Marines were posted around the edges of the big room. They wore highly polished but completely functional battle armor. Kwon told me they were complaining a lot about not having contributed to the fight, and I made a note to give them a pep talk about how much their presence and their work as a damage control fire brigade had meant to me—trust marines to feel slighted if they didn't get the chance to die in hand-to-hand combat.

In front of us, Klak and a contingent of his warriors had lined up in their military finery. The proud Raptor had insisted on presenting me and the rest of my crew with high awards, and I couldn't see the harm. All but one of his ships was busy doing relief work. I hoped that afterward I could talk to him about the future and our place in it. We could really use R&R on a friendly planet, and we had a lot of re-engineering to do on *Valiant*.

Klak, attended by several of his staffers, stuck awards on our chests. The medals reminded me of fishing lures with their colored threads and dangling bright metal symbols. He decorated me first, then the crew, saluting each in turn. I thought it was a classy gesture even though our success had only been partial.

Once finished, Klak took a position well in front of our ranks, facing away from us and toward some kind of civilian video news crew, so we became the backdrop. His comrades moved well away from him, leaving him alone on camera. I figured he was making a victory speech to his people—probably one tinged with sorrowful gravity at the loss of life.

I figured wrong.

"My people," he said, "I am Klak. With the help of these brave alien allies, what was once my fleet has saved many from death, although the cost was high."

He reached up and tore off his badges of rank, throwing them on the floor. We watched him do this for a full minute, frowning but saying nothing.

"I hereby give up my position," he continued when he stood in a plain harness, "because I abused it. Senior Field Director Kleed will take my place. I usurped authority and illegally forced others to obey my will in order to save as many as I could. However justified, my reasons are no excuse. In order that my mother, my sisters, my daughters and the rest of my family are not dishonored, I now atone for my crimes."

Hansen understood a moment after I did what was about to happen, and he broke ranks. He took a step forward, lifting his hands. I threw up an arm to bar his way.

"No," I said. "Don't interfere."

"But—"

"This is their culture. It's not our place."

I felt Hansen step back, and I dropped my arm. Then, gripped by the dread of inevitability, I cleared my throat and called to the Star Force personnel in my best parade-ground voice: *"Present—arms!"*

My crew's hands snapped upward in salute, and the marines presented their polished rifles with a textbook crash of boots on the deck. We stood that way while what I knew must happen, happened.

Klak saluted his comrades in arms. Then via the camera drones, all the people of his worlds living or watching this recording in the future were to see him commit ritual suicide. His tail curled forward between his feet and lifted. Reaching down with his hands, he pulled its spiked end upward to eye level, staring at it for a moment.

I dearly hoped no human would laugh because this stance did seem peculiar. I doubted they would be laughing in a moment, and I felt a lump form in my throat at what was to come.

Quickly, suddenly, without further ado, Klak opened his mouth hugely wide like a Tyrannosaurus Rex getting ready to seize its prey. Then he shoved the deadly end of his tail into his own mouth.

Klak bit down hard. The spikes penetrated the soft palate and pierced his brain, killing him instantly. He fell to the deck, stone dead.

None of the other Raptors moved for a long moment. Then an honor guard of eight unfolded a stretcher and ceremoniously placed Klak on it. They marched out with the body.

"Order—arms," I called. Marching to the front, I turned to address my people. "Ladies and gentlemen of Star Force, you did one hell of a day's work today. You saved many lives, but you couldn't save that one. Klak's life was his to do with as his honor demanded so none of you should blame yourselves. Aliens are aliens." I swept my eyes across the ranks once more. "Dismissed."

The formation broke up in melancholy conversation as people filtered back to their duty stations. Ritual suicide wasn't something humans watched very often, and none of us had realized what was coming, although I should have.

Adrienne turned to me with tears in her eyes and embraced me momentarily, her sweet-smelling hair brushing my nose. I patted her awkwardly on the back a couple of times, still conscious of all the eyes on us. I figured this small slip could be forgiven due to the emotion of the moment.

"Okay, Adie, okay," I said, grasping her arms gently. "People are watching."

Adrienne sniffed, rubbing tears from her eyes. Then she stepped back, searching my face. For what, I didn't know.

"It's just about keeping up appearances," I said. "You understand."

"All right. Yes. Thank you, Captain Riggs. I'll see you later."

She turned to accompany Sakura out, putting her head on the stocky woman's shoulder. I desperately wished it could have been mine.

We offered to help with the planetary relief, but we'd been turned down by every official. Even though we were heroes, I suspected that not every Raptor felt that way. People, especially those far removed from the action, always looked for someone to blame when disaster visited them. Klak had clearly pointed out the wisdom of staying away from a badly wounded alien world.

Klak. I'd only known him a short time, but I'd felt a kinship with him. He'd been a leader in a tough spot, and he'd done the absolute best he could with what fate had given him.

Back on the bridge I realized Marvin had dropped out of sight again. I almost suspected he'd developed a new stealth technology of some sort, something that made him hard for our sensors to see at long ranges.

"Keep looking," I told *Valiant*. "He's out there somewhere. Hansen, let's start cruising slowly out toward Orn Six where the next ring in the chain must be. Take a looping course away from Kleed's relief fleet." With Klak gone, I'd rather avoid any of the local politics if possible. I had no idea what Kleed would be like.

"We can't outrun them in this current configuration," Hansen pointed out. "We're ugly, unbalanced and underpowered for our weight."

"Outrun them? We're heroes."

"That won't help us against a hundred ships."

"XO, you have a pessimistic streak."

"Heroes turn into scapegoats awfully fast, I'm thinking. Just ask your old man."

I thought about what Hansen had said and grunted, not willing to give credence to his speculations in front of the crew. "What makes you think the Raptors are anything but grateful?"

Hansen input a script from his helm station and something lit up in the holotank. I saw it was Kleed's relief fleet.

"They've altered course to intercept us, sir," he said.

I stared at the projected course lines. My lips tightened into a line.

"Ingrates," I muttered.

-39-

I expanded the image of the relief fleet and saw Hansen was right. As we curved away to bypass them and head toward Orn Six—from which this fleet had just arrived—Kleed had turned thirty-two ships, about a third of his complement, to meet us. The rest were sliding into a protective orbit above their devastated homeworld.

"What do you think he wants?" I mused.

"If it was a friendly chat, would he need thirty warships?"

"Damn. Can we beat them?"

Hansen shook his head. "Not by the numbers. They might get tired of losing ships, but if they press the attack I figure they'll lose ten or twelve and then kill us."

"What if we fire first?"

"Then they lose twenty before we die."

I sighed and went over Hansen's data. I couldn't find a flaw.

"How long until rendezvous?" I asked.

"About ten hours."

I started running simulations, shaking my head. "I guess we'll just have to see what Kleed wants, then."

"I know what he wants," Adrienne said as she stepped onto the bridge behind me. "Our factory."

"Why?" I asked. I saw her point right away, but felt it was a good idea to let her explain it.

"Over the course of a few short days our weapons doubled the firepower of their home fleet. In their eyes, the factory worked magic. For whatever reason, they didn't get a working factory from their encounter with the Nanos. When Earth got control of Nano factories, it could not only build amazing new technology, it could build *more* factories. It's what launched us centuries forward and saved the human race. Now Kleed sees us floating off with the holy grail."

"Yeah." I rubbed my neck. "He doesn't even have to be a bad guy to insist we give him a leg up. After all, if Klak was willing to sacrifice his ethics to save his people, Kleed will, too."

"Klak *did* say Kleed's honor was questionable," Hansen reminded me.

I nodded, remembering. "Yes, he did. So what do we do? Can we come up with a detailed plan to construct a small factory for them? If we can give them a shopping list of the rare earths required and show them we can complete the project in a month or two, they should be convinced we're serious."

"Yes," Adrienne said thoughtfully. "We can include cannibalized materials from their own structures and equipment. That would speed up the process when compared to mining raw materials."

"That's good. *Valiant* is a bit bloated anyway. We laid on the armor quite thickly. Let's hope he'll be happy with that. Go ahead and start prepping it. Make sure it doesn't have the technology database, though. We'll give them what they need when we decide to, as bargaining chips. Can your report be ready in ten hours?"

"Yes, easily."

"Then compile the list! Recruit whoever you need to help."

Adrienne saluted me wryly and left to carry out my orders.

"Why do I get the feeling things won't go smoothly?" I asked Hansen when she'd gone.

"Things never go smoothly with you around, sir," Hansen replied.

I glanced at him, saw he was grinning, and returned the expression.

"It's the Riggs curse, Mister Hansen." I folded my arms and stared at the tactical situation. I'd hoped to see a solution, but there was none. "Order a crew rest period for everyone possible and notify them we'll be at battle stations in about nine hours. That includes you. Make sure you get some sleep. I'll take the first watch."

"Aye aye, Skipper," he said, and left. At least it was an improvement over constant backtalk.

When Hansen returned after four hours, I stopped by the marine spaces to drink a beer with the troops. I talked to Kwon in particular. I found him arm-wrestling playfully with Steiner, letting her use both her hands and her whole body while he used just one. The big woman flushed when she saw me and withdrew.

I smiled at Kwon. "Sergeant Major, you might get some real action soon."

"Good!" he roared, rising and slapping me on the back.

"If you do, though, we're going to be heavily outnumbered. The new Raptor boss is bringing more than thirty ships to the party."

Kwon's brow furrowed. "I thought we were heroes to the Raptors."

"We are, Kwon, but there's politics involved."

"I hate politics." Kwon slammed his ham fist into the wall to emphasize his point. He left a dent the size of a melon.

"Me too."

"Can we beat them ship to ship?"

I shook my head. "No, but that's where you come in. You need to be ready for anything—repelling boarders especially, but also a space assault with grenades." By grenades, I meant the specialized small nukes marines used for anti-ship use.

"Why would they board?" Kwon asked. "Why not just blast us?"

"We think they want our factory."

"Thieving bastards."

I clapped him on the shoulder. It was like slapping a Brahma bull. "Just let me handle the diplomacy, my friend, but be ready to pull my nuts out of the fire."

"That's what marines do!" Kwon roared. "We'll be ready, boss."

"Good man." Cheered, I headed to my cabin to catch some shuteye. It was always better to fight in a rested state.

When I reached my cabin and opened the door, I got another surprise. "Adrienne?"

She stood in the middle of my floor with her hands clasped oddly. She seemed a little nervous.

"Sorry," she said. "I know this isn't appropriate, but I wanted to see you."

"Okay..." I said, moving to sit on the bunk.

She took the only chair in the room.

I smiled at her and felt oddly relaxed. "What's up?" I asked.

Her hands continued twisting nervously as she gazed down at them, not meeting my eyes.

"You know, you're a bit of a..." She faltered.

"Prick?"

"No," she laughed nervously.

"Rogue?"

"Closer."

"Rascal? Scoundrel? Stud?"

Her laughter became genuine. "How about 'comedian'? No—that's wrong. I just meant, you're not my usual type. But..." She ground to a halt again.

I suddenly understood that I had this in the bag if I didn't blow it. I decided to give her a little help.

"Look, Adie, we've been dancing around this thing between us for a while, but is this really the best time to talk about it? In a few hours we'll have to face down an alien admiral and his fleet."

Adrienne's face rose, her eyes sharpened. "Damn it, Cody, we're always hours away from some crisis or another. Don't you think we'll both do our jobs better if we get a few things settled?"

"Okay, point taken. What first?"

"First? I'm tired of playing second fiddle to the memory of my sister. When we talk, I can see it in your eyes. It's like you're gazing at a princess on a pedestal in your mind. Do you realize that we've been on this ship almost as long as you and Olivia were dating?"

I hadn't thought of that before, and it wasn't completely true—but she had a point. I'd been serious about Olivia, but we'd only gotten together for about a semester's time. I decided quibbling wouldn't be a good play, so I nodded in agreement.

Fortunately, that was good enough of an answer for Adrienne.

"She had her faults too, you know," Adrienne continued, "but you've forgotten them all by now. I can't live up to an idealized version of Olivia."

I nodded encouragingly. "All right, I'll try to keep that in perspective. Second?"

"Second?" she demanded. "There has to be a second? Is this a relationship by the numbers?"

"This is a relationship?" I asked.

"It—it could be."

"Ah." That was the elephant in the room, so big and obvious it was difficult to see and hard to get the mind around. "If that's what you want, I'm helpless."

She frowned at me quizzically. "Why are you helpless?"

I shrugged. "You're in control of this situation. You always have been. How could I resist the advances of such an attractive young woman?"

"I'm not sure if you're seducing me or making fun of me. You're the captain."

I smiled, realizing at that moment I wanted her. I'd wanted her for quite some time but had been too guilt-ridden to take the proper steps. At times I burned for her, lying there alone in my bunk. But I'd been desperately afraid that I'd screw my command up by bending my principles.

Adrienne's voice grew thoughtful. "You know Cody, your problem is you worry too much about textbook solutions. This is your first command, but you need to relax. The Academy book never anticipated one ship and crew being lost and alone for months or maybe years. *Valiant* has become a society, and societies evolve their own rules. As long as they work, no regulation can say they're wrong. If you really—"

I grabbed her and kissed her. I'd only been half-listening anyway, and the urge suddenly overtook my caution. She stiffened up for a second in surprise, but then relaxed. We kissed for thirty nice seconds, then pulled apart. I kept my hands on her shoulders and we looked into one another's eyes.

"Looks like you made your choice," Adrienne said, smiling. "So much for me being in charge."

"Yeah," I said. "You think the crew can handle it if we do this? You and me, my favorite girl, and my ops officer as well?"

"What the bloody hell do you care what the crew thinks anyway? You fly this ship however you wish. You spend more time with Kwon and the marines than you do with the Fleet people despite the fact you're a Fleet officer. My impression is that Cody Riggs does whatever Cody Riggs wants to."

"So I'll ask again: what would the crew think about…about you and me?"

"Sakura and Hansen are already an item—then there's Bradley and Johnson. Oh, and Kwon's been shagging that tremendous woman from the missile deck. I'm sorry, I shouldn't say that."

"Tremendous woman?" I couldn't help but chuckle. "Steiner is big. I think they're a good match."

"She's probably the only female on the ship large enough to take him on without breaking," she agreed. "Anyway, my point is it's already happening all around you. You can't stop it even if you wanted to."

"This wouldn't be the same. None of the others are pairing up with subordinates. That would be wrong. The problem is that as the captain, everyone is my subordinate."

"I think that's just an excuse." Adrienne moved to sit on my bunk. We were almost touching.

"I think you're afraid," Adrienne said.

"Of what?" I scoffed.

"Of dishonoring Olivia's memory. Of not measuring up to your father. Of disappointing the people who know you. Of failing to get us home. Cody, you're just like all of us. We're full of worries, but that's okay. We're here to help each other overcome them."

She was right, I realized. I'd been blind, standoffish, perhaps superficial. I'd had valid reasons, sure, but good intentions never kept anyone off the road to Hell. "I can see that. And maybe…maybe this could work. But how do we not go too far? This has to remain a military organization with discipline. If not, we'll fall apart and never make it home."

"But maybe it's not *just* a military organization," she insisted, taking my hand. "Think of this as a deep scouting mission. Or even a colony mission seeking a new home for humanity."

The colony idea stunned me. What if we never found Earth again? What if we were destined to become a splinter colony, cut off from home and trapped on this highway of rings? I'd never considered the idea before now.

Her gentle touch brought me back to the here and now. She'd slid her hand up my right arm. This sent quite a powerful signal to my brain then down my spine again.

"We're not comrades marching in lockstep," she said, "or brothers in arms. We're real people with open hearts. A family."

"Every family needs a mother and father," I said with a slow smile. I realized she had me now. I'd told her she had all the power in this relationship, and whether she believed it or not, she did. I couldn't resist her.

"Grandpa Hansen and Grandma Sakura," she snickered. "Who's the batty uncle in the attic?"

"That would be Marvin," I chuckled along with her, feeling easy for the first time in a long while.

Adrienne leaned forward to put her head on my shoulder, and I circled her with my arms. "What now, O Mistress of *Valiant*?"

Although the tension had broken, I found myself not wanting to move too fast for fear of ruining this fragile thing we were building.

"Now, you kiss me again," she said, raising her lips to mine.

I obliged.

The kiss began gently, almost chaste, but rapidly progressed past lips to tongues and earlobes and necks. Then she finally pushed me away.

"No, not yet," she said.

Taking a deep breath, I swallowed my protests and turned an automatic frown into a smile. Play it cool, a voice kept saying in my head. I listened to that voice.

I stood up. "Are you hungry? I'm hungry."

Adrienne blinked at me in surprise. "Giving up so soon?"

"You said 'not yet.'"

"Yeah, but..." she looked disappointed, which was exactly how I was feeling.

"I'm sorry," she said. "I just don't want our first time to feel rushed. You have to deal with the Raptors in a few hours. You'll need some rest and a clear head. I wanted to help not muck things up for you."

"No problem." I forced myself to smile. "We'll start over later, when we have lots of time." If there was a later. The grandest irony would be getting one or both of us killed just before we consummated our passion.

"Very well, then," she said. She stood and kissed me once more before slipping out of the cabin.

I was left with a thudding heartbeat and a raging libido. Foremost in my mind was the unarguable fact that I wasn't as good at this sex stuff as my father had been. I'd heard plenty of stories about Dad's younger days, and Mom had always sourly hinted they were true. Somehow, he would have managed to get himself laid in this situation. I felt sure of it. I'd done my damnedest and failed.

My sigh turned into a growl of frustration. Adrienne's intention had been to help clear my head, but she'd failed spectacularly. Still, when in life does anything ever go the way we plan?

A long cool shower and a beer—okay, two—relaxed me some, and I was able to catch a couple of hours of sleep before I had to be ready. When I awoke without the distraction of hormones, I found I felt fine.

After a quick meal, I headed back to the bridge. The holotank showed no change. We remained on course and Kleed's ships were braking for rendezvous in about an hour.

If I wanted to fight, now was the time to decide. We could pour on the speed in order to blast through them as fast as possible, taking several out with our heavy weapons, but then we'd be the quarry in a chase against fast ships. They'd catch up with us according to Hansen's calculations. We'd kill a few more of them, and then they would take us apart. They would do it slowly in hopes of getting our technology intact.

No, this was to be a poker game, one in which both sides had advantages. They had more chips and better cards. On the other hand, I didn't have to win this one. I just had to limit our losses and leave the table alive. If we were lucky, I'd lose a couple hands, push my chips across the table and get out of the casino.

If I couldn't get away, they would demand we play for keeps. I wasn't sure what the human equivalent of tail-eating would be, but I was sure I didn't want to find out.

"Steady as she goes," I told Hansen. "There's no need to make it easy for them. Just keep heading for Orn Six. Incidentally, have we found the ring yet?"

"I believe so, sir. It appears to be lying flat on the surface of the planet." Hansen put up a fuzzy, long-range image of a circle against a gray background. It was impossible to tell the scale.

Ring orientations seemed mysterious when they intersected planetary bodies. Sometimes they buried themselves on end, forming vast archways. Sometimes we found them far below ground and even underwater. I'd never heard of one lying flat on the surface. That implied it had been placed there, or excavated. If it had fallen into the gravity well from orbit that would have caused a significant impact, and there was no crater around it.

"Got something else for you, sir. We found this exactly, precisely, on the other side of the planet."

"What's that?" I said, looking at the perfect square he indicated on the still image.

"Some kind of surface installation. Maybe a science lab or a defensive fortification, we're too far away to tell."

I couldn't do anything about it, so I grunted and put it out of my mind. "*Valiant*, hail Marvin. Be sure to encrypt the transmission."

"Channel encrypted and open. No immediate response."

"Keep trying." I sat down and spent some time strategizing while gazing into the holotank.

"Yes, Captain Riggs?" came Marvin's voice several minutes later.

I was about to chide him about not calling me "Commodore," when I realized I only commanded one ship again. "Captain Marvin, where are you?"

Again I waited through the long delay. "I am on my way to Orn Six as you suggested."

Had I suggested he go there? I was pretty sure I'd told him to stay near enough to help us, but if he was light-minutes away it would take several hours for even *Greyhound* to reverse course and get here. To do that he was going to have to light his engines and become easily visible. I decided a distant, unknown ace in the hole was better than none at all.

"*Valiant*, begin a continuous encrypted broadcast of all ship's data including video and audio feed. Whatever happens, I want Marvin to have a record of it. Captain Marvin, remember your orders are to get back home and pass on all data about this expedition if something happens to us. Also, *Valiant*," I said, struck by a sudden inspiration, "configure our antennas to broadcast full audio and video in Raptor format with beamcast boosting toward the three planets. I want every Raptor to see what goes on here. I'll let you know when to start transmitting."

"Scripting done," said the ship. "Channels opened and reconfigured."

"Captain Riggs," Marvin said, "we don't have the time for an extended conversation, therefore I need to point out something you may not have noticed. Please load the file I have transmitted to the holotank and follow along."

"Go ahead, *Valiant*, do it."

Marvin continued as the presentation came up, showing the situation at the end of the first battle with the Lithos right after we'd entered this system.

"Based on a great number of observations," he explained, "I've calculated the exact capabilities of the various Raptor ship types. You will note that the relief fleet is accelerating at a very conservative rate, stressing neither machine nor biotic component."

"What you mean is, the enemy commander isn't hurrying," I said.

"Correct," Marvin said. "One would expect a commander of reinforcements to push his ships to the limit in order to try to save his homeworld. I calculate he could have had a third to a half of his fleet join in the battle with the Lithos even if only for one high-speed pass. More to the point, he could have fired over a thousand missiles that would have easily reached and targeted the enemy in plenty of time."

"Holy shit. That might have done it."

Kleed had been willing to risk a whole planet so he could pick up the pieces. What a bastard. With the biggest fleet and just colony governments to deal with, he might be setting himself up as a new dictator.

"Hopefully this information hasn't disconcerted you in any way, but I thought you should know. Captain Marvin out."

He'd given me a lot to think about, that was for sure, but by this time we had less than twenty minutes until the Raptors matched course with us. I turned to Hansen. "Sound battle stations. I want everyone in suits, armed and ready to fight like hell. Hansen, you have the bridge. If Kleed calls, put him through to my battlesuit."

"Battlesuit?"

"Yup."

I didn't explain, but hurried down to the marine deck. No one was there. All the marines were already at their stations in anti-boarding teams. Most of them were placed near airlocks and the pinnace launch bay—or anywhere else an enemy was likely to enter.

I palmed the lock open, and my huge battlesuit opened for me to climb in. Over three tons of armor, weapons and survival systems were wrapped around me. Without servos, smart-muscles and built-in repellers, even I wouldn't be able to move in it. A moment later I had the HUD up and was linked in to the ship systems and the other marines. "Hansen, anything?"

"Nothing, sir," he said.

"Pass the word to our beam and missile gunners. No one is to fire on Raptor ships until fired upon. Keep them locked-on and ready. If they send something innocent over, like a pinnace, for God's sake don't shoot it down. But if they send marines to assault, you're free to fire—but on the boarding forces only, do you understand?"

"I understand what you're saying, but not why," he said.

"Look, as soon as it becomes a ship-to-ship action, all bets are off. They would have to respond, and they'll tear us apart and hope to get what they want from the wreckage. No, we have to play by their rules. Limiting our response to boarding defenses just might force them to stick to some kind of honorable rules."

As Hansen passed the orders, I clomped down to the launch bay deck. There I found Kwon and nine other marines. When it came to boarding, this was the weakest spot. The big space-doors were camouflaged and we'd slathered more smart metal over them, but they could not really be armored. If the Raptors located them and did try a storm assault, this was the easiest way in.

"Good to see you, sir," Kwon roared. "Just like old times."

"Right," I said. "Listen—"

Before I could finish my sentence, Hansen broke in. "Kleed's hailing us, sir."

I hardly cared what the backstabbing alien had to say, but I opened the channel anyway out of sheer curiosity.

-40-

Senior Field Director Kleed appeared much as Klak had. Perhaps he had a few extra decorations on his uniform, and I thought maybe he was bigger. When you're not used to them, aliens of a given race tended to look the same.

"Senior Kleed, this is Commodore Riggs. What can I do for you?"

"Commodore Riggs, you are a war criminal. You will surrender yourself and your technology to me."

I twisted my face into an expression of annoyance. This guy didn't beat around the bush. With an effort, I managed to keep my tone pleasant. "That's preposterous, Senior Kleed. My crew and I fought hard to save your planet."

"You interfered with our internal politics and incited an honorable officer to usurp lawful authority. The reasons behind these acts and their outcomes are immaterial. The law is the law. You will be tried, convicted and executed in accordance with our laws."

I smiled, although I was unsure if my expression would be interpreted properly. "How about we set that point aside for a moment. You said you want our technology. As a gift to your people, I've prepared a blueprint and a list of the components required to construct a fully functioning nano-factory. With your first factory, you can replicate more factories. Within a decade the production capacity of your planet could be multiplied tenfold. You will be a savior to your people. The name of Kleed will echo throughout history as the warrior who brought your people back from the brink of ruin."

Kleed's eyes shifted left and right in his head as if he was thinking. I got the impression he was concerned about what those around him would say.

"That is a noble gesture, Commodore Riggs. It may be that I can negotiate a reduction of your sentence. Perhaps mere life imprisonment in a labor camp can be achieved."

As far as I was concerned, Kleed had spoken the magic word: *negotiate*. So there was some wiggle room in the old buzzard after all.

"Would you consider a sentence of exile, for me and my crew?" I asked. "We'll pass beyond the borders of your system through the ring on the sixth planet. You can rightfully claim justice was done."

Kleed thought about that again. "No. That is no penalty at all. My people demand punishment for the billions of lives lost."

Starting to get angry, I said, "We *saved* billions, Kleed! Without us your home planet would be a smoking crater with nothing larger than a microbe living on it."

"I disagree. If you hadn't convinced Klak to mount your weapons, the Lithos would not have clung stubbornly to their massed ship. Instead, they would have followed their normal tactics and broken up. We would have defeated them, as usual."

"I don't believe that. The Lithos came in with a plan. They joined into their mass ship long before the new weapons fired upon them. Genocide was always their intention."

Kleed stood stoically, unmoved. "That cannot be proven, and my people will accept my interpretation."

"Well how about this, smartass," I said, opening the transmission feed to the general channel. "*Valiant*, translate and broadcast Marvin's findings about Kleed's fleet speed and lack of missile launches on every Raptor channel. Let's show his people what he really is."

Once his buddies saw what he'd done, I figured he had nothing to compel us but naked force. Unfortunately, revealing the truth might not be enough depending on the reaction of his troops.

"These allegations are lies and misunderstandings," Kleed blustered. "We didn't have the fuel to hurry to the battle and then brake afterward. Had we done so, the entire fleet would have been lost in space. Also, we left the majority of our missiles behind with a skeleton crew to guard the ring against attack, and the few we kept had to be used judiciously." I realized Kleed was speaking for the benefit of his subordinates and might be broadcasting to everyone else as well.

"Riggs," Hansen broke in, "we've got incoming assault troops. You've got two minutes left for chatter, tops."

I pulled up *Valiant's* tactical display on my HUD and swore. "*Valiant*, close the channel to Kleed. Kwon, prepare to repel boarders! Hansen, pass the word to the auxiliary defense teams. Make sure those anti-snowflake guns are operating, and no firing at the Raptor warships!"

When we'd welded the frigates to *Valiant*, we'd left all the anti-Litho APs intact. These stubby towers had the ability to sweep along the hulls of the ships. Hopefully, they would give the Raptor marines a nasty surprise.

"Hansen, you have the watch!"

"Yes, sir."

I went below decks to meet up with Kwon at the hold bay doors. Kwon made sure his troops were set to cover the outer doors, then dragged me behind the cover of a stack of constructive nanite barrels. I checked my laser rifle and readied myself.

With one minute to go, every light in my helmet was green. As the seconds ticked off, I reviewed the tactical feed.

"Hansen," I said, "it looks like our broadcast did some good. Did you notice not every Raptor warship launched troops? Some haven't sent out any boarders. Maybe not everyone is behind him on this."

"Either that, or they don't put marines on every ship. Or maybe Kleed's honor demands a fair fight."

"Maybe. What matters is that we've got about one hundred Raptors inbound. I think we can hold."

"Good luck."

On the HUD, I saw the Raptor marines landing on the hull. Our hull defense APs, originally made for snowflakes, immediately began to cut them down. A third of the enemy died before they were able to get into crevices and low spots to avoid the beams, which were programmed not to hit our own hull.

"They're on the hull," I said over the ship-wide channel. "They'll breach soon. Get ready!"

Before I'd finished speaking, a white-hot line appeared over the launch bay doors and what little air remained inside puffed out. Several objects sailed in through the orange melted metal, and Kwon yelled, "COVER!"

I ducked with everyone else as the enemy grenades blew, creating a storm of plasma that washed over us and ignited everything flammable. Fortunately, our armor was far too tough to yield to mere high heat.

"*GO, GO, GO!*" Kwon roared, and we opened fire into the smoke-filled hole. Several Raptors in armor fought their way in and died in our crossing beams. A handful of survivors got through the death funnel at the breach.

Up close and in battle, they moved with sudden leaps and more grace than a man would display. They sailed across the floor directly at us when they were close enough. They didn't seem to have beam weapons, just huge axes and those tails of theirs, which were encased in flexible articulated armor. Sharp flanges protruded at right angles and between the blades on the axes and the blades in the tail. The Raptors hit us hard.

One came straight for me, and my beam slashed across him reflexively, but the glancing burn hardly slowed him down. His huge space-axe, with a blade two feet wide from tip-to-tip, came slashing down in an enormous overhand blow that would have cleaved me from crown to crotch if I'd stuck around.

I leaped back as the axe flashed toward me while trying to keep my laser in play. The Raptor missed and buried his axe in the smart metal floor. I couldn't get a bead on him before he let go of the melee weapon and leaped again, swinging his bladed tail in a roundhouse sweep this time.

Reflexively, I blocked the spiked ball with my rifle. The tail flanges cut the weapon nearly in half. I realized in surprise the blades must have been enhanced. Maybe they had a molecular edge. The Raptor sailed over my head on his next bound, bounced off the wall above, and came back down toward me.

I ducked under the swinging tail and grabbed the abandoned axe handle. Roaring with effort, I pulled it from the resisting floor, ignoring my destroyed rifle, which now flopped, dangling from its power cable.

Taking a wild swing with the axe, I got lucky. The Raptor's tail was sliced clean off. Raptor blood spewed into the vacuum and began to boil in the low pressure. My opponent crashed into the far wall and flopped on the deck. He was out of action and dying fast due to shock and asphyxiation.

"*Valiant*," I gasped, "increase gravity to three Gs everywhere there are Raptors." Almost immediately, the floor pulled me toward it. I almost slipped and fell on my face. All around me others felt the same tug, and they staggered under their own tripled weight. I smiled grimly, as the Raptors were no longer flying around and leaping like berserkers. I was pretty sure my trick would hamper them more than us, especially since my marines wore powered battlesuits that assisted us automatically in every movement.

Now that the Raptors weren't hopping around like demented grasshoppers, I stepped forward to do battle with more confidence. Their armor didn't appear to have nearly as much power-assist as ours did. Soon, we'd dispatched the dozen or so that had invaded the launch bay. Out of eleven of us, seven were still on our feet. The others were too wounded to fight.

Kwon shook a bloody space-axe in my direction. "Not bad," he rumbled. "And with the higher gravity we'll do even better next time."

"Fifty down, fifty to go," I estimated. "Leave two marines and the wounded guys here. The rest of you follow me."

I could have told Kwon to take a team and split up, but I knew he'd just ignore my orders and stick with me anyway. The big marine had made it his purpose in life to watch Dad's back, and now mine—he'd already told me. As long as I was safe on the bridge he'd do what I told him, but with me in a battlesuit I knew he wouldn't leave my side.

We might be facing two to one odds, but fighting on home ground with an omniscient brainbox to guide us helped even the score. The gravity trick tipped the fight decisively in our favor. With five line marines in tow, I headed for the nearest incursion my HUD showed me. Four crewmen had barricaded themselves in a compartment and were defending it against three Raptors who were chopping at the smart metal walls with their axes. The stuff kept trying to seal up, and the crewmen blasted away with their laser pistols, but without our help they were done for.

When Kwon saw the situation, he elbowed past me, filling the corridor and flanking the Raptors. None of us even got to fire or swing before the huge man chopped them down like saplings. In the tight corridor, under three gravities, they were almost helpless.

"Why didn't they bring firearms?" Kwon asked me as he led the way toward the next fight.

"They're trying to capture our factory. Apparently, Kleed didn't feel like waiting around until we built one for him. This is the modern equivalent of a bayonet charge. On a planet they probably would have had us, but with our suits and the gravity we'll have the advantage."

"If they're trying to capture our ship's factory, shouldn't we meet them there?"

I was about to disagree when I realized he might be right. Normally, shipboard battles were centered on capturing the bridge and the engineering section. But in this case, we were off the page of the Academy textbooks. They might well steal our factory and retreat, figuring they had what they wanted.

On my HUD, several enemy squads looked like they were fighting their way toward the center of our ship where the factory resided. In fact, one group of sixteen had penetrated quite close.

"You're right, Kwon. Go, now—fast. I'm right behind you."

We pounded through the passageways and into the factory room just as three groups of Raptors burned their way in on the other side. It looked like these guys had lasers after all.

Then I saw something that made my blood run cold. The Raptors had seized a group of crewmen and disarmed them. I recognized two of the group: Adrienne and Sakura.

My marine team had only four rifles between us. On the marine channel I contacted my troops. "This is Riggs. Everyone, finish off the attackers as fast as you can and converge on the factory room. We have a hostage situation."

"*RIGGS!*" The translation software did its best to preserve inflection and intensity, so I knew this was a Raptor speaking over our channel. "This is Kleed. I have your females. You have no honor if you cannot defend them!"

My heart sank as I realized Kleed had recognized his hostages' gender. The factory room connected to Engineering, and the women's normal posts were in those two places. "Cease fire! Cease fire!" I called over the general com channel. "Keep back and await instructions."

As our fire slackened and our reinforcements gathered nearby, the Raptors stopped advancing as well.

"Kleed, is that you?"

"I am here." One of the Raptors, bigger than the others, stepped forward. "I have your mothers and your sisters."

I didn't bother to correct his misconception about our women, as it really didn't matter. If there was a way out of this situation without losing Adrienne, I had to find it. I stood up so he could identify me across the deck.

"I see, Kleed. But we're not like you. If you kill our females the rest of us will fight harder and will slaughter every one of you, and you will still not have gained our technology for your people. Where is the honor in that?"

"I've seen your people are not as soft and weak as I'd been led to believe by the video you transmitted. I'd thought you were merely clever technicians, but I see there are real warriors among you. In honor, I admit my error."

"Then stop this treachery. Release our females, and we'll escort you off our ship. I will still build a factory for you as a gift. You can still be the hero."

Kleed flapped his helmet from side to side in the Raptor equivalent of a head-shake. "Before, perhaps that was possible, but you have already called my honor into question with your broadcast. I cannot return with half a kill. I must have it all so that my people may feast on your bodies and know me to be worthy. Otherwise, I might as well eat my tail right now."

"I'd go for that," Kwon said loudly.

"No matter what happens, you can't possibly fight your way off this ship," I said.

"I do not intend to. As I said, I will have it all or none." Kleed waved forward a Raptor with an odd, pregnant look. The leader pushed a large button on the belly armor of that one and an oversized display lit up. "Now, if this one speaks a code word, we will all die in atomic fire. That is, unless you give me what I want. He is my eldest son, Kreel, so you know I am committed. You see, Riggs, it is *you* who cannot win."

"Great," Kwon said under his breath. "I knew he wouldn't fight fair."

Fight fair...

"Kwon," I said, slapping his arm with my armored hand, "did anyone ever tell you you're brilliant?"

"Nope. Never. Not even once."

"Well, you are today. You just gave me an idea. Kleed," I yelled, "Klak was ten times the Raptor you are. You're a dishonorable weakling, and I'll prove it. I call for trial by single combat."

Kleed stood there frozen, but I saw his troops looking at one another. I could tell I'd touched a nerve. Marvin's briefing to me about Raptor society had mentioned settling differences of honor with duels. Such contests were legally binding solutions to disputes based on the belief that whoever was right would be favored by the Raptor's god and granted victory.

"Sir, let me do it," Kwon said, trying to step forward.

"That's not how it works. I called Kleed out, and now he has to meet me," I hissed. "Get back to your place." I reached up and took off my helmet after making sure the air was good. "Kleed, I know your customs. If you don't agree, you forfeit. You'll prove I'm right about everything. And by the way, this is also being broadcast to all your ships and all your civilians—

to your mothers and sisters and daughters, too." I spread my hands dramatically, dropping my helmet to the deck with a clang. "Come on Kleed. I'm waiting for your answer. Are you as big a chicken as you appear to be?"

Kleed made the only answer he could. Reaching up, he took off his helmet, leaving only his nose mask on.

"I accept your challenge, Riggs," he growled, standing tall.

"Let's do this!" I shouted, and stepped forward to meet him before he could change his mind.

-41-

Meeting a raptor face to face was daunting. They were a head taller than humans even without that long, powerful neck.

Kleed hit a release on his armor, and it opened up in several places. His troops peeled it off until the Raptor stood unclothed on the deck.

"Because you have challenged me, I choose the battle-tools. Claws and teeth and tails it shall be, nothing more. But you must normalize the gravity, halfway between yours and ours."

I popped the releases on my own battlesuit, stepping out of it. "That sounds reasonable." I told *Valiant* to set the gravity, which turned out to be slightly higher than one G, favoring the Raptor.

"But there's one problem," I said. "I have claws, sort of, and some teeth—but no tail. That hardly seems honorable."

Kleed paced back and forth, glancing at his son and the other troops as if troubled.

"Great," Kwon said. "You get killed first, then we fight, then he blows the ship."

"Kwon, I'm hurt. Have you no confidence?"

"He's one big mother, sir, bigger than me even. With that tail...I know you're microbed like your father, but still... He's six hundred pounds if he's a kilo."

I smiled. "Don't count me out yet. Kleed's on the spot."

Kleed spoke. "I hear you, Riggs. What is the answer to this dilemma? There is no honor in slaughtering a tailless ape such as you, no matter how brave."

"How about if I grow a tail? Or something like one?"

"What do you mean?"

"Give me a minute, Kleed." I turned to Kwon. "Go get me a pool bat. My favorite one, with the wrapped grips."

"But—"

"Don't argue, just do it!"

Kwon turned and lumbered out of the room. In a moment he was back with the bat I needed.

"What is that?" Kleed asked suspiciously.

"It's my tail." I swung it back and forth in my hand. "Here, examine it." I rolled it across the deck to bump against his foot. "A titanium club with some sticky cloth to help me grip it. No power supply, no moving parts. Just a piece of metal."

"Metal is stronger than bone."

"And you outweigh me more than three to one. You have teeth and claws. Do you think this one object makes me your superior? If so you might as well concede the contest right now."

I forced a laugh and gestured to the crowd. My marines caught on and loudly joined in the laughter. Hopefully Marvin's translation program was good enough to get the point across.

"Agreed!" Kleed roared. "I have no fear of your puny club. Let us fight."

He kicked the bat contemptuously back to me. I picked it up, resting it on my shoulder. Across the room I could see Adrienne looking at me with naked fear. I blew her a kiss.

"Okay, what's the signal to start?"

"We start now," Kleed said, and he attacked.

Fortunately we were some distance apart, at least forty feet. Remembering the leaping tail attack his people favored, I immediately dodged to the left. As he was already in flight by that time, Kleed couldn't change course. I circled the inside of the impromptu ring that had formed around us, made up of marines and Raptors. Both sides had forgotten our dispute in the excitement.

When Kleed was back on his feet and charging close a second time, I found I'd already run out of bravado and plans. I had no idea of how I would beat him.

After a couple more abortive hops that I dodged, Kleed settled down to stalking me. I was faster than he was, but eventually he would get too close, and I'd have to go *mano-a-mano*.

My only advantage was the bat I'd scammed him into letting me have. I could block with it or maybe shove it into Kleed's mouth and break some teeth. But if we got in close, I knew that tail would nail me. No, my best bet was to keep him at range and try to catch him with a good hard swing. I knew I wasn't going to get more than one shot when he caught me.

Kleed stalked forward and I retreated until I was up against a bulkhead. Thinking he had me trapped, he came in clawing and biting. He performed a tail sweep, aiming low. I leaped over it, but the blades rasped against my left boot. The sole tore open and blood dribbled out. He'd scored first.

I jumped away, ignoring the pain. My toes would heal. Already, nanites and microbes were sealing up the slashes in my foot. My boot was even knitting itself back together.

Seeking to press his advantage while I was in pain, Kleed snapped at me with that toothy snout. I rocked back, wound up, and swung my bat as hard as I could for his jaw.

I knew I was going to pay for this move because Kleed's tail was like a third hand, always striking in combination with his claws and teeth. He got an arm up in front of the bat, taking some of the power out of my blow. It still broke a bone and smacked into the side of his head, but now I was off-balance with my follow-through. I tried to roll with it, but I felt those tail spikes snake upward, trying to gut me. The blades clattered over my ribs, tearing up my chest muscles.

Kleed staggered away, his tail pulling away a hunk of my skin on the embedded spikes. My gut burned and ran red. I wanted to scream in pain, and my marines were gritting their teeth and hissing in worry. I forced myself to straighten, ignoring the blood and the pain.

When I lifted my bat, I found my left arm didn't cooperate. The muscles and tendons there had been sliced away and that side no longer operated. I switched to using my right alone, wielding the bat one-handed like a sword or baton. To show I was still in the fight, I swung it in a figure eight and came on, trying to finish the Raptor off. Even with nanites sealing my skin, I could feel the loss of blood. Possibly I'd black out soon.

Kleed must have suspected my weakness. He kept his guard up. With only one hand, I wasn't able to generate the power I needed to smash through. His forearms were the size of my thighs.

The Raptor shook off the blow I'd given him and began to come back at me. Now I circled away again, rolling my left shoulder to try to get some feeling in it, urging my nanites and microbes to greater efforts. I could feel the strength returning, but I wasn't sure who would win the battle of the microscopic healers.

I felt a shock of pain. Kleed had lunged forward at great speed and caught me in the leg with his tail, in the back of the thigh this time. The flexible whip of it tended to wrap around any guard and do horrible damage, like a spiked ball on a chain. I stopped moving as I could barely stand. Running or jumping was out of the question.

I had to end this quickly. The next time his tail came at me, I didn't jump or duck or spin as I'd been doing. Instead, I took a little hop to one side and swung my bat, imagining the spiked end of Kleed's tail was a hard-driven pool ball. The wet smack when titanium hit bone and flesh at three hundred miles an hour sounded nothing like the crack of pool, but the effect was electrifying. The ball at the end of his tail slammed into his gut. Blood flew in a spray, and I could see several of those spikes buried to the hilt in his chest.

Kleed fell on the ground, thrashing. I advanced, hobbling over the floor. I suspected a trick. With his eyes closed, he cradled the end of his appendage and keened like a man with crushed gonads.

"He has been disemboweled by his own tail," I heard one of the Raptors say, and the others took up the call. They backed away, heads down as if ashamed.

"I claim victory!" I yelled, waving my bat above my head. "Kleed has lost the battle and is without honor."

"Kleed is without honor," echoed his son, the one with the bomb on his belly. Slowly, he took a claw and pressed a sequence. I thought we were goners.

The display on the device winked out. I gasped with relief.

The Raptors dropped their weapons. Adrienne pushed past her erstwhile captors to touch my injuries. Her face was wreathed in worry.

"Are you going to live?" she asked me.

"Only if you give me a kiss right here in front of everyone."

She did it. My lips had been split open at some point, but I didn't care. With blood in my teeth and a slightly sick feeling in my head, I grinned and faced the group.

"Round these bastards up and get them the hell off my ship!" I ordered Kwon.

To the cheering of the crew, Kwon and his marines marched the Raptors to the launch bay. They cheered even louder when I kissed Adrienne again. I had to hang onto her neck with my good arm. The other had gone numb, and I'd dropped my gory bat. But the only thought in my head was that I needed to rethink my policy on fraternization. After all, the captain had to have someone to share his confidence...and his bed.

I was hauled to the medical bay by Adrienne and Sakura. I was weakening fast, and I didn't think I could fight them off if I wanted to.

Lying on my back with a blinding white light in my face, I contacted the bridge.

"Hansen, let the Raptors come pick up their people. You're going to have to fly us out of here now. I'm—out of commission for a while."

"Yes sir. What about the factory plans? They're requesting that we honor our agreement and hand them over as a sign of good faith."

"Really? You know what I say to that? Screw 'em! They can fight the Lithos on their own next time around."

"Yes, Captain!" said Hansen. For once, he sounded very pleased with my orders.

I frowned for a second as the channel closed. Had that been the first time he'd called me "captain?" I thought that it might have been. At the very least, it was the first time he'd done so without at least a trace of sarcasm in his voice.

Adrienne fussed over my injuries after that, with Sakura lingering nearby, watching. I wondered why she was there. Maybe she wanted to personally thank me or to make sure I was properly cared for. After all, I'd saved her life.

A few minutes later, Kwon showed up and posted himself next to my bed as a guard. Adrienne played nurse—there were endless needles, sutures and unpleasant sensations.

Taking a last look around with half-shut eyes, I noticed Sakura had left. She'd never said a word. Mentally, I shrugged. She wasn't the most expressive person. I decided to take her gratitude as a given.

* * *

The Raptors left us alone after our refusal to share technology. They didn't even bother to make contact. I think they were embarrassed and ashamed, although whether by their champion's defeat or his behavior, I wasn't sure.

I was far from an expert on the nuances of Raptor honor, but by skill, luck or divine providence I seemed to have used it against them. I'd pushed all in with my paltry pile of chips and won the pot.

Deciding not to press our luck, I let the Raptors be.

That day we held funerals for our dead. Three marines and one crewman had died in the battle. I felt every damned one of their deaths. They were my responsibility. If I'd thought to challenge Kleed earlier, maybe there wouldn't have been a boarding action. Then again, it was probably only his supreme overconfidence and his trapping himself aboard *Valiant* that had forced him to accept the duel.

The next day I declared a holiday for everyone, letting *Valiant* run everything. As we were in deep space with nothing nearby, I felt like the risk was negligible. Getting up early, I packed all of Sir William's things up and put them into the cargo hold. I finally moved into the captain's quarters. For the first time since joining *Valiant*, I felt like I'd earned the position. From their responses, I knew the crew was ready to accept the change.

I'd spent the night after the battle with Adrienne, but I'd been too banged up for sex. She'd pouted a bit until I reminded her of what she'd said about making the first time special. Due to the miracle of nanites and Microbes—plus a little help from the autodoc—I invited her to breakfast in the morning.

The food was nothing special, but the company was excellent. Suffice it to say that we spent our holiday athletically making love. For once there was no looming crisis and no emotional baggage to push us apart. For the first time, I let go of my regrets that Olivia and I had never slept together. It was better we hadn't for now I would never compare the two.

Despite my itching, healing body, it was a day and a night I would always remember—and the next couple were pretty damn good, too.

* * *

We found *Greyhound* on Orn Six, at the location we'd suspected was a square-shaped Raptor installation. In fact, it wasn't of Raptor origin at all.

When we cruised into orbit, four Raptor monitors pinged us. They were missile-heavy mini-fortresses held aloft by repellers above the ring. They painted us with their radar, but held their fire.

Valiant edged closer. My gunners were locked on with our heaviest weapons—but nothing happened. Apparently Star Force and the Raptors were now at peace, or at least in a state of truce.

I felt better when we'd half-orbited the planet and landed next to *Greyhound* near the Square. That's what we ended up calling it: the Square. Resembling a city nearly half a mile across, it was composed of an infinite variety of dark gold-colored cubic shapes each placed upon or even within one another. Perfectly square openings dotted the cubes in seemingly random places—not only on the sides, but often on top of, or beneath overhangs. The doorways varied in size from too small to accept a fingertip to ten yards across or more. While always lined up with the associated cube's edges, the portals might be placed anywhere on any surface.

Our sensors had spotted Marvin's ship resting nearby. We'd been attempting to contact him intermittently, but he hadn't answered. *Greyhound* seemed to be undamaged, and I suspected he was still inside the hull.

I also suspected he was just too busy to bother answering us. Whatever this Square was, I was certain it fascinated him and probably for the same reasons it fascinated me.

That didn't mean I hadn't learned a few things since falling through the first ring back on Yale. This time I disembarked *Valiant* in a battlesuit with Kwon and a squad of marines at my back. Hoon joined us as well, representing our science team. I had more faith in his ability to survive a crisis than three clumsy civilians, nanotized or not.

Adrienne wanted to come along, but she hadn't been trained to use a battlesuit, and I wasn't going to let her out in a thin crew suit this time. There probably weren't any Lithos here as *Greyhound* hadn't been molested, but other dangers might lurk.

I decided not to fly close to the Square on suit repellers. I had no idea what we were dealing with here. It seemed a lot safer to walk, and only fly if we needed to jump out of there fast. The Square itself showed unusual, hard-to-pinpoint power emanations. It made me jumpy.

As we moved warily among the cubes, the doorways beckoned to us. Black as a void, they seemed to be made of liquid darkness with no depth. I'd seen something like it, but I wasn't certain where.

Choosing a large opening near ground level I walked up to it and stared at it for a time. I couldn't see inside the perfect, obsidian darkness.

Picking up a stone from the rocky surface—the ground was not paved or altered in any way—I was just about to cast it at the portal when I heard Marvin's voice over the close-range com-link.

"That may be inadvisable, Captain Riggs."

Marvin slunk out from behind a large cube. The core of his body was a lumpy cylinder ten yards long. His many tentacles and camera stalks sprouted from his central mass in a random profusion. He looked like a fifty-armed octopus sliding toward me.

"My, how you've grown," I laughed.

"I determined that an increased body mass could more efficiently explore this facility."

"And what *is* this facility?"

Marvin's appendages moved slightly faster in agitation. "I'm not certain."

"Got a guess?"

"I have a theory, but the evidence is very thin."

"Share it with me," I said.

"This place was built by a very advanced agency."

"Can we get to the point, Marvin?"

He didn't even bother to get huffy about not using his self-appointed title this time. Maybe he'd grown bored with the joys of playing captain.

"I suspect it's a station—possibly even a laboratory. More importantly, I'm fairly certain it was built by the Ancients."

I turned in a slow circle, eyes wide. "Now you have my full attention. What makes you think the Ancients built this?"

"All the technology we've ever encountered up to this point in our exploration has been comprehensible right down to the fundamental level. By studying it, I was able to determine core principles and work toward replicating and altering it. Every type structure I've encountered has been technologically straightforward—except for one."

I nodded thoughtfully. "You're talking about the rings."

Marvin moved closer, picking his way carefully across the rocky ground. "Exactly. While we've made some haphazard progress toward controlling them, like a primitive playing with a motor vehicle, actually understanding and replicating the technology is far beyond us. This facility is of a similar, perhaps even more advanced, nature."

"So what would happen if I threw this rock at the doorway?" I hefted a chunk of what looked like broken masonry.

"The results are highly unpredictable since I've not tested this particular portal. Let me show you what occurs when another is interacted with."

Marvin led us through winding non-streets. The cubes seemed to be set down randomly so there were no straight boulevards, only narrower and wider spaces between them. I could see tentacle tracks in the dust as if the robot had been here before, and they increased in number until we came to a large plaza. Here, the haphazard placement of the cubes had created an open space a hundred yards across.

I saw instruments all over the place. Devices were pointed at walls and doorways. I recognized small lasers, other beam projectors, and what I thought was a scanning electron microscope. There was a portable materials analyzer and a dozen other things less comprehensible. Smart metal wires snaked to several generators, and everything was connected together in a console at the center.

"You've been busy, I see," I said. "No wonder you didn't answer."

"This place is far more fascinating and important than mere interspecies politics," Marvin replied.

Hoon had followed me since landing but maintained his distance poking and prodding things. When he saw the equipment, he quickly moved to inspect it. Without permission, he began making adjustments.

"Professor," Marvin said, "please do not touch that equipment."

"I am merely recalibrating some of your sensors which are showing some evidence of maladjustment."

"Maladjustment? They're calibrated to twenty decimal places."

Hoon snorted—that's what the translated nonverbal sounded like, anyway. "A mere twenty decimal places? No wonder you've made no progress. I can improve your precision to at least thirty-five decimal places." The lobster continued to play with the consoles.

"You've got to love Hoon, Marvin," I chuckled. "He's at least as nosy as you are."

"I don't have a nose."

"It's an idiom, Marvin. Look it up."

Marvin's body language gave me the impression of patient longsuffering as he ignored Hoon.

"To answer your initial question, Captain Riggs..." He led me over to stand below a small portal. It was like a window a foot across and set about twenty feet up on the side of one wall. "Stay here," he said to me.

Then he grabbed Hoon and hauled him protesting over to a spot under a high overhang. Watching this reversal definitely gave me a sense of irony.

"Wait here," he said to Hoon, who sputtered and complained bitterly. Marvin returned to me. Extending a tentacle with a tiny laser, Marvin inscribed "CR" on the rock I held, my initials I guessed, and then pointed. "Toss the rock through that portal."

Aiming carefully, I gently threw the stone at the hole. It disappeared as soon as it crossed the plane of darkness.

"I've been assaulted!" I heard Hoon shout. He came scuttling over to me with a rock in his claws. "This was fired into my carapace. I don't appreciate humor of any kind, but personal assaults are too much, Riggs."

I took the rock and examined it. On one side I could see the inscription: "CR."

"It's a ring. A portal." I laughed aloud. "But it only goes from here to there?"

"That one does," Marvin said. "Others lead to portals around the Square, but some lead nowhere that I can see—and some appear to go nowhere at all."

"Huh?"

"Let me show you." Eagerly, Marvin seized a long metal rod lying on the ground. He led us to a three-yard-wide portal near ground level, he extended the rod's tip to enter the flat darkness, then drew it back. When he did, the piece he had shoved through did not return. Turning the end to me, I could see it was shiny, as if it had been sheared off—which I figured it had.

"Better not fall through that one," I said, backing away a bit.

"There are many other wonders here, Cody Riggs," Marvin said. "Areas of variable and twisted gravity, places where physical laws are bent—even some spots where time itself is altered. And can you guess what these cubes are made of?"

"Stardust, right?"

"Exactly," Marvin said. He seemed disappointed I'd guessed, but since that was what the rings were made of, I'd figured it was only logical.

"Well Marvin, I'm very impressed. You have yourself a mad scientist's playground here. I'd like a daily written report of your work, and I'll expect a weekly briefing in person. Carry on." I turned to go.

"But Captain Riggs, I have so much more to show you!"

"Marvin, I'm genuinely happy for you, I really am. You've finally found something to fully occupy your neural chains and networks. You might say, however, that I have too. So you and Hoon stay here and do your thing, and I'll do mine for a while." I waved an airy salute. "See you in a week."

We left him there with his tentacles half-raised, like a forlorn wiz-kid whose science fair project had only won second place. But I knew I could've spent hours listening to him and only scratched the surface. I planned to turn loose Sakura and the civilian scientists to be my liaisons. Marvin and Hoon might destroy the star system if they were left in this playground alone.

For the most part, I wanted to get more familiar with my new quarters and the king-sized bunk inside. Adrienne would play a big part in that exploration.

I felt of pang of guilt even as I had that pleasant thought. Had I forgotten about Olivia so quickly? So much had happened... I no longer was haunted by Olivia's memory, but I was still determined to find out how and why she'd died and who was responsible. When I returned to Earth—and I would—I'd seek justice on her behalf.

In the meantime, I had a large number of living people to worry about. We had a base to build, repairs and reconfigurations to perform, and information to acquire. For example, I didn't know what was on the other side of the ring the Raptors were guarding. Before we could dive through, we had to investigate the far side. I'd learned my lesson on that score.

One thing was certain…we weren't going through the ring until we were fully repaired and ready for action. Every star system we'd visited so far had been hostile to intruders. In fact, so far the entire universe seemed like a hostile place.

A private worry I didn't share with any of the others involved the Ancients. They were out there somewhere. They had to be. Right now, I was standing in the middle of one of their castoff toys. Maybe they were all dead—or maybe they were waiting for us. If we were destined to run into them, I didn't want to do it unprepared.

And most of all, I didn't want to accidentally lead them back to Earth.

The End

More Books by David VanDyke:

Plague Wars Series
The Eden Plague
Reaper's Run
The Demon Plagues
The Reaper Plague
The Orion Plague
Cyborg Strike
Comes the Destroyer

DavidVandykeAuthor.com for information

More Books by B. V. Larson:

Undying Mercenaries
Steel World
Dust World
Tech World

BVLarson.com for information.

Made in the USA
Lexington, KY
07 July 2014